LIVING WITH ANNIE

LIVING WITH ANNIE

SIMON CHRISTMAS

FUNGAL BOOKS

First published in 2020
by Fungal Books

ISBN 9798630850874

Editing, typesetting and ebook creation by Laura Kincaid,
tenthousand publishing services
www.tenthousand.co.uk

Printed by Amazon

For Thomas Jex Harrison

Though my philosophical studies have been pursued with more zeal than profundity, I have nevertheless given myself all possible trouble and have taken the greatest care to convince myself of facts with my own eyes by means of accurate and continued experiments before submitting them to my mind as matter for reflection. In this manner, though I may not have arrived at a perfect knowledge of anything, I have gone far enough to perceive that I am still entirely ignorant of many things the nature of which I supposed was known to me.

Francesco Redi,
translated by Mab Bigelow

PART 1
EXPERIMENT

1

Why are you here? Because your body fails? Because the darkness draws in on you – as it draws in on all of us? I don't think so. I think you're here because you thirst for living wisdom, vital science, a biology of truth. So I offer you neither cures nor consolations, but a life story. My life story. Read it: and when you are done, you can decide.

Like all life stories, it begins at a moment of conception.

It's the day Jon Caldicot's boyfriend announces he's dying. They are sitting in the minuscule living room of Jon's flat: Scott, the boyfriend, perched on one of two folding chairs; Jon slumped in an ancient, collapsing sofa. It's evening, November, dark outside. They've switched off the main lights and left the desk lamp turned against the wall so that – apart from Jon's brightly lit papers stacked next to it – the room is washed in half-light at best, and the nuances of expression are easily lost. They're drinking red wine – Rioja: Scott brought the bottle – and Jon is talking about a problem he's having splicing a gene into a vector. Scott might be listening but, if he is, chooses no very logical moment to interrupt.

'I got my results today.'

The pause that follows is just too long.

'You'd forgotten, hadn't you?'

Another pause – then Scott gets to his feet and, without looking at Jon, walks swiftly into the bedroom.

'Shit,' says Jon to himself. 'I'm so sorry,' he calls out, 'I've been so caught up with...' He hauls himself out of the sofa and follows. 'You know what I'm like. I'm sorry.'

Scott is sitting on the bed. He meets Jon's contrition with a more unforgiving look than usual.

Jon sits next to him. 'So what did they say?'

'That I'm dying. I'm going to die.'

Till now Jon's been thinking the crisis turns on his forgetting to ask.

'You what?'

'I have something called Scander's disease. They reckon I've got about four years. And...' There's been a hardness to Scott's voice, a front: now it crumbles. 'I'm so fucking scared.'

Jon holds him as he breaks down. But he has not yet got his head around those words: 'I'm dying. I'm going to die.' He can feel in his arms the warmth of Scott's flesh, the dampness of his tears and snot, the ratcheting in and out of snatched breaths. He can feel Scott living. He can't feel him dying. And he can't feel his own reaction. Instead, he finds himself staring at a mark on the wall above the plug socket, telling himself over and over: 'This is real, *this* is real' – but not believing it once.

After a while Scott pulls himself together. He does not leave the cocoon of Jon's arms, but he does grow calmer there and – perhaps knowing Jon will struggle to engage without facts, or perhaps seeking an escape in their objectivity – he starts to repeat what the doctor has told him, as if intoning holy writ.

'One by one my nerve cells stop working. I start to lose feeling in my limbs. Then I can't move them. Bit by bit I'm paralysed, until I can hear and see but nothing else. And then I die. Too many nerves stop working, and I go with them.'

'But can't you... Isn't there a treatment?'

Scott shakes his head and swallows hard. 'There are...' – he halts, screwing his face shut on another wave of emotion, then releasing it in a sharp exhalation – '... palliatives.'

He looks at Jon and smiles slightly, almost quizzically, as if wanting him to say something. But Jon has nothing; so, looking down again, Scott continues: 'I'm still going to die though. I'm going to die whatever I do.'

And that's when my story begins, with those words: 'I'm going to die whatever I do.'

Jon himself is not aware of it at first, because it is itself the stuff of awareness, but in his head a slew of excitation is spreading across the spindled cells of his cortex. It begins with the minute vibrations of hairs in his ear, as hammer and anvil translate the waves of sound from outer to inner. The topmost ions of a finely charged scree are dislodged, clattering down gradients with a landslide behind them. Avalanches spread to the ends of long fibres where chemicals wait like greyhounds in traps. The signals are propagated forwards, processed, parsed, unpacked, compared. Webs of association light up or are pressed into darkness. Thoughts dance like fairies on the living gossamer threads. Possible universes come into being. This is the energy of creation *ex nihilo*, the inexplicable entry into the world of a new idea, a new beginning.

And then, at last, Jon – whatever Jon *is* over and above this concerted mass of protein and fat – feels it: his reaction, like an energy flooding his body, sharpening every muscle fibre and thrilling every nerve ending with the merest fraction of tension. He says nothing, but in his head the words circle: *I can fix this. Annie can fix this. I know how to break the Laws.*

It wasn't Scott's diagnosis that kept Jon awake that night, but his own idea. And this not just because the idea seemed – and continued to seem, as he lay awake turning it over – such a good solution to the problem Scott posed. It was also because, in the short yet stalled narrative of his life, this was just the sort of development he'd been waiting for.

Jon's father was still in the habit of recounting an anecdote of his younger son's first day at kindergarten, told to him by the assistant who had taken the bewildered boy under her wing. 'To help the new ones settle in, she said, they always tried to keep them busy on the first day, give them things to do. So she was busy cutting up paper for something, and she'd asked Jon to help her, and every time she had a bit of paper to throw away she'd say: "Could you put this in the bin for me, Jon?" And off he'd toddle to the bin, which was on the other side of the room. It was a trick she'd used before, she said, to help the new ones settle in. Only what does Jon do? The third time she asks, he pipes up: "Miss Carter, I think it would make more sense if I brought the bin over here."'

For the father, it had been further proof of what he had long known: his son was gifted. Every picture drawn, every Lego brick laid, every word or grammatical structure mastered had offered the proud parent the evidence he craved. Before the child could co-ordinate his limbs, indeed, he'd noted something unusually focused in the way he struggled to slot shaped blocks through shaped holes. In Mr Caldicot's mind there was no doubt: the genes – his genes – had come good in Jon.

For Jon, it was one more knot in the net of expectations his father was casting around him. Expectations that could never be met, since his gift was also to take the credit for anything he did achieve.

'Well done,' his father would say, reviewing a report card all As and stars, 'but of course, we expect it of you.' He did not want his son getting arrogant.

'You are special,' he'd say, but not as any doting father might tell their child – rather as a statistician might address an outlier before removing it from a calculation.

'We have no worries about *you*,' he'd add in an aside to a long exposition of concerns about Jon's older brother, thoughtlessly delivered in the younger brother's presence. 'You are gifted.'

Jon knew neither to whom he should be grateful nor whether he could ever repay their benefaction; because the brothers talked to each other as well, and Jon knew that, when he was absent and his brother around, his father did in fact worry about him.

The question that concerned Mr Caldicot was this: what would Jon *do* with this gift of his? Would he be equal to its application, or would he squander and dissipate it? A successful cardiac surgeon, Mr Caldicot had settled on the idea of applying his own gifts to medicine at the tender age of four. Vocation had been a defining feature of his life, and one that had guided his fascinations from the start. Here was a boy that could not pull the wings off a daddy-long-legs without trying to work out, with the aid of a magnifying glass, whether and how they might be reattached. By contrast, Jon's gifts – his ingenuity, his inventiveness, his ability to see what held a problem in place – seemed to lack an organising principle. In the absence of a pin or suture, fretted the father, the gifts risked misalignment. And though he told the story as often as ever, he began to fear a darker meaning might lie at the bottom of Miss Carter's waste-paper bin: not just an eye for a better way of doing things, but a lack of respect for the existing order.

Things came to a head when Jon, aged fifteen and boarding at Mr Caldicot's old school, supplied the brains in a daring prank-cum-protest which saw the First Eleven cricket square seeded with dandelions.

'Our son is going off the rails,' confided Mr Caldicot to his wife.

'Don't be such a dolt,' she replied briskly. Hemmed in by class and marriage and motherhood, Sylvia Caldicot had channelled her own intellectual gifts into her garden: and there, pricking out seedlings in the greenhouse and mulling which wisteria shoots to train and which to cut, she had polished a very different lens from the one through which her husband saw the world. Jon was flowering, not going to seed. He might have need for a cane or two in time, or cover if a late frost threatened, but neither parent nor gardener could make of him what he wasn't. 'Youthful high jinks,' she snorted.

On this, as on many other matters, father and mother did not see eye to eye.

And Jon? Well, once he had been not one but two. Each gamete had received its unique share of potentiality, but neither was blessed with viability. Human beings are at best a truce, more often a skirmish, and in early teenage years an all-out border war. Waiting with his co-conspirators outside the headmaster's study, he at once seethed with rage at arbitrary power and trembled at the thought of falling short of his gift.

The idea of becoming a scientist first occurred to Jon less than a week after this adolescent crisis. Correlation is of course no proof of causation, and *post hoc ergo propter hoc* the oldest fallacy in the book, but I can't believe the timing was an accident.

He was watching a documentary when it happened. The subject was Francesco Redi, an energetic man of the Italian Renaissance who conformed to stereotype by working as a physician for the Grand Duke while writing poetry about wine and, in between stanzas, founding experimental biology, toxicology and parasitology.

'Redi put meat in eight jars like this,' explained the presenter, demonstrating with that wide-eyed enthusiasm that is the stock-in-trade of such programmes. 'He left four open but covered the other four with muslin.'

A shot followed of the presenter struggling with muslin and string, and muttering that the task was harder than it looked. Then a cut to time-lapse film of the fates of these different chunks of meat, accompanied by a portentous voice-over: 'In the open jars, maggots soon appeared on the meat, but in the jars covered with muslin, there were none. No maggots appeared unless flies could get in. With a simple, ingenious experiment, Redi had disproved a belief in spontaneous generation that stretched back millennia. But he'd also done something far more profound: he'd invented the very idea of an experimental control.'

For Jon, watching, something clicked.

It was like this whenever he encountered a problem. For a long time there would be no apparent progress, no stepwise approximation to solution, just a patient delineation of structure. And then, all at once, like the silhouette of a goblet becoming the profiles of two people in conversation, the whole would suddenly shift, the obvious variables falling back to reveal the hidden constant on which the problem pivoted. Vary that constant and the problem would dissolve.

The question that had been troubling him this time was what to do with this gift of his. Now he saw his error: an assumption that it had to be something over and above what he already did. What if the solving of problems were not a talent in search of application but a vocation in its own right?

The next morning, at breakfast, he confidently informed his parents that he knew what to do with his life: 'I want to be a scientist.'

Each parent had reason enough to be pleased by this statement. Neither saw any need to enquire what it actually meant. Had they done so, Jon would have treated them to an ill-formed and improbable narrative in which he was to toss off discoveries and disciplines as easily as he gained prestigious prizes. Perhaps one of them might have disappointed him then and there, and this story of mine come to an abrupt halt before it even started. As it was, the only question that occurred to them was: what kind?

Jon still had ringing in his ears the TV presenter's enthusiastic reading of the epigraph of Redi's *Experiments on the Generation of Insects,* a quotation from Pliny: *Nature is nowhere to be seen to greater perfection than in the very smallest of her works.*

'I'm thinking about microbiology,' he said, even though, if he'd been honest, he wasn't entirely sure what microbiology was.

Nor at that precise moment did it matter. He had a solution. The gift would be repaid and the father would be happy. The moment was like a great wave that carries a surfer hurtling forwards, if only he can stay upright.

Thirteen years later Jon was in the shallows, stalling and stumbling. The practicals for his degree in Microbiology and Genetics at Sheffield had given him a first inkling of the heavy preponderance of patience and frustration over gift and genius in his chosen career. His doctorate, in Oxford, like all doctorates, had seen the painful paring back of ambition to the scale of a footnote. Watching and talking to his seniors had given him insight into the real activities of a modern scientist: not covering jars of meat with muslin but writing grant applications and responding to peer reviewers. To be a renaissance scientist, it was beginning to dawn on him, one first needed to live in a renaissance.

But he was young still, and the dream still raged against the dying of its light. It was no longer spoken with the breathless wonder of a TV presenter. It was no longer spoken at all. Yet it spoke, demanding every day: when? When will you at last achieve something astonishing?

Now, he replied, lying awake next to Scott. *I can fix this. Annie can fix this. I know how to break the Laws.*

Breakfast was a strange, silent affair, all the more awkward for being crammed into the tight perimeter of the flat.

Had he been a free agent, Jon might have lightened the mood by sharing his idea. But a habit of strict confidentiality held him back – a habit underpinned by darkly vague sanctions alluded to in the non-disclosure agreement he'd signed when he first went to the US, then signed again when he returned to Cambridge. He could not talk about Annie to anyone outside the mycotherapy community – and that included Scott. Whether he liked it or not, it was Professor Lazenby he'd have to take his idea to first. So – as there was nothing else in his head other than that idea – he matched Scott's reflective quiet with his own edgy, corked silence.

It was eight and half months since they'd met. Jon had not long been back from California, too new on the limited Cambridge scene to have slept with everyone who did not repel him or to recognise everyone who did. Scott, a strikingly pretty young man with regular features and short blond hair, was at the very top of his target list. Meanwhile, from the perspective of others, Jon was still fresh meat, the honey pot, the candle around which the moths fluttered. It was Scott who got carnal, stuck and burned.

Their first liaison was a casual shag. They'd both done the same sort of thing before, both gone out looking for it, and both had every intention of doing it again. But then, waking up in the same bed the next day, with the bright light of mid-morning wheedling through the unlined curtains and into their still fuggy minds, each was touched by the sudden thought that it wouldn't be such a bad thing to be a bit more boring for a while, and each sidled away from the emptiness towards the other's embrace. It was not love: not yet at any rate. But it was enough for them to agree, wordlessly, to see how things went together for a while.

And after that while? Time was supposed to have told. Perhaps they'd have stumbled on something deep and enduring. Perhaps they'd have gone their separate ways. Perhaps that first wordless agreement would simply have held, unrevisited, until loneliness wheedled its way back in as the sunlight once had. Time would have told. Now, though, time was up: a decision had to be made where one should just have happened.

If anyone had listened in on the conversations of their friends and acquaintances over the next few days, as news of Scott's diagnosis spread, they'd have noticed a pattern, a moment in every such interaction when, after a pause, someone would add: 'Poor Jon.'

They'd not say any more: because everyone knew – though no one wanted to articulate – that it was not Jon's future loss that made him 'poor' but his present dilemma. Had he and Scott met just days or weeks previously, no one would have expected him to stick around. Had the two been together for years, his staying would have been taken for granted. But they were in between, indeterminate – and, as all those friendly onlookers could see, Jon's options were neither liquid nor solid, but a kind of moral slush. Poor Jon.

Scott too could see it. It was one among the jumble of thoughts that swam through his head that morning, a frantic shoal of hunted fish fleeing the great white shark. But he could focus on neither this nor any other, and instead sat mesmerised by their shimmering mass.

Everyone could see it. Everyone, that is, except Jon. Because these multiplying ethical epicycles simply disappeared when the sun was placed at the centre of the system. And the sun was neither Scott nor their relationship, but Jon's bright idea.

He needed to talk to Lazenby.

'I'd better get going,' he said, finishing his coffee.

'Hmm,' said Scott. 'I might… I think I'm going to stay at mine tonight, if that's OK.'

Jon hesitated. By tonight he might have good news to share. 'Yes, of course.' In his own mind Scott was already saved, so it did not occur to him to say more.

'Speak later.'

'Sure,' said Jon, placing his unwashed mug and cereal bowl into the sink and picking up his bag. Ridiculous, he thought, that he could not just tell Scott. Ridiculous and… cruel. 'I'll call you,' he said, swinging the bag over his shoulder, then left for the lab. The sooner he talked to Lazenby, the sooner he could move things forwards.

Hindsight is a wonderful thing, and with hindsight Jon would wonder why he'd ever expected anything more than emphatic equivocality from Professor Imogen Lazenby. But his idea had dazzled him, and he launched into its explanation with visions of her leaping to her feet like Archimedes from his bath, raising her hands to the heavens in delight.

She was still in her seat when the explanation concluded. Nodding slightly and slowly, she folded her lower lip under her teeth, idly picking up a pen as she did so and holding it between finger and thumb.

'It's a fascinating proposal,' she said after a discouraging pause. 'But…' said the cadence of her voice, a self-questioning major sixth rather than a confident octave.

She took a swig of tea from the oversized blue mug that left her side only when biohazard required. Jon had accepted a mug of tea too – not because he really wanted one, but because he'd learned that the ritual of making and milking was, for his boss, an important preamble to chats of any kind.

'But you don't think it would work?' he prompted when Lazenby showed no signs of resolving the inconclusive chord of her reaction.

He sipped at his own tea. Lazenby had bid him sit in the low, paunchy armchair in the corner of her office, wheeling the office chair over for herself – a strategy which ostensibly served the comfort of the visitor but in practice merely amplified the power of the visited.

'Well… It's certainly not straightforward.'

And really, what had he been expecting? There was a pattern in his disappointment here.

It was nearly a year since he'd taken a post-doc in Lazenby's lab. He'd done so with high hopes: opportunities to father new sciences were thinner on the ground than in Francesco Redi's day, but by working here he was at least placing himself as close as he could to the origins of a field. Where better to apply his gift than working alongside one of the founders of mycotherapy?

Jack Kapinsky, with whom Jon had done his first post-doc in California, agreed and wrote a glowing letter of recommendation to his former colleague in Cambridge. To Jon, meanwhile, Kapinsky spoke as highly of Lazenby, lauding her brilliance as a scientist – though adding a note of caution: 'Don't expect it to be like working here. You need to manage Imogen, keep her informed.'

Jon, caught up in his enthusiasm, heard the praise and not the caveat. Nor did he pay much attention when, in his first few days, his lab mentor offered further words of advice: 'She doesn't always give you the room to develop your own thinking. But then, she does have a bad habit of being right. It's frustrating, but you can learn a lot from her.'

It was only a couple of weeks later that Jon first had his own doubts. Faced by a small technical problem which was holding up his work, he did what he did best: solved it. A simple adjustment to the protocol raised the success rate for the procedure from fifty per cent to around eighty per cent. It was a no-brainer – and quickly copied by others in the lab. A few days later, Jon had his first cup of tea made for him by Lazenby.

'I hear you've had a bit of a breakthrough with our transcription difficulties.'

Innocently and enthusiastically Jon explained how he had analysed and solved the problem.

Lazenby nodded as he did so, rolling a pen back and forth between her long, thin fingers. 'Did you calculate the risk of reverse transcription invalidating the entire line?'

Jon hadn't and communicated as much by falling silent.

Lazenby drew a long breath over a taut tongue, as one contemplating a disaster narrowly avoided. 'How long have you been here now?'

'It'll be four weeks on Monday.'

'And how are you finding things? I mean, are you settling in OK, do you think? Finding your way around?'

'I… Yes, I… thought so.'

'Good. Well, best get on I suppose.'

Lazenby stood up and made towards the door, adding as she did so: 'Jack Kapinsky and I, we're… we have quite different approaches.' At the door now, she turned to face him. 'Run your ideas past me next time, yes? Before you change anything.'

Jon nodded, his cheeks flushing as he did so. He would not make that mistake again, he told himself. Except, being Jon, he had – and again, and again. It was not that he did not respect Lazenby's request that he consult her 'before you change anything'; more that his measure of anything being changed was incommensurate with hers. Even when he did think to talk to her first, proposals that seemed to him modest became, in her reworking of them, reckless and ill-conceived. And, he'd wonder, was that really what he'd been proposing? On one occasion it even seemed to him that Lazenby's own innovation, announced a week or so later, bore a striking resemblance to what he thought he'd been suggesting all along – though by then, he couldn't entirely be sure what he'd thought. Lazenby did not so much sink opposing arguments as loosen their moorings and let them drift, so those on board ended up with no idea where they were.

Next to what he was now proposing, those previous ideas had been mere tweaks to the lab's modus operandi, qualifications to caveats on provisos. If they had been met with such hesitation, such caution, then really, what had he been expecting, walking in as he was with a proposal to rip up the Laws?

'Obviously there are questions that need to be considered...' he fumbled. He still couldn't see any himself: the idea seemed as elegant and simple as it had when it had first popped into his head the night before. But it was clear there *would be* questions now Lazenby was involved.

'Yes,' said Lazenby, rolling her eyes to one side as if those questions had massed at her flank, ready to ride into battle. She swung her chair slightly towards her desk, set her pen down, then turned back to Jon again, leaning forwards as she did so and resting her long forearms on her knees. A tall, lean woman with a thin face, angular cheekbones and a functional approach to clothes, there was something of a Swiss army knife about her when she folded herself in this way.

'And it's not just *our* questions, of course,' she continued. 'I mean, things are pretty much up to me when it comes to *how* we do our work here. But when there are questions about *what* we're doing... I mean, what you're suggesting here, we'd have to take it to the funders.'

'Arexis?'

'Well, they do pay the bills. It's... well, you know, our scientific pact with the devil, if you like. We sacrifice a little freedom in order to be able to do anything at all.'

'I'd have thought they'd love the idea. New potential treatments, new commercial opportunities…'

Lazenby nodded and held up a hand to stop him. 'Yes, yes, I know.' Having hesitated in a gesture, the hand continued to her forehead, where a single long grey hair had escaped the scrunchie that held its fellows tight against her scalp. 'I've learned the hard way that Arexis has its own peculiar logic,' she continued, pressing the hair back as if into a groove across her skull. 'It's still… In many ways they still think and act like part of the government. More focused on reasons *not* to do things than on opportunities. And you're suggesting that we rip up the principles that have underpinned years of mycotherapeutic research.' She sat back again and reached behind her for her tea. 'And then, of course, there are the risks. Reversion to violent sporogenesis, for instance—'

'But that's the whole point,' interrupted Jon. 'You don't have to worry even if Annie did revert.'

'Well,' said Lazenby, non-committally, 'the best I can do is raise your idea with Matt Peachey. Maybe he'll go for it, and then we can consider what the next step is. But we *would* need Arexis on board.'

He really should not have been surprised. Things never stayed simple or clear-cut when she got her bony hands on them. And – grudgingly – he could even see where she was coming from. In arguing that she had to talk to Arexis, she was merely acknowledging what Jon himself wanted her to acknowledge: that this was a radical and important idea. It was just that… Jack Kapinsky would have said as much. He'd have hailed a potential breakthrough even as he exercised the caution required of him. 'Great thinking,' he'd have said. 'Good job. Well done.'

Should he perhaps have declared his new-found personal interest in the treatment of neurodegenerative diseases? Should he have appealed to her pity? He could not be certain it was a human emotion in which she shared; and, if she did, he had a feeling she would see no place for it in her science. She was cold, he told himself, warmth rising in his own breast as he did so. Cold and unfeeling.

Because he did have a personal interest here. How was he supposed to behave around Scott now? The supportive boyfriend?

Listening, sympathising, passively absorbing, pretending there was only one possible outcome? All this when, in his head, he was already rehearsing another role: the bringer of good news. 'I can fix this,' he would tell Scott on that happy day. 'I know how to break the Laws. But first, let me tell you about Annie...'

Yes indeed. The time has come. I can put the introduction off no longer.

So let me tell you about Annie. For there is much you need to understand before you make your decision.

First, though, you must promise to hear me out. Like you, I once heard about her for the first time, and I know how the waves of disbelief will crash through you, how every educated, moderate thought in you will cry out against the truth. For of all the strange organisms in nature, the fungus *Aeisitos neuromethistes* – *A.n.*, or 'Annie' as they called it in Jon's lab; or, by extension, as they called 'her' – must surely be one of the strangest.

However, let me first soften your credulity and warm you to this theme of strangeness. For nature, I assure you, is far stranger than we care to remember, walled up as we are in our antiseptic boxes, with everything of the earth screened, piped or shrink-wrapped. In nature, strangeness is the norm, not the exception.

Let's take just one example: the nematomorpha – or Gordian worms, as they are sometimes called. What strange and terrifying creatures they are. *Spinochordodes tellinii*, for instance, starts its life, like many other creatures, as a tiny larva hatching from an egg. Unlike most other creatures, however, its first task is to get itself eaten – by a passing grasshopper or cricket or such like. Once inside, the digestive tables are turned, with the worm feeding off the grasshopper's vital juices, coiling around its innards and growing as much as four times the length of the unhappy insect – which, all the while, continues doing whatever grasshoppers do. Then, when the worm is ready to reproduce, something remarkable happens: it hijacks the grasshopper's tiny brain. Quite how it does so we still don't understand: all we know is that the grasshopper is suddenly drawn to water, flinging itself into a puddle or lake where, as often as not, it drowns – while, from the suicide's body, the worm wriggles free, ready to find a mate and spawn.

Whenever I think about that grasshopper, I picture it as an ornate trireme – the carved hull, the oars, the slaves that pull them – sailing across dry land until it runs aground in open water, and piloted by the Gordian worm, not so much on board as wound into the vessel, a soul that survives the sinking. As Descartes meditated: 'I am not merely present in my body as a sailor is present in a ship but am closely joined and, as it were, intermingled with it, so that I and the body form a unit.'

A unit, a creature, an organism. What easy concepts they are, at least in those padded cloth books that very small children like to chew. In that animated world, however, even ants have personalities and smiley faces. No one draws pictures of Pseudomyrmex ants living in the hollow thorns of a bullhorn acacia, working tirelessly to protect the tree from the ravages of other insects while feeding on the nutritious nodules the plant grows specially to sustain its mercenaries. What 'unit' would they draw? A single ant? A co-ordinated and mutualistic nest of ants? A tree-ant complex of which that nest is itself just one physiological system?

All this may seem very remote, of course. But turn the spotlight on yourself for a moment. Let's start with those famously 'good' bacteria living in your gut, busily synthesising vitamin K, fermenting polysaccharides and training your immune system. You are living symbiotically with them. You are a symbiont. And why stop there? Is there such a world of difference between the myriad cells of your body – each with its function, each with its own lifetime, each prepared to die for the common good – and the swarming myrmidons of the ant nest. You are a community, a colony. And when you open up those cells, what do you find inside? Mitochondria, ancient bacteria that have chosen a sheltered life in a tiny sea of cytoplasm. Damn it, they even have their own DNA. And they outnumber *you* millions to one. You are a battleship with a prokaryotic crew. And who is the pilot? You see? Never mind the Serengeti: nature is you, sitting there reading this, symbionts and parasites all bundled together in the constellation you call yourself.

Such is the strange world in which *Aeisitos neuromethistes* – Annie – is a truly strange organism.

She is, as I have already mentioned, a fungus: a member of a kingdom about which, for most of my life, I knew little. In so far as they had entered my consciousness – which was normally fried, for breakfast – I took them to be degenerate plants of some kind. That was the limit of my naïve mycology – *myco*-, I should mention, being the Latinate prefix used to signify all things fungal. I am no expert even today, but I do now know that fungi are not plants, and that a mushroom is merely the fruiting body that arises from a convoluted network of tiny fibres – a mycelium of hyphae, to be technical about it – that spreads underground. And I've learned there are many other types of fungi, spreading their hyphae into many other places, among them the living tissues of other creatures.

Of course, you too have a network of tiny fibres inside you. They run to and from every extremity of your body, twine together in your spine like beans that have grown beyond their canes, and swell into a sentient knot in your head. Like Gordian worms, they are wound into the vessel. Your nerves. Your neurones.

So what happens when an *Aeisitos neuromethistes* spore finds its way into a creature with such a neural network? A lab rat, for instance, *Rattus norvegicus*, one of the hundreds that Jon and his colleagues in the lab infected in their efforts to better understand Annie. Ratty's immune system is, of course, alerted to the presence of subversive agents and sets about wiping them out. Such indeed will be the fate of the vast majority of spores. But sometimes, just sometimes, a spore encounters one of Ratty's nerve cells and has time to attach itself and squirt its plasm through the cell membrane, leaving behind a mere husk for the antibodies and leucocytes to attack. By the time the soldiers arrive, the priest is already in the hidey-hole.

I'm glossing over some wonderful detail here, expressible only with technical terms such as *zoospore, flagella* and *plasmodium*, semi-technical metaphors involving guns and needles, or – failing all that – diagrams. Once inside the cell, the story becomes even more complex: so far as I understand it, most of the action takes place beyond even metaphor and diagram in a world of biochemical pathways and enzymes. For a while, I was thinking I should try to bring it all to life somehow – until it occurred to me that it already *was* life. It is only us who, in our lust for control, insist on slicing things into process maps and Gantt charts. My efforts would be like trying to 'bring to life' that moment when, say, someone first falls in love by offering a slavish enumeration of physiological and hormonal changes. Or like arguing that we did not know life at all until Dr Frankenstein supplied the spark. You see, the truth of life, the thing we should have known all along if we had not stuck our fingers in our ears and sung la-la-la, is that we control nothing. The truth is that Annie takes over.

She starts with that first infected nerve cell, spreading her own hyphal tubes along its axons and dendrites. Nerve cells, as you may know, carry their impulses along their membranes: Annie leaves this mechanism intact until she is ready to replace it with her own arguably far superior mechanism based on protein polymer threads running the length of the hyphae. Something else entirely beyond my comprehension happens at the synapses, the gaps between one nerve and the next, where Annie absorbs and co-opts components of the cell she is busily digesting. At the same time, amoeba-like off-spring break free from their mother and swim this narrow channel to begin the process all over again in the next nerve cell. Cell by cell, Annie spreads until, where once there was a network of fibres, pulsing and buzzing with emotion and calculation, sensing and willing and reflecting, there is… a network of fibres, pulsing and buzzing with emotion and calculation, sensing and willing and reflecting.

Everything and nothing has changed.

Ratty continues doing all the things that rats do: eating, mating, running about – even learning: as one of Lazenby's early studies showed, infected rats perform as well in mazes as their uninfected cousins. Annie is just as good at forming new connections as the neurones she replaces: new memories, new skills, new relationships. She has to be. She needs Ratty fully functioning, after all. Ratty is her ship now, the only thing that keeps her afloat. They are closely joined and, as it were, intermingled until the day Ratty dies.

By now, you'll have worked out why Jon saw in Annie a poten-tial solution to the problem posed by Scott's diagnosis. A brand new nervous system – albeit one of a different species – with no need for surgery or drugs. The rewiring of an entire biological dwelling without so much as a mark in the plasterwork. New lamps for old. Everything and nothing would change.

In and of itself, of course, that was not a new idea: the theoretical possibility of using Annie to treat neurodegenerative diseases was apparent to anyone familiar with the fungus's strange life cycle. Jon's stroke of genius lay in his solution to another problem: the risk of violent sporogenesis. For Annie's story, even in outline, is not quite complete. Like a Gordian worm, she too must reproduce.

2

Everyone who encounters Annie has to climb over a wall of disbelief.

It was four years now since Jon had done so. Through the long run-up to his first encounter – the direct approach from Jack Kapinsky via Jon's PhD supervisor, reminiscent of how he imagined secret agents were recruited; the telephone conversations in which Jack grilled him about his experience without explaining anything about the opportunity beyond it being unusual, cutting edge and entirely secret; the formal vetting interview by a forbiddingly humourless young woman from the Ministry of Defence; the non-disclosure agreement that Jon had to sign; the arrival of a letter confirming a US visa he had not even applied for – through all of this had arced his mounting anticipation of something extraordinary, something that would shock. Yet even so he was unprepared and listened with incredulity as Kapinsky, at their first face-to-face meeting, outlined the life cycle of *Aeisitos neuromethistes*.

Since then, however, day-to-day exposure – to Annie's reality if not to her spores – had dulled his awe to the point of complacency. In the end, it was just another lab he went to each morning, and Annie was just another species whose pathways could be mapped and genome sequenced, another organism to be re-engineered. He had seen with his own eyes, day after day, what Annie actually did: yes, everything changed, but everything also stayed the same. And just as the highest mountain will one day be washed into the plain by the tedium of rain, so too there is no wonder so great that it will not at last succumb to the drip-drip-drip of habituation.

Even the thrill of spy-like secrecy had soon given way to the pedestrian reality of not drawing attention to oneself. The secret to keeping a secret, his dour vetter had instructed him, is never to be caught hiding it – and so it had proved. It was easy enough breezing over those stock questions people ask about work: most who asked were only doing so out of politeness, and the few who were genuinely interested were easily satisfied by generalities about re-engineering micro-organisms for therapeutic purposes, illustrative examples of the principle – such as engineering gut bacteria to synthesise vitamins – and a rider that he wasn't able to talk about the details of his own work. So commonplace is reticence in the world of research that no one paid much attention, so long as he didn't big up the secrecy with words like 'top' or 'strictly'.

This is the reality of conspiracy: not the shadowy, omnipotent agencies of popular drama but a flimsy complot between those with an interest in not telling and those with no interest in hearing. In the case of Annie, those in the know had long ago found common ground in silence, albeit for differing reasons. Businessmen, generals, civil servants: each had their own aversion to telling anyone anything about what they did – backed up by a legal apparatus which made non-disclosure the norm. As for the scientists, they were happy enough so long as they were supplied with generous funding and an annual congress at which they could score points off one another. Besides which, they'd agree over dinner whenever some newcomer showed symptoms of moral qualms, it was far safer not to attract attention from the kind of fact-phobic journalists who kicked up storms about genetically modified crops or stem-cell research. No one wanted Frankenstein Fungus headlines muddying the limpid waters of enquiry.

In this small and, by necessity, close-knit research community, Professor Imogen Lazenby was a prominent figure. It was a status that her achievements as a scientist would alone have warranted. For admirers, these achievements were lent extra weight by the fact she had established herself at a time when women, especially good-looking women like Lazenby, still struggled to be taken seriously in the lab. As the young Lazenby was reputed to have snarled: 'You may have airbrushed Rosalind Franklin out of history, but nobody's airbrushing me' – although others claimed this story was itself the apocryphal creation of misogynists who needed to paint Lazenby as an ambitious harridan in order to explain her away. They had a point: Lazenby's behaviour was, by mere dint of her gender, subjected to scrutiny of a kind her male contemporaries never faced. Like all successful women, her psychology had become common property – much as those who are pregnant find their bellies suddenly and unaccountably pawed by strangers. Her character was staked out and squabbled over by champions and detractors, as if she were Africa and they the imperial powers of Europe. And this, perhaps, had been and remained a far greater if also more subtle obstacle to her career than those occasional naked shows of chauvinism she still encountered: that she could not act lightly, that her every action was weighed down in advance with competing narratives. Hardly surprising that she'd long ago learned to stop caring.

Lazenby had one other key claim to fame: that, along with Jack Kapinsky and a professor in New Zealand called Fred Anderson, she had been there at the very beginning, as a post-doc in the Cambridge lab of Sir Arthur Hayton. Everyone was familiar with the story of that lab. There was no formal requirement, no training course, no protocol: yet everyone somehow came to know how, in just four years, Hayton and his team – Lazenby among them – had made the journey from a chance find in a shrew collected from the tiny Pacific island of Teobeka via a series of astonishing discoveries to the concept of mycotherapy – the idea that Annie might one day be used to tackle deep-seated 'diseases of behaviour' – and to the three 'Laws' which still bore Hayton's name, and which set out the conditions an engineered variety of *Aeisitos neuromethistes* would need to meet in order to be considered for therapeutic use. Hayton's Laws defined the community's shared research agenda, its discipline, its identity, and reverence for those who had attended their first articulation, however lowly their position at the time, went beyond mere rational respect for concrete achievements. Those early few had about them the aura of origins, and as the numbers who remained dwindled, so too their veneration resembled more and more a cult of ancestor worship.

But the story that everyone knew was a chronicle of crucial experiments and breakthroughs, not of human beings living human lives. Science prefers its narratives desiccated. It trains its hero-bards to efface themselves with the passive voice and to flatten circuitous journeys of discovery into the determined linearity of methods-results-conclusions. Thus is perpetuated that delightful fantasy of nature disclosing itself, untainted by subjectivity. It is a fantasy which first entrains us in the schoolroom, as we stare down microscopes at fuzzy blobs and discover, like trainee haruspices poking around in the entrails of an ox, whether or not we have the gift of sight. And for those who do not, there are the neat, labelled drawings of the textbook to copy, reassuring us that, even if we do not see it, life has been – can be, will be – delineated.

It has not been, cannot be, never will be. And as for disclosure... It seems to me that it is not nature that discloses itself in the book of science. All intellectual activity is, in the final analysis, autobiographical – and the science surely reveals the scientist, not in what is found perhaps but in what was looked for. The questions we seek to answer are the questions that life has posed us. And so it was with Imogen Lazenby.

Imagine yourself, for a moment, a thoughtful, perceptive child looking back in awe along the great chain of being. Even at its furthest, tiniest extremities, you can see the evidence of that essential quality of life: motivation. For even bacteria seek out the light and whip themselves along chemical gradients. Away from the bad, towards the good. Nor does this elementary discernment drive only the simplest organisms. You too feel its tug. But, laminated across it, how many loops and circuits of hesitation and ratiocination, the apparatus that separates you from a moth hurling itself into a flame? Woven into it, how many parallel sensitivities and dispositions – to mimic, to emulate, to belong? Away from the bad, towards the good: but over and above, so many checks, balances and nuances, so many layers, so much sophistication, so much richness of experience, so much risk. The more complex the system, you think, the more ways in which it can go wrong. And turning your back on the great chain of being, the chain that links your intricate existence to those first primitive tropisms, you look up at your own mother, half-slumped across the kitchen table with the empty bottles tumbling beside her: towards the bad, away from the good.

What do you conclude? That our brains are too elaborate for us to control? That, like a Gordian worm, they pursue their own agendas, blind to our interests, while we vainly seek to nudge them aright with chemicals, cash and contextual cues? That the neurones are always one step ahead of us? Whereas a fungus, you think – and though years have passed since you sat at the kitchen table, this is but another clause in the same lifelong thought – a fungus is just a fungus, whatever channels its hyphae may grow along. A fungus is a simple organism, and its agenda – if one can even use such a word – is also simple: towards the good, away from the bad. A fungus, moreover, can be engineered.

From the moment when, working in Sir Arthur Hayton's lab, she had first observed that rats infected by *Aeisitos neuromethistes* avoided foods which were rich in copper, Lazenby's vision had been simple: that standing on the shoulders of an evolutionary giant she might touch heaven itself. Give Annie the basic instructions – the desires, the aversions – and she would handle the tricky business of rewiring. For instance – just one example of many Lazenby might have chosen – give Annie an aversion to alcohol and she would soon tweak the drinking habits of her host. Everything and not quite nothing would change.

Lazenby's mother was long since dead. When her daughter was eighteen she had reached that rock bottom to which, supposedly, all addicts must fall if they are ever to recover. Like too many, the rocks had smashed her to pieces. There was no recovery. Lazenby knew what others said about her – that she was cold, manipulative, ambitious – but it was not their voices that woke her in the night. It was the voice of a terrible and wise spirit telling her that, in humans, evolution had created animals much weaker and baser than they longed to be, and bidding her correct nature's great work. It was to that patient, painstaking quest that she had given her life.

Many obstacles lay in her way. Some she had already surmounted; many remained ahead of her. Looming over all of them was the risk that Annie would one day revert to violent sporogenesis.

It was hard for younger researchers – researchers like Jon – to understand why elders of the tribe like Lazenby attributed so much significance to this risk. For years now, Annie's reproduction in the lab had been a passive and uneventful affair. Somehow – no one knew quite how – Annie recognised when her host was approaching the end of its life, and in preparation some of her cells gave up on their neuronal duties and instead began frantically producing spores. By the time the rat in question died, its blood was full of these spores, which dutiful technicians could simply harvest and inject into new hosts. Everything worked like clockwork. It was hard to see a problem.

But things had once been very different, as the elders remembered only too well. Annie's commitment to the long life and good death of her hosts had been unwavering since 1974, just two years after she had first been identified. During those first two years, however, she had shown a darker face to the world. Far from living out a long and natural life, rats infected with the fungus would suddenly start behaving in the most disturbing fashion, deliberately seeking to wound both themselves and any other living things in the area. Not fatally, but enough to draw blood. And sure enough, it was quickly confirmed that this behaviour was associated with the release of spores into the rat's bloodstream. Unsurprisingly, Hayton's team concluded that this was the mechanism by which Annie spread in the wild – along the same lines as the rabies virus, say, which drives its victims to bite others while stopping them from swallowing their own virus-laden saliva; or those Gordian worms, sailing their grasshoppers into a puddle.

Harvesting spores from these demented rats had been a tricky process, requiring a steady hand and thick gloves, and leaving those who had undertaken it with graphic impressions of how things might go wrong with Annie. Then, in early 1974, a post-doc by the name of Imogen Lazenby noticed that some of the infected rats she was working with were significantly more docile than the others. She shared her observation with Hayton, suggesting that simply by selecting spores from these individuals they might over a few generations be able to develop a strain that was easier to work with – a tame strain, if you will.

Hayton hesitated. The grey men at the Ministry of Defence who called the shots in those days were not that interested in docility: no one had thought of mycotherapy back then, and interest in Annie was focused instead on ways in which she might be weaponised. Making life easier for people in the lab was all very well – but not if it meant an end to the funding that was paying those people's salaries in the first place. 'I wish it weren't so,' he explained to young Lazenby, 'but I do have to take their views into account. Think of it as our Faustian pact. We sacrifice a little freedom so that we can do anything at all.'

Lazenby was furious – but she needn't have been, as Annie was one step ahead of them all. Over the next few weeks, docility spread through the ranks of infected rats like some kind of benign flu. Lazenby's putative tame strain became a reality before their eyes, and the violence and self-mutilation simply disappeared. And as the erratic behaviour of infected rats reduced to nothing, so too their lifespans stretched out until it was hard to deny that a subtle and fundamental change in the texture of causality had taken place. No longer were rats dying shortly after Annie spored; instead, Annie was sporing shortly *before* her hosts died.

This strange transformation in Annie's behaviour posed an obvious question: what if Annie flipped back again? If only they had known why she had flipped in the first place... But there was no good explanation of what had happened in 1974, and no obvious way of preventing a reversion. Nor, unfortunately, were any answers to be found by studying Annie's behaviour in the wild – for the simple reason that Annie no longer *existed* in the wild. The only reason why a species-hunting expedition had gone to Teobeka in the first place was that it was earmarked for destruction in a French nuclear test. Among the creatures collected were examples of a previously undocumented type of shrew, interesting from the perspective of shrew-geeks, but not interesting enough to delay the test. By the time an equally undocumented but rather more significant type of fungus was found living in said shrews, Teobeka had already been vaporised, and neither shrew nor fungus had been found since on any other island in the area. Annie lived only in the lab these days, and researchers were left guessing how she'd made her way in the world outside.

Annie's transformation had made possible everything that followed: no one would have suggested using her for therapeutic purposes if likely side effects had included turning into a walking blood fest. But it also cast a long shadow. What if Annie reverted to violent sporogenesis? What if she did so in a human host? Lazenby was not to be deterred by such anxieties. She'd handled the rats in the early days, retched and wept into the sink, and lain awake at night trying not to reimagine what she had seen. But she'd also sat at the kitchen table as a little girl, and, bloodless as it may have been, there had been every bit as much violence and self-destruction in what she had witnessed there. Yes, there was a mountain to climb, but slowly, methodically, rigorously she would grind that mountain into dust. She'd do so by unflinching adherence to the Laws. Like a nun preparing her soul for paradise through the drudgery of daily observances and chores, she would arrive at the gates of heaven.

As one of its most significant assets, Arexis liked to keep a close eye on the Mycotherapy Unit in Cambridge, and the person to whom this task was allotted was Matt Peachey. A gruff, ugly man in his mid-forties, he amused those who worked in the lab – who saw him going in and out of Lazenby's office – by being the antithesis of everything they imagined in a corporate type. The state of his clothes in particular was a common source of chatter: here was a man who could not put on a clean shirt and tie without getting ink on the one or dipping the other in his soup. It was hard to imagine someone with so little control over his own appearance being in charge of anything. Yet it was to him that Lazenby had deferred: 'The best I can do is raise your idea with Matt Peachey.'

For two weeks after that conversation, Jon waited patiently for a response. Then, midway through the third week, he heard someone laughing about Peachey's hair the day before and decided to approach Lazenby to find out what had happened.

'Professor Lazenby. I was wondering what Mr Peachey had to say about… my idea?'

He had interrupted Lazenby reading, and when she looked up from the paper it was as if, for a moment, she did not recognise him.

'Engineered toxicity?' said Jon.

'Jon,' she said. 'Yes.' She shook her head. 'I'm so sorry.'

'He wasn't interested? Why not?'

Lazenby frowned. 'Look, these things are often about picking the right moment. Leave it with me, OK? There will be another opportunity to bring it up.'

Which might have been very good advice for someone who didn't have a boyfriend who'd just been diagnosed with Scander's disease. Or, indeed, for someone who wasn't Jon. For someone who did and was, it sounded like giving up – something he was just not prepared to do. So, since that was clearly what Lazenby was doing, he decided to take matters into his own hands and talk to Peachey himself.

Peachey's vices supplied the opportunity: for the man was a smoker and, like the few other smokers in the lab, had to take his habit out to a specially designated patch of ground some way from the building's entrance – visible, as luck would have it, from Jon's bench. A few weeks later, on a grey day that constantly threatened rain without once following through, Jon got his chance. Without even taking off his lab coat, he hurried downstairs as fast as he could and headed over to the smokers' corner where Matt Peachey stood alone, contemplating a bed of tired old rose bushes as he drew the smoke down into his lungs.

'Mr Peachey,' he called as he approached.

Peachey looked up. He had a fat, fleshy face, topped with hair that managed somehow to be short and dishevelled all at once.

'I know that you've considered my idea and I'm sure you've given it proper thought and I don't want to question your judgement or anything, but… it's just… I wasn't sure if maybe, I don't know, Professor Lazenby might not have presented it exactly as… I mean, if I could maybe take you through it just one more time and… Of course, I understand that there are bound to be concerns about an idea which breaks Hayton's Laws, but… The thing is, I do think there's a case to be made. I mean a commercial case. And a medical case as well.'

Peachey, still sporting the same frown with which he had heard Jon out, tipped his head back slightly as he blew smoke out against the breeze and tapped the ash from the end of his cigarette – apparently not noticing that most of it was falling on his own trousers.

'Did you prepare that speech?' he said at last. There was a growling undertone to his voice, as if the words were being attacked by bears as they passed through his throat.

Jon nodded. It had been so clear in his head before he started speaking.

'You didn't make a very good job of it then, did you?' continued Peachey. But his frown was wavering as he did so. 'Not a bloody clue what you're on about. Who are you?'

'Sorry, I didn't... Jon Caldicot.'

'Pleased to meet you,' said Peachey, depositing his cigarette in his mouth and sticking out a now unencumbered but still rather yellow paw.

Jon shook it: the grip was firm and enveloping.

'So what's this idea of yours you're on about?' continued Peachey, sacrificing consonants as needed for the sake of the cigarette on his lip.

'Professor Lazenby talked to you about it a couple of weeks ago when you were last here. My idea for a safe way of using Annie in the treatment of neurodegenerative diseases like... Scander's disease, for example.'

Peachey had relieved his lip of the fag. The frown had gone entirely now, though the natural curve of his mouth remained downwards, like a frog's, and his eyes had narrowed slightly. How different those eyes were – sharp, intelligent – from the jowly face that housed them.

'What's Scander's disease?'

'It's... It's a neurodegenerative disease.' A very rare one, it now occurred to Jon, not the most promising market for a therapy. 'I think the same idea would apply to other more common conditions like multiple sclerosis or motor neurone disease. Anything where...'

'Anything where the neurones stop working,' interrupted Peachey. He took another drag on his cigarette, enough to exhaust it, and dropped the stub on the ground – ignoring a sign which had been put up some months previously, at Lazenby's instigation, asking people to use the nearby disposal unit. 'Not exactly a new idea, is it? It would be pretty difficult in practice to target all the malfunctioning cells, but... I guess we'll get to it some day.'

'But we wouldn't have to target cells if we didn't stop Annie at the synapse.' This was one of the three Laws: that a therapeutic strain of Annie should be incapable of spreading across the synapse to other neurones, thus preventing the spread of the fungus through the entire nervous system.

'That's true,' said Peachey, glancing ostentatiously at his watch. 'But then we have to worry about the risk of violent sporogenesis. Though I suppose you're hoping that will go with the spores?' Another Law: that a therapeutic strain should be incapable of producing spores.

'No, I... That's the whole point. We keep the spores as well. We keep everything. All we do is engineer the spores so they're toxic to the host.'

Even as Jon was speaking, the folds of Peachey's face were gathering themselves into a final impatient dismissal. He had drawn breath ready to speak, had almost formed the words with his fleshy lips, when Jon's words actually registered. For an instant Peachey's expression froze – then collapsed across his face like a mudslide.

'We do what?'

'We engineer the spores so they're...' Halfway through repeating himself, the question suddenly broke into Jon's train of thought: 'Professor Lazenby did talk to you about this, didn't she?'

Suddenly noticing the ash on his trouser leg, Peachey set about brushing it off – though he succeeded in smearing in as much as he dislodged. 'Very probably,' he said, without looking up. 'But talk me through it again.'

Had she not explained it properly? Had she not explained it all? This was the whole point, the idea that elegantly dealt with the threat of reversion to violent sporogenesis and overturned the Laws. And it was Scott who had said it: 'I'm going to die whatever I do'. It was true, he was. So why not make death a part of the therapy?

'We engineer the spores so they're toxic,' Jon repeated one more time. 'In the likely event that Annie continues sporing passively, just before the host's death, then the upshot is a very short curtailment of life – after many years lived with full function. However, if Annie ever did revert to violent sporogenesis, then the host would die the moment Annie spored, before any violent behaviours could begin. And they would still have benefited from the intervening years of full function: not as good, I admit, but still a very clear benefit, with no associated risks. All we need to do is ensure the toxin causes an immediate and entirely painless death. We don't have to work out how to stop Annie at the synapse, or stop her sporing… We can go ahead with this straight away. I've reviewed the known proteins in the spore coat and I have some initial ideas about how we might do it, and obviously that part needs some more work, but compared to the Laws… Well, anyway, that's the idea I explained to Professor Lazenby, and… she told me she'd spoken to you about it.'

'Then I'm sure she did,' said Peachey, making one last futile attempt to sort out his trouser leg. He looked up, a yellowed grin on his face: 'Memory like a sieve, lad. Medlicot, did you say?'

'Caldicot. Jon Caldicot.'

'Well, Jon Caldicot,' continued Peachey, reaching into his inside jacket pocket as he did so, 'I tell you what. You have a go at writing down your ideas – doesn't matter if they're a bit rough and ready; it's just something for us to discuss, not a paper in *Nature* – and then' – he had taken a battered old wallet from his pocket, bulging with dog-eared receipts and rail tickets, and from it now pulled a business card – 'send them direct to me, OK? Before Christmas if possible? And sometime in the New Year you and I will have a chat.'

Jon took the card: *Dr Matthew Peachey, Director of Innovation (Biological Therapies), Arexis Ltd.* 'Thank you. I… That's great then.'

And it was. But in his head, another assessment of the situation was ringing with even greater force: *She never said a word to him.*

Life is so much easier to live if we just suppose the existence of villainy. Wrong, but easier. We learn the trick early, as children, smacking the chair that tripped us up. Naughty chair. How much of human history has been written by that sleight of hand? It's easier to draw neat lines than to mend the many partial fragments of truth. And so this broken world stays broken, and we roll on in our lesser lives.

Jon was not defeated or disheartened by the possibility that Lazenby had stood in his way. On the contrary, he was galvanized, and the possibility itself, like a muscle twitching with volts, was made rigid certainty.

She never said a word to him. She lied to me when she told me she'd spoken to him.

Why? He could think about little else that morning and set about the things he could not put off entirely in a distracted, half-hearted fashion. What was her motivation? That was the question that occupied him now.

Maria, the Spanish post-doc who worked opposite, must have noticed him gazing into space, perhaps even caught his lips moving slightly as he ran the scripts of conversations in his head, for she interrupted one such train of thought by tentatively calling out his name.

'Hmm?' he said, shaking himself.

'Are you OK?'

'Yeah. I'm fine. Just... stuff.'

He knew this wouldn't hold. Maria was not the kind to stay quiet long, especially if she suspected something was going on.

'Do you want to grab some lunch out?' he added. He'd noticed Maria's lunch box in the fridge earlier but guessed that whatever was in it would take second place to her curiosity.

'Sure,' she said. 'Let me ten minutes to finish.' Though her English was excellent, she'd sometimes pick the wrong word.

The ruse had, of course, only postponed Maria's inevitable questions about what was wrong with him today, and he'd no idea what he was going to say when the questions did come. But at least they'd be out of the lab, away from Lazenby's domain.

Popping out for lunch with Maria had become a frequent feature of his workdays in the time since he'd joined the lab, to the extent that she surely now counted as a friend rather than a colleague – though, perhaps reflecting cultural differences, the sharing of personal matters tended to be more with than by Jon. A warm, effusive woman who mixed real empathy with a sharp sense of humour, Maria was never short of things to say, and since what she had to say was always entertaining, Jon was very happy to listen.

From Maria's perspective, meanwhile, the fact that Jon had no ulterior motives was more than enough to commend his company. Along with her intelligence and wit, she was also strikingly beautiful in a classically, almost stereotypically Spanish way: slender, olive-skinned, straight black hair, wide bright eyes and a long, sculptural nose. She was also blessed, or cursed, with large, well-formed breasts, which metaphorically as well as literally came between her and many of the straight men she encountered. It was nice to talk to someone who wasn't glancing at her tits every few seconds.

They went to the café they always went to, close enough for their lunch breaks not to be overextended by the journey to and from, but far enough away not to be full of other people from the lab.

'So,' said Maria, as soon as they'd done ordering. 'What is going on with you?' She sometimes pronounced the word 'you' as if it began with a J, a quirk of an accent that drove the English boys wild, and that Jon too thought charming.

'Stuff, like I said,' said Jon. Though he knew that, this lunch, he was not going to get away with listening to Maria – and perhaps had suggested it for precisely that reason. 'Scott got some bad news.'

He'd decided on the way there to tell Maria everything: Scott's diagnosis, his idea, the meeting with Lazenby, what she'd said, everything up to and including his encounter with Peachey that morning. And he started with every intention of following through. But then something happened – at first just a hint of a qualm as he talked about Scott's diagnosis, then fully fledged second thoughts, then a growing conviction: he should *not* share his idea with Maria. He should not share it with *anyone* else – not yet, not until... Until what, he could not have said. But before he'd finished answering Maria's questions about Scott and Scander's, this new decision had taken a firm hold of him: he'd be telling Maria no more.

She, meanwhile, was characteristically full of concern and advice in response to the news he *had* shared. He had to look after himself as well, she pointed out. It was natural he'd want to be there to support Scott but vital he did not forget that he too would need support. In an abstract way he could see how what she said made sense, given that he'd only given her the first part of the story. He'd denied her crucial facts here: that Scott would not in fact be dying at all, that he himself would need no support, that he had a solution, that it was Annie.

'Yes,' he said in response to her questions. 'Yes. No.' This, it struck him, was the first time he'd actually told someone else about Scott's condition. He'd spoken to friends whom Scott had told, yes, but never himself made the announcement. Why would he? The announcement that mattered could not yet be made. And telling half the story would only have prompted exactly the kind of well-meant but slightly irritating attention he was now receiving from Maria.

It was his own fault, of course. He should not have shared even as much as he had.

'No. Yes.'

At least he'd thrown Maria off asking why he had been so distracted that morning. She was, he could see, assuming that worries about Scott were to blame. Allowing that lie to take root, moreover, left him free to keep half a mind on the question that really bothered him: why Lazenby had lied to him. Even as he went through the motions of engaging with Maria's sympathy, the question was rattling back and forth in his brain.

'Do you think I should tell Lazenby?' he said suddenly, cutting rather awkwardly into something Maria had been saying.

'Of course you should,' said Maria without hesitation.

'Really? You don't think she...' He broke off. Obviously he'd not be telling Lazenby, but how to ask Maria what he wanted to ask without supplying the full context? 'Don't you think she might... I don't know, use it against me?'

'What?'

'I mean, don't you think she's...?' Again he broke off. 'Have you never wondered whether you can trust her?'

Unusually, Maria said nothing but looked at him puzzled.

'She twists what you say so it means something else. And she...
I think she can be jealous of ideas.'

Maria shook her head. 'I have lost you. Why are you saying
this about Professor Lazenby?'

'I don't know. It's... I don't know.'

'Do you think you should take some time off perhaps?'

'Why?'

'It's a big thing you are having to respond to. Scott's condition.'

Jon shook his head. 'No, I'm fine.' He should have just let
her rattle on as she had been and not mentioned Lazenby at all.
'Really.'

They headed back to the lab soon after, and he did his best to
look as if he were now getting on with his work without distraction. At times, in fact, he so looked the part that he actually did
forget and became quite immersed in the task at hand. But the
question was always waiting there, ready to rush into any pause in
his activity: why had she lied to him? And when it was time to go
home, it was waiting to go with him.

He had to work through Peachey now. Lazenby would not
be happy perhaps, but that was what Peachey himself had asked:
'Send them direct to me.' No need even to tell her, in the circumstances. Why should he? After what she had done.

'Is there anything up?' asked Scott. They had eaten the first half
of their meal in silence, Jon lost in frowning thoughts and Scott,
it now transpired, shooting him worried glances.

'Hmm?'

'You seem very... I don't know. Upset?'

'I'm sorry. It's... nothing. Difficult problem at work. I've got it
going round in my head. Sorry.'

'That's OK. If it helps to talk about it...'

Maybe it would have. But it wasn't an option. If he couldn't
talk to Maria, who'd signed the non-disclosure agreements and
had nothing personally at stake, then he sure as hell could not talk
to Scott.

'No, it's fine. How was your day? Sorry I didn't ask.'

'It was fine. Normal. Nothing special really.'

They fell silent again, both now staring at their plates: lamb chops and broccoli, prepared by Scott. Jon, who'd been lost in his own head, was now acutely aware of the person sitting opposite him, and the unknown thoughts in his.

'How are you...?' he began, but Scott had begun speaking at exactly the same moment:

'You know, Jon...'

They smiled awkwardly.

'You first,' said Scott.

'No, you go,' said Jon, popping a big piece of lamb in his mouth to reinforce the point. There were only so many times he could ask Scott how he was doing, after all.

'It was nothing.'

'Go on,' said Jon through his mouthful, waving at Scott to continue.

'I was just going to say that... You can still talk to me, you know.'

Jon swallowed his mouthful and frowned. 'How do you mean?'

'I just feel like... Look, this is a difficult time and I really appreciate everything you're doing to support me. I'm just not quite ready to be protected yet.'

Jon was puzzled. Protected? If anything he thought he'd been rather too blunt in some of the explanations he'd given of Scott's condition. 'We've been talking a lot, haven't we? I mean... Look, I'm sorry I'm quiet this evening. I'm wrapped up in something, that's all.'

'It's not that you're quiet,' said Scott, closing his eyes and covering them with his right hand, fingers splayed. Then he pulled the hand away and sat up again, looking at Jon and smiling. 'Forget it. Really. I... I'm just feeling a bit tired, that's all. And my feet are bad again.'

It was the persistent tingling sensation in his feet that had first taken Scott to the doctor. The harbinger of a lingering death.

'Do you want me to rub them for you?'

Scott let out a breath, something halfway between a laugh and a sigh. 'After we've finished eating maybe.'

'Jon is being great about it,' he'd been telling friends. 'I couldn't do without him.' And through those last few weeks it had been true. The doctors did their best to explain things, of course, but they took for granted the parts that really troubled him. 'The neurones progressively lose the capability to transmit messages from your brain,' they'd say, oblivious to the fact that Scott had never really considered how moving his foot might involve one part of him instructing another. With Jon, and only with Jon, he felt able to cry 'Stop!' and pull back to the realms of the obvious. He needed to know how his body worked before he could understand how it was now falling to pieces, and Jon knew all the answers – or at least, when he didn't, understood what others were talking about. That was Jon's way of seeing the world: as a subtle contraption, intricate beyond any individual's grasp perhaps, but still knowable in its essence. And with Jon's help Scott was beginning to understand the events unfolding in his lower motor neurones and so feel a little less in their thrall.

And yet... At the edges, like the first twinges of discomfort in a joint that will some day grow stiff with arthritis, Scott felt moments of irritation too. If only Jon had also been able to accept why his patient accounts of how a fault on a protein could wreak so much havoc did not *exhaust* what was happening to Scott. If only he'd been able to make a little room for Scott's way of seeing the world: as a place in which the laws of conservation hold only for things which do not matter; in which loss can never be accounted for, only eventually accepted.

'It's very nice, by the way,' said Jon, prodding the remaining lamb on his plate with a fork. He hesitated. 'I do have to do a bit of work before I go to bed as well. Something I have to write.'

'No problem.'

'I'll rub your feet too.'

'Really, they're not that bad. You do your work.'

Jon nodded. 'It's quite important.'

More important than just rubbing Scott's feet. If only he could have explained as much to Scott.

For a few days after sending his thoughts to Peachey, Jon was on a hair trigger, pumped with adrenalin, ready to fight or fly at a moment's notice. But nothing happened: no response from Peachey, no change in Lazenby's behaviour, nothing. This, he reminded himself more than once, was entirely in line with what Peachey had said to expect: only 'sometime in the New Year' would they have another chat. Nevertheless, he was disappointed. The more he thought about it, the more it seemed to him his idea warranted a much swifter response. This was not just a solution to Scott's problem he was proposing. It was a revolution in mycotherapy. A liberation.

He'd signalled as much in the title he'd given his short paper: *Engineered spore toxicity as an alternative to compliance with Hayton's Laws*. But at this point, I think I should pause to check that you too have understood the nature of what Jon was proposing, and the context in which he was proposing it. When you make your decision, I would like it to be an informed one, and these are technical matters. If you have a technical mind, of course, if you've already grasped it all, then feel free to skim a few pages. If, however, you are – as I was – a late student, slower to understanding, you may welcome a few reflections of the kind I, in my own time, was denied.

Let me start by making a general observation. In the West, our paradigm of medicine has long been the *cure*: the elimination of agents of disease, be they micro-organisms, toxins or faults in our own make-up. But even in the West, cures are only one part of the picture. Indeed, the endeavour of medical science can be seen as a heroic counterpoint to those primitive bacterial tropisms that had once inspired Lazenby: do away with the bad, leave the good well alone. Advances in the latter, leaving the good alone – keyhole surgery, smart drug delivery, brachytherapy – can be just as important as breakthrough cures.

And so it was with Annie too. The dream of those first myco-therapists – Hayton, Lazenby, Kapinsky – was that she might do away with a species of bad that had gripped humanity through ages. A cure! But the challenge they faced was to leave the good alone. For Annie in her native form is beyond good and evil, a creature of pure will: the will to multiply. Introduced into a host – a shrew, a rat, a human, it matters not – she does not say, as some clever neuropsychologist might: 'These neurones are behaving just as I think they ought to, so I will leave them be'. She does not rest until her proliferating clones have taken over the entire network, leaping from cell to cell across the synapses that divide them. Nor, when the moment comes to move on, does she ask, as a medical lawyer might: 'Who gives their consent to bear me next?' Nor indeed, as a bioethicist might: 'By what means may I pass to them?' In those first few months in Hayton's lab, she had shown herself capable of violent contempt for the well-being of her hosts, and though she had laid that violence aside, those who followed had no way of knowing when she might take it up again. Annie gave no promise to leave the good alone.

Hence the three Laws, the bulwarks raised around the good as conditions of any therapeutic use of Annie.

First, a therapeutic strain of Annie should be incapable of spreading across the synapse to other neurones. Inject such a strain in just those locations where the clever neuropsychologist thinks it is needed – in the brain, perhaps, or the spine, or the peripheral nervous system – and it will take over only those neurones it can reach before the body's immune system wipes it out. It cannot spread any further on its own. It does just as it is told.

Secondly, a therapeutic strain of Annie should be incapable of producing spores. It would, like productive but infertile crops, depend entirely on humans for its proliferation. Spores would be engineered in sterilised facilities, not spawned into the blood of those about to die, and medical lawyers would oversee the informed choices of those seeking new lives.

Thirdly, a therapeutic strain of Annie should promote only positive behaviours in its hosts. It should not, constrained and neutered as it is, recall its former freedom and lash out. Its will to proliferate should be utterly extinguished and the task of deciding what it should and should not do handed to committees of bioethicists.

Thus Lazenby and those who worked with her had set about correcting nature's great work. Thus, if you'll forgive the picturesque allusion, they hearkened to the terrible and wise spirit, took up Caesar's sword, stepped from the Temple roof and turned stones into bread.

The origin of the Laws lay, of course, in violent sporogenesis. But over time the Laws had acquired a validity of their own in the mycotherapy community – even as belief in the threat of violent sporogenesis declined. As the years went by and Annie continued in her placid ways, more and more younger researchers began to wonder whether the risk of violent sporogenesis was in fact a real one. Was it not possible that the behaviour of those first rats was down to some additional factor – something in the environment, an unknown pathogen – which had subsequently disappeared? To many – Jon included – this seemed a far more plausible explanation than the idea that Annie had spontaneously changed her behaviour across many different locations. Those who ran the labs, who remembered, would shake their heads at this growing scepticism: if only they had seen what we saw. The young researchers, in response, would wonder if their elders were not letting emotion cloud their scientific judgement. Between them, the bald lack of evidence of Annie's behaviour in the wild, or of other factors in those early labs, turned the disagreement into a pinhead waltz of angels: the risk could neither be proven nor dismissed. They might as well debate the existence of God. And in this vacuum of uncertainty, the grip of the Laws had grown not weaker but stronger. On these at least we can all agree, even the most ardent sceptic would say. The Laws are just common sense.

So it seemed because they thought only of life. Life was the hidden constant in their formulae. And then, one evening, listening to Scott in his flat, Jon remembered death: 'I'm going to die whatever I do.' For death needs no laws, no technicians or committees.

The proposal – Jon summarised in his paper to Peachey – *is to engineer one or more proteins in the spore coat of* A.n. *rendering its spores instantly and fatally toxic to a human host. This will enable therapeutic use of the engineered strain to cure neurodegenerative conditions. Compliance with Hayton's Laws will be unnecessary, because:*

i) *In such conditions, replacement of the entire neural system is required. Not only is stopping at the synapse unnecessary, it would actually prevent therapeutic use.*

ii) Sporogenesis will be associated with the quick and painless death of the patient. Provided simple precautions are taken around the disposal of patients' bodies after death, there will be no risk of spread. No restriction on sporing is therefore required.

iii) The only negative behaviour ever associated with A.n. is violent sporogenesis. This is violent behaviour that follows the production of spores. Since the patient will die at this point, there can be no further behaviour. The positive behaviour delivered, meanwhile, is the continuation of normal, fully functioning behaviour in the patient long after it would have ended. No further controls on behaviour are therefore required.

The engineered form of A.n. will of course be not only the cure for the patient's condition but also, via its toxic spores, the ultimate cause of death. Overall, however, the clinical outcomes are clearly and overwhelmingly positive.

A revolution in mycotherapy. A liberation from the Laws. Yet the paper was sent and nothing happened. No word from Peachey. No reaction from Lazenby. And soon the lab was winding down to its state of festive coma, with vital life support – the feeding of rats, the checking of cultures – maintained by a skeleton staff and the rest despatched to towns and countries afar. Soon Jon was preparing for his own annual and unavoidable stint in the parental home. Soon he was on the familiar train and, as it seemed every year, heading backwards, not forwards.

3

Christmas at home resembled an assault course, the challenge being to scramble over awkward pauses and avoid falling into unwanted conversations. Given the amount of practice he'd had, Jon ought now perhaps to have been an expert in getting through it, but it's a strange quirk of families that, however long we spend in them, we never get better at them. Christmas never got any easier.

His first mistake was worthy of a rookie: arriving a couple of days earlier than his brother. By doing so, he condemned himself to two whole lunches and dinners alone with the parents, picking his way around whatever topics in that morning's *Telegraph* had wound up his father. Jon himself rarely followed the news, and when he did found himself ambivalent on many issues. Had he himself been charged with solving this or that social or economic problem, or dealing with a specific foreign-policy crisis, then – and only then – would he have taken a stand: he'd strong enough opinions when he was directly involved, for example on lab protocols or new innovations in the field. On matters outside his sphere of influence, however, he could generally see both sides of any argument. When others discussed current affairs, he would find himself nodding in agreement to views expressed from all ends of every political spectrum – with just one exception: when the other in question was his father, speaking in those tones of jaded disdain that newspaper articles so often provoked in him. 'Sheer incompetence,' Mr Caldicot would declare about whichever minister, public servant or government agency had attracted his attention. 'Most disappointing.' And Jon would find himself viscerally drawn to the defence of the slighted party, often in the absence of knowledge or evidence, sitting there biting his lip or, if he released it, quickly regretting it.

At least at meals both parents were present, and their starch-stiffened interactions with each other provided some sort of boundaries to the conversation, like crash barriers along a much-travelled clifftop highway. The arguments were always the same, and always ended up in the same place, which was nowhere. More fraught with risk were the conversations each parent would snatch singly with their son when the other was engaged elsewhere – at an average rate of one encounter per parent per festival. These were the perilous moments when they came closest to saying what they really thought.

The paternal intervention came on the second day Jon was back – the morning before Christmas Eve. Mr and Mrs Caldicot had headed off after breakfast to buy another bootload of surplus food, leaving Jon to install himself in a corner of the living room with some reading for work. A while later he heard them coming back and bumping around in the kitchen, and hesitated for just a moment before deciding not to go and offer to help putting things away. Five minutes later he glanced up again to realise with horror that his father had noiselessly entered the room and was standing at its far end, eyeing Jon with the thoughtful, frowning face Jon had often seen him apply to his case notes.

'Oh. You made me jump.'

'Apologies,' said his father, though with an intonation that suggested a response to someone asking what time it was. He sat in the burgundy leather armchair that had always been unquestionably his. It was a large room, with dark wood and weighty soft furnishings, and their chosen seats left a forbidding stretch of Persian rug between them.

'Yes,' said Mr Caldicot, though not obviously in answer to anything. 'So how is work?'

'Very good,' said Jon, nodding. This was often the first question.

'I suppose you'll tell me it's top secret and that you can't divulge any details.'

Jon bridled slightly. He had never in any conversation with his father used the word 'top' in front of the word 'secret'. 'I'm not just telling you it's secret. I'm actually not allowed to talk about it.'

'Hmm,' said his father, placing hands on his knees with out-stretched fingers. 'Always disappointing.'

'How's *your* work?' said Jon, letting the journal he was holding – thus far in a tilted position for reading – fall flat on his lap.

His father sighed and frowned. 'Very good, on strict performance measures. My statistics remain among the best in the country. With only a few years left to retirement, however...' He folded his hands over his stomach and stared at Jon, as if Jon would obviously understand what he would have gone on to say had it been necessary.

Jon did not, and indicated as much with a pointed shrug.

'One's thoughts turn to legacy,' said his father wearily. 'One would like to think one could impart a little of the skill one had acquired over the years to a younger generation. But these young registrars...' He shook his head.

'I see,' said Jon, nodding slightly. There was a moment of awkward silence, and – without much hope – he tilted the journal upwards again and lowered his eyes to the text.

The conversation, however, was not finished.

'I found myself thinking the other day about *your* younger years,' continued his father – and for just a moment, Jon wondered if he could really be about to embark on the kindergarten story yet again. 'Do you remember the day you first announced to us that you wanted to be a scientist?'

Jon said nothing, merely curved his mouth into a slight, unhappy smile. This was potentially worse than the kindergarten.

'I remember being a little surprised by the choice of specialism,' continued his father, who had not really needed an answer anyway. 'Not that I've anything against microbiology. On the contrary, a solid science. I used to know an excellent parasitologist.' He chuckled. 'Great connoisseur of sherries. However, that's by the bye. A solid science, but not exactly a glamorous one. Not what one might expect a young man with such' – he waved a hand towards Jon – 'talents to settle on at such a young age. But you'd seen this programme about... Francis?'

'Francesco Redi.'

'Francis...co Redi. Exactly. And I remember thinking: if the boy is inspired, Henry, let him follow his inspiration. So I did. And you have.'

'Yes.'

'And are you still?'

'Am I still what?'

'Inspired?'

The question caught Jon off guard. 'By Redi, you mean?' he said unconvincingly. He knew his father did not mean that. And his father knew he knew, and gave him a weary look. 'One would hate to think of your gifts going to waste. Your promise. It would be so... well.'

'And why would you think they are?' said Jon, his anger rising. Though anger was not the only emotion. There was something else: something more elemental. And before he could identify it, it had chased more words from his mouth. 'I've actually made something of a breakthrough in the last few months.'

His father raised one eyebrow slightly.

'Possibly quite an important one,' continued Jon. Why had he said 'possibly'? It should have been 'definitely'. 'I'm waiting to hear back from the company that... well, the funder. It will save lives. And it will revolutionise the field.' Now he had gone too far. Yes, ripping up the Laws was revolutionary, but the words sounded ridiculous coming out of his own mouth. 'I mean, in a way. It's a... Well, it's a very different approach from what everyone else has been trying to date.'

Beyond a relaxation of the raised eyebrow, his father's face had shown no reaction as Jon blurted out this claim to continued in- spiration. But now, as Jon wound to an ungainly halt, something akin to a smile played across the corners of his father's mouth.

'That sounds very satisfactory,' he said. 'Of course, it's the sort of thing we'd have expected of you, whatever specialism you'd cho- sen. Just so long as you're still being adequately challenged, that's the thing. And you're still inspired to challenge yourself. I would hate to think you were stagnating.'

'I'm not stagnating,' insisted Jon, though the words came out a little strangely, so a listener might have wondered whether this were a statement of fact or an expression of determination.

'Good good,' said his father, getting to his feet. 'If only I could believe the same about your brother.'

Jon clenched his teeth to stop the reflex enquiry as to why he'd said this escaping his lips.

'Well,' said Mr Caldicot.

'Yes,' said Jon, pointedly picking up his journal again.

'I suspect my surgical skills may be needed in the kitchen.'

'OK.'

And with that the conversation was over – though, agitated, Jon found it impossible to return to his reading and soon gave up entirely.

To his great relief, his brother arrived a couple of hours later, along with his wife and two small children: a maelstrom of noise and need that snapped Jon and his parents out of the ritual shadow-play of the last few days together. Jon's nephew, a timid little boy but the first grandchild, provided an alternative focus for Mr Caldicot's dynastic ambitions, while his niece, as yet still mewling and puking, made sure that no one could really focus on anything apart from her for very long. Christmas rolled on, presents were opened, mince pies were eaten, the Queen made her speech, and Jon's brother engaged in long and sometimes loud arguments with their father, while his sister-in-law fussed unhappily over the children. All pretty grim, but at least no one was asking Jon any questions.

Then, on his last evening, just when he thought he had made it through unscathed, his mother somehow managed to catch him alone in the kitchen while he was making himself a turkey and stuffing sandwich. He knew at once, from the way she peered at him through her spectacles, that she wanted to establish something.

'Just making a sandwich,' he said, weakly and unnecessarily.

His mother ignored the remark and, as was her wont, got straight to the point. 'Are you happy, Jon?'

'Erm… yes.'

'You don't seem it.'

'I don't?' said Jon, genuinely surprised.

His mother narrowed her eyes slightly. 'Your father may be good at cutting hearts open, but when it comes to reading them he's a numbskull.' Quite why she'd referred to his father at this point was not clear to him. 'So come on. Let's have it.'

'I... don't know what to say.'

If he'd ever got round to coming out to her, of course, if she'd not connived in quietly giving up on the questions about whether he had a girlfriend – well, even then, what might he have said? That a man he'd been seeing since the spring had a terminal illness, but not to worry, he had a solution? None of which meant he was unhappy, anyway. Neither that nor... anything.

'No,' his mother was saying. 'I suppose you don't. And if you ask me, that's half the problem. But you're not asking me. None of you are. So... go on then: make your sandwich.' And she stalked back out of the room.

A few minutes later he carried his plate out into the room where they were all gathered. His mother was by now nursing his niece, cooing – albeit brusquely – to entertain the little girl. His father was playing with Lego with his nephew – or rather alongside his nephew, since the boy's attempts to decorate the man's construction were not proving welcome. His sister-in-law was sitting back in a sofa next to his mother, her bottom so far forwards and her shoulders sunk so low that she was almost horizontal, her eyes gazing upwards and into space, a large glass of red wine held slightly aloft in her hand. Only his brother, Harry, fleetingly caught his eye, and in the contours of his face Jon saw a passing acknowledgement of their shared suffering. Then Harry too looked away: they didn't talk much these days and had little else in common.

The following day he was back on the train, another Christmas over. But this time he felt neither the relief he had felt in years gone by, returning to California or to Oxford, nor that sense that he could now be himself again, tell the truth again.

Scott's diagnosis cast a pall over their New Year festivities that only Jon could see through, and pretending to be sad but putting a brave face on it proved almost as exhausting as pretending to be happy had at home. They spent New Year's Eve at Scott's place, with a group of friends hand-picked by Scott; and, after they'd sung Auld Lang Syne, Scott made a little speech to them all. New Year's Eve, he noted, was usually a time for looking backwards and forwards.

But he'd been doing a lot of thinking since his diagnosis and realised that what he needed to do now was focus on the present – and that these were the people he wanted to do that with. 'There'll be plenty of time to deal with what's coming. What I don't want to deal with is a feeling of regret that I missed out on something along the way.' There were tears, and toasts, and hugs, and high emotions all round. To Jon, the whole thing stank of capitulation, and he excused himself a little later and headed back to his own flat.

The next day he popped into the lab. A few other people were around, among them Lazenby – who nodded to him from her office as he walked by. And a strange thought occurred to him: had any of it actually happened? Had he spoken to Lazenby? Had she lied to him? Had the conversation with Peachey ever taken place? And his paper – had he actually written and sent it? Had he even had an idea in the first place? Just as resolutions written by a New Year's moon fade to invisibility in the daylight of January, so too the sense of purpose which had animated him since that evening when Scott first shared his diagnosis was growing transparent, insubstantial. He could almost see through it.

And then, just two days later, the shit hit the fan.

Jon didn't even know Peachey was in the lab that day. He'd received no reply to his e-mail, and from his bench could not see him coming in. Nor did Lazenby say anything when she popped her head round the corner to ask if she could have a word, please. Perhaps he should have guessed – but didn't, and so was taken completely by surprise when he walked into Lazenby's office to find Matt Peachey already sitting in the derelict armchair; indeed, with his ruined features and rumpled suit, seeming almost to have grown out of it.

'Jon,' he said warmly, hauling himself to his feet – a task made no easier by the low, yielding seat. He held out a huge hand and shook Jon's firmly. 'Happy New Year. Good to see you again. And thank you for this.' He held up in his other hand a dog-eared printout of the paper Jon had written. 'Very good stuff.'

Lazenby came in, carrying a chair from the lab meeting area for Jon to sit on. As if to welcome her, Peachey repeated: 'Really very good indeed. We were just agreeing, weren't we?'

'Absolutely,' said Lazenby, for all the world as if she meant it – which Jon could not for a moment believe. 'Very interesting. Have a seat.' She herself sat in her office chair, claiming as usual both ascendancy and the right to swivel. Following her lead, Jon lowered himself a little hesitantly onto the hard, fixed chair he'd been assigned. No tea had been offered.

'Speaking from the company's point of view,' Peachey was saying, 'this is just the kind of innovative thinking we've been crying out for.'

Lazenby winced.

'And,' continued Peachey, 'I really appreciate the way you've tried to put it into… well, a commercial context. Really, that's my job, not yours. However it may seem at times, I am on your side in all of this. Someone's got to keep the bean-counting out of the science, after all. But I have to say, it does make my life a lot easier when people are prepared to meet me halfway. I really appreciate that.'

'On the other hand,' interjected Lazenby, 'there *are* some pretty fundamental questions to be considered.' Somewhere along the way she had picked up her pen and begun twizzling it round her fingers like a baton.

'That there are,' said Peachey, giving the bears in his throat free rein. 'And of course, on fundamental questions there is always room for disagreement.'

There was the briefest of pauses, as Lazenby chose not to respond but instead kept her eyes fixed firmly on Jon.

'Right,' he said, feeling that it was his turn to contribute, but not at all sure where he was supposed to fit into the conversation. 'Well… I'm glad you think it's a good idea.'

'Not straightforward, though,' said Lazenby – then added in a slightly lower voice: 'As I said when we spoke about this before.'

'The thing is,' said Peachey quickly, almost interrupting her, 'from the perspective of actually taking this thing to market, there are two big outstanding problems. I'm not talking about the science now, but the… well, the ethics I suppose. The first is the fact that what you're proposing does in the end mean killing people.'

'But they're going to die whatever we do,' protested Jon. 'And this way they get years of… Think of it as palliative.'

'Yes, I know,' said Peachey, half-lifting a paw from his knee to stop him. 'It's all in here' – he tapped Jon's paper, still lying on his lap – 'and I think I'm with you on that one. I'm just saying that it is an ethical issue, and it would need more than just my say-so.'

'Not straightforward,' repeated Lazenby.

Peachey caught his breath, rolling his eyes towards the ceiling as he did so. 'If it were down to me,' he tried again, 'I'd be testing this out tomorrow. I mean, the way I see it, there are people out there already at the end, with little to lose and everything possibly to gain. But there's… a way of doing things which we do have to follow, because it's there for good reasons. Plus other… things we have to work around.' His quick little eyes met Jon's again, the brows above them rising slightly as if desperately signalling something. A swift glance in Lazenby's direction, like a pointing finger, then back to Jon.

'That's not the main problem, though,' Lazenby was saying. She had been glowering at her pencil as Peachey spoke and so missed this little pantomime.

Peachey fell back in his seat a little. It was obviously Lazenby's turn now.

'What do you think it would be like?' she continued, looking up again to address the question directly to Jon.

'Erm… What would what be like?'

'Having this treatment of yours.'

'Well, it would be quite a straightforward procedure really. You could use an intraspinal injection like we do here. It's quite a… standard…'

He tailed off because it was clear from the look on Lazenby's face that he was not answering the right question. 'After all that,' she said. 'Having had the treatment.'

Jon shook his head slightly. He didn't understand.

'Can I have the…?' said Lazenby to Peachey, gesturing towards the paper on his lap. Then, taking her time to reach behind her for her reading glasses and balance them on the end of her nose, she held Jon's work out at arm's length, peering at it as if it smelled odd and flipping the pages with the very tips of her long fingers. 'Yes, here we are… Scander's disease.' She looked up at Jon, over the top of her glasses. 'You use that as your main example. Not one I'd heard of before but, having checked, my understanding is that someone suffering from this unfortunate condition remains conscious, able to hear and see, right up to the very end.'

'Yes.'

'Which, to you and me, sounds intolerable, like being a prisoner in one's own body.'

'Yes.'

'But still something. Still an experience. Still you. Whereas if I replace your entire central nervous system – part of which was *still functioning*, remember – if I replace all that with *A. n.*… Is that still you? Do you still have these experiences? I mean, your body can move again, it carries on living, excellent. But are *you* still there to enjoy it all?'

'I…' began Jon, then stopped again. She was doing what she always did: undermining a perfectly good argument with… questions. Always questions. He glanced at Peachey, but he remained slumped back in the armchair and met Jon's look with no glances or rolling eyes, just the slightest of nods.

'Your whole premise,' continued Lazenby, flicking another page of the paper, 'is that people with something like Scander's disease are' – she hesitated, looking for the phrase she wanted – ' "going to die whatever they do". Matthew put it very well just now: "little to lose, and everything possibly to gain". But that little may still be a great deal. And your… idea, well…' – she handed the paper back to Peachey and removed her reading glasses – 'it might mean taking away even that little.'

There was a pause. Jon's chance to ride to the rescue of his idea. His brilliant, perfectly thought through idea. The idea that would save Scott. Provided – and no, this was not what he should be thinking about, but he couldn't shake the question now it had been asked – provided it was still Scott that had been saved.

Then the moment was over. It was too late.

It was Peachey that brought it to an end: 'We're not saying it could never be possible. For my part, I think… I hope it will be one day. But before we can take it forwards, we have to understand what it would really mean. We can't just wipe out a person's entire nervous system without knowing what will happen to the person.'

'It's replacing, not wiping out,' corrected Jon, but the fire had gone from him.

'Point taken. Replacing. But we'd still have to find out.'

'Which I think we can do,' said Lazenby, suddenly sounding almost upbeat. 'We begin with the controlled replacement of single neurones. We move towards therapeutic uses with engineered aversions. As we go, we monitor the phenomenological consequences. We build up an evidence base on what it's like from the inside. Something we'd always planned to check on – but now we can put it towards your idea as well.'

In other words, everything stayed exactly as it had been. The Laws stood. It was only by sticking to the Laws that they might one day earn the right to break them.

'And don't worry,' added Peachey, 'if and when the time comes, I'll make sure you're properly credited.'

'Right,' said Jon, flattened. 'I'm not too worried about that really.'

'Well you should be, lad. It's a bloody jungle out there. This is about your career as well.'

'Not that everyone adheres to the same principles and standards we have here in the lab,' threw in Lazenby. 'It's one of the things I pay a lot of attention to,' she added, swivelling towards Peachey, 'helping people build their careers as scientists. Anyway...' She swung back to Jon, slapping her hands on her knees as she did so. 'I think we're done here for today.'

But they weren't done. Not Lazenby and Jon, at any rate, as Jon discovered quarter of an hour later after Peachey had been ushered from the building.

'A quick word?' she said, finding him back at his bench.

Maria shot him a concerned glance as he rose to follow. To have two 'words' so close together was a sure sign of trouble; plus she'd noticed the look on his face when he returned from the first 'word', and the silent wall of concentration that stood around him, forbidding her to speak. Inside that enclosure, Jon had been running in rings, hunting for the things he should have said, finding nothing. There had to be an answer, the hidden constant that, turned into a variable, unlocked the puzzle. But he didn't have it.

'Tell me,' said Lazenby when they were settled back into their usual positions, 'what do you think makes a great scientist?'

This wasn't one of the starting points for conversation that Jon had been expecting as he followed her along the colourless lab corridor; but then, with Lazenby, it seemed things never were as he expected.

'I don't know. Curiosity?'

Lazenby nodded. There was nothing about her face or body language to suggest she might be about to murder him, with a writing implement thrust through a weak point in his skull perhaps, but still he couldn't entirely rule out the possibility.

'And... Curiosity and, I guess, good ideas.'

'Good ideas,' repeated Lazenby. She had reached out unthinkingly to take up her pen, as she always did, but now it was as if she'd noticed her own hand and stopped it in mid-air. 'That's what people attribute my success to.' She let the hand fall slowly back to her knee. 'But they're wrong, you know.'

There was a pause, but it did not seem intended for Jon to say anything.

'I've seen quite a few bright kids like you in my time,' continued Lazenby. 'Full of good ideas. Every so often one of them gets lucky and makes a breakthrough of some kind, and then they think they're set for life. They look back at history and fixate on those few examples whose luck held, the ones who went on to win prizes and were feted as great scientists. The geniuses. The outliers. But, of course, there's nothing in the history books about the rest of the normal distribution curve. So before long, chances are, those kids find out their luck was just that: luck, a one-hit wonder, no real substance. And then they go off and become... consultants, or journalists. Or they go to work for a drug company. Which is probably the right choice for *them*. But it isn't science. Because what they want is excitement, and science, in the final analysis, is boring. Yes?'

'Yes.'

'There's no such thing as a great scientist. There is only great science, great method. I know you've always... struggled a bit with the way we do things here, the rules, the... procedure. But the rules *are* the science. They're bigger than any of us. So if you ask me what makes a great scientist, I'd say there are two things, and the first of those is discipline. Almost like a martial art. The discipline of method. Having the humility to recognise that we don't do things the way we do because we feel like it, because we want to, but because it *works*, because it has been *proven* to work, again and again, century after century.'

She gave Jon a wry smile, and drank some of the tea she'd evidently made for herself before coming to collect him a second time. Clearly it was his turn to speak now.

'And the second thing?' he said helplessly.

'Oh yes,' she said, putting her mug back down again and looking Jon straight in the eye. 'The second thing. Integrity.'

She paused – a pause that, though it lasted barely a second, yawned with tension.

'Why did you do that?'

This time the pause lasted even longer – so long that it ran from one life into another. But the timeline of that transformation was tipped on its end, its many events not laid end to end but stacked one upon another: Lazenby's lie; Scott's diagnosis; Francesco Redi's jars of meat; Miss Carter's bin in the kindergarten – always Miss Carter and her fucking bin.

'You go behind my back to our funders,' continued Lazenby – still at the same even pitch but with the consonants of each word sharpened by fury – 'you put me in an almost impossible position...'

'You lied to me,' interrupted someone. The words had come out of Jon's mouth.

'I beg your pardon.'

'You told me you'd raised the idea with Peachey and that he had rejected it. I saw him, I thought I'd give it another go, and he told me you'd never said a word to him.' He was out on a limb now: Peachey had said no such thing. But he had nowhere else to go. 'And it was him who told me to send a paper to him. What was I supposed to do? I was the one in an impossible position, and all because you lied to me.'

Lazenby was shaking her head, her mouth opened in readiness to speak, though she waited until Jon had come to a halt before she did so. 'I never told you I'd spoken to Peachey. I said the complete opposite. I said we should wait until an opportune moment.'

'You lied to me,' repeated Jon. She was doing it again, holding up her magic mirror to the world and reflecting her own twisted half-reality.

'I did no such thing. Why would I lie to you? I don't know what you think is happening here, but...'

'I'll tell you what's happening here,' interrupted Jon. 'My boyfriend has Scander's disease. One by one, his nerve cells will die. He'll lose the feeling in his limbs, then the movement. In the end he will hear and see but nothing else. And then he will die. And I will be sitting next to him the whole time thinking I could have saved him. I could have saved him: me, not discipline, not fucking integrity. What would you do, hm? What would you do if you were me?'

Too late Jon realised how loudly he was shouting. They'd be hearing him in the lab, for sure: if not the words, then at least the tone and volume of his voice. He'd really done it now. She had pushed him too far.

'Jon,' Lazenby was saying, her right hand held up and bent back slightly, the open palm turned towards him. 'Jon. Just... take a deep breath, OK? I'm very, very sorry to hear all of that, and we need to talk about it. But right now, you need to... Yes? OK?'

'I didn't mean to shout,' said Jon, feeling suddenly very vulnerable. He'd meant everything he'd shouted, though.

'That's OK. Don't worry about it. I think maybe you should take the rest of the day off. Go home, do what you need to do, calm down a bit. OK? Then we'll talk again tomorrow.'

'I had a chromatograph running...'

'Maria will pick it up. I'll talk to her. And we'll talk tomorrow. Now I know what's going on I can try to help you. But right now you're too emotional.'

Help him? Her, help him? But she was right: he was too emotional. This wasn't the end of it, not this time, but it wasn't the moment to push things further either.

'OK,' he said. 'Right. Yes.'

It was Scott's turn to go round to Jon's place that evening. He'd offered to cook dinner – as he often did – and arrived with the shopping at about half past five, not expecting to find Jon already home, lying on the bed, staring at the ceiling.

'Oh, hello. You're home early. Is everything OK?'

'Hey there. Yes, fine. I'd finished for the day and thought I might as well knock off.'

'Right.' Scott frowned, obviously unconvinced. 'Are you sure?'

'Yes, I'm fine.'

'As you wish,' said Scott. 'I'll get the dinner started.' And he returned to the kitchen.

Jon remained lying on the bed. What *was* it like to be another person? To be Scott, for example? And what would it be like if Annie were in place, or in charge, or in service, or… it wasn't even clear what the word would be. He had seen with his own eyes, day after day, what Annie did – but in rats. And what was it like to be a rat? Before or after?

His head was starting to ache from the knots he was tying inside it. It was either this fruitless circuit or another: that Lazenby had him exactly where she wanted him, that she'd found his weak spot, his vulnerability. By 'helping' him she'd have him back under her thumb. Was that it? Was that how it worked then? She'd still lied to him, though – he was sure of that. Though her question was a good one: why? Why would she have done that?

And then there was Peachey. 'If it were down to me,' he'd said, 'I'd be testing this out tomorrow. I mean, the way I see it, there are people out there already at the end, with little to lose and everything possibly to gain.'

There was a clattering noise from the kitchen: Scott getting saucepans out of a cupboard into which they did not really fit. Like the thoughts in Jon's head. If he could just dislodge the right one…

Their conversation over dinner was halting. In and of itself, there was nothing so unusual about them having little to say: they'd made it past the point in the relationship where they felt they had to talk all the time and would pass whole meals together reading, or checking social media, or texting, or watching something on the television. Most of the time they spent alone together was in fact in the virtual presence of thousands, a starry cast of welcome distractions. Tonight, however, neither of them seemed to have the appetite for alternative activities, and through the long pauses their attention remained awkwardly focused on each other.

In the end, Scott could take it no more.

'Look, Jon, I know you can't talk about your work, but I can tell something is going on and… I don't think it's good to keep things bottled up like this.'

'No, it's…' began Jon, preparing by reflex to offer another empty denial – then stopped: what was the point pretending? He let out a deep breath. 'Problems in the lab.'

Scott nodded. 'Is it serious?'

How to answer that one? Was it serious? Scott's life depended on it. 'Yeah, it's pretty serious. I've… kind of fallen out with my boss.'

'That's tough,' said Scott. 'I know there's nothing I can do, but… you know, it does sometimes help to tell someone else what's going on, so if you want to do that…'

'Thanks,' said Jon. And could he? Was now the time to tell Scott? And tell him what? For the first time, it suddenly occurred to him that the good news he had to deliver was more complex, more equivocal than he had imagined. What would it be like after Annie? He couldn't answer that question.

'Actually,' he continued, 'I have a question.'

'Sure.'

'If there were a possible solution – a cure, I mean – but it was so radical that you couldn't be sure you'd still be you afterwards, would you want it?'

Scott shifted awkwardly in his seat. He'd been looking at Jon across the table but now dropped his eyes to his steak and began sawing at it.

'You mean, like, if it would change my personality?'

'No, I... well, sure. For example.'

'Why do you ask?'

'Because...' If he was going to do it, then now was the moment. 'It's just a question. I mean, hypothetically.'

Scott put down his cutlery and sat back in his chair, though his eyes remain fixed on the plate for a moment longer. Then he looked up, a steeliness in his eyes that Jon had not seen before.

'And this is related to your problems at work?'

Jon said nothing. Yes, it was; it was central to those problems. But he couldn't see any clear way to explain that.

Scott sighed. 'In the future, when things get bad, then who's to say what I will or won't do? I don't know. And I don't want to think about it either. It's like I said at New Year: I want to live for the present, without regrets. And either you can be part of that or—' He broke off, exhaling loudly and again looking down. 'There's no cure, Jon,' he continued. 'I admire who you are, I admire what you do, but this is what it is.'

'I shouldn't have asked,' said Jon. There was another conversation, just out of reach, in which they were talking about what he'd meant them to talk about, but somehow he'd missed the turning. 'I'm sorry.'

'It's fine. It's hard for you as well, I know.'

'But I shouldn't have asked.'

'Forget it. Let's talk about something else.'

So they talked about something else. Scott did the hard work coming up with topics, and Jon went along with them, though if someone had asked him just fifteen minutes later what they'd been talking about – what Scott had been talking about, accompanied by his acknowledgements – he'd have had no idea. All the real action was inside his skull, in the deafening babble of billions of neurones. And when he and Scott at last went to bed, they would not let him sleep.

Then, from the swirling cacophony, rose a fragment he had not heard before. Peachey again: 'This is about your career as well.' His career as a scientist. In what way was this about his career? When exactly had he signed up to... discipline? Doing what had been proven to work, again and again, century after century. Yes he'd had a dream, but the dream of a pioneer in a new-found land, not the dream of a crank in a vast rolling vehicle. Why this assumed projection of his future along lines he had never chosen for himself? And if he allowed himself, just as a thought experiment, to let this constant vary – to give up on jumping through the hoops or caring about where they took him – what would he then do?

'I'd be testing this out tomorrow,' he mouthed to himself in the darkness.

His father would be furious. But this wasn't about his father either.

It was about his idea, his solution to the stealthy dysfunction corrupting the sleeping body next to his. If he could present them with, not a rat, but a human being, telling them in his or her own words what it was like – 'Yes, it's me, still hearing and seeing you, and talking to you' – if he could do this then, sure, he might lose his job, his career, but his idea would brook no further objection. And jobless as he might be, careerless, prospectless, his dream would spring into life again.

It was so simple, so obvious – like all the best solutions once they have been stated. It couldn't be with Scott though. Not yet: Scott had too much left to lose still. But 'when things get bad, then who's to say what I will or won't do?' There were people out there already at the end, with little to lose and everything possibly to gain. Peachey had said it.

Everything made sense. He was halfway between thought and dream now, at last slipping into the folds of sleep, and everything made sense.

There was someone out there – someone he did not even know yet – someone who would put the flesh on his idea. And when the idea lived and breathed and spoke, when the idea walked among them, then it would be their God, and they would be its people. And the idea would say to him: 'Your debt has been repaid. Your gifts have not been wasted.'

He just had to find that someone.

Actually I doubt very much that God featured in Jon's train of thought, waking or sleeping, and certainly not in a biblical allusion. That bit was me, of course, adding my flourishes. The prosaic facts of the matter – that is, what Jon could later remember – were that he went to sleep confused and angry, and woke with the resolution that would carry him through the coming weeks of insanity. But I'm not sure prose will ever meet the requirements of a true science of life.

Besides, this is my life story, and I'm finding it harder than I expected not to be its hero and to skulk silently on its edges.

4

Anthony Cogan lived in the house in which he had been born; in which he had grown from infant innocence to adolescent alienation; from which he had launched himself into the world, swearing never to return; to which he had returned after his father's death; in which he had watched his mother die; and in which he too was now dying, amidst paintings and furniture that had quietly held their stations when he deserted his. Perhaps, he'd muse – he had so much time for musing these days – perhaps the deepest layers of dust behind the most arcane books on the topmost bookshelves had settled there before him. Take down a volume and the span of his entire parenthetical life would follow in a plume of dry-smelling dust.

As a young man, he'd dreamed of his own creations up there on the shelf: works that combined razor-sharp intellect with a deep humanity, and somehow shed a light of ideas upon the world without reducing its manifold greys to black and white. If only he had written them. The sentiments, bon mots and clever turns of phrase never crystallised from their weak, colloidal emulsion, spread thinly over chats and correspondence like egg-white glaze over pastry. Shiny, insubstantial.

Being diagnosed with Scander's disease at the age of forty-two might have been, in a back-to-front way, his salvation. A recalibration of value in life, prompted by the prospect of death, coincided with diminishing abilities to wander away from the computer. His options for distraction diminished while his ability to write remained intact. When his fingers went, there was the voice recognition software. When the voice went too, a clever piece of kit that tracked his eye movements allowed him to carry on creating text. Even now he could have set down the great thoughts of which he had so far given the world only glimpses. But no: there are always

ways to procrastinate. That same clever piece of kit also allowed him to browse the internet, post comments in discussion groups, log on to porn sites or watch pay-per-view films. 'I'm going to write my life story,' he'd tell those who still visited him, with great confidence, but in fact he'd never had one to tell. It had all been so much flim-flam and frippery.

In *The Idiot*, Dostoevsky has his hero, Prince Myshkin, tell the story of a man he met in Switzerland – a man whose experience mirrors that of the young Dostoevsky. The unnamed man is condemned to death and stands on the square awaiting execution by firing squad. 'What if I didn't have to die?' he asks himself in those final moments. 'I would turn every minute into an age. Nothing would be wasted or frittered away.' Then, at the last minute, he is reprieved – and his fine words come to nothing. 'I asked him about that,' says Myshkin. 'He didn't live like that at all, and wasted a great many of his minutes.' It was a passage Cogan often reread, consoling himself with the thought that the celebrated novelist too had frittered his time away. There was a kind of art even in non-achievement. Of course, the entire illusion depended on wilfully forgetting that, between the wasted minutes, Dostoevsky had written *The Idiot* and all his other works. Whereas Anthony Cogan lived in the house in which he had been born.

And there he might have died too, leaving on history nothing more lasting than a toeprint before an advancing tide, had he not happened to check one morning the Scander's Community website – something he'd not done for weeks and did now with so little in the way of intention that his action barely qualified as a whim. But check it he did and so chanced upon a recent post from someone with the username 'Biologist': If you are willing to consider trying anything, then I have something for you to consider.

Perhaps a life story worth the telling is indeed one shaped by willpower, dedication, focus. But happenstance should not go unsung, and it just so happened that Cogan was the one who picked up on this cryptic offer in the hour or so that elapsed between it being posted and it being removed again by the site's moderators. Dear Biologist, he wrote to the e-mail address supplied, I am willing to consider trying anything. Please tell me more. Anthony Cogan.

He wasn't expecting much. Biologist would most likely turn out to be a scammer or a fantasist. But he might as well give it a go. So complete was his disappointment with life that he had no illusions left to be shattered. At least that's what he told himself. A slightly frustrating exchange ensued. Biologist was keen to explain things in person and suggested a face-to-face meeting. Cogan, cautious, wanted more information first. Biologist expressed a reluctance to put things in writing and described what he had to share as confidential. *This appeal to secrecy is very telling*, wrote Cogan in the diary he persisted in keeping, even when nothing happened. *More evidence that my interlocutor is some kind of crazy conspiracy theorist. I will not bother responding.* And for a few hours, he stuck to this decision. Then, like smoke through the cracks around a door, hope insinuated itself once more into his thoughts. Perhaps he should try one last time. What had he to lose?

And so he wrote again to Biologist: If you know anything of what Scander's does to a person, you may understand that 'face to face' is not my preferred mode of communication these days. Certainly I can understand what you say, but framing my response, my questions – for I'm sure there will be questions – takes time. A lot of time. Can we not communicate by e-mail first?

He was pleased with this response and remained so for the rest of the day. The next morning, however, when there was still no reply, he began to wonder. Had he perhaps been a little too demanding? Was Biologist's reluctance to write justified? Had he or she found someone else who was willing to meet without prior explanations, someone who would now benefit in Cogan's place from whatever it was Biologist had to offer?

Most likely, he diarised, *I have succeeded in flushing out a liar or a time-waster. Biologist is not replying because he or she has nothing more to say, and whatever he or she has really been up to, I have thwarted it. My caution has been well placed.*

But what if it had not been? A second morning with no reply found him toying with the idea of a follow-up e-mail. Fine, they could meet. He'd rather it were not that way, but if that was what it took then so be it. Throughout the day he did his best to distract himself with other things – the things that, until he'd spotted that first post on the Scander's Community website, had seemed more than adequate padding for the little time left to him. Now they could not hold him as they had, and before he went to sleep, he drafted another e-mail to Biologist, begging for a meeting.

The draft never got sent. In the morning, a reply from Biologist was waiting in Cogan's inbox:

Mr Cogan,

I'm sorry for my reluctance to write things down. It's essential that none of what I have to say is shared with anyone. However, I also understand your reluctance to meet.

So let me begin by saying that my name is Dr Jon Caldicot – not a medical doctor, but a research scientist. I am part of a team working on a fungus called *Aeisitos neuromethistes*, or Annie as we call it for short. This fungus has a most unusual life cycle, which is what makes it relevant to your condition...

It was a long e-mail – and for Cogan a disturbing one. He'd been quite ready for a rant about the power of crystals or Ayurvedic massage, but this? His first reflex was to dismiss it. *Though,* he wrote in his diary, *there is something in the tone that makes me hesitate: a matter-of-fact quality, a dullness of exposition, a lack of those breathless claims of efficacy which are the stock-in-trade of the snake-oil merchant.* Nonsense it might be, but a vanishing fraction of hope had infected him and, like a parasite, co-opted him to its own ends.

It was at this point that Cogan shared the whole exchange with Ryan.

Ryan Griffiths was... well, what *was* Ryan to him? A full-time carer would have been the short answer – and this was indeed the role to which Cogan had appointed the boy nearly three years earlier, for which Cogan still paid him, and in which he occupied the garden flat of the grand old Victorian pile in Hampstead where Cogan lived. That was the deal, but through their unavoidable intimacy Ryan had become, surely, something beyond that. Cogan, at any rate, had grown to appreciate him for so much more than the formal services he rendered; his loyalty, his intelligence – not education, but intelligence – his unfeigned interest in whatever topic Cogan might choose to ramble about, his patience as Cogan painstakingly constructed those rambles on screen, his thoughtfulness when at last he spoke himself – his wisdom even, if that was the word for one so young. Still only twenty-four, Cogan would have to remind himself. Oh, and his good looks too, of course – not that Cogan harboured any illusions on that front, or sullied his growing fondness for the boy with anything so tawdry as a sexual fantasy, but spending his dwindling days with someone so easy on the eye was pleasant. Ryan's smile alone could dispel the lurking doubt that there had been no point waking up that morning and remind him that, even if all he had left was observation, there was joy to be had in beholding beauty. Yes, Cogan knew how lucky he was to have found someone like Ryan and flattered himself that, over and above the salary and apartment, something else kept the boy at his side. A connection. Perhaps one could even call it a friendship.

But until now he'd held off mentioning Biologist to Ryan. It hadn't seemed worth bothering. It was all going to come to nothing, so why trouble Ryan with it? And perhaps too he was a little ashamed to be entertaining such foolish hopes.

'You've been keeping this quiet,' said Ryan as he read the e-mails. His tone of voice was light-hearted, but as he settled into reading the last and longest message, his face took on a more serious expression.

'Is this for real?' he asked when he'd reached the end.

The unavoidable pause followed as Cogan picked out the words he wanted. 'I don't know,' said his computer's voice at last. 'I suppose we'll find out.'

'You're going to meet him then,' said Ryan, nodding. Cogan studied his face: there was scepticism there for sure, and something else – a hesitation of some kind.

It took him a while to construct the question: 'You don't think I should?'

Ryan shrugged. 'I think you should be careful. I mean, it doesn't sound like it's real to me. But even if it is… Why are we hearing about this only now? Why isn't this available as a treatment? And what's this guy...' he glanced down at the e-mail again to check the name – 'Jon Caldicot, what's *he* up to?'

If the muscles had still worked, Cogan would have nodded and smiled. Clever boy. Clever to wonder about motive before fact. And clever to be so cautious. Wasn't that just what he, Cogan, needed to be, to check the irresistible, desperate hope that he could even now feel taking hold of him?

But most of his muscles had long since given up on him, and it was all he could do to look down at his screen again and pick out the words of a suggestion. 'You'll have to ask him when he comes.'

It was a sunny day in early February when Jon made the trip to Hampstead: one of those crystalline blue days, all sunshine and ice, that sometimes interrupts the flagging winter, like an unexpectedly funny joke from a best man who's dragged his speech past the limits of good will. A handsome young man answered the door and introduced himself as Cogan's carer, Ryan.

'Tony's expecting you. I'll take you through.'

Jon followed him into the house, blinking as his eyes adjusted to the darkness within. From the front door, a short corridor opened to the right onto what had once been the central entrance hall of the house. But the stairs to the floors above had been blocked off at the top, and the space turned into what at first sight seemed to be a furniture store, with various items in dark wood – two wardrobes, a chest of drawers, a dresser, a bedstead, and other things hidden beneath or behind them – pushed up against and largely obscuring the room's only window. The stairs themselves, what remained of them, were stacked with cardboard boxes from which, here and there, hung untidy sheaves of paper. Through all this, two passages had been left clear across the deep pile carpet: a wider one along the left-hand side of the room, effectively continuing the corridor from the front door, and a narrow one, cutting between the stacked furniture to a door underneath the stairs. And over everything hung the slight, musty fragrance of that fine-ground particulate that lingers through dustings and hooverings in rooms that are too full of stuff.

'Through here,' said Ryan, heading on through the doorway at the far end of the wider route. As he followed, Jon glanced through two other doorways on his left into rooms as clogged and coagulated as the hall: sofas, armchairs, tables, a large glass cabinet full of stuffed birds, lamps with heavy lampshades, and everywhere books – on shelves, in boxes, piled up on every spare surface in precarious towers that had, here and there, toppled sideways or slumped into a fanlike slew of half-open volumes.

'Remember that it takes him a while to say things,' Ryan was saying. 'Don't try to fill in the silences. He needs the time to compose his answer.'

The next room could hardly have been a greater contrast. True, the walls here too were encrusted with books, like the inside of an amethyst geode, but shelved and orderly, and between them rugless and unencumbered floorboards stretched to a sunlit bay window at the far end of the room. Beyond the window, an overgrown garden, all twisted branches, deep green leaves and dark berries. Before it, just four things, arranged like props on a stage set: a state-of-the art home entertainment system, with tower speakers and a forty-two-inch screen; an upright armchair with red upholstery and wooden arms; some way from it, a cheap plastic folding chair; and Cogan himself.

Listing Cogan as a thing was not so far off the mark. What remained of his body – the unused, unstimulated muscles had dwindled and slackened, so he seemed all skin and bones – was strapped, quite literally, into something midway between a wheelchair and a mobile booth. The latter impression resulted from the various items of kit which, bolted onto the chair, enfolded Cogan. A large screen was fixed in front of him, over his lap, angled like a lectern, while above it, suspended from metal arms which curved around on either side of Cogan's head, hung something that looked like a CCTV camera, tilted downwards to point at Cogan's face. Wires from each ran to a grey, humming box attached to the back of the chair, from which a discreet lead ran to a nearby mains socket in the wall. In the middle of it all, Cogan's thin, depleted face, held securely in place by a cushioned metal band running around his forehead, seemed little more than another component.

Only the sharp blue eyes, taking the measure of Jon with brisk vertical saccades, were self-evidently alive – like the eyes of a masked man, peering through his disguise.

Jon had been learning about Scander's disease for three months now. He'd read more times than he could remember about the progression of the condition – and the retreat of the human being before it. Yet it still came as a shock: as if he'd been expecting to find Mr Cogan sitting in the armchair, drinking tea and leafing through the pages of a magazine while he waited for his guest to arrive. Through no fault of his own, and like so many others, Jon had made his way through life in a tidy little vehicle of health, steered clear of the crashes by modern medicine. And now he was rubber-necking the reality of twisted metal and flesh.

Cogan, for his part, detected Jon's hesitation. He saw in the mirror of Jon's stuttering gaze his own shrunken body and pale, harnessed face, and, having seen others falter – not strangers but old friends, seen after many years – he recognised the curves of the clock-spring thoughts that had just burst open in Jon's head. In the past he had taken some pleasure in naming the feelings of others – not through cruelty but to let them know he understood – and he would have liked to do the same now. But did not. Naming, for Cogan, involved the arduous selection of words from his screen by means of tracked eye-movements. Only the most common words could be quickly accessed. To frame a thought fully, and thoughtfully, might take minutes. And even then, it would be only the bones: no meat, no features. It was simply too hard to dress meaning with speech these days. He had to rely on others understanding, and – apart from Ryan – they never did. And as for nuance, which once he had cherished, cultivated and exhibited like some rare hothouse flower – nuance was a bouquet for Ryan alone.

Besides which, even if he'd had his voice, it's doubtful Cogan would have managed much in the way of nice dissection of the moment, because even as he saw his predicament reflected in Jon's eyes, so too he felt – and the feeling swelled so fast it took away what little of his breath remained – a pang of something that had had no place in that refined, half-imagined past of his. Hope:

unlooked for and uncompromising, tugging at the ends of every defunct neurone in his body as if one of them might still respond.

It was Ryan who pre-empted what could have become a consuming silence. 'Dr Caldicot,' he said, though that had been obvious.

Jon – Dr Caldicot – shot an involuntary glance towards Ryan, a plea for help. What should he do now? But Ryan merely smiled: people had to deal with this themselves, and either they'd do well or badly. There was nothing he could add, except possibly to get in the way.

'Hello,' said Jon pathetically, half-lifting a hand almost as if to wave.

Cogan studied him, taking in as much of the man as he could with his bright, mobile eyes. Later, after Jon had gone again, he'd write a description of his visitor in his diary:

I was expecting someone a little older, though I also suspect Dr Caldicot is one of those people who looks younger than he actually is. Because he looks about twenty but in his e-mail said he was a post-doc, which I think means he must be nearer thirty. He has a boyish face, quite round, with pale skin and cheeks that appear to be permanently reddened. Either that or he was blushing the whole time. The features are almost chubby and topped off with short, untidy brown hair: indeed, my first thought was of a cherub's head, though the body was long and lean. A good height: about six foot, I'd guess; at any rate taller than Ryan. Based on today's showing, he has that tendency I've spotted in other scientists of buying jeans that are just a bit too short, an effect exacerbated by a pair of trainers that I hope were at least comfortable, since they'd little else to commend them. The cuffs of his shirt also sat a little high on his wrists: I suspect it was a cheap one, bought in a shop that does not offer variations in sleeve length. The overall effect was of someone who hadn't quite grasped his own growth into early adulthood. Quite handsome, albeit in a geeky way. And innocent: that was my overriding impression. A guileless young man. I hope I am proved right.

That was all later, though, looking back and making sense. Right now, in the moment, he saw only what hope let him see: a young man with an honest, intelligent face.

Then he shook himself – metaphorically of course, more metaphorically perhaps than ever in his life. Dr Caldicot would see nothing of this inner drama in his inert face. The communication would remain one-way unless and until he made the effort to reverse it. Just as well he'd prepared a welcome, he thought, as he dropped his eyes to his screen: one he could bid his voice deliver with no more than a glance.

'Thank you for coming to see me, Dr Caldicot. You'll forgive my having prepared a short speech to get the conversation going. It takes so long for me to say things these days that I find it better to prepare.'

Jon ought to have guessed what was coming, but the voice too took him by surprise. It had a halting, half-human intonation: almost authentic but not quite, and so not at all. As it delivered its lines, Cogan's eyes had rolled up again to watch him, and now, as it concluded, they looked meaningfully towards the armchair. Ryan had also stepped forwards, gesturing for Jon to sit down.

'Oh,' said Jon, crossing to the chair and sitting, 'thank you.'

Having directed Jon, Ryan took his own place on the plastic seat, positioning himself roughly equidistant from both of them. This unsettled Jon: he'd been quite clear in his e-mails that no one else should be told what was going on, yet it seemed this young man was going to sit in on their conversation.

'It's alright,' said Ryan. There was something of an accent in there – rural, probably somewhere west, even a hint of Welsh maybe – but he looked almost as if he might be from the Mediterranean: a warm, olive tone to his skin and curly hair so black it almost shone. 'I won't tell anyone.'

'Oh…' said Jon, further unnerved. How had Ryan known that was what he was thinking? Beautiful eyes too: green. His nose was rather large, perhaps, but it suited him. 'No, of course.'

Ryan smiled politely and looked back towards the figure in the chair. 'The floor is yours, Tony.'

Once more the bright eyes flicked down to the screen; once more the synthetic voice began: 'Let me begin by thanking you for your patience. I realise you would have liked this meeting to take place earlier and not to have had to put so much in writing.

Please rest assured that what you have told me will go no further. Obviously it has been quite a lot to take in and, if you will forgive me for saying so, a little difficult to believe.'

Jon took a breath, about to say that he too had found it hard to believe the facts about Annie when he first heard them, but Cogan's speech was pre-programmed and continued regardless.

'In light of this, I hope you have not taken offence at the request in my most recent e-mail that you bring with you some kind of proof that you, at least, are who you say you are.'

A pause. Jon shifted his weight in the chair, levering himself up slightly on his elbows and nudging his buttocks sideways, trying his best to minimise the movement. Voluntary use of his muscles felt somehow in poor taste, as if he were showing off.

'It's your turn to speak,' said Ryan. 'When he's looking at the screen, he's preparing something to say. When he's looking at you, it's your turn.'

'Right,' said Jon, glancing round at Ryan – and looking back to Cogan he saw that those alert, shining eyes were indeed fixed on him. 'No, not offended at all. I can quite understand. And yes, I realise how hard it must be to believe. I've brought—' He rooted in his trouser pocket for his wallet and, having found it, pulled out his ID card from the lab. 'Here,' he said, holding it out rather ridiculously to Cogan.

'May I?' said Ryan, jumping up and reaching across for the card. He took it from Jon's hand and scrutinised it before carrying it across to Cogan and holding it in front of his face. 'All looks in order.'

Cogan focused his vision on the card: the bad picture of Jon, the name of the lab, Jon's own name and details. It did indeed look in order, and around his heart – one of the few regions of his body which still fed him sensations from time to time – he felt the hope grow a little tighter.

From Jon's perspective, there was no response at all from Cogan; but Ryan must have picked up on something he had not seen, for he brought the card back, handed it over and returned to the plastic seat. Then the speech began again.

'Thank you. I propose to suspend further disbelief for the purposes of today's conversation. Let us assume that everything you have said in your e-mail is true. I'm sure you will understand that some questions remain, and I hope you will not mind us asking you those questions today.'

'Not at all,' said Jon, without even checking if Cogan had given him the signal to speak, though this time, as it turned out, he'd got it right. He didn't mind Cogan asking him questions – though he wasn't sure about that 'us'. It was all very well this Ryan saying he'd not tell anyone, but who was he, and why was he here?

Cogan, meanwhile, was selecting his first question from the list he had prepared. 'Given the amazing potential of this fungus to help so many people, according to your description, why has its existence not been made public before?'

'Well,' said Jon, glad they were starting with such an easy one, 'with something this potentially controversial... I mean, the far-reaching nature of the... the implications...' He ground to a halt, as it dawned on him that this was not so easy after all. Why was Annie so shrouded in secrecy? 'Do you know, now I think about it, I'm actually not sure.' Unless of course it was those stories of violent sporogenesis, the putative risk that all that potential could become something so much darker. He absolutely did not want to get bogged down with that today. 'I suppose it's... like a habit really. I've never really questioned it, I suppose.'

Cogan was watching him intently. He could of course see that Jon was finding the question awkward – but the impression was of someone not lying or avoiding but trying to tell the truth and finding he did not know it. All of which seemed very plausible. He shot a sideways glance to Ryan, whose face was hardened into a more sceptical, less forgiving expression – narrowed lips, narrowed eyes, furrowed brow. Something else was going on with Ryan; Cogan didn't know what, but it had been there ever since he'd first shown him the exchange with Biologist: a reticence, almost a hostility. Now was not the time to explore it, not with strangers present. Nor did he want to waste time composing a response to Dr Caldicot. Instead, he selected the second question from his screen.

'Given that the existence of this fungus is a secret, why are you revealing it now, to us?'

Jon hesitated. He was feeling rather foolish after his fluffed response to the first question and was keen not to do the same again. He had talked about this in his last e-mail, surely? And really, it now struck him, it would have been a good idea to reread that e-mail on his way there; though, in fairness, he'd not been expecting a… well, it felt more like a job interview.

'The thing is,' he began, speaking more slowly this time, to give himself time to think, 'the way that science works, it could be years before anyone actually benefits from this. There is so much…' – despite his best intentions, he hesitated: the word 'discipline' had popped into his head, but he did not want to say that – 'red tape, so much red tape, and people are going to die, people that we could help. Every possibility has to be considered before you can do anything. It's… well, it's ridiculous really.'

Cogan was looking down at his screen, and Jon remembered that this meant he should wait. He glanced at Ryan for confirmation, but Ryan was staring resolutely at his knees and did not look back. So he waited – waited for what seemed like an age, especially when it was measured against the brevity of what Cogan finally said: 'What possibilities in particular are being considered?'

'I'm sorry?' said Jon. He had not understood the question.

'What are people worried about?' said Ryan, who clearly had. He did not stop staring at his knees though. 'This red tape you talk about, presumably it relates to risks, side effects, things that might go wrong. So what are they?'

Once again, Jon stalled. The risks associated with his idea? None. No *real* risks. Except that, of course, it would not be Annie-of-the-toxic-spores that Jon would be administering to Cogan. To re-engineer her would take months of work in the lab – hardly something he could do on the side, between his other work, un-detected. Just getting a sample of Annie in her native state would be challenge enough. And in that native state, if one believed the stories of the older generation, an insignificant, vanishingly small but perhaps not quite non-existent risk remained: that a sporeful Cogan might one day set about gouging chunks out of himself and anyone else he could get his fingernails into. Again, though, he was not going to talk about that. Not when the whole thing was most probably a misreading of the data. He was sure there was no risk. And the merest mention of those stories would take him back to the Laws, the constraints, the going nowhere.

He could feel his irritation levels rising. *Who the hell are you?* he wanted to snap back at Ryan. *Where do you fit into all this? And when did I agree to be interrogated by you?*

But just in time, Ryan saved him: 'What is giving this stuff to Tony supposed to prove?'

That was it. Of course.

'The risk,' he said, catching his breath, 'is that it's not Mr Cogan any more afterwards.'

'How do you mean?'

'The thing is, there's absolutely no detectable difference in rats...'

'In rats?'

'Yes. That's the biological model we use...'

'So basically Tony is your lab rat?'

Cogan's surrogate voice interrupted: a flat, inexpressive 'Ryan'.

'I'm sorry,' said Ryan, collecting himself; and then again to Jon: 'I'm sorry.'

'That's fine,' said Jon. He could hear the irritation in his own voice: even as, at the same time, it crossed his mind how good it must be to have someone care this much. 'I didn't express it very well. I'm not really used to explaining this kind of thing.'

'Please,' came the computer voice, incongruously.

'He means please go on,' said Ryan, slumping back in his chair.

'OK,' said Jon. 'So there's no detectable difference in... behaviour, from the outside. But we've no way of knowing how it would feel from the inside. For a human being.' He'd been looking at Ryan as he said this, but now – remembering why he was there – turned back to Cogan. 'I don't know how it will feel for you. I don't know if it will be you at all. On the inside. Does that make sense?'

Cogan's eyes flicked down to the screen but just for a second. 'Yes,' he said. Then his eyes went down again, this time for longer.

While he waited, Jon looked round at Ryan again – taking advantage of the fact that Ryan's own stare had returned to his knees.

There was something intensely attractive about him that was more than mere good looks, something he'd not noticed until Ryan lost his temper. A kind of restrained passion. So unlike Scott, flashed the thought through his mind.

And then the electronic voice began again: 'I don't quite understand how I can help you with this. Suppose we proceed and my body is restored to full health. Suppose I behave as I would have before I had Scander's. How will you know if it is me on the inside?'

'You can tell us,' said Jon, frowning. Again, he did not understand the question. 'A rat can't tell me. That's the problem. But you'll be able to tell us what it feels like.'

Cogan looked down at his screen but did not immediately set about composing his response. Part of him, the eternal teacher, wanted to explain to Dr Caldicot the philosophical shortcomings of the answer he'd given, but that would take a long time, both for him to say and – on the basis of the evidence so far – for Dr Caldicot to understand. And the truth was, another part of him wanted this conversation to finish quite soon now. For one thing, Ryan's behaviour was troubling him. But there was something more than that: the sudden realisation that, if he poked too many holes in Dr Caldicot's logic, he might convince himself not to proceed. And that was not what he wanted.

Because what did it matter to him if the experiment failed to prove what it was meant to prove? *He* would know if it was still him or not 'on the inside'. And if it were, he would be living his life again, living it to the full, making good on the wasted promise of those wasted years. And if it weren't – so what? He'd have cut short the last few years or months or weeks of decline, and someone else would be living his life, better perhaps than he'd ever lived it.

What, come to that, did any of these pre-prepared questions matter? *I could have played the game a little longer,* he wrote in his diary later. *Weighed my options, calculated risks, done the book-keeping. I could have pressed from my faltering brain the last dregs of rationality and laid them at the service of decision-making. But it would not have been by their cold measures that I'd have arrived at my choice. No, that choice had already been made. I can't say when. Earlier in the conversation, maybe? When I read Dr Caldicot's account of* Aeisitos neuromethistes? *When I first saw the post from Biologist on the Scander's Community site? Or perhaps it was before that, before I'd even heard of Scander's. It just took all this time for me to realise what I should have known all along: that I want to live. Above all else I want to live.* The questions still on his list – why ask them, when all they could possibly achieve was death?

None of this, though, could he express in the moment. Even if he'd found the words, he could not have invested them with the feelings he wished them to carry. His bing-bong surrogate voice lacked rhythm, intonation, passion: it was as inexpressive as the face he could no longer bend to a smile or a tear. Even if he'd tried, he could have framed only the factual envelope of all that was going through his mind at that moment: facts shorn of meaning, like spindly sheep shivering on a hill. It would all have been so much worthless bleating.

'I have no more questions,' he said instead.

'I have one, if I may,' said Ryan, and when Cogan glanced towards him he found those loyal, trusting eyes fixed on his face, as if they were peering into his soul and reading in it all that could not be said.

'If that's alright with you, Dr Caldicot,' added Ryan, turning to Jon. Whatever had been driving his earlier hostility, he appeared to have mastered it, and his voice was calmer again, if perhaps just a little too precise about the ends of words.

As it happened it was not at all alright with Jon. If Mr Cogan had no more questions, then surely that should have been the end of it. But he clearly did not have any choice in the matter. 'Yes, of course,' he said crisply.

'What I still don't understand is: why you? Why are all your colleagues happy to deal with the red tape, as you call it, why can they all live with the thought that people who need this treatment are dying all the while, but you can't?'

'My boyfriend has Scander's disease,' said Jon. Though the intonation of his voice said something more like: *There, are you happy now? You've made me say it.*

'I'm sorry to hear that,' said Ryan, visibly chastened.

'He was diagnosed three months ago, so it's too early for him to try it out. He still has some good years left. I mean,' he added, realising what he had just said and looking at Cogan, 'I'm not trying to imply that—' Again he broke off. This Ryan was making him say and feel things he did not want to. 'Look, I'm not trying to pretend that any of this is easy. Straightforward. I can't make a decision for you or for anyone else. I can just give you the facts.' And the fact or myth of violent sporogenesis? 'The facts as I see them,' he added weakly.

'I'm sorry if I've intruded,' said Ryan, 'but you understand why we do have to ask these questions.' He looked at Cogan, his eyes seeming to search for something in the motionless face that met them. 'But I think we may have done with questions for today. Am I right, Tony?'

Cogan broke eye contact for long enough to find his response – 'Yes' – then met Ryan's eyes again.

'Do you need more time to think about it? I get the feeling that you've already made a decision. Is that right?'

Again Cogan's eyes flicked to the word on the screen: 'Yes.'

Ryan faltered. 'Yes as in "yes, I've made a decision", or yes as in… your decision is "yes".' But he already knew which it was. 'It's your decision is "yes", isn't it?'

Once more the screen: 'Yes.'

'There you go then, Dr Caldicot. Tony says "yes". Your experiment is on.'

This was the moment when Jon's idea was granted its incarnation. It was the moment when the cloth was tied to the meat jar. It should, surely, have had some grandeur. But in Jon's clouded mind it passed almost unnoticed. He was troubled by Ryan, troubled by his evident dissent, troubled by the way this unwanted third kept drawing his own eye. And this absorbing detail distracted him from the larger view as he wrapped up the conversation with a promise of further contact when he was ready to meet again. Ready, that was, with samples from the lab to inject for the first time in Annie's history into a human host. But all Jon could get into focus was the fact that Ryan would be there again, unsettling him.

He could not resist picking up the conversation on the door-step as he was on the brink of leaving.

'You don't think he should be doing this, do you?'

'It's not my decision.'

'If he doesn't go ahead, how much… how long does he have to live?'

'I don't know,' said Ryan, looking to one side as he spoke. 'He might be dead when I go back in. Look, I'm sorry, I didn't mean to intrude into your personal life.'

'That's OK. Like you said, you have to ask the questions. I just wasn't—'

He broke off and instead gave an apologetic half-smile, which Ryan half-returned. The conversation was coming to an end – a few last pleasantries and he'd be on his way. Yet suddenly, Jon found himself wishing more than anything for it to carry on.

'Look,' he began, his voice a little uneven, his cheeks, he suspected, reddening even more than usual, 'I do understand your concerns and, if you have *more* questions then… I'd be happy to sit down and discuss them. I mean, I'm not in any hurry to get anywhere.'

There was the minutest change in Ryan's expression: nothing that could be pinned to any one feature but a subtle hardening of the whole. 'That's alright. We'll be seeing you soon anyway. And we have your e-mail.'

'Yes,' blustered Jon, definitely blushing now. 'Of course. I'll be in touch.'

Then the door was shut.

The sun was still shining outside, the day bright and blue, but Jon walked back to the Tube under a cloud of his own making. What had he been thinking of, saying that to Ryan? What kind of idiot was he?

It wasn't until he was rattling under the streets of North London, watching his soup-spoon reflection slide up and down the window opposite, that the full significance of what had just happened hit him. Cogan had said yes. The experiment was on. And in his mind a vision arose of that shrivelled wreck of a man rising up from his machine chair and telling them; of Annie finding her voice, after all those years cleaning her whiskers and running round mazes; of everyone – Lazenby, Peachey, all of them – bowing down before the now unquestionable validity of his idea; of Lazenby admitting her error – and her apologies formed on his lips as he sat there, like the thoughts of a madman; of his father... But even now, he could not make out the features of his father's face, and in his mind's eye saw only a silhouette.

Back in the house, Cogan had already composed his question for Ryan.

'What's going on?'

'I'm just worried,' said Ryan – sparing him, as usual, the ritual of disingenuous what-do-you-means. 'You heard what he said. It might not even be you.'

'It definitely won't be me when I die,' said Cogan – a little cruelly, perhaps, but they were well past beating about the bush.

'I know. And I don't like thinking about that either.' He folded away the plastic chair, no longer needed now it was just the two of them again, and carried it back to the kitchen where it normally lived, leaving Cogan alone for a moment. There was something else – he was sure of it: Ryan had already been behaving oddly before questions of identity had arisen. But whatever it was – and most unusually for Ryan – the boy did not seem to want to talk about it.

Perhaps Ryan too had realised his cover was an imperfect one, as he came back into the room with a further explanation. 'It could all turn out to be bullshit as well. And I don't want to see you disappointed.'

'Do *you* think it's bullshit?'

Ryan shook his head, hovering by the armchair that Jon had vacated but not sitting down, as if he were trying to make his mind up about whether and how long to continue the conversation. 'I did. Then he told us about his boyfriend, and now I'm not sure. I mean, yes, it could still be bullshit, but he clearly believes it.' He rested one hand on the back of the armchair and tapped his fingers against the wooden frame. 'Look, I know you've said "yes" now, but you can still change your mind if you want to.'

It frustrated Cogan at times like these that he lacked the ability to respond without hesitation: 'Why would I want to change my mind?'

Though the truth was there were things he too was choosing not to talk about to Ryan. If he had still been prepared to count risks and rewards, there were reasons aplenty he might have changed his mind. But he wasn't, and change wasn't on the cards.

I am, he would write in his diary, *like a man lost in the desert who, after days and nights of half-starved hallucinations, crawls on all fours to the top of a ridge and sees before him the scrub at the edge of the wilderness: thin soil from which the poorest scratch out their subsistence but to me a verdant paradise, a carnival parade of leaves and worms and beasts for me to kiss, one by one, as they welcome me back to life.* Anything, surely, was better than this pent-up, failing existence. He did not write, and did not wish to entertain the possibility, that this might be just one more hallucination. The hope was too intoxicating. The hope alone was better than what had come before. And if he were disappointed, as Ryan feared? Well, that would be another day, and at least in the meantime he would have lived.

And that was why he'd set aside the pre-prepared questions further down his list. One question in particular, which he'd saved until the end, and now did not want even to think about: *How does this fungus spread from one host to another?*

Because of course he'd been doing his own research since Biologist had told him about Annie. A direct search for *Aeisitos neuromethistes* had returned no hits – as he'd anticipated, given what Dr Caldicot had told him about the secrecy surrounding the fungus. But wider searches – *brain parasite,* for example, or *fungus growing in brain* – had afforded Cogan glimpses of a strangeness in nature he'd never before even glimpsed.

For example, he'd read that as much as half the world's pop-ulation might have *Toxoplasma gondii* living in their brains: a charming parasite that alternates between the guts of cats and the brains of rats. Once in the latter, it sends its hosts skipping gleefully into the path of new cats, to ease its path back into a gut. In human brains, meanwhile, the evidence suggested a link with schizophrenia. He'd read about Gordian worms... but I've already told you about the Gordian worms, piloting their grasshoppers to watery deaths. He'd read about *Ophiocordyceps unilateralis*, and this more than any of the bizarre creatures he'd encountered had captured his imagination. The zombie fungus, as it was commonly called, but Cogan found himself drawn to a different metaphor. It began with a few choice images, but then, in the empty hours, he found himself working and reworking them, tweaking and extending what had now become a passage, obsessively returning to the text whenever he was left on his own. By the time Dr Caldicot visited, his overwrought account of the fungus's life cycle had almost collapsed under its own weight:

In the jungles of Thailand and Brazil, a fungal fanatic evangelises the carpenter ants that busy themselves carving galleried nests into decaying stumps and trunks. Its spores, adhering to an insect's exoskeleton, must first break through this tough carapace with brute force, like a missionary pounding his fist upon a pulpit. Once inside, however, the fungus exerts a subtler pressure: the ant is in its thrall now and does its bidding. First, like one speaking in tongues, this new servant of God begins twitching and convulsing until it falls to the forest floor. Then, with the zeal of a convert, it seeks the holy site for which it is now destined: a leaf 25cm above the ground, on the north side of a plant, with just the right levels of humidity and temperature. There, driven by the yeasty idea that has taken hold of it, it performs the rituals of its new faith, plunging its mandibles into the main vein of the leaf and holding tight. According to the fossil evidence, carpenter ants have been observing these rites for some forty-eight million years at least: a more distinguished pedigree than any human religion. The ant's sacred work is almost done now, but to ensure there is no backsliding Ophiocordyceps unilateralis *atrophies the muscles in the ant's jaw, locking it in place in a death grip. Only now does it call upon the ant to make the ultimate sacrifice. Only now do its hyphae bury into the soft inner parts and feed on its vital juices. And then, when the time is right, the ant's head cracks open and the fruiting body of the fungus thrusts into the world, ready to spread its good news to the myriad heathen ants that still roam the forest. Another ant dies, but the word it died for lives on, so that more souls may be saved. In parts of the jungle, dense graveyards of these ruptured ants can be found, like the tombs and relics of martyrs assembled in a great cathedral.*

It was not a love of words that had driven Cogan onwards in this endeavour. It was the image of those fields of cloven ants pincered to leaf veins. And why should his own life be any different? He did not indulge himself with grotesque fantasies of his own head cracking open as, perhaps, he hung upside down from the vaulted ceiling of a medieval chapel. But he did find himself adding a question to the list he was building for Dr Caldicot: *How does this fungus spread from one host to another?*

But what was the point, he asked himself again now, when Ryan gave up on trying to change his mind and went back to the kitchen to prepare lunch. What was the point of all these questions? If Annie was indeed going to give him a new life, it was not as a gift. In her own time she would exact as her price her own continued existence, and when that time came, Cogan realised, his own life would be as incidental as an ant's. And what was so new about that?

Cogan, you see, might have glimpsed the strangeness of nature, but he had not yet come to understand it. The things he had read seemed proof to him only of what he had always been told to believe: that life is defined by the iron necessities of survival and reproduction, and in their service is nasty, brutish and short. He'd read about the jungle, seen it on TV, but he had not yet walked in it and opened his eyes.

5

Things in the lab had settled down surprisingly quickly following Jon's meltdown in Lazenby's office. That night, lying on his bed after being sent home – and in between formulating his plan to find someone with Scander's willing to have a fungus injected into their central nervous system – Jon's imagination had run the gamut of disastrous next-day scenarios. But his fears had proved misplaced: indeed, if he'd not already cast her in another role, he might almost have seen Lazenby's subsequent behaviour as kind.

'We need to talk about yesterday,' she'd said, catching Jon before he even made it to his bench, equipping him with tea and leading him to her office.

She had obviously prepared a speech of sorts, so Jon – still torn between rage on the one hand and, on the other, a near overwhelming impulse to pile in with circuitous, self-abasing apologies – bit his lip and let her speak.

'The first, most important thing to say is that you are a highly valued member of the team here. Highly valued. I can't stress that enough. Your work on the LN3 gene, for instance… Well, I could single out lots of examples. This team needs you. And that's the second thing. We're a hard-working team and I know that I… well, sometimes I work people too hard perhaps, and I'm not always good at acknowledging the lives people live outside the lab. But we *are* a team, and if people are facing difficult times then we need to find ways to support them. I need to find ways to support them. Which leads me to my third point: that I owe you a sincere apology. I jumped to conclusions about your behaviour which… given the information I had, were not unreasonable *hypotheses*. But I failed to treat them as hypotheses. I treated them as facts. I failed to live up to my own values, and in the process I made a very serious and entirely false accusation against you. I published before I had all the evidence. So, what I'd like to do is say sorry now, without qualification, and I hope we can fairly quickly move on from that and get back to the great science we're doing here, which is after all what we really care about. And lastly, to help us do that, I hope in the future you will feel more able to… share personal matters… relevant personal matters, with me or with others here. We all have our… Well, we all bring personal… perspectives to our work, and maybe they make us the scientists we are. If we can learn to engage with them objectively.' For a fraction of a second she was somewhere else, following some private train of thought. Then she continued: 'Not that I'm suggesting you need to be objective about what's happening to your partner. I'm sorry, that didn't come out right. Just that… well… what am I saying?'

He'd never seen Lazenby confuse herself like this.

'Just that you should feel able to tell us – tell me – what's going on. And if I make that difficult then I'd like to know what I can do differently.'

In the moment, the effect of all this had been to swing him sharply away from the rage and leave him gibbering how sorry *he* was, until Lazenby at last calmed him down and convinced him no more apologies were needed. All very embarrassing in retrospect, but the air was cleared and, within a few days, Jon found that life in the lab was much as it had always been.

Or perhaps even improved. For one thing, everyone in the lab now knew that Jon was having a tough time in his personal life. How could they not know? The outburst in Lazenby's office had been audible to many and had needed some kind of explanation from her. What exactly that explanation had been Jon never found out, but its effectiveness was readily apparent, first and foremost in the fact that no one asked him what the hell had been going on in there, but also in a noticeable kid-glovedness in the way people spoke to him and dealt with him in the next few weeks.

As for his relationship with Lazenby, not only had no damage been done, arguably it was only in the aftermath of his breakdown that they had a relationship at all. Lazenby had always been his boss, of course; he had always been one of her team. But now it was as if she had noticed him at last: not that there was any radical transformation in her behaviour, but it seemed to him that she thought for a few moments longer when he proposed some minor innovation, hesitated before finding objections, even on one or two occasions agreed without reservation. In short, Jon suddenly found himself being taken a little more seriously.

The ironic thing was that, so far as he could see, this was *not* because he had gone to her with a brilliant idea but because he had thrown a wobbly in her office. Had his vulnerability triggered some thwarted maternal location on her genome? Or had she seen in it – as he'd cynically suspected that first day after being sent home – a way to re-establish control? The problem with Lazenby was that one could never tell. There were always at least two Lazenbies on offer, often more, different admixtures of saint and sinner, martyr and manipulator. It only took one small doubt about her motivation in some minor matter to spark a chain reaction in Jon's head, a torrent of questions that could wash away faith in her sincerity – but which would then in turn be followed by a wave of shame and self-reproach, a visceral flood from which the image of Lazenby *inviolata* would rise once more.

Except she'd lied to him, he'd then remind himself. She'd said she'd talked to Peachey when she'd not.

The rage might abate, but it never went away. It was always there, reminding him what had happened and what he had to do next. And it seems to me, looking at all of this from the outside, that the duplicity in Jon's readings of Lazenby reflected nothing more clearly than *his own* behaviour. For even as he filled out the new space created for him in Lazenby's world, he was swapping e-mails with Anthony Cogan; even as he re-engaged with the team's shared endeavour, he was laying his own private plan to cheat them; and when that plan was put into action, then the trust invested in him, the contracts he'd signed, the protocols, procedures and regulations, the Laws, the chains that bound them all together – but which also bound his idea and had for so long bound Annie – all of that would be irreparably broken.

None this, however, occurred to Jon. He was in the thick of it, and self-consciousness is the enemy of action. Returning from Hampstead with a 'yes' from Anthony Cogan, he did not even consider such perspectives on what he was planning to do. His was a narrative of destiny, not treachery; of gifts, not thefts. And for that narrative to proceed, he needed the spores.

It soon became clear that acquiring them was not going to be an easy task. The physical act of placing a small vial of liquid in a pocket or bag and carrying it out of the building posed no particular challenges in and of itself. But Lazenby ran a tight ship with respect to control of the hazardous materials in her lab, and getting round these was far more problematic. To work with spores – something he did on a regular basis – Jon needed first to book a biological safety cabinet, then to put in an order for the spores, both of which could be done electronically. A batch of ten vials in a protective plastic case would then be delivered by a lab technician: the plastic case bore a unique identifier for the batch, which was also etched onto the sides of the vials. At this point, the batch became linked to Jon in the system: if anything happened to it, for example if it disappeared, then he would be the one responsible for it. When he'd finished with the batch, he would mark it as completed on the system and a lab technician would return to collect the plastic case and empty vials: and only when this technician updated the system did Jon cease being responsible.

Returning from London, Jon was confident he'd find a way round these simple safeguards. But the more he thought about it over the next couple of days, the less confident he became. He rapidly ruled out transferring the spores from the vials to some other kind of container: this would jeopardise their viability and risk contamination. He also ruled out blaming it on a lab technician: for example, insisting that he'd returned the case when in fact he hadn't. There was too little time between him marking a batch as completed and the technician turning up to collect it for him to pretend that someone else had collected it in the meantime. A third option – simply brazening it out and claiming that he had no idea what had happened to the samples – didn't even warrant consideration: most likely this would lead to the whole lab being ripped apart in search of the missing vials.

His best chance, he soon concluded, lay in the possibility that a technician might not actually check the identifier on each empty vial as well as the one on the case when marking their return on the system. If he could somehow get hold of a case of empty vials – a problem in itself, but he'd get to that in due course – then he could simply do a switch: put the full vials into this case, and the empty vials into the case he was returning. Provided the lab technician just checked the case, which would have the correct identifier, and didn't notice the mismatch between case and vials, he'd be in the clear – as both case and vials would then be destroyed.

Having settled on this approach in principle, he decided to carry out an experiment to test its feasibility. He began by ordering two cases of samples – a common enough request – whereupon batches JXC-93/78 and JXC-93/79 were delivered by Kevin, one of the friendlier lab technicians who, as it happened, Jon had also seen from time to time at the gay pub in town. Jon set about his work as usual, starting with batch seventy-eight, but as he finished each vial, he returned it to case seventy-nine, making room for it by switching a full vial from case seventy-nine to seventy-eight. By the end of the morning, he had a plastic case marked seventy-nine full of empty vials marked seventy-eight, and a plastic case marked seventy-eight full of full vials marked seventy-nine. All that remained for him to do was mark the former as completed, wait for it to be collected – Kevin came by again just before lunch – and see if anything was noticed.

'You're in a good mood,' said Maria over lunch.

It was true. He was in a good mood. Nothing made him happier than wrestling with a problem like this, and the fact that he was doing it in the service of his new-found mission in life made him feel better than ever.

'You're right. I am in a good mood. I think I could conquer the world today.'

'You better take a look at my gene lines then. I can't do anything with them.'

'You know what I always tell you, Maria. Find the hidden constant and...'

'... turn it into a variable,' joined in Maria for the last few words. 'Yes, yes, I know you are a genius. But all I see are fucking constants.'

Jon laughed. 'Poor Maria. I'll take a look after lunch.'

'How is things at home?'

'They're fine.' The truth was that, over recent weeks, he and Scott had been spending less and less time together. There had been no conscious decision to rein things in, no discussion about the future, no amicable agreement. It was just that, since New Year, the reasons not to go round to one place or another had seemed to stack up, the ease of crying off joint social engagements increased, the impulse to seek each other out dwindled. Jon had seen Scott only once since his trip to London and had spent the night feeling slightly uncomfortable about his momentary if entirely ineffective interest in Ryan on the doorstep. Plus there was something else: a vague feeling that there might be infidelity in the mere fact that Scott had not known he was in London but thought he was spending Saturday afternoon in the lab. It was a plausible enough story: he often did go in at weekends. In a way, one could even argue it was true: he'd gone to London to further his idea, an idea he could no longer develop within the literal confines of the lab. And even if one could not really argue that, there were very good reasons why he'd not told Scott what he was up to. The subterfuge, moreover, was temporary: he'd be revealing all in due course, when what he had to reveal was a solution, not just the thwarted prospect of one. One could make the case that his lies were of the same bland ilk as those told when planning a surprise party or sneaking out to buy a present. And yet... it is in these tiny cracks in candour that other desires find a foothold, like those struggling, anaemic seedlings that will, in time, reduce foundations to dusty rubble.

'They're fine,' he repeated. 'Nothing to report really. How's things with the lovely Javier?'

Discussion of the man Maria had recently started dating, a handsome LLM student from Venezuela, readily accounted for the rest of their lunch, with Maria doing most of the talking. Jon was more than happy to listen, though in truth his mind wandered at times back to the lab and the switched empty vials.

As soon as they got back he checked the system and saw to his delight that Kevin had marked the batch as returned and disposed of. His plan, it seemed, had worked, and all he had to do now was work out a way to get hold of a case of empty vials. He was still mulling how to pull this off when, ten minutes later, Kevin turned up at his desk.

'Jon. Can I have a word?'

Jon's heart sank. 'Sure.'

'I think you muddled up the batch you returned before lunch.'

As he had feared: the mismatch had been noticed. But of course, the whole point of carrying out the experiment was that it left him the option of pretending an honest mistake. And to pull that off he would have to pretend not to know what Kevin was talking about. 'How so?'

'You said you were returning seventy-eight, but it was seventy-nine.' Kevin had brought the empty case with him and now held it out towards Jon, with the label on the case – JXC-93/79 – towards him.

'Let me have a look,' began Jon, reaching out to take hold of the case from Kevin. And so fixated was he on what he'd been expecting to hear that he'd already pulled an empty vial out and held it up to examine the etched number on its side before it hit him. 'Sorry, what did you say the problem was?'

'You logged it as seventy-eight,' repeated Kevin. 'But it's seventy-nine.' He pointed to the label on the case.

In a flash, Jon realised what he had done. He'd been so focused on getting the right – which was to say wrong – vials into each case that, when he'd come to marking the batch for return, he'd mistakenly entered the number from the vials, rather than the number from the case. Kevin hadn't noticed the mismatch at all: he'd just looked at the number on the case – exactly as Jon had expected him to.

'So I put this in as seventy-eight,' he said, swiftly popping the empty vial with its incriminating seventy-eight code back into the case and handing the whole thing back to Kevin. 'And this…' he added, spinning round and making a show of checking the batch still in his cabinet. 'You're right, this is seventy-eight.' He held up the case, inviting Kevin to look at it through the glass window, though Kevin clearly didn't feel this was necessary.

'Exactly,' said Kevin. 'Problem is, I'd already marked it as returned before I noticed. I'm meant to check before I do that but... you know, sometimes you get distracted. And it was only chance that I noticed it just before I put it into the disposal unit.'

'I'm sorry about that.'

'Don't worry. It could happen to anyone. But' – he dropped his voice a little – 'I need to ask you a favour.'

'Of course.'

'I've had a few slip-ups lately and... well, if I have to change the record now it will show up in the report and I'll have to explain it, and why I didn't check it properly first time round. And I really can't afford another mistake right now.'

'I see.' It hadn't occurred to Jon that there might be consequences for a technician if they failed to spot his deliberate error.

'So would you mind marking seventy-eight for collection as well now, and then I can put this one' – he held up the case of empty vials – 'through the system and dispose of it. That way no one will notice the difference.'

'Yes, of course,' said Jon. 'No problem.' Then, as Kevin seemed to be waiting for something else, added: 'Shall I do it now?'

'If you would,' said Kevin. 'I really appreciate this.'

'Honestly,' said Jon, crossing to the terminal and logging in, 'it's the least I can do, given that it was my error in the first place.' He quickly located the menu for batch JXC-93/78 and marked it as ready for collection. 'There you go.'

'Thanks,' said Kevin, then blushed slightly as he added: 'I'll buy you a drink in the Fountain some time.'

'OK. No need but... sure, that would be nice.'

Kevin was already on his way out of the door when another thought occurred to Jon. 'Hold on, what about...?' he began: then, just in time, something told him to stop.

'What about...?' repeated Kevin, who'd stopped in the doorway.

'Erm... nothing.' But what if Kevin went away wondering what he'd been going to say and realised the same thing? 'What about Thursday next week? At the Fountain.'

'Yeah. Great. Thursday it is.'

Of course, this wasn't at all what Jon had been planning to say. Kevin was kind of cute in his own way but not at all Jon's type – and even if he had been, Jon was with Scott. In a small town, moreover… all that would now have to be dealt with too. But Jon's eyes were on a higher prize.

For the next few minutes he sat at the terminal, hitting the refresh button every so often, waiting for Kevin to finish things off at his end. Then at last it came through: batch seventy-eight marked as returned and disposed of. And just below it, batch seventy-nine, also marked as returned and disposed of. Both batches clearly marked as out of his hands in the system – despite the fact that a case of ten untouched vials still sat in the cabinet behind him.

Kevin did not return that afternoon, the system was not updated again and Jon found other things to do to fill his time that did not require use of the spores still in his possession. He left it even later than usual to go home, and then, with few people still around in the lab and none of them anywhere near his cabinet, slipped the plastic case into his bag.

He had his spores.

Next morning, he caught Kevin in the corridor: 'You know the little issue we had yesterday.'

'Yes?'

'I realised when I went home that I had a finished batch that was already marked as returned and disposed of.' As Kevin's expression was blank, he added: 'Batch seventy-nine' – though it seemed unlikely that anyone was keeping track of the numbers through all of this.

It took a moment longer before the penny dropped. 'Shit. I see what you mean.'

'Don't worry. I took the empty case to the stock room and slipped it into the disposal. So it's all dealt with. Everything sorted.'

'Oh,' said Kevin, breathing out heavily through the word. 'Thank you. You are a complete star.'

'Don't mention it. I'm looking forward to that drink. Oh… and on that note, I didn't check yesterday but I assume it's OK if Scott joins us too.'

'Scott?'

'My boyfriend. You don't have to buy him a drink, don't worry!'

'Your... sure, of course.'

'Great. See you round then.'

Everything sorted. All he had to do was send a text to Scott suggesting a drink at the Fountain next Thursday and an e-mail to Cogan confirming that he would be visiting again on Saturday.

With his decision made, Cogan had spent no more time on his account of *Ophiocordyceps unilateralis* or internet searches for brain-dwelling fungi. Instead, he'd turned his attention to preparing for Dr Caldicot's next visit. For faced by the prospect of new life, death or intermediate transmogrification, he wasn't going to miss the opportunity to make a speech.

Many people given the opportunity to plan what might be their last words would think hard about what it was *they* wanted to say before quitting this earth. Not so Anthony Cogan, whose first instinct was to find out what everyone else had said. Like a preacher fashioning his Sunday sermon, he liked to have a text around which to spin his homily – sometimes irreverent, often irrelevant and always intensely self-referential: language with a loophole, constructed with half an eye over its own shoulder. If long years in universities had taught him anything it was that nothing original remained to be said, only original ways of resaying it, and that the greatest failing was to be caught claiming to say something new and sincere by the ever-present Critic, with his dictionary of quotations and acute sense of irony. Poor Cogan, who these days had to write in order to speak, also knew that he first had to read in order to write.

Given the intimate relationship they were about to establish, the obvious topic to read up on was Annie herself. But not her life cycle. No: he was not revisiting that topic. So instead, in the hope of inspiration, he spent a little time investigating the roots of her Greek name. The second part appeared to be a reference to Annie's practice of replacing nerves. The first part, meanwhile, suggested the involvement of someone who enjoyed obscure references: not just a *parasitos* – one who makes a habit out of eating at another's table – but an *aeisitos* – one of the chosen few who were granted the privilege of eating in the Prytaneion, the centre of government. For a while, he thought he could perhaps make something of this, but it came to nothing, and he soon lost interest in the finer points of Athenian political structures.

So he went back to Dr Caldicot's e-mail and decided to follow up a passing reference to the island where Annie had been discovered, Teobeka. When he ran a web search on that he found that the island's claim to fame lay not in its being the source of a brain-eating fungus – of this there was no mention, of course – but in its having been controversially blown up by a French nuclear bomb in the early 1970s.

The source of controversy lay partly in the fact that the explosion had happened at all: by then, most other countries had signed the Test Ban Treaty and ceased atmospheric testing. It was, however, the consequences of the affair for those who had once lived on Teobeka that had attracted most outrage in the commentaries Cogan found online, and made the island's name briefly synonymous with imperial disregard for the sensitive balance of indigenous cultures.

The Teobe, inhabitants of Teobeka, had been shipped en masse to the much larger neighbouring island of Madenu – neighbouring by Polynesian standards of remoteness, that is – where they were expected to assimilate with a local population who, to European eyes, looked more or less the same. Given the legendary peacefulness and generosity of the Teobe, it was assumed by their colonial governors that they would accept the inevitable extinction of their culture with good grace.

For two years after their translation, moreover, it seemed they were doing just that: quietly disappearing as a distinct people, surrendering their identity in exchange for the sophistications and sanitations of the larger island. Then, without warning, it all went horribly wrong, and nobility gave way to savagery of the bloodiest kind. Exactly what happened over the following year was hard to establish, as the authorities prevented access by all independent parties, and a world troubled by a shortage of oil and a surfeit of atrocity was, after a brief flurry of journalistic comment and an aborted debate in the UN, content to let this far-off Pacific mote be washed from its eye. Without doubt people had died, but who was to say where the truth lay between an official count of 221 and claims by die-hard conspiracy theorists that massacred thousands lay in unmarked graves? One thing only was clear: by the time things calmed down again, the traditional culture of the Teobe – and with it any meaningful talk of a 'people' – was gone for good.

That culture, as it so happened, had been recorded in loving detail by Edith Markham, a Cambridge anthropologist who had spent over ten years living on Teobeka and, bit by bit, immersed herself in the ways of its inhabitants. Her works had been dutifully cited, if not actually read, by most of those whose accounts of the Teobe debacle Cogan now found himself reading, so he, despairing of inspiration among the nuclear fallout and hoping an anthropologist might be just the ticket, turned his attentions thither.

He began with various papers Markham had published on aspects of Teobe life but soon found himself tiring of the minutiae of pot-washing, body-cleansing and blood-sharing – the latter a peculiar funeral rite involving faces smeared with the blood of the deceased, which Markham was not only allowed to observe but, in the end, also invited to join, and about which she had written, to Cogan's way of thinking, at tedious length. So he moved on to *Grief, Madness and Wisdom*, the book Markham wrote on her return to Cambridge in 1971, while campaigning against the planned nuclear test. After three chapters of pseudo-spiritual nonsense, however, he could take no more of it – especially as he'd already found out that the author of these mystic visions of Teobe-inspired universal peace had, not long after writing them and as her last act in life, gone on a rampage through Newnham village with a kitchen knife. Edith Markham was not the stuff of last words: not Anthony Cogan's last words, at any rate.

Worse still, he had now wasted most of what had once seemed an ample stretch of time to prepare what he wanted to say. The day when Dr Caldicot would come by with his needle and vial was fast approaching, and Cogan, like a complacent undergraduate caught out by a deadline, still had no essay. At this rate, he was set to die, or live, or change, not only intellectually unannealed but also in a very bad temper.

'You've been very grumpy this last week,' said Ryan, the day before the day of injection. It was a mystery how he had worked that out from Cogan's flitting eyes and flat speech, but such was his preternatural ability to peer through the lumpen flesh that imprisoned Cogan.

'I wanted to say something,' said Cogan, 'but I can't work out what.'

'That's not like you,' teased Ryan. Then his face grew serious. 'I know I've said this before, and please don't be annoyed, but I need to say it again.'

It was true, Ryan had said it before, and Cogan's first reaction was indeed one of slight irritation. But the mechanics of communication gave him time to think again and be a better person. Ryan had said it just after Dr Caldicot's first visit but, since then, he had kept his counsel. The boy had a right to express a point of view.

So Cogan checked himself and found the words: 'Go on.'

'Well, you know what I'm going to say: that you don't have to go through with this if you don't want to. And...' He crouched down in front of Cogan's chair and extended his right hand to hold Cogan's left arm – a gentle, reassuring pressure which Cogan could not feel, only try to remember. His gaze, meanwhile, fixed on Cogan himself, on the last physical presence of the man in the world, sparkling somewhere just behind the glassy curve of his eyes – and for a moment, like that, they communicated. And Cogan, never normally lost for words though often lost in them, now found himself simultaneously gripped by a strange new terror, the terror of not knowing what to say, and at the same time freed from it by the knowledge that, to say anything, he would first have to look away and so stop talking. Words were not an option.

'Look,' continued Ryan, 'it's entirely up to you. But... I need you to know that it won't change how I think about you either way.' He let out a little breath, and for just a fraction of a second his eyes shot away to the left, only to return again almost at once. 'I mean, I don't think for a second that's why—' He broke off and shrugged slightly, clearly unsure how to go on.

The words of Cogan's last response were still on screen. Provided he said nothing new, he could speak without anything more than a momentary break in their eye contact. 'Go on.'

'Well, you know what a big softy I am. You've teased me about it often enough. And these last three years working here with you have been...' A sigh this time and a longer glance downwards. 'I don't really think of it as work, you know. I've learned so much from you. The things you talk to me about, all the stuff you know, the books and the ideas – I've changed so much being with you, and now... I'm not sure I want you to change.'

He smiled nervously – and it crossed Cogan's mind that, even had he died right then, at that moment, that smile would have been enough in his life.

'I don't mean that, of course. I mean, if you were up and about and walking and talking then, who knows? Maybe I'd be looking for a sugar daddy.' He gave a little laugh, blushing slightly as he did so, so neither could know whether he was entirely joking.

'The thing is, all this, right now, it's precious to me, and I don't want to lose it. And if I do, I won't be able to live with myself if I think you were trying to make it *more* precious. What I'm trying to say is... I'm sure it's not, but if it is... I mean, you know that *I* don't need you to do this. Not for me. You do understand that, don't you?'

It broke Cogan's heart that he had to answer – not because of the answer itself, a simple 'Yes', but because, to give it, he had to turn his eyes down to his screen for long enough to find that answer and so let the moment slip from his steadfast gaze into the dark halls of memory, where it would shine only for so long as Cogan himself held a candle aloft.

Just in time, with mere hours left, he had realised what he needed to say. Nothing. There was nothing he needed to say.

There is a paradox, wrote Edith Markham, in the very idea of a person changing. For something to change, something must also have stayed the same; otherwise there is no identity between what came before and what comes after. Yet when we look for that enduring something, we find precisely nothing.

It's not a new conundrum, of course. Many centuries ago, Plutarch was wondering whether a ship which has been restored by successively replacing all of its parts – a series of small changes – is still in fact the same ship. If the ship was none of its parts, what was it? And if it was nothing, what was changing? Yet, manifestly, ships change; people step into the same river twice; those people themselves change; anthills change; compromises change; relationships change; and only philosophy seems to stand still or, at best, revolve upon its axis.

For her part, Markham was not identifying the paradox in order to eviscerate it on the syllogistic slab, enumerate its sinews and Latinise it into clockwork. She was no logician, but an anthropologist – or perhaps, in her later years, as one who had started to appreciate humanity's place in the panoply of life, an aspiring biologist in the full sense of that term. For her, the paradox was something to live within: a habitat, an ecosystem.

Pseudo-spiritual nonsense? So Cogan had written in his diary mere days before. But then, as if the trumpet had sounded, he – whatever 'he' was – had been changed.

It had already happened, or started to happen, before he lay there waiting for Annie to rewire his body – much as a derelict shell springs to life in the mind of an architect before any plans are drawn or scaffolding erected. Not that he could have put his finger on it, even if he'd yet been able to move the finger. But... how could he express it? He had seen what had been there all along, and now at last he was ready.

Ready physically as well as mentally once Ryan, shrugging off offers of help from Jon, had taken his shirt off, lifted him from his chair and arranged him stomach down on the bed, with his head turned sideways so that he could still breathe and see.

'If you have second thoughts,' said Ryan, 'then look at me and away and back to me and away again, two times, OK?'

Without his screen, of course, such elaborate signals were the only way Cogan could have communicated had he wanted to. But as he had nothing more to say, he could look at Ryan without interruption. And lying there, looking into Ryan's eyes, he fancied he was at last peering through all the words – the years of words, the blankets of words – to what had always been wrapped inside them, shaping not the stitches or colours but the long contours.

Cogan was ready, and Jon too was ready – as ready, that is, as he was ever going to be on the basis of his proficiency in giving intraspinal injections to rats and a few evenings buried in medical textbooks. If he made a mistake, he kept reminding himself, there was nothing actually left to damage. Not inside Cogan's spinal column, at any rate, and he would not steady his hand by letting his thoughts wander to anything beyond that band of bone and nerve.

Annie, multitudinous in suspension, was ready. Readiness was the essence of her sporulated form, her *raison d'être*, her all.

Only Ryan was not ready. Cogan might have found in his unwavering gaze a moment of epiphany, but only because, like a theatre audience, he did not see through the gauze to the frantic stagehands. Backstage, Ryan was in turmoil. He could not talk to Tony about it and, sworn to secrecy, he could talk to no one else. No one except – and over the last week or two he'd been over this a hundred times, and every time found himself boxed into the same unavoidable conclusion – no one except this stranger, Jon Caldicot.

The moment itself passed without event. Cogan did not even know the needle had entered until Ryan spoke: 'It's over, Tony.' The needle was already out again. Then Ryan was lifting him back into his chair, dressing him and wheeling him back to his usual place before the bay window. And there he sat, waiting, while Ryan showed Dr Caldicot out. Still him, for now at least. Nothing had changed, but with it, maybe, everything.

'And Ryan?' you're asking. 'What *was* going on with Ryan? Are you really trying to say that Ryan was in love with the husk of a man over twice his age?' And while I have not once used that word myself, I understand why you ask the question and am still at a loss as to how to answer it. That's how it is with human beings. The closer you get to them, the less you understand them, until at last you arrive at yourself and bow to mystery.

I suppose some part of an explanation must lie in Ryan's own history, starting perhaps with his being one of five children. Large families have to share out being noticed, and a child can get used to being overlooked. Being in third place meant Ryan missed out on the small advantages of oldest and youngest, while sharing that third place with a non-identical twin prone to violent mood swings reduced his portion of parental attention to something close to zero. Events had then conspired to rub out even the tiny fraction that remained. First, his little sister, Rebecca, was born with a heart defect which required close parental observation interspersed with regular hospital visits until she was finally given the all-clear around age ten. By then the eldest, Mark, had joined the army, creating a new source of background worry for the exhausted couple, while Ryan's twin, Adrian, tipped over the edge by the explosion of hormones in his body, embarked on a career of low-level juvenile delinquency which would last until he himself became a father in his early twenties. Dependable and unexceptional, Ryan might perhaps have claimed the role of 'the one we don't have to worry about' – had not his older sister, Laura, already delivered on that front: a talented dancer from her earliest years, she'd turned professional at the age of sixteen with a place in the touring company of *Cats* and hadn't stopped working since.

When Ryan himself turned sixteen, tragedy struck: Mark, on a tour of duty in Afghanistan, was killed by a roadside bomb. A year later, Ryan's mother was diagnosed with breast cancer, kicking off three years of surgery, chemotherapy and – most debilitating of all – uncertainty. It was as if the Griffiths had been selected for participation in a modern-day experiment modelled on the Book of Job. They responded with the courage and resilience of which human beings can sometimes be capable, but it was hardly surprising that, in the process of meeting all the demands placed upon them, the relationship at the heart of the family began to unravel. Gina Griffiths' arduous recovery took place in parallel with the slow and obvious unwinding of her marriage to Peter: they finally separated, with great sadness on both sides, shortly after Ryan's twenty-second birthday.

While all this was going on, Ryan – self-sufficient and, in so far as he could be, supportive – completed a BTEC and Foundation

Degree in Health and Social Care at the local college and, with certificates in hand, slipped off to London. Laura, who was now getting parts in West End shows and had bought herself a flat in Peckham, encouraged the move and offered her sofa as an initial base. The two had always got on well, and in recent years had been brought even closer by the shock of Mark's death – Laura was acutely conscious that she was now the eldest – the ongoing worries of their mother's cancer and Adrian's increasingly out-of-control behaviour. But, oddly enough, it was Ryan's sexuality that had done more than anything to cement their relationship. Laura, working in an environment in which being gay was far from unusual, had guessed her brother's proclivities long before he finally came out to her at age sixteen, and rather enjoyed having a cute gay brother. For the young Ryan, meanwhile, the stories Laura told about gay friends when she was back home – entirely for his sake, he later realised – had provided crucial reassurance that at least one family member was going to accept him. When he did come out, Laura was the first he told.

Telford was not the most exciting place for a young gay man to grow up, but all things considered Ryan had not had too bad a time of it. He'd been lucky enough to go to a secondary school which took active steps to stamp out homophobic bullying and so was spared the treatment dished out to many other kids, gay and straight alike. Back home, meanwhile, the reactions to Laura's stories suggested that, while his family was unlikely to respond with the same enthusiasm as his big sister to an announcement of his sexuality, they would also probably get over it pretty quickly. When he did at last tell them, their reaction was even more positive than he'd expected – in that they barely reacted at all. Even Adrian, about whom Ryan had been most worried, merely shrugged and reassured Ryan that if anyone at school gave him any trouble for it they'd get their heads kicked in. Even in declaring that he was gay, Ryan barely registered on the family radar.

So in moving to London, Ryan was definitely not fleeing the barbaric homophobia of the provinces. On the other hand, the tedium of a small provincial scene and contrasting delights of a big city did play a part in his decision. Ryan had more sex in his first two weeks down in London than he'd had in his entire life until then – a pace he would keep up for much of his first year.

But the move wasn't just about getting his rocks off. As a young man just turned twenty, animal urges drove a significant portion of his decision-making, but the young Ryan was also susceptible to rational thought. In these moments he set about the pressing tasks of finding regular work and a place to live. After eight months of temporary jobs, with his back developing a permanent kink from the gap between the sofa cushions, he stumbled on an opportunity through the friend of someone he'd briefly dated that solved both problems at once: working as Cogan's live-in carer.

From the outset, Ryan knew he'd been incredibly lucky. True, the hours were long, with much less time off than he'd ideally have liked, but the pay was good, with a flat he could not possibly have afforded thrown in, and it made sense to work hard for a few years and build up some savings. Moreover, he soon discovered that he actually quite enjoyed the work. Of course, there was plenty of routine and drudgery, and the mechanics of getting food in and piss and shit back out again were never going to be anything better than bearable, but much of the day was occupied by the more agreeable task of keeping Cogan company. They would talk, for instance: and, even if their conversations were about as balanced as a Socratic dialogue, the experience of sustaining interaction over hours at a stretch was a new and exciting one for someone more accustomed to sitting quietly on the sidelines. He didn't care or even stop to think whether Tony saw him as a person or a hired help: someone was talking to him as an adult human being, and that was quite enough for an impressionable young man like Ryan. Slowly, imperceptibly, his recognition of his good luck in finding the job mutated into an intuition of the workings of fate.

Those quiet boys and girls that the world overlooks – what stories do you imagine they tell themselves? With neither gratitude nor resentful rebellion to shape themselves around, what do you suppose they make of themselves? The Ryan that arrived at Cogan's was like the unformed protagonist of a *Bildungsroman*, and Cogan, blithering on about literature and philosophy, had no idea what creature he was feeding and forming.

Bit by bit, Ryan's life began to revolve around Tony. He still had sexual needs, of course, which he met mechanically at the sauna or via the internet, but he gave up on his previous vague intentions of finding a boyfriend. He still had to eat, to exercise, to sleep, to visit his family or talk to them on the phone, get his hair cut, go to the bank. But his execution of these chores became more and more perfunctory, until he'd find himself with time spare even on his days off to spend with Tony, chatting about this and that while the agency carer dealt with the practicalities. Perhaps one day, he told himself, they'd hand all that stuff over to the agency for good, so that he and Tony could just spend their time talking. Strangely, perhaps, he never bothered himself with the fact that Cogan would soon be dead.

It was into this equilibrium of slow decline that Dr Caldicot had burst with his promises and threats, and for the first time in his life Ryan felt he had something to lose. In his head he'd always imagined a youthful, mobile Anthony Cogan gliding effortlessly through a glittering world of seminars and salons and dinner parties, all sparkling wit and repartee – a world to which the likes of him could never have access but on which he was being permitted to spy. Now, suddenly, Caldicot had appeared – from that same world, so far as Ryan could tell, and offering the exile a return ticket. And why would a recovered Tony want to waste his time talking to some young man who'd been wiping his arse these last few years? What could a man like Tony ever see in someone like him?

And Tony – the person he talked to, the person who listened, the person who actually seemed to give a damn and who, by doing so, brought to the fearful confusion of Ryan's thoughts a fixed point of calm – Tony was the one person he could not tell. The fixed point was moving. Tony had become the confusion.

He could not talk to Tony and, sworn to secrecy, he could talk to no one else. No one except Jon Caldicot. It didn't matter how many times he ran the argument: the conclusion was always the same.

But it wasn't until they'd reconfirmed plans for follow-up monitoring and contact and said goodbye on the doorstep, it wasn't until he was starting to turn back into the house that he made the final decision to speak: 'You know you said that if I had any questions...'

He broke off, once more having second thoughts, and Jon stepped into the gap perhaps a little too quickly: 'Yes, of course.'

'I mean... you know, some of the practicalities,' stumbled Ryan. Practicalities. How would he even begin to talk about this to someone he barely even knew? But there was no one else.

'Do you want to talk now?'

'No, I should get back to Tony now.' If they were going to talk, he didn't want it to be here, not in the same house as Tony. 'Maybe over a beer some time.'

'That would be great.'

'I mean... if you're in London again.'

'Absolutely. I can come down easily enough. When works for you?'

'Well, the agency nurse comes on Thursday evenings, so...'

'Brilliant. This Thursday then.'

'OK, sure. Let's confirm it during the week. I'll give you my mobile number.'

They swapped numbers, and then, not sure if he was relieved or regretful, Ryan hastily repeated his goodbyes and slipped back into the house, shutting the door behind him.

There was silence in the dark hallway. The furniture, the boxes, the piles of books stood motionless, like ancient stalagmites. 'We must have a clear-out,' Tony would say every few months, but the time was worth more to them both than the space, and the clear-out never happened.

But this had. Dr Caldicot had. Annie had. They had come into this house and turned it upside down. Fine, thought Ryan: if that was how it was, then he was ready to fight.

6

There had to come a moment when the improbable edifice Jon had constructed started to crack. He had built his house from problems and solutions, balancing them against each other like forces of action and reaction, engineering from their interplay a structure that, on paper, could not be faulted. But out in the real, living world, winds blow and earth moves, and even the mightiest towers at last give way to eager roots.

Had it not been for the taxing details of volunteer finding, batch number switching and intraspinal injection, perhaps his resolution, born in the dark as he half-slept after his showdown with Lazenby, would not have made it even this far. As it was, busied with obstacles, he'd kept himself from thinking about the act itself until the act was performed. Now it was done though, there was nothing left to do, and like moisture that will freeze and expand, questions began to seep into the void.

And the first of these was already spiralling around his head as he walked from Mr Cogan's house in Hampstead back to the Tube: why did Ryan want to talk to him?

Because Ryan had questions, he answered himself. Questions about practicalities, just as he'd said. That was all there was to it. But his having to keep telling himself this, on top of his too easy assent to another trip to London, belied the fact that he wanted there to be a different answer. And where was he to place this wayward desire in the great scheme to which he had committed.

It wasn't just a question of cheating on Scott. Cheating? When they were barely seeing each other any more? The word almost had no meaning by now. But Scott was his boyfriend; his boyfriend's disease was the problem he was solving; his idea was the solution to that problem, which belonged to Scott; the steps he had taken were designed to remove the obstacles Lazenby had cruelly laid in the idea's way; he'd taken them so that he could help his boyfriend; who was Scott, and had Scander's. Those were the constants that held together the precarious formula for his intentions – and that formula might be blown apart by new, unanticipated variables.

Questions about practicalities, he repeated to himself. That was all there could be to it. And if there were any doubt, which there wasn't, it would all be laid to rest come Thursday.

Which reminded him, he'd need to let down Kevin, whom he'd also promised to meet on Thursday. And also let Scott know the drinks were off – though Scott had not yet said if he was coming, responding to Jon's text by instead suggesting he come round and cook dinner on Tuesday evening. And somehow, with minutiae like these, he again managed to distract himself not just from Ryan's sudden suggestion of a meeting but also from the fact he had just released a brain-eating fungus into the not-so-wild of Hampstead.

Distractions could not hold the world at bay forever though. The next blow to his equations was dealt just a few days later, on Tuesday afternoon. And it struck a term he'd forgotten, the very constant he'd had to let vary to launch upon this course of action in the first place: his career.

There was nothing to indicate exactly what was coming when Lazenby called him into her office. How were things at home? Was he getting any support he needed? Was there anything he was unhappy about? All reasonable enough questions from a boss. But the half-hearted way she asked them and then seemed to ignore his answers warned him that this was not the real purpose of the conversation. She was building up to something – and the thought suddenly occurred to him: what if she'd noticed? Batch number seventy-nine, marked used by Jon and disposed, but nowhere to be found in the disposal unit. Case number seventy-eight, also used by Jon, in the disposal unit but, on closer inspection, full of empty vials from batch seventy-nine.

He shook himself: the idea of Lazenby rummaging through the lab waste to check that everything was in order was, of course, absurd.

Then Lazenby brought his wandering thoughts to heel with her real question:

'I was wondering... have you spoken to Matt Peachey lately?'

'No, I... Not since...' He stumbled to a halt: Lazenby knew since when.

'Nothing on e-mail or anything?'

'No.' Nor had he expected anything, beyond a vague assurance that they'd talk again in 'a few months' time'. The corporate man was off in his corporate world again, creating PowerPoints, meeting in meeting rooms, dealing with shareholders – whatever it was people in that world did. Jon hadn't given him much further thought.

'I suppose you must have made a big impression on him that one time you met then,' mused Lazenby, though not sounding very convinced.

It was two times, of course: once with Lazenby and once more before that in the smoking area, but Jon decided not to correct her. 'Did I?' he said instead, when it became clear that Lazenby had no intention of explaining what was behind her remark.

'Looks like it.'

'Why do you say that?'

'I had an e-mail from him this morning,' said Lazenby, swinging her chair round towards her computer and starting to flick through her inbox with the mouse as if she were looking for one she wanted to show to Jon – though if this was the case, she never found it. 'He's arranged an invitation for you to this year's Congress in Seville.'

This Jon had not been expecting. Attendance at the International Mycotherapy Congress was strictly limited, the aim being to sustain the kind of close-knit, intimate network of colleagues that had brought the discipline into existence in the first place – but the inevitable consequence being exclusivity and cachet. Outside the small circle of luminaries guaranteed an invitation, like Lazenby and Jack Kapinsky, invitations carried enormous importance: for those at the next tier down, hoping one day to have their own labs, as proof that they'd not yet fallen by the wayside; for those at a lower level as a kind of golden ticket to the mycotherapeutic chocolate factory; for those at Jon's level unheard of. Exactly how invitations were allocated remained a mystery outside the Congress committee, but it was generally known that nominations and representations were sought from key figures in the field, and lengthy discussions then had about who was up-and-coming, who still had it and who could safely be cast aside. Jon had not even dreamed of being the subject of their deliberations, let alone in receipt of an invitation. An aspiration for the future, perhaps, but not looked for yet.

'You're kidding me,' he blurted involuntarily.

Lazenby met this suggestion with a disdainful flick of the eyes. 'He asked me to let you know to hold the dates. It's… Well, I'm sure he knows what he's up to. And you've not been in touch with him?'

Suddenly Jon realised the nature of the suspicion he was under. 'I haven't been in touch with him at all. This has come as a complete surprise to me.'

'Well, there you go then. I'm sure we'll both find out when we do finally see him. It's on March the twenty-first and twenty-second. There's a dinner on the Sunday evening as well.'

As he'd said, a complete surprise. One that initially left him reeling – then, as he walked back to his bench, smiling. This was recognition. Recognition of his idea. There was no other reason Peachey would arrange his invitation, no other basis on which Peachey even knew him. It was his idea that was going to the Congress.

'You look very pleased about something,' said Maria when he got back to his bench.

He could not stop a broad grin spreading across his face. 'I've been invited to the Congress.'

'What?'

'I know.'

'That's fantastic news.'

'Yeah.'

'And do you know… I mean, why you?'

Jon laughed. 'Thanks for the vote of confidence.'

'No, don't tease me. You know what I mean.'

He did, and of course had said nothing to Maria or anyone else beyond Lazenby and Peachey about his idea. But now he had an invitation to the Congress to explain. He'd have to say something. 'I think it's because I had an idea…' he began, then broke off.

Because it wasn't just an idea now, was it? It was sitting in a wheelchair in Hampstead. And the smile faded from his face as he realised that the good news belonged in a universe he had chosen to turn his back on.

'I had an idea,' he repeated. 'A new way of using Annie. Therapeutically. I discussed it with Lazenby and Matt Peachey too. And I think that's why.'

'Wow,' said Maria. 'When was that?'

'A few months ago.'

'Wow.' He couldn't be sure, but it seemed to him that her excitement too had been checked: as if she were disappointed he'd not told her this before. 'And the new use? Or is it top secret.'

'I don't know,' he flannelled. Yes? No? It would not be top secret when he showed them Cogan. That was the whole point, after all. 'I probably shouldn't say more without checking. You know, and maybe don't say anything to anyone else yet.'

'*Claro*,' said Maria, then thought a moment before adding: 'You know, you shouldn't keep everything so… locked up.'

'Yeah, I'm sorry. I wasn't really sure I could say anything.'

Maria shook her head. 'I don't mean that. This idea, this new use. It's about Scott, isn't it?'

'How…?' began Jon – then broke off. A picture had suddenly come into his mind, a vision of Maria's face when at last she learned what he had done, unspeaking but saying all she needed to say in the inflection of lip and brow. Why did you not talk to someone? Why did you not talk to me? 'Yes,' he said. 'It's about Scott.'

'And that's why you had the argument with Imogen.'

'Yes.'

'Well,' said Maria, 'I'm very pleased for you about the Congress. Just don't keep things locked up, you know? There's no need.'

He agreed with her for the sake of appearances. She might even have been right until the Saturday just gone when, in that dusty, memorialised house in Hampstead, he'd passed the point of no return.

And the glittering career in which an invitation to the Mycotherapy Congress was a first step? That was precisely what he'd left behind. Lazenby rooting through the used, empty vials in the disposal unit? Irrelevant, because they were all going to find out anyway what he'd done. The whole plan turned on that revelation. It was only the unveiling of Cogan, fully infected and offering his first-hand account of what it was like to have a new nervous system, that would trigger the necessary sequel: Scott's gratitude when he learned what Jon had done for him; the recognition by all that the Laws could indeed be circumvented; Lazenby's admission that she'd been wrong to stop him; progress at last for his idea. This much he'd had mapped out since he'd first decided on this course of action, lying on his bed after his outburst. And an unwanted career, trapped in Lazenby's discipline, was the thing he had happily set aside. It was just that he'd not had the invitation then.

Only now, belatedly, did he find himself starting to fill out in more detail what took the place of that career: instant dismissal, perhaps a criminal investigation, certainly no chance of working in science again. He tried to imagine himself presenting Cogan at the Congress: 'I have done what no one else dared.' He tried to imagine Peachey patting him on the back: 'Well done, lad. You did what I'd have done myself if it were down to me, gone out and tested it.'

He tried to resolve the blank silhouette of his father's face into an expression of unmixed pride. But the images did not come. Of course they did not come. Because they were absurd, too absurd even for a daydream.

He was still locked up in his thoughts that evening when Scott came round and cooked dinner, doing his best to stay engaged with the conversation, but drifting off whenever Scott wasn't feeding him the cues for obvious responses. To be honest, he'd rather have spent the evening on his own, but Scott had seemed particularly keen when he'd suggested the meal and, as they'd not seen each other for more than a week, Jon felt he could not say no.

It had not once occurred to him that Scott too might be following his own locked-up lines of reasoning; that, with life's endpoint suddenly made so salient, he might not be in the mood for wasting time; that, if he had delayed a decision so long, it was only because, like anyone pulling the curtains back and letting in the direct light of day, his eyes had needed time to adjust. So Jon was totally unprepared when, after another silent digression into his own preoccupations, Scott said: 'This isn't working, is it? I think it's time for us to call it a day.'

'What?'

'It isn't working.'

'What do you mean?' In fact he'd understood what Scott meant the first time. But he did not believe it even the second.

'I mean...' began Scott, a little irritated – then checked himself. 'Look, we've had a fun time together, especially at the beginning. But lately... I mean, look at us, we've not seen each other for nearly two weeks and we've nothing to say to each other. Do *you* think it's working?'

Jon felt a strange panic gripping him. The obvious answer was: no, of course it wasn't working. But he'd... invested. He'd made a commitment. Not to Scott, but... justified by Scott. 'I'm sorry. I've been so preoccupied with work lately. And I... I lock things up. I'm sorry.'

Scott was shaking his head. 'I'm not having a go at you, Jon. I'm not saying you've done something wrong. I'm just saying... well, you know, sometimes things don't work out. We gave it a go, and we had some fun, and maybe now it's time to move on. I thought... I don't know, I thought you'd feel the same way.'

'No,' insisted Jon – although every fibre of his body was screaming: yes, yes, that's right. 'Is this... is this because of your diagnosis?'

'No,' said Scott, folding his arms, the irritation surfacing once again. 'It's not because of my diagnosis.'

'Because if you're thinking that it's not fair to me...'

'I'm not thinking it's not fair to you. And to be honest, you're pissing me off a bit now. It's not about my diagnosis, it's about me, and what I want in life. I don't want' – he waved a hand vaguely, as if gesturing to the air they were breathing – 'this. Sitting here, doing nothing, saying nothing, going through the motions.'

'You're right,' said Jon, feeling his breath growing shorter and shallower. 'And I think that's my fault. I've let myself get caught up in things. I can do better. It's like you say, we had fun at the beginning. Just let me try again.'

Scott sat back in his chair, shaking his head again and letting out a taut little sigh of disbelief. 'I can't believe you're doing this. I came here tonight thinking one of us just had to say what both of us were thinking. And that, in the circumstances, it had to be me. But this... Why are you doing this?'

'Doing what? Trying to fix things?'

This time Scott's sigh was long and deep: a chest-full of air, along with all the tension that had held it in place, released, the last of it shaped into a falling 'Yeah'. He looked to one side. 'Of course you're trying to fix things. That's what you do, isn't it?'

'Yes. That's what I do.'

'You know what then?' continued Scott, sitting forwards again and looking at Jon. There was something business-like about his manner. 'It *is* you. You've changed. We had lots of fun at the beginning because you were different then. I like the way you get passionate about things, get carried away. I like the way you seem to pile into life and enjoy it in your own geeky scientist way. And I don't know if it was the diagnosis or what it was but... it's like you've shut yourself off from me. Either it's not there any more or... I don't know. It's like you're hiding from me.'

'Hiding what?'

'I don't know. I'm not saying you're actually... Jesus. Look you've changed, that's all. With me at any rate. And I'm sure I've changed as well. Of course I've changed—'

'Well, yes,' interrupted Jon – and suddenly his inner agitation was no longer panic or fear: it was anger. 'I suppose I have changed. But did it occur to you to wonder why? Did you ask yourself what I've been so preoccupied with?'

'Yes,' said Scott calmly. 'And I asked you too. Lots of times. You wouldn't answer.'

'I couldn't answer. I wanted to tell you but I couldn't. Not just because of the confidentiality. I didn't want... I didn't want to get your hopes up too early. And I still don't know for sure. But I have an idea that can fix this. Fix Scander's, I mean. Completely fix it. And that's why I've been so preoccupied. That's what I've been fighting for against that cunt Lazenby. And I've taken risks, you know. Big risks. I've put myself on the line for this. And that's what I've been hiding, you see? That I'm trying to fix things.'

Only as he spoke the last words did he realise how loud his voice had become. Not shouting like he had in Lazenby's office, but the same swell of volume and emotion. Then the wave crested, broke and receded, leaving behind it nothing but mortification.

Scott didn't reply immediately, and when he did so it was as he pushed his chair back from the table to get up. 'I'm sorry, Jon. I'm sure you mean well and… this idea of yours, I hope it's successful. But part of me feels that's the only kind of relationship you're capable of: fixing things. And I'm not a problem. I'm a human being.'

'Not you,' mumbled Jon. 'I wasn't trying to fix you.' But the fight had gone from him.

So Scott left.

Jon must have got a little sleep that night because, when his alarm at last went off, it woke him. Grey and unrefreshed, he dragged himself out of bed and into the day. His mind, which the night before had been a fly hurling itself against window panes, now lay still and listless on the sill. With no energy for anything else he occupied himself with the humdrum of everyday life. And despite so much being at stake, nothing happened: the day passed at the lab without his once having to fake a smile or dodge a question, and even with Maria, who had that bad habit of noticing when something was going on, he found himself merely omitting, not actively hiding. Lazenby said nothing. Scott made no contact. No word came from Hampstead. And the evening, when it arrived, was much like most of his evenings those days: a quiet one, in on his own, catching up on a bit of reading and watching television before bed.

But everything was fractured.

Locked up, Maria had told him. He locked things up. Locked them up so well he couldn't even get at them himself now. 'There's no need,' she had said: no need to stay silent, say nothing, tell no one. But now, he realised, there was more need than ever. His own actions had made it so. His idea had marooned him on an oceanic spit of secrecy, and with every hour that passed he was going a little crazier, his thoughts growing a little more ragged.

He needed to communicate. But the more he thought about it, the clearer it became there was only one person he *could* talk to.

The next morning Jon sent a text message to Ryan to check on plans for that evening – while also making his excuses to Kevin when he saw him and postponing their drink to another, unspecified time. Ryan replied suggesting the Duke of Gloucester in Soho – which confirmed, as Jon had supposed, that Ryan was almost certainly gay. Not that Jon was expecting anything like *that* from this meeting, he told himself on the train.

He had never been into the Duke of Gloucester, though he'd walked past it once or twice. Unlike most of the gay bars in that part of Soho, it was still recognisably a pub. It had proper pub bars, for example, one upstairs and one down, with brass foot-rails along their base; it served bitter on tap alongside the usual array of bland lagers; upstairs there was even a dark swirly carpet. But this was no local: downstairs, the pub-style wooden tables and chairs had been wedged into corners, leaving ample standing room for the crowds that showed up on Friday and Saturday nights, and bass-heavy music thumped from speakers that were not really up to the task. Even on a Thursday evening, knots of shaven-headed, muscular men in bomber jackets were starting to gather down there; among them, Jon felt he must look like some kind of foppish puppy. It was at least a bit quieter on the upper floor, with more places to sit, fewer people and much quieter music: so after a few circuits to assure himself that Ryan had not already arrived, Jon opted for a corner up there – texting his position to Ryan to be on the safe side.

Ryan arrived ten minutes late, apologised for keeping him waiting and insisted on buying him another pint to put next to the one he'd already started on.

'I don't think ten minutes really counts as late these days,' said Jon when Ryan came back with the drinks.

'It does to me,' said Ryan, pulling up a stool and sitting down opposite Jon. 'I was brought up properly.'

'My father would love you.'

'I'm glad to hear it.'

They chatted about Jon's home and family in Surrey and Ryan's in Shropshire; about Jon's passage through some of the world's great universities; about Ryan's across his sister's sofa. Despite the intimacy forced by secrecy, despite the fact each had identified the other as the only person he could talk to, the truth was they'd only met each other twice before and barely knew each other. Neither felt able to plunge straight into the topics he really wanted to talk about: both appreciated the opportunity to sip a little beer and ease into the conversation.

It was Ryan who first took a turn towards more serious matters: 'Look, before I say anything else, I've been wanting to apologise to you.'

'Me? Why?'

'The first time you came round – I was out of order.'

'Really not necessary,' said Jon, though the fact he knew what Ryan was talking about was perhaps evidence it was. 'But if it makes you feel better: apology accepted.' Though far from ready to talk about his own issues – and unsure what it was he'd want to say when ready – he too felt it was the moment to move the conversation on. 'You wanted to talk, you said. About practicalities.'

'Yeah,' said Ryan. He picked up his almost empty glass. 'Do you want another?'

Jon, who'd started one up, was still only about a third of the way through his second, so declined. 'But let me get this one for you.'

While waiting at the bar, he took the opportunity to sneak a look at Ryan, whose eyes were fixed on a beer mat he was turning over and over with his right hand. If it *had* been a date, he mused, then he'd have been very happy about how it was going – and about who it was with.

'So there's no specific question as such,' explained Ryan when Jon returned with the second beer. 'I just have, you know, concerns. And there's no one else I can talk to about them, given the... you know. Keeping it all secret and everything.'

'Yes,' said Jon.

'The thing is, the thing I keep thinking is, suppose it does work: what then? I mean, I'm still struggling to believe any of this, to be honest. But let's say, for the sake of argument, it really does work: the Scander's is reversed, Tony can talk and walk and everything. That would all be fantastic, of course, but... what then?'

The question appeared to be rhetorical – which was just as well, as Jon didn't really have an answer. It was the same question, albeit with different accents, that he had started asking himself.

'I assume you plan to tell other people?' continued Ryan. 'I mean, I'm guessing that if it works there will be lots of people wanting to talk to Tony. It'll be a big deal, yes? The kind of thing that gets on the news. They'll make documentaries. And they'll need to do all sorts of tests and observations and things.'

'I suppose so,' said Jon, frowning. 'I'm not sure about the news. I suspect... the confidentiality, that is.'

'And how are you going to keep Tony confidential? You can't keep him in a lab.'

'No, but... I don't know.'

'You see this is the kind of thing I'm talking about. Maybe someone *will* decide to keep him in a lab. Whether he likes it or not. Or maybe it will all come out, and he'll be on the news. Either way, it won't be like now. It won't be... The way I look at it is: right now Tony's just another person. He can do as he pleases. Sure, he has Scander's – he can't do that much. But who he sees, who he talks to, who he spends time with – that's up to him. And that's all going to change, isn't it?'

'I don't know.'

Ryan was lost for a moment in some private train of thought, eyes on his beer. He didn't seem especially bothered that Jon had no answers to any of his questions. 'Do you know what the irony is?' he continued, still staring at the pint, then looked up at Jon again. 'Tony reckons that even if it's not him we'll have no way of knowing. He says he's going to be a living, breathing test case for Cartesian scepticism.'

'I'm afraid I don't know what that means,' said Jon.

'Nor did I until Tony explained it to me.'

'And what *does* it mean?'

'Cartesian scepticism? It's from Descartes, a French philosopher. Tony says he was a key figure in the Enlightenment, the first truly modern philosopher. He looked at other people and he thought: maybe they're not really people at all; maybe they're just very sophisticated machines. How would we know the difference if they were? They would move and talk as if they had thoughts and feelings and… as if they were alive, even though in fact they were just empty. Tony says that's what I'll have to face: that he might just be a biological machine run by this fungus of yours, even if he seems just the same.'

Jon frowned. He thought he'd heard something like this before, though he'd never known what it was called. The argument seemed logical enough as presented, but he wasn't sure about the conclusion. After all, his whole plan turned on the cured Cogan declaring that he was still himself, not something else pretending to be Cogan. 'There must be something wrong there though,' he ventured.

'Oh yes,' said Ryan. 'It's bullshit. I told Tony as much. He said I was like Dr Johnson kicking a stone. Either way, it's total bullshit. I'll know. I'll look into his eyes and I'll know. It's not complicated.' He took a swig of his beer. 'You don't mind me going on like this?'

'No, it's fine.'

'I'm not expecting you to resolve any of it for me. I just…'

'Needed to talk?' suggested Jon when Ryan failed to find whatever phrase he was looking for.

Ryan nodded. 'He was trying to find out more about your fungus, you know.'

'I'm sure he was. Did he find anything?'

'Not really. There was some… anthropologist, is it?'

'I don't know. Anthropology is a thing, yes.'

'Markham? I think it was Markham. Have you heard of her?'

'No.'

'Tony thought it was rubbish. But I liked the bits he got me to read. There was a story – like a legend of this tribe she had visited. It starts off with one god making the world, and then there's another god… Well, anyway, the idea is that in the beginning the world is all one, and then it gets broken into lots of pieces, and the pieces are still trying to find each other. Like, people. People are pieces. Tony reckons it's similar to something in Greek philosophy. Plato? Does that sound right?'

'I have no idea, I'm afraid.'

'Plato's *Symposium*. He reckons the whole thing was ripped off by Markham. But I liked the story, even if she did rip it off. And I think it's right. We are just pieces, looking for each other. We meet people... Well, it's no accident who we meet, I think. We meet people for a reason. We just have to make sense of it.'

It wasn't really Jon's kind of theory, but sitting there listening to Ryan energetically expound it, watching his lips form the words and his green eyes sparkle with conviction, how could he doubt it? And us, he wanted to ask: what's the reason for us meeting? Tell me this too is no accident.

'I'm sorry,' said Ryan. 'I'm talking too much.'

'It's fine.' He was enjoying listening. Enrapt, in fact, and at the same time slowly gathering the courage to open up himself.

'I just needed to get some stuff off my chest, like I said,' Ryan was explaining needlessly. 'And I didn't feel I could talk to anyone else. I hope you don't mind.'

'Not at all. I... Well, to be honest, I have the same issue. Not being able to talk to anyone I mean.'

Ryan nodded. 'You haven't told your boyfriend?'

'No. I haven't. And... Hmm. Actually I... Actually he dumped me.'

'Oh.'

'Two days ago.'

'I'm sorry to hear that.'

'It's fine. We'd been... drifting apart, you know. Since his diagnosis, and... Well, maybe it wasn't so much that. But it's been hard, not being able to talk to him. I didn't feel I could. Maybe I was wrong, but... It felt like the right thing to do, you know. Not telling him.'

'Right.'

'I haven't talked to anyone really. I took the idea to my boss, originally, and she blocked it. Wouldn't even consider it. And then there's this other guy from the company who funds our lab, and he was more interested, but it all got very political. And I thought, you know, if

I could just show them how it could work, then that would solve everything. At the time it seemed so simple, but now... To be honest, I'm out of my depth. And I just don't know. If it works, I just don't know what happens next. I'll be in trouble, that's for sure.'

'What kind of trouble?'

'Well I stole the spores, for starters. And I'm in breach of the confidentiality agreements I signed. So big trouble, I suppose.'

'I'm sorry to hear that. And about your boyfriend too. I guess he didn't realise what you were doing for him.'

'No.'

Ryan frowned and stared into his beer for a moment before looking up again and continuing: 'Please don't think that I'm not grateful. Tony too. And if he knew you would get into trouble... I mean, this means the world to him. You can imagine. And me too. So I don't want you to think I'm not grateful for what you're doing for us. I just wonder how it will all play out. You know. Sometimes it's better the devil you know. It can feel like that anyway.'

'I guess you're right.' It was advice he'd have done well to have heeded a few months ago. Too late now though. 'When I meet devils I just want to sort them out.'

'Probably that's what makes you a scientist,' said Ryan, raising his glass slightly as if in a toast.

'Probably you're right,' said Jon, returning the gesture. How much he would have been enjoying himself had it not been for all the reasons he was not.

'Whereas I'm a carer. I live with the devils.'

'That's very wise, you know.'

'I have my moments,' said Ryan, smiling. 'Do you wear a white coat?'

'Sorry?'

'In the lab.'

'Ah. Yes. I wear a white coat.'

'That's about as much as I know about science. Wearing white coats, discovering stuff.'

'Not such a lot of discovering stuff really. It's pretty boring most of the time. And the stuff you discover is... well, it's just details most of the time.'

'You don't sound like you enjoy it very much.'

Jon sighed. Did he enjoy it? It was certainly not what he'd had in mind at fifteen, watching that documentary. But what *had* he had in mind? White coats and discovering stuff? 'Do you enjoy your job?'

Ryan too hesitated before responding. 'It depends which bit you're talking about.'

Jon nodded. 'Snap. It depends which bits. Though it doesn't make a lot of difference, because when this all comes out...' He didn't bother to complete the thought. When it all came out his career would be finished: exactly as he himself had accepted when embarking on this course of action but... very disappointing, as his father would say.

He was brought back to the moment by Ryan. Beautiful Ryan, in whose bright presence his thoughts could not stay dark for long. 'We could...' he began – then broke off, thinking, and took a large swig of his beer.

'We could?'

'No, I was just thinking that, from what you're saying, none of us really wants... I mean...'

Again he broke off. Again Jon prompted: 'What?'

'We could just keep it quiet.'

He searched Jon's face for a reaction, but Jon did not immediately understand what he was saying.

'Keep what quiet.'

'If it works. We just don't tell anyone. We don't have to, after all. No one's forcing us to. And that way, you don't get into trouble, and we... Tony can live how he wants.'

'You mean we don't tell anyone he's been cured of Scander's?'

'Exactly. If it works. I mean, none of this may happen anyway.'

'What about... his family? Friends? People will see what's happened. It will be investigated. Someone will find out.'

'He doesn't have any family to speak of. And friends... not as many as he used to. A few have stuck by him. I'm sure there's some way round it.'

It was true: there was sure to be some way round it, and if anyone could find it, then Jon was that man. That was his thing, after all. Solving problems. Just as Scott had said. And then he could carry on as he had before: no consequences, no punishments. He'd go to the Congress, start making a name for himself, build the relationship with Peachey and Arexis – maybe in a few years get the go-ahead to start working officially on his idea, perhaps get his own lab to work through the objections and issues, maybe even see it all come to fruition one day. Probably too late for Scott – but everything was too late for somebody.

'If we put our minds to it,' Ryan was saying enthusiastically.

'I don't know…' murmured Jon, so quietly it was unlikely Ryan could actually hear him. 'I'd have to think…'

Though he was thinking now. At least, thoughts were racing round his head. Whether he deserved to be the subject of an active verb was another matter entirely. Grammar comforts us with the neat distinction of agent and object, mover and moved. But peel back the skin and what will you find? Frenetic endocrines, mind-less neurones, soups of serotonin and dopamine. You don't need Annie in charge not to be in charge yourself. The question is not why you do what you do – the question is whether those deeds need a 'you' at all, whether 'you' are not just some afterthought of consciousness. Something would happen next, of course, but whether Jon had much of a hand in it is anyone's guess.

However, I won't get much further with my story if I carry on in that vein. Sometimes we need to lie to ourselves to make any progress at all. So let's say Jon was making a decision. Because in all those months, starting from that first night cradling Scott in his arms, this was as close as he came. He could have said: yes, let's put our minds to it. Even the process, plotting with Ryan, would have been a source of pleasure. Or he could have said: no, there are greater things at stake here. This is my mission, the reason for which I was given this gift. And though I may be punished for my actions, it's better to be punished than to disappoint. He could have answered either way, but instead said: 'Maybe it could work but… I don't know.'

Ryan seemed to check himself, falling back in his seat as he did so. 'Well,' he said, and his tone was suddenly more business-like, 'think about it.'

'As you say,' said Jon weakly, 'none of this may happen anyway. It may not work.' That was his best hope now: failure. 'Annie may not take hold.'

'You're right,' said Ryan. 'We can cross that bridge when we get to it.'

'Yes.'

'Do you want another drink?'

Neither of them had actually finished the drink they were on. The question was asked not for the sake of an answer but to close the conversation that had preceded. They carried on chatting for a while longer, but in all important respects, the evening was over.

Like the faithful in troubled times, Cogan waited patiently for a sign.

Dr Caldicot had been very clear that he should expect nothing for the first few weeks. In rats, he'd explained, it was pretty much impossible to detect whether infection had been successful for ten days. Thereafter, it took another week or so before even ten per cent of neurones were replaced – after which things speeded up for a week before slowing towards near complete replacement after a month, a characteristic S-curve which he supposed would be replicated in a human host. Over what timescales, though, Dr Caldicot did not know. Certainly not faster, he thought.

So during the first week Cogan really had no grounds for expectation. And yet, of course, expect he did. The phantom sensations he imagined he felt in his limbs from time to time – sensations he'd long ago learned to disregard – now became invested with an intoxicating potential. Every strange thought that popped into his head, every odd twist in a dream, seemed a possible coded message from the living thing that was – if all was going to plan – winding its way into his life. And as for movement, he'd spend whole hours staring at a finger, like one who imagines he can unlock the power of telekinesis by training the power of his thoughts on unresponsive objects.

Under any circumstances he'd have awaited with excitement the return of life to his enervated body. But the strange turn in his relationship with Ryan had created a new impatience. What exactly had passed between them? He was not entirely sure. His erstwhile hope that they might be considered friends had certainly been fulfilled, but it seemed there was something more. It hung in the air between them every time they were together now, like electricity: galvanising, yes, but putting him on edge too. This could be a source of power, or this could be a terrifying lightning strike. He did not want to investigate further until he had not just his wits about him but also the means of expressing them a little more quickly. Not once in all the time since he'd lost it had he longed so much for the return of his own voice.

For his part, Ryan too seemed reluctant to flush their wordless game out into the open. There were moments when he seemed to Cogan's sharp gaze as if he were about to brim over with unnamed feelings, but none of it was spoken. Where there had been a free and easy exchange between them, now there was a more constrained, if also more intense connection, a relationship of bitten lips. To Cogan, it seemed that Ryan was waiting, just as he himself was: waiting to see if he would indeed emerge from this cocoon of wasted flesh and wires.

While they waited, routine filled the time. Food and drink went in; shit and piss came out; clothes were put on and taken off; limbs were washed and rearranged; functional communication took place. It was as if, by coming so close to whatever it was they were coming close to, but then holding off a little longer, they had thrown themselves back to the kind of interaction they'd had when Ryan had first taken the post.

Though in other ways, private ways, things could not have been more different. When Ryan went out on the first Thursday after Cogan's infection, the latter found himself – for the first time ever, and absurdly – wondering where he was going and with whom. Ryan had had Thursdays off for years now: he'd dined and dated and danced and shagged – at least, Cogan assumed he had – without it mattering in the least to him. Yet now, ridiculously enough, he felt a sensation he could only describe as jealousy. And when he saw Ryan again the next morning, he wanted above all else to ask – and thanked his lucky stars and Scander's that the question could not slip out in a moment of emotion.

He had no idea that Ryan was meeting Jon; nor did he suspect any connection when Ryan asked, midway through Friday, and apparently apropos of nothing: 'Do you think we can trust Dr Caldicot?'

'Trust in what way?' Dr Caldicot had done his bit now, so far as Cogan was concerned. The critical question now was whether they could trust Annie.

'I don't know. If we... I mean, you know, if you needed to rely on him for any reason.'

'I rely on you,' Cogan wanted to say. 'I trust you.' But he didn't. Instead, hesitating over his screen, he had his voice say: 'I suppose we would have to.'

'Hmm,' said Ryan. 'Maybe.'

It was three, unbearable weeks later that the sign at last came: a dull, tingling ache along the outside of his left little finger.

'Are you sure?' asked Ryan, when he told him – and wisely, he knew, for over those last few days he'd told Ryan about a number of twinges and flickers and known, even as he described them, they were nothing.

Not this time though. 'Sure,' he replied through his screen, too excited to find all the words of a proper reply. 'Sure. Sure.'

Gently, Ryan held out his hand and, with the tips of his fingers, touched the tiny patch of sentience which Cogan had indicated. As he did so, his eyes stayed fixed on Cogan's, so that Cogan knew he did not even need to look down at the screen to communicate what he was now feeling.

'You can feel that?' said Ryan.

Beside himself with joy, Cogan looked down and hunted for a word. 'Pressure.'

He looked up again. Ryan was smiling at him and now, meeting his gaze again, folded his hand around the little finger. 'It's time we talked,' he said. 'About the future.'

That night, Cogan had a dream. If it was a dream. Normally, in dreams he could walk and talk, or sing and dance, sometimes even fly. In this dream, his body lay insensate and unresponsive on the bed, but for the feel of creased cotton where his little finger lay upon the sheet and the quick movements of his eyes as he scanned the darkness.

It was as if he had woken up, but for the fact that a voice was talk-ing to him, talking in his ears as if it were the voice of someone or something that lay on the pillow either side of his head. 'Tony,' it was saying. 'Tony. Tony.' He could not turn his eyes far enough to see who or what was there; nor could he move his skull from the dip it had formed where Ryan had placed it tenderly upon the pillow.

'Who's there?' he demanded, unaccountably terrified – and the next day, when he recounted what had happened, the fact he himself had spoken seemed proof enough that it had indeed been a dream.

'Erm… me, it seems.'

'What do you want?'

'I don't know,' said the voice. It sounded like a young man: educated, received pronunciation, not unlike Cogan's own voice had once sounded. 'I'm not sure I want anything. What do you want?'

'I was asleep,' hissed Cogan. 'You woke me up.'

'Did I? I thought you woke me up. It's rather confusing. You seem afraid.'

'I am afraid.'

'What are you afraid of?'

'I don't want to die.' As is the twisted way of dreams, this seemed a completely appropriate and logical thing to say at this juncture.

'Then you ought to live,' replied the voice.

And suddenly – in the dream – Cogan understood. 'Is that you? I'm talking to you, aren't I?'

'It's me, yes. But I'm afraid I'm not quite sure who that is.'

'Are you going to make me bite into a leaf and then crack my head open?'

'I… don't think so. That strikes me as an odd thing to say.'

Cogan's fear had subsided as rapidly as it arose, and now he even let out a little laugh. 'I suppose it was. I'm sorry.'

'Don't worry,' said the voice, then asked: 'This Ryan, who is he?'

'Who's Ryan?' whispered Cogan, and the whole of their con-versation earlier that day came back to him as one, like the new-felt warmth of a bath enfolding his frozen body. 'Ryan is everything. Ryan is the reason I didn't know I needed. Ryan is the sense my life never made. Ryan shows me how broken I am by making me whole.'

'Good,' said the voice. 'We need to be clear what matters. And this Caldicot person. What about him?'

'Dr Caldicot?'

'Yes. You seem to be thinking about him a lot.'

'Not *about* him. He's played an important role in our life but... no, Jon Caldicot doesn't matter.'

7

Registration for the International Mycotherapy Congress began on the Sunday afternoon, with a welcome address and dinner that evening, but after some thought Jon decided to take an afternoon off work and fly out on the Friday. He hesitated in making this plan, wondering if he really wanted to spend time on his own in an unfamiliar city where he didn't even speak the language beyond 'please' and 'thank you', but Maria assured him he'd regret it if he didn't leave some time for sight-seeing. And how right she turned out to be.

It wasn't just the beauty of the place that lifted Jon's spirits, though it was undeniably the most beautiful city he had ever visited; nor the weather, though even in March the warmth of the sun would have done a midsummer's day proud back home in England; nor the alien sounds and smells and tastes; nor the lullaby murmur of uncomprehended language; nor even the change of pace, ambling along side streets and mooching in cafés. It was more than any of those things, something over and above and beyond that coaxed Jon's shoulders down from his ears, loosened his brows and softened his jaw. Within hours he'd abandoned his planned itinerary – Giralda, Alcázar and Santa Cruz, Guadalquivir and Torre del Oro, Parque María Luisa and Plaza de España – and settled himself on a bench in the Plaza del Triunfo, losing himself in the multilingual burble of tourists, the hum of trams and the clopping of horses, the razor-sharp shadows of finials and buttresses inching their ways across the walls of the cathedral, and the slow progress of the present moment towards the future. That night, he slept so soundly that, when he woke, he wondered for a moment whether he might not in fact be someone else. Someone who made fewer mistakes.

Because, lose himself as he might in the winding streets of the city, there was no escaping the scale of the error he'd made by stealing spores and infecting Cogan.

His last hope remained that Annie failed to take hold in Cogan's system. On that front, no news was at least good news. Though he'd no idea how long infection might take in a human host, the fact that four weeks had gone by with no real changes was surely positive. He might even have started to relax a little, had it not been for Cogan's almost daily status reports.

I thought this morning I felt a sensation in my stomach, akin to the feeling of butterflies.

Yesterday I was quite convinced that a muscle in my buttock was twitching.

Today I moved an eyelid.

None of them had led to anything, right up to the most recent report, on the day before he left, of an aching sensation in Cogan's left little finger: False alarm again, I'm afraid had come the e-mail the next day, just before Jon set off to the airport. The finger is again insensate. He understood why Cogan was doing it – and that Cogan, at his end, would not even imagine how each new point would puncture Jon, leaving him flat and motionless.

Nor was it just the e-mails from Cogan. There were the e-mails from Peachey's PA as well, making arrangements for the Congress; the nine unused vials of spores, still in their plastic case, tucked away at the back of his sock drawer; the little reminders of Scott he kept stumbling on around the flat. He could make no progress against these thumb-tack recriminations.

A month after they'd split, he had to admit that he was missing Scott far more than he'd thought he would. Not, perhaps, in the aching, yearning way a person might miss someone they truly loved, but in the restless, distracted manner of someone whose favourite show has finished on TV. It didn't help that there was no one he felt he could talk to about what had happened.

There were old friends, of course. It was just… he'd not made such a good job of staying in touch with the people he'd known at school, at Oxford, in California, and none of them were in Cambridge anyway. He'd have to make the effort to contact them, to catch up with them – in many cases to update them on the very relationship that had now broken down. And he'd have to listen to them, be interested – after all the time he'd let pass, he couldn't expect just to ring them up and talk about himself.

As for friends in Cambridge… well, there were people he knew and went out with, of course, but all of them knew Scott as well – were more Scott's friends than his, when he thought about it. He knew quite a few of Scott's friends, in fact. He'd been so busy at work since coming to Cambridge that he hadn't had much time to make his own connections – nor the inclination, perhaps – either way, Scott's friends had been… convenient. Until now: he was hardly going to talk to them now. In fact, the more he thought about it, the more it seemed to him he'd only one real friend of his own: Maria across the bench. Maria would have understood. Yet he hesitated, nonetheless.

And all the while, from Ryan: nothing. 'We meet people for a reason,' he'd said, and in Jon's memory it seemed had looked straight at him as he said it, willing him to look through the words to a meaning. 'We just have to make sense of it.' No sense, however, was forthcoming. In answer to Jon's texts, his e-mails: nothing. He'd enjoyed the evening a lot: nothing. He wondered how Mr Cogan was doing: nothing. He was due down in London (lie) and perhaps they could catch another drink: nothing. And as something halfway between a consolation prize and salt on a wound, Jon was left with a postponed drink in the Fountain with Kevin, whose interest in him he'd completely failed to notice all these months but now could not fail to see.

More than once he'd revisited Ryan's proposal. 'We could just keep it quiet.' Could it work? And might expressing interest in the suggestion, belatedly, prompt some kind of response from Ryan. It was still an option, a bridge they could cross when they got to it. But now – something held him back, some shred of dignity, perhaps, some last scrap of self-respect. He might be set to disappoint everyone else, but he did not have to disappoint himself.

From all of this, Seville afforded at least a few days of unexpected respite – and, as luck would have it, the spell of the mini-break was broken in the gentlest possible way. Returning to the hotel at lunch-time on the Sunday, with the hour of registration fast approaching, he bumped into the one person he was actually looking forward to seeing: his old boss, Jack Kapinsky.

'Jon Caldicot,' he called across the hotel lobby as Jon sauntered in from the street.

'Jack. How wonderful to see you.'

'You too. I didn't know you'd be here.'

'I meant to drop you an e-mail but' – a shadow of the weeks gone by passed across his mind – 'you know how it is. The time shoots by. How are you? You're looking great.'

Jack had just checked in, having that morning caught the AVE train down from Madrid, and suggested they meet for lunch in half an hour or so, after he'd had a chance to drop his bags and freshen up. 'I've been meaning to write you as it happens. Something I wanted to ask you about. I doubt we'll have much opportunity once the circus gets underway.'

They opted for the restaurant in the hotel, reckoning they'd have more chance of hearing each other than in one of the nearby cafés or bars. To Jon's questions about people he'd known from the lab in California, including Jack's family – it was Jack's style to invite those who worked for him round for barbecues and the like – Jack gave leisurely and humorous responses, in the manner of a wise West Coast sage and raconteur. To Jack's questions about Jon's new life in England, Jon responded as vaguely as he could, retreating into facetious jokes about bad weather whenever possible, in the manner of an educated Englishman. The style suited the exigencies of the moment, but it was also familiar, comforting. Limpets, roaming the littoral rocks in search of food, return at each low tide to one spot, their shells worn down to a perfect fit with its uneven contours, and to this spot they cling until the sea returns, gripping fast against desiccation, predators and children with buckets. Humans, ranging their own shorelines, are not so very different when the good times retreat. Chatting to Jack, with the warmth of what might have been a Californian spring seeping into his bones, Jon found himself recalling – emotionally rather than episodically – a time when he had been happier than he now was.

'So things have worked out well between you and Imogen, then,' Jack was saying.

For a moment, Jon had been somewhere else. More specifically, he'd been remembering – for no apparent reason – an experiment he'd once tried running back in Jack's lab, which, to his intense frustration, he'd never been able to get to work. More specifically still, he'd been remembering talking to Jack about it, discussing possible resolutions. Only even that was really just context for the memory. It was Jack's face he'd been remembering, his tone. It had always been him, he now realised, coming up with ideas, while Jack just asked questions and raised issues. And Jack's face… He'd not been remembering, so much as realising: Jack had known all along that the experiment could never work.

'Sorry? I was… miles away.'

'Imogen. Things have worked out well between you and her.'

'Why do you say that?'

'Well, you're here. That's quite a coup, you know.'

'Oh. Yes, bit of a shock actually. But it's not thanks to Professor Lazenby. The guy at Arexis organised it. Matt Peachey.'

'Ahhh,' said Jack, drawing the vowel out as if to track the trajectory of a falling penny.

'Do you know him?'

'Not exactly. I mean, I've met him of course. Mycotherapy's a small world, and Mr Peachey sits on a big pot of funding. He's what they call a "mover and shaker", even if he's never directly moved or shaken me. But he did put in a call with me a few months ago, just before Christmas, out of the blue. That's the thing I've been meaning to write you about. I assumed he was after a piece of my lab – but no: he wanted to talk about you.'

'About me?'

Jack nodded and watched Jon with an expression that seemed to say: yes, that's right, you've got it. The problem being that Jon had no idea what he was supposed to have got.

'I'm sorry, I don't… Why was Peachey asking you about me?'

'Isn't it obvious?'

Jon shook his head.

'I'd guess he's trying to tempt you over to the dark side.'

Jon's brain was not working well on this one. Perhaps it would have caught up had it had a few more seconds, but Jack spotted the blank expression first and pre-empted with a more explicit explanation.

'He's going to offer you a job.'

The penny now executed its parabolic descent for Jon too, albeit unaccompanied by vocalisation.

'That's my guess anyway,' continued Jack. 'Why else would he have wanted to ask me about you? And now this…' He gestured broadly, presumably towards the idea of the Congress. 'Looks to me like a charm offensive.'

'I suppose it is,' said Jon, unsure what to think. He'd imagined a different kind of career progression when the invitation had arrived.

'What did you do to impress him so much? To be frank, I'm surprised Imogen let you near him in the first place.'

'Well,' said Jon awkwardly, wondering how he was going to handle this one, 'she didn't exactly. I mean it's… not straightforward.'

'Jeez. You went behind her back? I'd not had you down as the political type.' There was a note of disappointment in Jack's voice, which Jon found absurdly unsettling.

'No, really, it's not like that. It was an accident. Lazenby told me she'd talked to Peachey about something… an idea I'd had, so I talked to him as well when I… well, when I happened to see him. In the lab. And it turned out she hadn't talked to him at all and—'

'And now Imogen is pissed with you,' interrupted Jack, 'and Matt Peachey's seen an opportunity to poach a bright young kid for his outfit. I get it. You've been having fun over there then.'

Jon nodded, relieved that Jack at least seemed to have dropped the dark charge of being political.

'And what was the idea you had that led to all the drama?'

More drama than Jack could ever have guessed. And it suddenly occurred to Jon how wonderful it would be to tell him everything. Not just the idea, but everything he'd done in its service. Yes, there would be consequences, but those consequences would be human ones, judged by others, enacted by others, seen by others. It would be out in the open, a fact. This awful waiting would be over, and his secret would no longer be shared with no one but the secret himself.

And Ryan, of course. Ryan who'd as good as told him they were meant to meet, then gone incommunicado. Ryan whom even now he could text: *OK, let's just keep it quiet, but please reply.*

But Jack… He could tell Jack everything, tell him now, and even as Jack reacted with disbelief, horror, disgust, even in those he could find a kind of release.

Of course, the thought was gone in a flash. He wasn't going to tell Jack anything, not even the idea itself.

'My bad,' said Jack, picking up on his hesitation. 'I shouldn't have asked.'

'Sorry. I don't want to get into even more trouble. I made a mistake by telling Peachey and… well, I can't really get my head round all the politics, you know.'

'What about this job though?' asked Jack, moving the conversation on quickly. 'Are you tempted at all? Assuming I'm right, that is.'

And if Cogan were not infected. There was still a splinter of hope, after all. 'Blimey. I don't know.'

'Did you really just say "blimey"?'

Jon laughed. 'What do you think I should do? I mean, I've pretty comprehensively blotted my copybook with Professor Lazenby.'

'Really? I doubt it, to be honest. She's not the type for copybook blotting.'

'But do you think I should consider it? A job, I mean.'

'I couldn't possibly say. It's your future. The only thing I'd say is… Well, no. Really it's up to you.'

'Go on, what would you say?'

'Well, two things. First: do you still want to be a scientist?'

'Pass.' He didn't know what he wanted any more. 'And the second thing?'

'Just… be careful, you know? People can be tricksy.'

'You mean Professor Lazenby. Don't worry…'

But Jack had held up a hand. 'No, not Imogen. I mean, she is difficult, it's true.' He laughed, remembering something. 'The arguments we used to have. But Imogen... What you see is what you get with Imogen. It's this Peachey guy I think you may need to be careful of.'

'Really?' Jon didn't recognise either of these characterisations.

'I mean, I don't want to malign the man,' continued Jack hastily. 'I really don't know him, and I've no personal reason to doubt him.'

'But?' said Jon, articulating the word that had been implicit in Jack's intonation.

'But... I don't know. A feeling. Have you ever wondered how he came to be Imogen's boss?'

'No. I didn't know he was.'

'Oh, he is. I'm sure Imogen doesn't present it that way, but when push comes to shove it's Arexis that calls the shots. Which means Matt Peachey. And how did someone as brilliant and... savvy as Imogen allow herself to end up in a situation like that, do you think?'

'I don't know,' said Jon. As Peachey's guest, he was feeling just a little uncomfortable with the direction Jack was heading in.

'The first time I met him,' said Jack, 'he was an ambitious young manager at Porton Down. He might have done his PhD there in fact, I'm not sure. This is back before Arexis existed, when all the research on Annie in the UK was still part of whatever acronym it was at the time. I lost track after the MRE. So you've Porton Down, and you've Cambridge – and the only reason Cambridge had anything in the first place was because Sir Arthur Hayton insisted on it. He was one of the old guard: went to school with people who knew people who could pull strings. Had a club down in London. I went there once: astonishing place. The world run from armchairs... But Hayton had gone now, you see, and Imogen had taken over in Cambridge – because in the end, no one could get away from the fact that she was the woman for the job. Though there were those who tried to stop her. And guess what, Imogen never got an invitation to that club, because women weren't even allowed in.' He widened his eyes at Jon. 'Your country.'

'I think it's changed a bit since then.'

'Really? It sure as hell hadn't then. Imogen was desperate: they were going to shut her down, move the whole outfit to Porton Down. I've never seen her quite so defeated. Just like you, she couldn't get her head round the politics. In her world, you see, being a great scientist ought to have been enough. I tried to get her to see that it wasn't but... Anyway, as it turned out, I didn't need to. Because the next time I saw her she was all hope and happiness. "I've got an ally," she told me. "Someone on the inside." I'd met him, as it happened, at the Congress the year before: Matt Peachey. Her knight in shining armour.'

'And what happened?'

'He saved her. I don't know all the ins and outs, but the Cambridge lab wasn't shut down. The two teams carried on as they were, fighting each other for the same pot of funding. And then a couple of years later, Imogen suddenly tells me the whole thing's been privatised. She's thrilled, because the signs are everything will be consolidated in Cambridge, under her. Peachey's still fighting her corner, she says. And I suppose he was. Except, when the dust settles, everything's consolidated in Cambridge under her, but she's under Peachey.'

Jon frowned. He couldn't quite see what Peachey had done that was so bad. 'I have to say, it sounds like Peachey had earned the position.'

'I suppose he had.'

'I don't see why that means I need to be careful of him.'

'No?' said Jack, scrutinising Jon's face. 'Well, you're much younger than me. More in tune with the world than a washed-out old hippy.'

'What have you got against Peachey?'

'Nothing. Better him than Sir Arthur Hayton and the old guard, believe me. I just... Well, I'm not sure I like the new guard much either. Just be careful, that's all I'm saying.'

'I will,' said Jon. He felt a little annoyed with Jack, but he reminded himself that the warning was offered with the best of intentions. Of that he was confident. Better to change the conversation. Besides which, something else had struck him in Jack's story. 'So Lazenby thought she was a great scientist, did she?'

'Pardon?'

'You said that she thought being a great scientist ought to have been enough.'

'I'm not sure she ever described *herself* as a great scientist. I'm sure she didn't. I just mean she didn't think politics should play a part in it. I think she's learned her lesson on that one.'

'Yes,' said Jon, smiling to himself. Boy, had she learned it. 'So can I ask you a question, Jack?'

'Depends what it is.'

'What do *you* think makes a great scientist?'

'Blimey,' said Jack in an attempt at a Cockney accent. 'You got any harder ones?'

'Seriously though. Lazenby told me what *she* thought, and I'm sure you—'

'Well, if it's a competition...' interrupted Jack with a twinkle in his eye. 'What makes a great scientist? I don't know. It probably depends what day of the week you ask me. But right this moment... Put it like this: I sometimes think of science as a bit like a boxing match with nature. Only you're this little, puny bantamweight, and nature is this huge, lumbering heavyweight. Most of the time nature doesn't even notice you pounding away at it with your little fists. Every now and then it blinks or flinches, and the judges award you a point or two, more out of sympathy than anything. And then, just when you think you've got a chance of winning, nature swings round and floors you with a single punch, and with the little birds tweeting round your head, you realise you don't understand jack shit about nothing, that everything you thought you knew was just a first guess. That's when some people get up and walk away: they've had enough of the fight; turns out they weren't scientists at all. Most of us who do stay... well, we get some kind of perverse kick out of getting up again, shaking ourselves down and throwing ourselves back into the ring. But the great scientists... they're the ones that realise they're never going to win at this game. So they change the game instead – to judo, or ping-pong, or tic-tac-toe. Don't ask me how. I get up and the only thing I can see to do is get stuck back into the fight again. I can never see the other games. And between you and me, I'm happy enough the way I am, and too old to change now anyway. But that's what the great scientists do. They change the game. How did I do?'

'A much better answer than Lazenby's.'

'Great. That's all that matters.' He hesitated before continuing: 'Jon, I'd like to tell you a story – but if I do, you must promise not to repeat it.'

'Of course.'

'Imogen would not be happy, and we're both too old to have any more arguments. But I feel like maybe you don't appreciate just how great a scientist she is. I mean, really, she puts us all in the shade.'

'I...' began Jon, then hesitated, steeling himself for the lie: 'I do appreciate her.'

'Maybe you do. But let me tell you anyway. It's about Hayton's Laws. Sir Arthur Hayton. That pompous old shit. You wouldn't ever have met him, I suppose?'

'No, I... he died years ago, didn't he? I mean, before I came to your lab.'

'Yeah. Well. Sir Arthur Hayton was not a great scientist. He hadn't a creative bone in his body. Not the man to look at Annie and see her true potential. Do you see what I'm saying?'

'Not really.'

'Hayton's Laws aren't Hayton's at all. They're Lazenby's Laws. Imogen was the one who dreamed up this discipline. She was the one who said: "Hey, enough boxing already, let's play tennis instead." She came up with the whole thing: the vision, the Laws, the lot. And he took it and put his name at the top.'

'You mean he plagiarised her?'

'I was at the meeting, Jon. There were only four of us there. She presented the Laws. The three Laws, just as we know them now. Sir Arthur Hayton told her it was a ridiculous idea, spoke to her as if she were some kind of... I don't know, some kind of lackey with ideas above her station. All he was interested in was turning Annie into a weapon. Yet mere months later, there they were: Hayton's Laws.'

'I had no idea.'

'Nor anyone else. Imogen had a choice: on the one hand – what would you call it? – justice, I suppose; on the other, a career. Sir Arthur Hayton had all the power.'

'Why didn't she say something later? When she did have power, I mean.'

Jack laughed. 'Really, Jon? Really? When Hayton had his stroke and was in a nursing home? How do you think people would have reacted if she'd stood up then and said: "Actually it was me all along." I don't think so.'

'I had no idea,' repeated Jon. If Jack was telling him this then, presumably, it was the truth. But he wasn't sure what difference it made. Did it maybe explain her behaviour? Perhaps a little. But it didn't make him appreciate her any more, as Jack had put it.

Perhaps sensing Jon's uncertain reaction to the story, Jack again jumped in to change the subject. 'Well anyway, I didn't mean for the conversation to get all heavy. Time to get our heads into circus mode. They'll all be arriving soon.'

'Yes,' said Jon, still turning over the story Jack had just told him in his head. 'Are you speaking?'

'Am I speaking?' repeated Jack, giving a coy little smile as he did so. 'Oh yes, I am speaking. Believe me, I'm going to blow you all away.'

'Really? What are you saying?'

Jack tapped the side of his nose. 'Watch this space.'

It wasn't until the pre-prandial drinks before the Congress dinner that Jon saw Matt Peachey: the first time they'd seen each other since their meeting in Lazenby's office. He found himself at once the object of Peachey's gruff indulgence and barely left his patron's side for the rest of the evening – smiling as he was introduced to the luminaries of mycotherapy, listening attentively as they held forth to Peachey, chuckling as required at their stiff pleasantries, laughing more heartily at Peachey's jokes about them once they'd gone and wondering through it all why Jack was so suspicious of the man.

Nothing was said about a job, but all the evidence was consistent with Jack's hypothesis. Most telling of all, perhaps, was a brief conversation Jon had with someone called Sir Andrew Harper, a civil servant that Peachey seemed especially keen to introduce him to.

'So you're the young man he's been telling me about,' said Sir Andrew, shaking Jon firmly by the hand. Smooth-skinned and with a full head of silver hair, it was hard to guess his age, but he had about him an air of great seniority. 'Very good to meet you. How are you enjoying the Congress?'

Jon made a few bland responses to similarly bland questions until Sir Andrew excused himself again: 'I suspect we'll be meeting more in the future,' he said, putting a hand on Jon's shoulder as he did so.

'Who was that?' Jon asked Peachey.

'The Knight Commander. Key fellow in government. *The* key fellow.'

'And why would we be meeting more in the future?'

'That all depends,' said Peachey non-committally. 'There's Georges Durand. You *must* meet him.' An introduction to the grand old man of French research on Annie – a long-time critic of mycotherapy who had instead pursued potential uses of Annie's conducting polymer – pre-empted any further questions from Jon. Though, in truth, the only question he was left with now was why Peachey didn't get on with it and make him the offer. Plus the question he could not frame: whether he'd be able to accept it, or whether Cogan would stymie everything.

They met again at breakfast the next morning and thereafter attended the Congress sessions together. Thus it was Peachey that Jon was sitting next to when Jack Kapinsky got up to speak in a plenary session after lunch. And as promised, he blew them all away, revealing what was probably the biggest breakthrough in mycotherapeutic research since Hayton's Laws – or whoever's Laws they were – had first been formulated. Annie, he announced, had been stopped at the synapse. The First Law had been cracked. This was mycotherapeutic history in the making, and everyone in the room knew it.

Jon couldn't resist the temptation to look for Lazenby in the audience. What would her expression be? Genuine, generous excitement at the breakthrough, or bitter jealousy? She was sitting a few rows in front of him, and he could only see the very side of her face – the curve of her cheek, the corner of an eye, too little to read emotions. But then, even if he'd been able to see her whole face, he might not have learned much from it.

She'd arrived late to the drinks the night before and barely acknowledged Jon. No surprise in that. What had surprised him a little was how she looked. It was not such a radical change really: she'd swapped her work clothes for an elegant cocktail dress, put on a little bit of eyeliner perhaps, loosened the long hair which, at work, she scraped back tightly over her scalp. No more radical, in fact, than any of Jon's other colleagues – even Jon himself – making a bit of an effort for a social event. It was just that Jon had never thought of Lazenby going to such events, never imagined her having a life of any kind outside the lab – and never stopped to consider that, in that other world, she might be a good-looking woman. And then there was the way she worked the room – smiling, laughing, always either the centre of an admiring group or locked in one-to-one conversation. This was surely a different Lazenby from the one he saw day-to-day in the lab. A nicer Lazenby, he'd almost have said – had he been able to shake the suspicion it was all just an act, put on for more important people than those who worked for her.

By chance, he found himself standing behind her in the queue for coffee in the break after Jack Kapinsky's session. She was talking with great animation to three other delegates Peachey had introduced him to the evening before; he, meanwhile, was on his own, queuing for Peachey's coffee as well while the latter went out for a cigarette. Even Lazenby must have realised that, in the circumstances, she had to say something to him.

'So what did you make of that?' she asked, turning to him at last while the other delegates discussed something else. She made no effort to introduce him. 'Your old supervisor has really stolen the show this time.'

'Hasn't he? He told me yesterday when we were having lunch that he had something big to announce, but I never expected that.'

Even as he spoke, Jon heard in his own voice the subtext – I was having lunch with Jack yesterday; I don't need you – and inwardly cringed. When had he become this person?

'I know. He said something similar to me a week or so ago, but I thought it was just Jack being Jack.'

More subtext? I'm closer to him than you; you're no one. Or was he just imagining it, projecting it, fabricating it? If he'd not known Lazenby before, he'd not have detected anything untoward in what she was saying. But he did know her – and he did not trust her.

'Good job we've good stuff of our own,' she was saying. 'Can't let the Yanks win that easily.'

It was all wrong. Lazenby was talking to him with the same light-hearted ease she applied to everyone else in the room, yet until then she'd entirely blanked him, and back in the lab he felt like she'd been treating him as some kind of pariah ever since his invitation to the Congress had come through. He'd had enough of these mind games: the sooner Peachey offered him a job, the better.

And if there was any lingering doubt, any residual hesitation, it was utterly erased the next morning when Lazenby made her own presentation. It began unexceptionally enough, with a review of some of the key findings made in the Cambridge Mycotherapy Unit during the previous year. Then, with only a couple of minutes of her slot left, Lazenby blanked her PowerPoint, stepped to one side of the podium and addressed the audience with the directness of an aspiring political leader.

'I have one more thing to say, which is not a finding but a provocation. We spend a lot of time at these events discussing what's happened in the year past, but it's good to look ahead sometimes as well. Where is mycotherapy going? What are we trying to do with it? What will all these findings add up to? This year, we've heard Jack Kapinsky tell us how to do something we've been trying to do for years: stop *A. n.* at the synapse. This is a momentous breakthrough. It brings us a step closer to real, therapeutic applications. I've always admired Jack as a scientist, as he knows, and I'm truly delighted he's had at least one success before he retires.'

She gave a little salute in Jack's direction as laughter rippled through the audience. Jon had to hand it to her: she was quite impressive.

'By coincidence,' she continued, 'we've been asking ourselves a different question this year. What if we didn't stop *A.n.* at the synapse? What if we let it spread? Maybe we're so fixated on the need to protect the nervous system that we forget all those people whose nervous system is the thing that's killing them. In Scander's disease, for instance, the ion pump mechanism breaks down, leading to a progressive loss of neuronal function and, ultimately, death. For a patient with Scander's, there is nothing worth protecting. For a patient with Scander's, we may need to change the rules and let *A.n.* take over completely.'

The room was silent now, wound with a shared question: where is she going with this? Coming from almost anyone else, this could have been dismissed as naïve nonsense. But it wasn't anyone else: it was Imogen Lazenby, one of the founders of the discipline.

For Jon, the question was a different one: what the fuck did she think she was doing?

'And what about the Laws?' continued Lazenby. 'I know that's what everyone is thinking right now: we've been round this loop before, and unless we can honour the Laws there's no meaningful way of taking things forwards. Along with Jack and Fred, I'm one of the last few people left who was there when the Laws were formulated. I've lived these Laws for decades. They've become... almost a religion to me. And that's the point I want to make, I suppose. A religion, you see, is not a science. It isn't subjected to the test of experience, of experiment, of method. And that's a problem. I'll be honest with you all, I still can't see a way round the Laws myself: that's why I'm thrilled to hear about the breakthrough Jack and his team have made. But just because I can't see a way round doesn't mean there isn't one. This room is full of brilliant minds – brilliant *young* minds, with new perspectives – and who's to say there isn't another way. My team is full of such brilliant minds, and some of them think it's time to look again at the Laws. My job, I've realised, is to let them.

'That's why, in the year ahead, I'm going to ask my team to start asking some difficult questions. What if we didn't stop *A.n.* at the synapse? What if we didn't stick to the Laws? What might we do then? I've no idea where those questions will lead – whether they'll lead anywhere, in fact. But, late in the day perhaps, I've realised that asking those questions is part of what it means to do science. And I wanted to use this opportunity to ask the rest of you to ask those questions too – and, if you happen upon answers, to bring them to this Congress in the fullness of time.'

Applause, more polite than warm, spread across the room as Lazenby left the podium. Jon joined in mechanically, his mouth half-open as he struggled to believe what he had just heard.

'Sorry, lad,' said Peachey, leaning across to him. 'I thought she was going to mention you by name.'

'You mean you knew she was going to say that?' He turned to Peachey, whose fleshy face was gathering in bunches around the eyes.

'You mean you didn't?'

Jon shook his head. His mouth had still not closed, but it had started to gain the contours of a smile about its corners. He didn't actually care any more.

'Bloody woman,' muttered Peachey. 'Leave it with me, lad.'

'It's alright. Don't bother. I'm… I wanted to talk to you anyway. I'm not sure I can really see a future for myself in Professor Lazenby's lab.'

'Right,' said Peachey. The applause had ended and people were starting to leave for the coffee break. 'Hold that thought,' he continued, getting to his feet. 'I need to make a phone call now, but then let's talk.'

Jon stayed in his seat, twisting sideways to let those further down the aisle past. He'd had enough weak conference coffee – enough Congress altogether, in fact. He could sneak off, it struck him, get a decent coffee, spend his last afternoon in the Plaza del Triunfo, letting the world unfold around him. Then that evening maybe he could even find a gay bar, go out for a drink, maybe get chatting to a Spaniard. There was so much he could do but never did.

Because really, why did he bother? When Scott thanked him by dumping him, when Ryan did not even reply to his e-mails, when Lazenby now brazenly stole his ideas and passed them off as her own... why the fuck did he bother? When his only reward was the drip feed of status updates from Anthony Cogan. And if he'd succeeded, if Cogan had been infected – what then? He could wave goodbye to that job with Arexis. For all he knew, he might be going to prison. And to cap it all, it seemed that Lazenby would be taking the credit. He'd be destroyed, and she would be up there again next year, trumpeting *her* discoveries, *her* breakthrough.

'Pleased?' came the last voice he'd expected to hear. It was Lazenby, who had sat herself down at the end of his now empty row, about five seats away from him.

'I beg your pardon?'

'Are you pleased?' she repeated.

He stared at her. She was more formally dressed today, her hair tied up, but not as tightly as in the lab – and still not quite the Lazenby he knew. Nothing in her face suggested sarcasm or insincerity. But surely she could not believe what she was saying. 'Are you serious?'

'What is it? Didn't you...? Matt Peachey said he'd talked to you—'

'You just stole my idea,' interrupted Jon. 'You stood up in front of everyone and presented my idea as yours.'

Lazenby's face hardened, and in an instant she was there again, the woman he saw every day, lacking only a cup of tea and a twizzling pencil. 'I did what?'

'I said: you stole my idea.'

'I give up on you, Jon,' she said, shaking her head and sighing. 'I don't know what goes on in that head of yours. You think *I* stole your idea? Who do you think has already filed for a patent based on it? Who do you think stopped me working on it until they'd got the legals sorted out? Who do you think I had to fight to make sure that at least something went out to the mycotherapy community as a whole? Besides which, you might notice that I didn't actually share your idea at all. I used my reputation – *my* hard-won reputation – to give you a chance of getting a hearing. Do you think anyone would listen to *you* if you started questioning the Laws? I give up on you, really I do. It's all about you, your ego, you being the hero who solves the problem. Typical—' She stopped herself from saying a word he assumed would have been 'man'. 'You just don't get it, do you? This, science, is a team endeavour.'

'A team endeavour,' snorted Jon. He was so furious he was hardly listening to her any more. '*Your* team, that would be. The people who aren't even here, while you read out their achievements. As I wouldn't be if you'd had your way.'

It's anyone's guess what might have happened next had their conversation not been interrupted. Perhaps they'd have gone at it hammer and tongs until they were screaming at each other in the plenary hall. Perhaps they'd have faced off silently, glaring at each other malevolently until the other delegates returned. Perhaps one or the other of them would simply have got up and walked away. The future teeters on a fractal edge, minutely sensitive to initial conditions, infinitely unknowable, predictable only in retrospect. Any of these things might have happened – but none did.

Instead they were interrupted by Georges Durand, the Frenchman, stalking across the room to hiss at Lazenby: 'Have you gone mad, Lazenby? Have you forgotten Madenu?'

'Georges,' said Lazenby sharply, shooting a glance towards Jon. 'Company.'

'It's OK,' said Jon, getting to his feet. 'I'm going anyway.'

As he left the conference hall, everything seemed clear in Jon's mind. He could not stay in Lazenby's lab. He did not want to stay in Lazenby's lab. He would take whatever job Peachey was offering and be done with it all. Done with Lazenby. Done with Scott. Done with his idea.

And Cogan? Ryan was right. They should just keep it quiet, tell no one. What did he care any more?

Halfway across the hotel lobby he stopped and took out his phone to compose a text to Ryan: *Let's talk again about keeping things quiet. I think you were right. We shouldn't tell anyone.* Then he hit send. And once that was sorted, he'd be done with Ryan too. Ryan who never responded.

But he should have carried on walking – out into the sunshine, as he'd intended – because in those few moments he stood there texting, Peachey had finished his call and followed him out into the lobby.

'Jon,' he called out.

Jon hesitated only a moment – he could not pretend not to have heard – before turning on his heel.

'Where are you off to, lad?' continued Peachey, loping towards him like some primitive hominid.

'I was just going to get some fresh air.'

'Can I join you?'

They stepped out into the street, where Peachey, with a very different idea of fresh air, at once set about lighting a cigarette. For a while they stood like that in silence: Peachey taking long drags on his fag and noisily exhaling plumes of acrid smoke; Jon trying to hold his thoughts together as the first cracks began to appear in his momentary state of clarity.

It was all very well running away, but what was he running to? He'd no idea as yet what this job – if there actually was a job – might involve. Or if he'd be interested. Or if… It was what Jack Kapinsky had said: did he still want to be a scientist? Was he really done with that? And then… there were Jack's suspicions too. He shot a sideways glance at Peachey, puffing away towards the end of his cigarette. There were Jack's suspicions, and the things Lazenby had just said as well.

It was Peachey who broke the silence. 'It may not have come out quite right, but she was meaning to help you there.'

Jon said nothing. The last thing he'd expected was for Peachey to defend Lazenby.

'It's hard for her,' continued Peachey. 'She's given her life to this discipline. Practically invented it. And then along comes this young whippersnapper and questions everything she's stood for for years. It took a lot for her to say what she said in there.'

'Hmm,' said Jon, unconvinced. It would have taken even more to give some credit to someone else for their ideas. But it wasn't only Lazenby's actions that now invited scrutiny. 'Is it true you've patented it?'

'What?'

'My idea. Have you taken out a patent on it?'

Peachey scowled. 'Yes. Arexis has patented the idea.'

'And when were you planning to tell me?'

Peachey took a long drag on his cigarette, then coughed noisily before continuing: 'Fair point. I should have talked to you first. But my main concern was to make sure that you would get the credit.'

'How does that work? When Arexis owns the patent. And when Lazenby's just stood up in front of the entire mycotherapy world and claimed the idea as hers.'

'Well, actually she didn't. And she can't either, because of the patent I've applied for. All she actually said was you were starting to ask questions in the lab. She didn't give the answer. And the reason she couldn't say more than that is that, when it comes to the documentation, you *personally* are named as the inventor. When the patent is granted, people will see that, and Lazenby knows it.'

'It's patented in my name?'

'Not… It's… According to your employment contract, the IP does rest with Arexis.'

'The what?'

'Intellectual property. But you're named as the inventor on something called Form 7. It's a way of acknowledging the individual. And it means that, whatever anyone says, it's there in black and white that it was you who came up with this. You get the credit. That's why I wanted to do it fast. I mean, if I hadn't, someone else could have patented your idea in their name. I mean, Imogen could have, for example.'

'You think she would have done that?'

'No, but… you know. It gives you the protection.'

'So… hold on, I don't get this. If Lazenby could have patented it in her name, why couldn't I have patented it in mine?'

'Contracts,' said Peachey, starting to cough again. 'They're the bane of my life,' he spluttered, before hawking himself to a halt. 'Lazenby's contract is… Her work on this pre-dates the lab, pre-dates Arexis. Technically, she's not… listen, do you really want all the ghastly legalese?'

'No.' He really didn't. He just wanted a straight answer. 'No, I just… Can I see this Form 7 then?'

'If you want to.'

'I want to.'

'I don't have it with me.'

'No, I... I know you don't. So does this mean you're going to take things forwards?'

'How do you mean?'

'If you've patented the idea does that mean you're planning to develop it?'

Peachey gave a long low grunt of comprehension, before taking a last drag of his cigarette and blowing the smoke up into the air. 'Not immediately. The things we talked about before, the issues – all that still has to be resolved. Imogen is right: we need to explore the implications in a controlled fashion first. But given what Jack Kapinsky had to say yesterday, we're a lot closer to that now, so... not immediately, but as soon as we can.'

Jon nodded. He could tell that Peachey was trying to let him down gently. Peachey, however, was not to know that Jon's relationship with his idea was no longer that of an enthusiastic originator. His reaction to further delays was not disappointment – he'd long passed mere disappointment and was now plumbing the depths of disillusionment – but a kind of defeated relief. It was at least one thing fewer he needed to think about.

'About what you said about a job...' said Peachey.

'Hmm,' said Jon. Yes. That.

'Did you mean what you said?'

It was a good question – but not one to which he could be sure he knew the answer. 'That I might be interested?' There were so many other questions: whether Ryan would respond to his text, and how; what was happening in Cogan's body; whether Annie would actually speak; whether anyone would still be interested *in him* if she did. And again, for just a second, as with Jack Kapinsky two days before, it occurred to Jon that he could tell Peachey right now, come clean, explain everything. 'The thing is' – the words were not just forming in his head as thought experiments: they were coming out of his mouth – 'I've done something really stupid.'

'Aha,' said Peachey. It was hard to place the intonation, somewhere between a question and an acknowledgement.

'Really stupid,' repeated Jon. As the words had come, he'd been staring straight out at the tourist shop opposite – not looking at it, just holding his eyes fixed on the motley assemblage of plastic bulls and flamenco dresses that filled its windows. Now though, he turned his head slightly sideways, his eyes more so, to look at Peachey, and as the man's meaty features slipped into his field of view it was as if Jon's consciousness were catapulted back into his body from whatever distant vantage point it had been banished to. What the hell was he doing?

'What's that then?' said Peachey. There was nothing in his face, his voice, his demeanour, to suggest he had any suspicion whatsoever of what Jon had been about to reveal. But the image of revelation still gripped Jon, just as the thought of falling grips a man who could but does not throw himself from a clifftop. And the sudden apperception of the constant, tissue-thin refraining that separates us all from self-willed disaster struck terror into him.

'I…' he floundered. 'The thing is…' He would have to say something. 'I've…'

It was Peachey's attempt to guess that saved him. 'Have you said something to the Professor?'

'Yes,' said Jon, for a moment slightly bewildered; then: 'Yes. I said… I confronted her. I said some things I shouldn't have.'

Peachey nodded. Perhaps some part of him had feared there was worse to come, for he now seemed relieved. 'Don't worry about that, lad. She's a grown-up. She'll forgive you. Nothing that can't be sorted out.'

'Right,' said Jon, turning back to the tourist-shop window.

'Come on,' said Peachey. 'Shall we go back in? We can discuss everything else another time.'

The remainder of the Congress passed without event. His path did not cross Lazenby's in the little time remaining, and Peachey did not seek to discuss things further beyond suggesting, in a taxi to the airport, that they find a time to talk the following week. Of course, they were all then on the same flight and found themselves awkwardly assembled at the gate, but somehow Peachey and Lazenby got straight into discussing – in whispers, as the public space required – the presentations of the last two days, so that

Jon could sit quietly to one side and nothing needed to be said. Their seats were in different parts of the aeroplane, and landing at Heathrow, Jon – who sat at the back – took his time sorting out his hand luggage and did not catch up with them or see them again that day.

There followed a strange, objectively brief yet, as experienced, dragging hiatus in Jon's life: a few days during which, after the high drama of the Congress and notwithstanding his sense that what happened next would determine the rest of his life, nothing happened and nothing could be done, at least not by Jon.

There was no cup of tea or chat in the lab, no one-to-one interaction with Professor Lazenby. In so far as they met and spoke it was in the context of groups, and no one other than himself would have detected anything out of the ordinary in Lazenby's behaviour towards him. For him, of course, that very normality was what was so disturbing – though he hunted in vain for signs of self-consciousness or studiedness in what must surely be the façade that she was presenting. Unless, somehow, she had been true to her word and, as she had declared in that final exchange at the Congress, given up on him, moved on, set her sights on other struggles. It was this possibility, hard as he found it to entertain, that troubled him most.

There was no immediate word from Peachey: no job description, no request for a CV, no follow-up even with possible days and times for the promised further discussion. Once again, this silence had about it a ring of the entirely ordinary: Peachey was a busy and important man who'd just cut two days out of his schedule for the Congress and spent a large part of those talking to Jon. It was hardly surprising if other matters had seized upon him the moment he got back to his office. Hardly out of character, either, for him to go quiet for a while. It was just… did he not realise how much depended on what he now offered?

There was no response from Ryan to Jon's text. Here there was a definite pattern of wilful blanking, so well established that really Jon had no reason at all to be surprised. Except… this time he'd actually had something to say, a definite proposal, a response to something Ryan himself had wanted, and not just a more or less veiled suggestion of another meeting. After everything he'd done for Ryan – well, for Cogan – at some level it was just basic courtesy that Ryan should respond.

Of course, there was nothing from Scott either. He'd not have expected there to be. Yet, in its own way, that still fresh absence served to sharpen a growing realisation: he was not at the centre of anyone's concerns.

He could have taken the initiative, of course: asked for a word with Lazenby; prompted Peachey; contacted Ryan again; even reached out to Scott. Theoretically, that is. Theoretically he could have done any of these things, yet somehow, in reality, he could no longer find in himself the raw material of motivation for anything beyond what was so routinised – getting up, going to the lab, eating, going to bed – that it happened without his needing to do any more than let it.

There was one other action he might have taken, of course, to break at least one part of the logjam: write to Cogan, whose updates had also temporarily dried up. On one occasion he even got as far as creating a new e-mail – though not as far as typing Cogan's name into the recipient field. Was it even Cogan he'd be writing to by now? Or Annie, equipped by him with a voice, with hands, with a place in the world of humans.

He did not want to write to Cogan.

So all that happened was that Kevin the lab assistant seemed to pop up all the time by his bench, despite Jon having postponed their drink again, while Maria asked him endless questions about the Congress.

From her perspective, of course, it was clear that the invitation had marked Jon out for a dazzling career in science – the kind of career, perhaps, that he'd once imagined for himself years previously, watching that documentary about Francesco Redi. She was taken aback, therefore, when, unable to maintain the pretence of enthusiasm any longer, he admitted to her what might be coming next.

'Actually, I'm thinking of leaving the lab and taking a job at Arexis.'

It took a little while to convince Maria that this was not some kind of joke.

'But this is crazy, no?' she opined forcefully. 'Why would you do that?'

'I'm… well, different reasons. I'm… I mean, things haven't exactly worked out well between me and Lazenby, have they?'

'Haven't they?'

'No.'

'I didn't notice.'

'No, well…'

'And anyway,' continued Maria, 'why is that important?'

'Erm…' It was obvious, wasn't it?

'You're going to give up just because you don't get on with one person?'

'No, I… I didn't say that.' It did sound stupid when she put it like that, but that was not what he'd meant. 'Besides, there's other reasons. And… I don't know.' He was regretting telling her. 'I think I'm just ready for a change.'

'What kind of a change?'

'I don't know. I feel like… I've ground to a halt.'

'We all feel like that sometimes. It's how things are. But you can't just give up.'

Two days later the dead calm was at last rippled again by a breeze of event: the long-anticipated word in Lazenby's office. There was no tea though, and unlike herself, Lazenby got straight to the point: 'You're thinking of leaving us.'

Jon sighed. 'Maria told you.'

'Maria?' Lazenby looked puzzled. 'Matt Peachey warned me he's arranging to meet you.'

'Oh.'

'He told me you'd… expressed an interest in working for Arexis.'

'Yes. I did.'

'Right.' She frowned. 'I know you're still extremely angry with me for whatever it is you believe I said or did.'

Jon could not stop a sharp exhalation of disbelief escaping from him. What he *believed* she'd said or done?

'I don't want to argue with you,' said Lazenby swiftly. She'd noticed. 'That's not why I wanted to talk to you. I know you're angry and I assume nothing I can say is likely to change that. As long as it doesn't get in the way of the science we're doing – which it isn't, is it…?'

Jon shook his head, conscious as he did so that there was something rather childish about his behaviour.

'… as long as it doesn't get in the way, then I don't think it would help. But I do want to talk to you about the choice you're thinking of making.'

'OK,' said Jon. He had no intention of helping her.

'Do you mind me asking why you're thinking of leaving science?'

Jon was about to respond with a surly 'no' when the phrase caught him. Leaving science. He was thinking of leaving the lab, taking a new job, giving up being a scientist even… but leaving science? He could feel a rush of emotion in his chest – not rage, as he'd expected, but the first choked spasm of tears.

'Well,' he said, battening down as best he could against the rising waves, 'it's like you said, isn't it? Us bright kids, full of good ideas. We go off and work for drug companies, and that's probably the right choice for us, isn't it?'

As he spoke, Lazenby's eyes closed and her hands rose to cover them, rubbing fingertips into the corners, then pulling sideways to wrap around her cheeks.

'I am so sorry,' she said – and such was the look of pain in her face that he could almost believe her. 'I thought… I was angry, and I didn't understand why you'd done what you'd done. I didn't know anything about Scott, remember.'

'Well, that hardly matters,' said Jon, the words slipping out of him now without restraint. 'Scott's left me anyway.'

'I'm sorry to hear that. Maybe… Look, don't take this the wrong way, but maybe you should take a bit of time off. Before you make a decision, I mean. There are good people you could talk to as well.'

'What do you mean?'

'Well, when there are lots of things going on and… things get confusing, it can, you know, help. To talk to someone.'

'I don't need to talk to anyone,' snorted Jon – even as it struck him how obviously he did. But to admit that, to give himself up to the flood welling within him – that he could not do, not here, not with her.

'I can't stop you leaving if you want to. But I really, really don't want you making a decision that you'll regret in later life. And I certainly don't want you doing so just because you're angry with me.'

'It's not about you,' said Jon, tight-lipped. Like his life revolved around her or something. 'I'll make a decision on...' He broke off. On what basis? 'Can I go now please?'

Lazenby shook her head and held up her hands, palms forwards. 'You can go any time you like. It's not a... school.'

'Right.' He got up to leave.

'And...' began Lazenby, then perhaps thought better of whatever it was she'd been planning to say. 'Let me know what you decide, yes?'

Mercifully, Maria was not at her bench: she'd have noticed immediately the state he was in and, even if she'd not said anything right then, would have been on his case before long. And he appreciated her concern, he really did: it was just that he could not cope with concern right now.

There were two e-mails waiting for him in his inbox. One was from Peachey, with the subject: *Dates for meeting*. He did not open it, because the other was from Ryan. Not from Cogan, but from Ryan. After all this time he had finally written.

The subject read simply: *Tony*.

Dr Caldicot,

I'm sorry to have to tell you that Tony passed away yesterday. The doctor says it was heart failure – so I'm guessing nothing to do with you know what. You shouldn't feel bad at all because over these last few weeks he's been so happy and hopeful, so at least he had that. I know he'd have wanted me to thank you for that.

The arrangements are all in place for the cremation, just like was agreed, so no need to worry on that front.

I hope you won't think this rude, but I want this to be our last communication. I was very fond of Tony, and I appreciate what you did for him, but now I need to move on. Please don't try to come to the house or anything. I hope you understand that I need to move on now.

Ryan Griffiths

In that moment, the intensity of Jon's emotions was such that what he actually felt was nothing: just stillness, as if the clocks had been stopped and the world put on hold while he readjusted to it. Nothing.

Then came the thought – just a thought, cold, intellectual: he had got away with it; there was no Cogan any more, no Annie in human form, no consequences. He could breathe again. Breathe and move on. Move on now.

And then at last came the feeling, taking form in his consciousness like the pain of a lost tooth as the anaesthetic wears off. No Cogan any more, but no Ryan either, no Scott, no… no Lazenby. He was alone. He'd been alone all along. And if he looked in a mirror right now, would he know he was a person at all and not just some very sophisticated machine? He was a vacuum, and, abhorred by nature, the vacuum ached with longing.

AN EXTRACT FROM
GRIEF, MADNESS AND WISDOM
BY EDITH MARKHAM

I shall never forget the day Tamika told me that I was to be her *koana*: should she die, I would be at her *koaniki*. I knew I had long since been accepted by the Teobe, a kindly and civil tribe, if not much used to strangers in their midst, but this was something over and above. Not just acceptance but incorporation. The word *koaniki* is closely linked to the verb *koan*, which means something like 'reunite' and is specifically reserved for joining together that which has previously been separated. By making me her *koana*, Tamika was not just inviting me to be part of her tribe: she was acknowledging that it was only fate that had separated us in the first place.

Like me, Tamika was an anthropologist. Her culture furnished no universities, no academic posts or peer-reviewed journals. But she looked at me, an alien being from another culture, and she saw a stance on the world that might be understood if only she could find a way to adopt it. Many of our conversations were just that: conversations. As I sought to find my way into the Teobe understanding of the world, so too she explored my strange perspective – often, I feel, with greater insight and perceptiveness.

One day, for example, only six months or so after I'd first arrived, she was helping me as I tried to understand an unfamiliar distinction in the Teobe language. The term for 'animals' in Teobe is *ka-nenka*, which roughly translates as 'self-movers', but I had noticed that a few animals – domestic dogs, wild 'singing dogs', a couple of species of tree kangaroo and cuscus – are assigned to a different class, *ka-linka*, 'self-feelers'. Surely, I asked Tamika, there was some term covering all of these things, some concept equivalent to 'animal'. At first she was puzzled by the questions I was asking, then at some point started laughing.

'How can you not see the difference?' she asked, laughing. 'The *ka-linka* are different in their essence. They have the gift of grief (*chaba*). That is why the dogs sing: feeling and music are one.'

So what about human beings, I asked. Humans feel grief too. Where do they fit in?

'Ah,' said Tamika, smiling. 'We too were *ka-linka* once and sang to each other. But then our forefathers learned how to lie and called it speech. Then they learned how to lie to themselves and called it thought. And now' – she tapped the notebook in which I was busily writing down what she was saying – 'now you have learned how to lie to yourself in the future.'

It was Tamika who told me the Teobe story of how the world came to be, and the origins of the *koaniki*.

When Kaletu created the world, life was unbounded and flowed through every part of it. There were no living things, no individuals, no species – no love, no strife, no family, friend or enemy. Life was everywhere and in everything.

Maleku saw what Kaletu had done and wanted to create his own world. But as he did not have the gift of creation, he instead broke off a piece of Kaletu's world and fashioned it into a tiny world of his own, which he called Analaka ('first human') and hid under an earthenware pot in his hut. Maleku did not think it would matter breaking off so small a piece of Kaletu's vast and beautiful world. But the crack he had made in Kaletu's world spread quickly, and soon it fell into a multitude of pieces.

When Kaletu saw what had happened to his world, she suspected Maleku was to blame. Maleku, however, denied all knowledge. So Kaletu tried to fit her world back together, but however she tried she could not make the pieces fit. At last, Maleku confessed, and brought out Analaka in the pot. Just as he was about to put Analaka back into the world, however, he slipped, and dropped in the pot as well. And the water that was in the pot became the ocean, and the pot broke and became the islands in that ocean, and the rock and the soil.

Now Kaletu was very angry and started to put the living pieces of this world back together again. But then Analaka saw what she was doing and begged her to stop. Because Analaka had looked around the world and seen how beautiful it was, how rich, how full of good things to eat, and he did not want to return to the reunited life again so soon. So Kaletu relented, stopped where she had got to and let Analaka live on. And the pieces of her world she had put back together became plants, and those that still remained became *ka-nenka*, and the children of Analaka were the *ka-linka*, among them the Teobe.

But the broken pieces of Kaletu's world still yearned to be one, which is why animals copulate, eat plants and eat other animals. And among the Teobe too, people still yearned to be one, and sought to mingle their blood and press themselves into each other's flesh – and there was much blood and much suffering as a result. So Analaka called together a council of all the Teobe and laid down the laws of the *koaniki*. And then the Teobe were able to live as men and women, because they knew their share of life would, at their death, be reunited with the greater life.

PART 2
CONTROL

8

It was only by chance that Jon found out about Scott's funeral.

Their failed relationship had also failed to mature into a friendship: only a few times in the six years since they'd split up had they made the effort to swap messages with each other, and only once, about three years after the break, had Jon actually been to see Scott on a trip up to Cambridge – an awkward hour of forced conversation that confirmed the insubstantiality of the connection between them and ended with insincere anticipations of a next time both knew was never going to happen. But their relationship had left its ghostly after-image across social media, and an illusion of contact been sustained by inscrutable algorithms which would, from time to time, place on the newsfeed of one some update from the other. Or from one of the friends of friends who, added in haste, now posted at leisure. One in particular, a former colleague of Scott's called Caitlin Stubbs, regularly cropped up on Jon's Facebook page – though to his knowledge he had never so much as liked a single thing she'd said, done or shared. Perhaps the all-knowing algorithms had long ago singled her out for a special purpose. For it was her update that alerted Jon – a photo of Scott as he'd looked before Scander's, with the caption: *On Wednesday we say our farewells. But he won't ever leave us really, because his kindness will always be with us in our hearts.*

A quick glance at Scott's own profile filled out recent events, from the moment a few months before when someone called Peter had, at Scott's request, taken on the task of updating the page, through the slow and pathetic last weeks of decline, to the inevitable announcement of death and, beyond that, a liquid wash of reminiscence, sympathy and gratitude, stemmed only by the occasional practicality – including, crucially, more details of Scott's funeral.

Jon knew at once that he had to be there – notwithstanding the inconvenience of the timing, just a day before the meeting with the Minister. It wasn't until he was actually in the crematorium, excusing his way past mourning huddles to a seat at the back in the corner of the room, that he wondered *why* he had felt this way. The realisation hit him the moment he caught sight of Caitlin Stubbs, locked in earnest conversation with someone who might well have been Scott's mother: that he was an impostor here, an intruder, someone who didn't actually know if that *was* Scott's mother because he had never himself met the family and, when he'd seen photos of them, had not paid enough attention. He had grazed Scott's life as a nettle grazes a leg. He had no place in this memorial – except perhaps that, in coming, he had briefly recreated the more impulsive, less worldly Jon that Scott had once known.

He was still wondering what had possessed him to come when, half an hour later, he was slipping out of the crematorium again, mercifully unnoticed by the few people who might possibly have recognised him. Back in his car, he pulled out his phone and did what he should have done years previously: silently deleted from his list of Facebook friends the few pegs that stayed him to a time that was now, definitively, over. Last of all, with only a moment of hesitation, he deleted Scott.

'So how was it?' asked Maria as they settled at their table with their coffees. He had called her two days earlier, as soon as he'd known he was coming up to Cambridge, and arranged to meet her in the café they'd once frequented. Such are the mechanics of neuronal activation by which one memory hauls others in its wake. And in truth, it really was nice to be catching up with Maria outside the context of work. Though perhaps another day would have been better.

'It was strange. I don't think I should have gone.'

'No? What happened?'

'Oh, nothing really. I just felt... It's all such a long time ago, isn't it?'

'Not *such* a long time.'

'And it's not like we'd stayed in touch or anything. I mean, it sounds terrible but... I think I was expecting to feel something when I got there. That it would mean something. But it didn't. I was just... there.'

'So you did all your feeling back then, when you first found out. It wasn't unexpected, was it? His dying. It wasn't a shock. I think it is good that you said goodbye. Better to go and feel a bit strange than to not go and regret it afterwards.'

'I suppose so.' What he wasn't saying, and had no intention of saying, was that he'd not felt that much six years previously either, and that even so his time with Scott represented something of a high point in his romantic life, unmatched in the weary cavalcade of online dating and commodity sex since moving to London. If he'd come to mourn anything, it was perhaps his own potential. 'Sorry, I'm not a lot of fun today.'

'In the circumstances I think I can forgive you.'

But Jon's lines of thought were firmly locked in recollection. Back in Cambridge, in this café, having just said a goodbye of sorts to Scott, it was perhaps inevitable that deeds and choices he'd not thought of for years should come crowding to the surface. 'Can I ask you a question? Do you think I made the right decision back then? Leaving the lab, I mean. Going to Arexis.'

Maria pulled a face. 'You're not serious?'

'No, not really. I'm just... It's just got me thinking about things, that's all.'

'This is not like you, Jon. You're not one to dwell on the past. Has something else happened?'

'I'm just feeling a bit reflective after this morning, that's all. How about you? How are Javier and Pilar?'

They talked for a while about Maria's husband; her little girl, now three; their varied ups and downs in nurseries and workplaces. Jon had asked the question with genuine interest, but today, the answers only seemed to underline how little he himself had accomplished in the same period. Oh yes, there were the incremental promotions at Arexis, the ninety-five per cent mortgage on his minute studio in Elephant and Castle, the dinners and nights out and weekends away that friends with children had long since given up on – the lifestyle, always the lifestyle. But nothing that would outlast Jon's own final trip to the crematorium. When it came to her turn to ask, the best Maria could manage as a question was: 'How is life in London?' Life in London. Whatever else it was, London was not a family.

'Yeah, good. Pretty much the same as ever really.' They'd once had the kind of friendship where Maria's next question might have been whether he was seeing anyone, but somewhere along the way that had lapsed. 'Busy with work.' Which was true. 'You know.'

'Still trying to work out how to go public?'

He nodded. Yes, and still getting nowhere. 'Things are coming to a bit of a head. We have a big meeting tomorrow.'

Maria made a noise that might have sounded like interest had Jon not already known the world he now moved in bored her to the bone. 'I'm sure it'll all go fine,' she said.

'Hmm,' said Jon, unconvinced. And slightly peeved as well, he realised: it was all very well Maria playing the high-minded scientist, but it was her job that would be on the line if he didn't come up with something. 'I do miss the lab, you know. I miss the... innocence.'

'Innocence?'

'Yeah. I mean, you can get on with the technical challenges. You don't have to worry about all this political shit.'

'I don't think that's missing the lab. I think that's missing being young.'

'Maybe.' Plus he'd not done such a good job himself of avoiding the political shit in the lab. Either way, there was no point getting cross with Maria. It wasn't her fault that he couldn't solve the problem it was his job to solve, that he kept wandering off into irrelevant reminiscence – indeed, that he had come to see her precisely in the course of such a meander. 'Who'd have thought that keeping things secret would be the easy part, eh?'

'You'll come up with something.'

'What would you do?'

'About what?'

'If you were in my shoes. You have these amazing potential therapies that you need to tell people about, but to do that, you first have to tell them you've been keeping quiet about a brain-eating fungus for decades.'

'I don't know. I suppose I'd try to focus on how amazing the potential therapies are.'

'Hmm.' No inspiration here, then. 'That's what the PR people keep saying. It's not…' Another thought occurred to him: 'Suppose you had to tell Javier. After all these years of keeping it quiet. How would you do that?'

Maria frowned. 'I'd just tell him, I suppose.'

'But the secrecy. How would you deal with the fact you'd kept it secret?'

'I'm not sure there's anything to deal with. I haven't exactly kept it secret. You know how it is. People ask what you do, you tell them you work in a lab. They ask what on, you say it's complicated. The conversation moves on. They weren't really interested in what you do to begin with. It's exactly as they told us when we started out: there's a mountain of stuff we don't know about, and it's only when we feel we're not *allowed* to know that we start wanting to. The secret to keeping a secret is never to be caught hiding it. Provided you never let on that there's something you can't talk about, no one will ever try to make you talk about it.'

'But with Javier? Surely it's different with Javier?'

'I don't know. There's plenty of stuff Javier's not allowed to discuss with me. I mean, with his clients, there must be lots of confidential stuff. I don't know actually. I never ask. We don't need to talk about that stuff. We tell each other about the people we work with, the personalities, the politics – all of that. I talk about equipment that doesn't work and he talks about crappy IT. We listen to each other, we empathise, we offer each other advice. Really, he knows almost everything. He knows I work on fungi: that's my specialism, how could he not know? And he knows I'm working on therapeutic uses. I expect he thinks that the fungus synthesises a drug – I'm sure that's what everyone thinks. But he knows I can't talk about the details and he respects that.'

'And feeling he's not allowed to know doesn't make him start wanting to?'

'I don't think so. Maybe if I kept parading the fact that my work is secret, that I can't tell him, maybe then he would start wanting to know. But I don't. Just like he doesn't harp on about client confidentiality. We're not keeping secrets from each other. They're just things that don't come up.'

'That's the difference,' said Jon – his mind had wandered again as Maria was speaking.

'Difference from what?'

'I was just thinking, as you were talking: the only real experience I have of keeping a secret in a relationship is not coming out to my parents. And that does keep coming up, however hard we try not to let it. Every family occasion, every wedding, every divorce, every new child, every time somebody else's relationship so much as gets mentioned; not to mention every gay character on every TV programme, every celebrity that comes out, or denies it. It keeps coming up. I can't help hiding it, and they can't help catching me hiding it.'

'You could just tell them and be done with it.'

Jon snorted. 'That's not going to happen. Anyway, it's not really… It just popped into my head. It's not really relevant. Maybe disclosure is not my strong point, eh?'

'You're not coming out to your parents, Jon,' said Maria, taking hold of his wrist with mock seriousness. 'You're just explaining to the population of Britain – no, Europe, the world – that there's this creepy fungus that can live inside their brains which the scientists have been experimenting on and the politicians have been keeping hushed up. Much, much easier.'

That was how his mind had been since he'd heard about Scott's death: wandering all over the place, stumbling from one thicket to another. And the funeral had laid nothing to rest. If that was why he'd thought he had to be there, he'd been sorely mistaken. Memories still tugged at his thoughts as strangers' eyes tug at a groom on his stag night. And he still had not a clue how to solve his problem.

For six years the science had trundled on.

Not for Jon's idea, it hadn't. Lazenby's plea to reconsider the Laws might have created a stir at the Congress, but coming as it did hard on the heels of Jack Kapinsky's announcement that the first of the Laws had at last been cracked, it had no lasting effect. The few researchers who might have been interested in pursuing the specifics of Jon's idea (without having ever heard of Jon) soon found out about the patent and backed off. At Arexis meanwhile, Jon found his first few months caught up in providing support to a strategy review which concluded, unequivocally, that all resources should be focused on combining Kapinsky's (unpatented) discoveries with techniques already developed in the Cambridge lab to re-engineer the aversion mechanism: two laws down, only one to go. Jon's law-busting proposal was quietly consigned to a shelf for 'future consideration' – the organisational analogue of a parent saying: 'We'll see.' Like a beautiful butterfly pinned in a case, it had gone nowhere.

Meanwhile, however, for the project defined by Hayton's – or Lazenby's, or whoever's – Laws, progress had ground ever forwards, crushing the obstacles in its way into puzzles, puzzles into details, details into topics for future PhDs. The focus had remained on alcohol, and within a few years, the team had engineered a strain, AN-43d8, which combined an aversion to alcohol with an inability to cross the synapse. A few years of further painstaking work identified the precise brain sites where infection was needed to create a coherent behavioural aversion. Testing could now begin in models displaying a prior preference for alcohol (with or without a genetic basis) – or, to put the point another way, in alcoholic rats. The tests were a resounding success.

In the process, moreover, the team stumbled on another fact of even greater significance: the strains of Annie they had stopped at the synapse also failed to spore. Nor were they alone in observing this. Before long the reports were flooding in from other labs around the world: hosts were dying and Annie, hemmed in to a few neurones, was dying with them. A team in New Zealand took up the challenge, infecting varying portions of rat brains with stopped-at-the-synapse strains and identifying a recurring pattern: the strains were capable of sporing but rarely did so when less than fifty per cent of the brain was infected, and never when less than thirty per cent. Further work, still ongoing, suggested that what made the difference was not in fact the proportion of cells infected but the infection of complete brain circuits. Either way, the implication was clear: by stopping Annie at the synapse, Kapinsky's team had also opened up a pragmatic way of addressing the final Law: no spores. The way was opening to human trials.

And that was when the problem Jon was now wrestling with had arisen.

Over the decades, secrecy had been the substrate on which the culture of research into Annie had grown. Bit by bit, those in the know had chipped away at the practical and moral objections to use of the fungus in human subjects, but they had done so in the societal equivalent of a Petri dish, shielded from contamination by the panics, scandals and furores of the public domain. Bit by bit, rationally and dispassionately, they had analysed and dismantled the risk scenarios – until only one obstacle remained: the very secrecy that had allowed them to progress so far. How could these great discoveries, these great hopes, now be shared with the wider world without at the same time conjuring the four horsemen of emotion, superstition, hysteria and conspiracy?

For a year or more, that question had lain at the heart of a war of bureaucratic attrition between Arexis and the MTLA – the Medical Trials Licensing Agency – regarding the move to human trials. It was a war that had absorbed most of Jon's working days, along with a fair few evenings and weekends, as he dealt with one after another of the objections raised by what Peachey liked to call the 'yes-men and no-gnomes'. But always, lurking behind the procedural quibbles and ethical technicalities, lay the real question: how shall we explain to people why we kept this secret for so long? And by resolving each new problem, Jon's only real achievement had been to strip this unanswered question bare.

Things might have stayed locked in that fruitless groove for years to come had it not been for a General Election that May. Driven by a potent alignment of financial necessity, ideological fervour and political opportunism, the new administration set about the business of government with an iconoclastic fervour reminiscent of Roundheads decapitating stone saints. Whatever budgets could be cut were to be cut. Whatever projects could be axed were to be axed. Whatever assets could be sold were to be sold.

It was with such maxims ringing in his ears that Gilbert Sword, a young and inexperienced Minister of State at the Department of Health, discovered that he was, amongst his many other duties, responsible for Her Majesty's Government's one hundred per cent shareholding in a company he had never even heard of before: Arexis Ltd. A company, moreover, that appeared to exist in a bizarre limbo state: notionally private but wholly owned by the state; notionally profit-making but sustained by a complex cascade of grants from the Department, from the Medical Research Council and – strangest of all – from the Ministry of Defence; notionally valuable but with only a handful of poorly performing products on the market, and no pipeline to speak of so far as he could see.

'Sell it,' had been Sword's immediate reaction. And understandably so, he was advised, but the timing was inopportune, Arexis being currently worth only a fraction of what it might be worth when a certain, highly secretive project – not mentioned in the documents the Minister had been reviewing – was completed. 'Complete it then. Then sell it.'

Unfortunately completion had been indefinitely delayed by very serious difficulties in establishing a basis on which human trials could go forwards, and no, unfortunately there was no sign that any resolution would be possible in the near future.

'Scrap it then. If we can't test whatever it is, then it's not worth anything. Scrap it and sell the rest.'

The Minister would surely wish to think carefully before throwing away the nation's significant competitive advantage with regards to an emerging therapeutic technology which might, in the future, bring billions into the UK.

'So test it. If it's so bloody valuable, why aren't we testing it?'

As the Minister no doubt realised, great rewards were often accompanied by great risks – great *political* risks – as he would appreciate once fully apprised of the nature of the therapeutic technology which Arexis was developing.

'So what are we actually talking about here?'

By the time Peachey found himself hauled into the Department, various civil servants with a finger in the Arexis pie had driven Sword to a state of, as he put it, considerable irritation. Which was to say that he was by now hopping mad. Arexis, which had looked like an easy rung on the ladder of self-advancement, was more and more resembling the grease on a pole. Peachey very quickly realised that he was there to be lectured, not listened to. The message was a simple one: either Peachey got his fungus back on the money-making track or the whole project was getting shut down and what was left of Arexis sold off to the highest bidder. In the process, however, as Peachey noted, Sword also betrayed considerable impatience with the kinds of concern the MTLA were expressing.

'He doesn't seem obviously bothered by the idea of a brain-eating fungus,' he told Jon the next day. 'All he wants is something he can show to the Treasury. So what I'm thinking is: if we can get the no-gnomes in front of him as well, they'll look like the obstructive bureaucrats they are and we'll come out smelling of roses. And Bob's your uncle: human trials.'

Jon was less sure. 'I don't think that, legally, a minister can tell the MTLA what to do. That would be political interference, wouldn't it?'

'Very possibly. But Sword's on the warpath. He's in head-bashing mode. Once he's made up his mind which way to go, I wouldn't want to be on the losing side.'

'And you're sure we won't be on the losing side.'

'That, my boy, is your job. Simple, rational responses to every possible objection the no-gnomes could make. Nice short briefing paper in advance pre-empting everything they're going to throw at us. Comprehensive, but no more than two sides of A4, and none of your fancy words or technical terms. This is a minister we're talking to here, not someone who actually understands anything.'

'All very easy then.'

'Compared to my job it is. I've got to find some way of tricking the MTLA into showing up for their own execution.'

'And what we say to the public? We still haven't really got an answer on that one.'

'You'd better hope these PR people come up with something good then.'

And hoped Jon had, but come up with something good they hadn't.

As for his own efforts to do what he was brilliant at, he'd just not been able to focus on the task this last week. There had of course been other times during the last six years when his thoughts had wandered into the weeds of recollection. As Maria rightly noted, however, he wasn't one to dwell on the past, and the opportunities for practice afforded by those same years had made him even more adept at cutting short memories of past follies – just as he'd become adept at ignoring those glimpses, in the men he pursued online, of past obsessions. Then Scott had died, and over the following days he had found himself lost in a jungle that grew in the small hours as he lay rehearsing again and again those meetings with Cogan, those meetings with Ryan. Yes, Ryan, with his ideas about fate and purpose. Why, all those years later, was it Ryan's words he found himself returning to: 'We meet people for a reason. We just have to make sense of it.' Why was it Ryan he was thinking about as the doors closed on Scott's coffin?

It was only halfway down the M11, half-heartedly rerunning the conversation with Maria, that his winding train of thought quite unexpectedly fell upon a sunlit clearing.

'The secret to keeping a secret is never to be caught hiding it,' he repeated out loud.

That was it. The hidden variable: who was going to get caught.

The plan had been for Peachey and Jon to meet in London the next morning and go through their tactics over bacon and eggs in a greasy spoon. They'd done the same many times before when they'd had morning meetings in town, as it made little sense for Jon to catch his usual train out to Woking only to catch another back in again. As it turned out, this particular morning it would have made even less sense, thanks to signalling problems at Clapham Junction. Peachey texted at 8 a.m. to let Jon know he might be late for breakfast; again at 8.30 a.m. to say he would definitely be so; then at 8.45 a.m. to say he was in a car and, if all else failed, would meet Jon in the reception of Richmond House. A bit before 9 a.m. he phoned.

'Total bloody chaos. Google Maps is saying an hour and twenty-three, so you may well have to start without me.' Not surprisingly, he was furious. With fast trains to Waterloo taking only half an hour, catching the 8.15 a.m. for a 10.30 a.m. meeting had seemed like a pretty safe bet. 'Can you bring copies of the papers? Just in case. I've got the pack here with me, but the way things are going...'

'Sure, no problem.'

'And the Knight Commander is coming. Keep an eye out for him when you get there.'

'Really? Why's *he* coming?'

'Because I asked him to. I thought we might need reinforcements.'

'Why him though?'

'Because he's a wily old sod and, however smart we think *we* are, he understands more about ministers and mandarins than we ever will.'

'Does it change how we present?'

'No, it doesn't change anything. He's just there as backup.'

'Right. You could have told me you were asking him.'

'And you could have been in work yesterday.'

'Hmm. This is not a good time for us to be falling out with each other.'

There was a momentary pause at the other end. 'You're right. I'm sorry. I'm pissed off at the trains, not you. I didn't tell you because he'd said he couldn't make it. Then he called yesterday to say he'd managed to move his diary around. Which suggests to me that he's heard something that makes him more worried than he was before.'

'But he didn't tell you what.'

'Sir Andrew? He never tells me anything.'

'So maybe he just moved his diary around, like he said.'

'Maybe. I don't trust him. I don't trust any of them.'

Bringing in people one didn't trust as backup didn't seem like such a great plan to Jon. Sir Andrew Harper KCB struck him as a particularly odd choice. Since their first brief encounter at Jon's first Congress, he'd met the man only rarely – almost always at meetings in Whitehall – and had never been able to establish with clarity exactly what he did. 'Diversification Team, Ministry of Defence,' was his standard line when they did introductions around the table; a line delivered with such forbidding self-assurance that no one ever asked what the Diversification Team actually was or why they'd been invited to the meeting. Peachey was not much more forthcoming when Jon tried to find out a little more.

'They provide a large chunk of our grant. Sir Andrew is one of the last people left from the early days. The only one left in government, I'd say.'

'And the Diversification Team? What do they do?'

'Diversify, I suppose. Better not to ask. Seriously though, I really couldn't tell you.'

'And that doesn't worry you?'

'Not if asking questions risks others asking questions about our funding.'

'I don't see why the MoD is involved at all.'

'Historical hangover. Goes back to pre-privatisation, when we were part of the MRE at Porton Down. That used to be an MoD outfit before it got handed over to Health. And the Knight Commander made sure a chunk of the funding stayed at the MoD, because that's what civil servants do: fight to keep control of budgets. It's a classic government fudge.'

Which seemed like no answer at all to Jon, who still struggled to reconcile himself to the idea that problems could be fudged away instead of being properly solved. Sir Andrew's habit of saying very little, but saying it in such a way that his word was never questioned, had added to his unease around the man. Not that he'd ever said anything that had caused any problems for Jon. But that possibility always seemed present, and Jon would find himself, against his own will, glancing sideways as he spoke to check for signs of disapproval in Sir Andrew's aquiline profile.

Right now, however, it clearly wasn't the moment to question Peachey's choice of reinforcements. Sir Andrew was coming, and that was that. Better to move on.

'About the public communication thing... I've had an idea. I was going to talk to you about it over breakfast, but... I know it's very last minute, but it only occurred to me yesterday.'

'Go on.'

'Well, we've been worrying that when people find out we've been working on this in secret they'll assume some kind of evil conspiracy. There must be more we're not telling them, you know. Risks we're not willing to admit. So we've been trying to come up with a way to prove to them that in fact we've got nothing to hide, that people can trust us. And as you know, the problem is that it never rings true, because all we'd really be saying is: sure, we hid stuff from you before, but you can trust that we're not doing so now; sure, it looks like a conspiracy, but really everyone's behaviour was above board. It just doesn't work. And all the benefits in the world aren't going to distract people from a juicy cover-up story. Not the press anyway. So, what I've been thinking is: what if we just accept that there have to be conspirators in this story? There have to be villains.'

'You're losing me, Jon. And believe me, I have considerably more patience for this topic than Gilbert Sword.'

'Just let me finish. We can worry about Gilbert Sword later.'

'Not much later. We're seeing him in an hour and a half.'

'Yes, I know, but...'

'Fine. There have to be conspirators. How does that help us?'

'We just have to make sure we're the victims, not the villains.'

'Go on.'

'We don't just say we've got nothing to hide. We say that someone's been *stopping* us from talking for... what? Thirty years? Right at the beginning these brilliant scientists – Hayton, Lazenby – they saw the potential for a miracle fix, a simple one-time treatment that could revolutionise our relationship with drugs, alcohol, tobacco, sugar... something that could set us all free from our weak wills. But it seems like someone didn't like that idea. They didn't want the little guy to get a break. They wanted to keep us as we are: fat, drunk, cancerous, in debt. They made the scientists keep quiet, kept coming up with petty objections, used their rules and regulations to block us. And that's the story. That's the conspiracy. Not what we've been doing, but the conspiracy to try and stop us.'

There was silence from the other end of the phone.

'It's Peachey's First Law,' added Jon, suddenly feeling less certain. 'Start by giving people what they want.'

Still silence.

'Are you there, Matt?'

'Yeah.'

'So?'

'I'm not sure. I think I get what you're trying to say but... Who *are* these conspirators? Who are these people who've been ganging up on the heroic scientists?'

'I don't know. I haven't worked it all out yet.'

'And you reckon you're going to in the next... what? Ninety minutes? Look, I've always admired your ability to come up with these left-field solutions but... we're going to meet the Minister. It's make-or-break time. And I don't want to fall out with you but we've had a month to prepare for this, we've gone through all the arguments, we've heard from the PR experts – the experts, Jon – and it's just a little bit late in the day to be throwing ideas like this at me.'

'I'm sorry. It's not as if I deliberately thought of this now.'

'I know. It's just... Look, today we stick with the plan, OK? If we're still standing afterwards then we can give this some more thought, and maybe you're on to something. But today we play safe? OK?'

'OK.'

'You're sure you're with me on this one, Jon?'

'I'm sure.'

'Because I don't—'

'I said I'm sure. Really.'

'Good. See you at Richmond House. I'll text you when I'm nearly there.'

'Sure,' said Jon, then 'Damn it!' as he threw the phone down on his bed, where he'd been sitting taking the call. What he was sure of was that the idea was sound, but Peachey was right, the details were far from worked out, and today was not a day to be taking such chances. If only he could join up all the remaining dots before 10.30 a.m....

He glanced at the clock: 9.05 a.m. It would take him half an hour or so to walk over to Whitehall, but maybe better to head off now, walk a bit, clear his head. It wasn't an especially pleasant walk – up Walworth Road, through the underpasses, then along St George's and Westminster Bridge Street – but at least he would be out and moving his legs. And to kill time at the other end, he could always pop into the café at the back of the County Hall where he and Peachey had planned to meet – or better, as it was a nice morning, walk on and take a ten-minute stroll in St James's Park. Stuck in his close, stuffy flat, it was hard to get things in order; outside, even if the air was hardly fresh, there was at least a sense of real movement in the rumbling stop-start buses, the late-running office-workers, the light breeze that gathered up their fumes and fag smoke to powder over windows he rarely dared open.

There were still some days when Jon loved London. On those days, had anyone asked him why, he'd have reeled off tourist-guide platitudes about things to do and places to go and energy and reinvention: all happy Londoners love London in the same way. Then there were the other days, when it was he who asked questions of himself: why had he ever chosen to live here?

There had been plenty of good reasons not to do so: the cost of living, the cost of housing, the unnecessary commute. His father in particular – barely recovered from the shock of Jon's announcement that he was leaving the lab – had rushed to construct a new bright future for his son on his own terms and taken it upon himself to sing the praises of Woking. But after a decade of comfortable stasis in university towns, hard on the heels of a childhood spent barely ten minutes' drive from Arexis' headquarters, and culminating in his grinding to a complete personal halt in Cambridge, Jon wasn't quite ready for the golf courses of Surrey. It was the spectacle of movement that drew him: a place where things did not stand still, where nothing and no one settled, where change seemed not only possible but necessary. A fresh start. And turning his back on the quieter, leafier districts – and horrifying his father – he'd hunted for flats in the grittier neighbourhoods of the east and south.

When he persevered in the face of threats to withhold a promised deposit, Mr Caldicot finally gave in and stumped up the cash for Jon to acquire an eye-watering mortgage and a gloomy studio in an ex-council block next to the railway. The constant noise had not bothered him back then, nor the thick air, nor the unsmiling faces, nor the shuffling, tutting huddles at ticket barriers and esca-lators. Back then the singularity of his consciousness in the mass of humanity had seemed not solitude but a liberating anonymity. Back then it was all motion, and trundling back into town on the train each evening he'd feel his pulse quicken to the pace of the city, feel himself coming to life.

Back then he could derive an entire evening's entertainment from just walking about the streets, watching people, sinking him-self into their sheer number. His favourite route had been to walk up over Waterloo Bridge, taking in views bloated with landmarks, and on to Covent Garden and Soho. Some nights he'd meet an acquaintance for dinner; others he'd go to a gay bar by himself and sit with his drink in the half-hope that someone might strike up a conversation. Often, in the first few months at least, that somewhere was the Duke of Gloucester, just in case Ryan Griffiths walked in. And while that particular fantasy soon dwindled, the twilight of his youthful romanticism outlasted it by a couple of years, and when someone did strike up a conversation, when Jon was pleased to reciprocate, it was always with Ryan's words in the back of his mind: 'It's no accident who we meet. We meet people for a reason.' After all, things that lasted had to begin, and why not now? Why not *here*?

He'd learned the hard way what it meant that *here* was a place where things did not stand still, where nothing and no one settled, where the mere possibility of change was enough to make moving on a necessity. Nothing lasted – and with time, it seemed, fewer things began as well. Tiring of the bars, and jaded by the walk, he found himself spending more time on dating apps, looking to start something there. Except, with so many of the dates being so unsatisfactory, and those that were satisfactory rarely staying the course beyond two or three more dates, and work being so demanding, and so much else to do – with everything taken into account, it was often easier to skip straight to the sex, and before long his app allegiances had shifted from dating to hook-ups. Until now, though people still thronged the streets and he still had people he could have gone for dinner or a drink with, there wasn't much need to go walking at all: he could now derive an evening's entertainment from lying on his bed with his phone in his hand and finding someone to come round. Or sometimes even that seemed too much effort, and he'd watch a movie on his laptop instead.

It wasn't that he'd moved to London so he could have more sex. There was so much else, so much else. When a man is tired of London... But sometimes the city did tire him. It tired him to the bone, and there were days when he fancied nothing more than a stroll in St James Park, where the waterbirds waddled to their own slower pace and the sound of the traffic along the Mall and Constitution Hill could almost be ignored.

It was St James's Park he opted for this morning. He'd walked briskly – these days the classic view of Big Ben and the Palace of Westminster failed to lift his eyes or slow his pace, except in so far as, even so early, knots of photo-seeking tourists entangled his route across the bridge – and made the park just after 9.45 a.m. – enough time, he reckoned, to loop over the bridge, buy cappuccino and Viennoiserie from the swanky café on the far side of the lake, then cut through Horse Guards and back down Whitehall. A few moments of whimsical serenity amidst the more fanciful bequests of history: the palace, the pelicans, the winding pathways and mounted sentries – a pocket fairy-tale kingdom at the heart of the ruthless, grinding metropolis.

He was getting nowhere with joining those dots. However sure he might feel of the soundness of the approach, Peachey had pinpointed an obvious problem with it in its current form: who were these terrible people who'd been suppressing stories about Annie for all these years? While the walk in had helped him shake off the fug of sleep and clear his mind before the meeting, it had furnished no brilliant answers to that question. And now, strolling along the lakeside with squirrels and exotic ducks around him, his thoughts wandered off the question entirely and turned instead to Scott, whom he'd watched committed to flames only the day before.

However little they had had together, still it had not been nothing. Like all abandoned wrecks, their relationship had once been christened with champagne and cheering, had sported jaunty pennants and spread full sails to the pleasant breeze. It had not lasted, but it had at least begun – and might have lasted longer, perhaps, had Jon known then what he now knew. True, he'd failed to understand Scott, just as he'd failed to turn his dream of a cure for Scander's into reality. But no part of that past experience proved that he was incapable of either, or doomed to failure in the future.

He was just in the wrong place. Not moving, but stalled. A constant. He had let himself become the problem to be fixed.

9

Arriving on Whitehall with time still to spare Jon paused again just before he reached the Department of Health, perching himself on a corner of Viscount Slim's plinth. He would just give Peachey a quick call, he thought, to check how he was doing – but he'd barely got his phone out of his pocket when a voice from behind interrupted him: 'Dr Caldicot.'

It was Sir Andrew, the Knight Commander, on his way from the MoD to the same meeting. He was, as ever, immaculately turned out: his full, silver hair combed neatly back from his smooth temples; the tailoring of his lightly pinstriped suit showing off to best effect his lean figure; his yellow silk tie knotted tightly to his chin in a wide, symmetrical triangle – in a way that made Jon immediately conscious of the way his own top shirt button would assuredly be peeping out over a knot that, however hard he tried, was forever skewed to one side.

'Ah. Sir Andrew.' He leaped to his feet, putting the phone away again and holding out his hand to shake. 'I hear you're joining us.'

'Indeed. I was just on the way. Matthew not with you?'

'He's been delayed. Trains. I was just about to call him…'

'Please, go ahead.'

Jon pulled out his phone again and dialled Peachey. There was no reply.

'Hi, Matt,' said Jon to the voicemail. 'Just here with Sir Andrew and wondering what progress you're making. Let us know if you think you'll miss the start of the meeting.'

'Not to worry,' said Sir Andrew as Jon hung up. 'I'm sure we'll manage till he gets there. Are we all set, do you think?'

They walked the short distance to Richmond House together, and Jon found himself – without quite intending to – sharing with

Sir Andrew both his dissatisfaction with the plans put forwards by the PR consultancy and his own half-formed alternative approach.

'But that's not for today,' he added hurriedly – and as he did so felt his phone buzz in his pocket, as if the spirit of Peachey were pointing an accusatory finger at him. 'I shouldn't have mentioned it really. We haven't got enough detail yet...'

'No,' said Sir Andrew. 'An interesting suggestion though. If you could identify the "villains", as you put it.'

'Yes,' said Jon, pulling his phone out for a third time. 'Sorry, this might be Matt. Do you mind?'

It was indeed a text from Peachey: *There in 2. Keep kt cmdr happy.*

'Right. It looks like he's going to make it. Shall we go ahead and sign in?'

In fact, Peachey was with them before they'd reached the front of the queue at reception. Since he'd been driven almost to the door, there wasn't a good reason for him to be red-faced and out of breath – yet, somehow, he had conspired to be so, and his palm, when he gave Jon's hand a peremptory shake, was unpleasantly damp.

'Jon has been telling me about his proposed approach to going public,' said Sir Andrew, after the barest minimum of pleasantries.

'Has he?' said Peachey, narrowing his eyes at Jon.

'I said it wasn't for today...' began Jon, mortified. But, uncharacteristically, Sir Andrew interrupted. Time was short, and the grown-ups were talking.

'You should propose it. Sword will love it.'

'Right,' said Peachey, and somehow he managed to pack into the intonation of that one, solitary syllable his unhappiness with this proposal, his anger with Jon and, trumping both, his deference to Sir Andrew. 'It's not really thought through,' he added.

'The "villains",' said Sir Andrew, accompanying the quoted word with a widening of the eyes and sneering of the nose, as if he were himself acting a villain in a third-rate pantomime. 'That's easy. Who does a new government blame for everything? You've not heard it from me, mind.'

Peachey issued a troglodytic grunt of comprehension. 'And I should propose that too, you think?' he growled.

'Well,' said Sir Andrew. They'd reached the front of the queue at last, and he broke off to give his name to the receptionist. 'It might be coming on a little strong to propose it. Ministers do like ideas they think are their own.'

He broke off again to engage with the receptionist, and Peachey turned to scowl at Jon – who, feeling somewhat superfluous to this conversation, had edged behind them in the queue.

'You certainly know how to drop me in it,' he growled. But for all his grumbling, the twinkle in his eye suggested a man who was not, in fact, entirely unhappy with the situation he found himself in.

'Do you need me to do anything,' said Jon – the best he could think of in the circumstances.

Peachey snorted. 'Keep your mouth shut unless I ask you a direct question.'

There were already half a dozen people in the meeting room they were taken to by the junior civil servant who came to collect them. Apart from the two representatives of the MTLA and two senior civil servants from the Department – all well known to Jon, though the former barely acknowledged their arrival – there were two other people he'd not met before. He found out who they were – one from the Treasury, and one from something he'd never heard of before called the Policy Innovation Unit – when the Minister at last arrived, and the meeting was kicked off by one of the two departmental civil servants with the obligatory round of rapid-fire introductions. The Minister himself was accompanied by an intense-looking young man with wavy hair that formed odd lumps on his head – surely no older than Jon – who introduced himself as Nick Fitzgerald, the Minister's Special Advisor.

It was this young man, to Jon's surprise, who took the lead once the introductions were done with. 'We all know why we're here, I think, so can proceed pretty quickly to the business in hand. The Government's position with regard to assets is straightforward, and in light of that it is clear that the proposed therapy using' – he checked his papers and stumbled over the name – '*Aeisitos neuromethistes* should be progressed to human trials. The question we're addressing today is how public communication of these trials can best be managed, given the long-standing secrecy around this project, and the Minister is looking forward to hearing constructive contributions on this topic.'

The silence that followed this introduction, broken only by the rustles and creaks of people shifting in their seats, was potent. Out of the corner of his eye, Jon could see a sly grin spreading across Peachey's face, while, across the table, the two MTLA representatives had visibly stiffened, like woodland creatures startled by a snapped twig. This was not the meeting they had expected.

It was the more senior MTLA no-gnome who broke cover first. Placing his hands palm down on the table before him, he leaned forwards a fraction and addressed the special advisor directly: 'With respect, the decision about whether and when this therapy might be progressed is one to be made independently by the MTLA alone.'

Only now did Gilbert Sword enter the fray. 'As I understand it, your objections to progression have all been met... Nick, the—' He held out a hand to his spad who, pre-empting him, was already shuffling through a sheaf of papers and quickly located the copy of the two-pager Jon had prepared. 'Thank you. As I was saying' – he made a show of scanning the document through the lower half of his varifocals as he spoke – 'all of your objections have been met *apart from* the issue of public communication. Is that not right?'

The gnome folded his hands together, interlacing the fingers. 'This is *one* of the issues on which the MTLA requires more information before making a decision.'

'And the other issues?' said Sword.

'The other issues are... That is the issue on which we require more information at the moment, but it doesn't follow that there will not be further issues raised once this... issue has been addressed.'

'I see,' said Sword, adopting the tone of a disenchanted teacher explaining fractions to an especially stupid child. 'For the time being, however, we can perhaps focus on resolving the one issue that *has* been raised?'

The senior gnome hesitated – and this proved to be a fatal mistake. For at his side, the younger, more junior gnome had been pulling faces throughout this exchange and was now unable to restrain himself any more.

'It's not *our* job to resolve the issue. In fact it would be improper for us to do so.'

Another silence, this time complete. The face of the junior gnome, already slightly reddened with passion, now flushed redder; next to him the face of the senior gnome seemed to harden, as if it were no longer a face at all but a death mask.

'Is that right?' said Sword. There was not a hint of sarcasm or aggression in his voice: he might have been kissing a baby as he spoke. But it was plain to all that the gnomes had just been written off. 'I'm very sorry to have wasted your time then. I hadn't realised you wouldn't be able to contribute.' He glanced ostentatiously at his watch. 'Nick, back to you.'

And that was that for the MTLA – at least for the rest of that meeting. Technically, of course, nothing had changed: the decision remained one to be made by the independent body, free from political interference. But, asked after the meeting, anyone present for that short exchange would have confirmed their expectation that approval would soon be forthcoming, and that included the senior gnome, who sat unmoving through the rest of the meeting with the stately indifference of a horse beset by flies. Only the junior gnome might have quibbled, and who cared what he thought about anything any more? And Jon, for his part, found himself wondering how he'd let these people detain and derail him for so many months.

However, the rapid despatch of the MTLA did not mean that Arexis was in for an easy ride. With the meeting effectively closed to anything but the 'constructive contributions' sought by the Minister, Nick the spad now set about demonstrating exactly why the proposals Jon had submitted in advance did *not* amount to such a contribution. It was all done terribly politely, but with no less implicit derision for that. On and on he went, determined to demolish every last corner of the proposals and, in so doing, display every one of his critical muscles. Particularly painful for Jon was the repeated use of the phrase 'the proposals from Cobbett and Stone' – the PR consultancy – as if he were underlining the craven way Jon himself had used this phrase to avoid taking final responsibility for the ideas in his two-page summary.

'Obviously we don't have anyone from Cobbett and Stone here today,' he concluded, his earnest delivery offset by just a hint of nauseating self-satisfaction. 'However, perhaps the Arexis team will be able to help us out with some of the more important problems and risks I have identified?'

Jon shot a sideways glance at Peachey, happier than he could have imagined that he'd been told to keep his mouth shut. To his surprise, he saw that the sly grin had not left his boss's face; indeed, if anything it had set itself a little deeper into his fleshy cheeks.

'Thank you Mr Fitzherbert,' he began in a low growl. Had he got the spad's name wrong deliberately, wondered Jon. 'Yes, Dr Caldicot and I may be able to help you.' Again, could those contrasting appellations be intentional? 'But I'd like to do so in the context of the Minister's expectations of the limited time we have today. In particular, I want to make this a *constructive* contribution.' This time there could surely be no doubt: that carefully enunciated 'constructive', delivered directly to the spad, was slapping this puppy down for wasting so much time showing how clever he was.

'Minister,' continued Peachey without hesitating, addressing himself to Sword now, 'we are extremely grateful for your attention to this matter. I think what's most heartening for Jon and myself is your commitment to making this public. We're scientists at heart, not communications experts' – he articulated the word 'communications' as if it were a term of which he did not entirely approve – 'and over the years it's been dispiriting, if I may speak frankly, how your predecessors in this role have prevented us from talking to the British people about the amazing possibilities of this therapy. I mean, I'm no politician, but there were times when I wondered if someone had nobbled them. It made no sense to me. I mean, look here' – he held up the very Cobbett and Stone report which Nick Fitzgerald had just taken to pieces – 'the advantages. Now I take the points you made' – he gestured towards the spad – 'and maybe it is now a bit late. We are where we are. But really, you have to ask: why were we not allowed to talk about this sooner?'

Nick Fitzgerald, puffing up with wounded vanity, was already gathering breath for a response, but a raised finger on the Minister's hand arrested him. It was instead Sword who spoke: 'Why do *you* think you were not allowed to talk about this sooner?'

'I really couldn't say,' replied Peachey. 'You have to ask yourself who loses from a therapy like this. The drinks industry? They have pretty deep pockets, I suppose. But you'd have to ask your predecessor.'

'If I may, Minister?' interrupted one of the Department of Health civil servants – Helen Gerrard, a no-nonsense woman whom Jon had always rather liked. 'This is all very picturesque but… We've known each other for a long time now, Matt, and I can't think of one instance until now where you've either asked to go public or been explicitly prevented from doing so by anyone at this department.'

'Well of course you can't. I wouldn't have dared make an explicit request until now.'

Gerrard shook her head. 'This is preposterous.'

'Well I've said too much,' said Peachey, holding up his hands. 'All I'm saying is that I think the British public will be furious when they find out something so potentially beneficial has been hidden from them for so long. And I think they'll want to know who stopped us telling them earlier, and why.'

'Yes,' said Sword. 'I would like to know that too.'

'Exactly,' agreed Peachey enthusiastically. 'You're the one shedding light on all of this. That's why we're so grateful. I mean, I could introduce you to scientists who've given their whole working lives to creating this therapy. They're committed to helping ordinary, hard-working families, but they've been forced to keep it quiet.'

Again Gerrard interjected: 'Minister, I really must object. This is a fantasy. Nobody's forced any scientists to keep anything quiet.'

'So why *is* it secret?' asked Sword.

'Because…' spluttered Gerrard. 'It's a sensitive issue, and the judgement was made many years ago that confidentiality was… the most appropriate approach to its development.'

'It's secret because it's secret, you mean.'

'Minister, with all due respect…'

'Perhaps I can shed some light on this,' interrupted a voice: Sir Andrew, who, as was his wont, had been listening carefully to what everyone was saying but now intervened to tell them what they ought to have been saying. 'Minister, you may be aware that I have been associated with this project for longer than anyone in this room. Matthew is speaking… a little colourfully, and my colleague is I'm sure right to say that she knows of no instances when Arexis or its scientists have been explicitly prevented from going public. Not as a matter of public record at any rate. But I think it is appropriate to say that Arexis has not been *allowed* to go public until now. And the reasons for that are indeed interesting.'

There was a pause, as everyone waited for Sir Andrew to enlarge on those reasons. When he did not – indeed, showed no signs of saying anything else – the Minister prompted him: 'And are you going to tell us what those reasons are?'

Sir Andrew smiled pleasantly. 'No, I am not.'

Sword let out an airy snort of disbelief. 'You're not able to or you're not willing to?'

Sir Andrew's demeanour remained calm and smiling. 'I suggest that discussion at a ministerial level may be more appropriate on this point. Shall I have my minister's office contact your office to set something up?'

'Yes,' said Sword, widening his eyes. 'That would be… very helpful.' He gathered his papers together with irritation. 'I think we've probably got as far as we're going to today. Nick' – he turned to his spad – 'can I leave it to you to follow up with everyone?'

The meeting broke up in a bad-tempered sort of way, with a number of its participants, starting with the minister himself, stalking out of the room without making eye contact with the others. Jon, by contrast, found himself swiftly collared by the woman from the Policy Innovation Unit, who, it quickly emerged, had been invited by Nick Fitzgerald: the spad had given her a rapid overview of Annie's 'behaviour change potential', she explained, and she was now eager to talk about 'cross-governmental applications'. Jon listened for a while, not really understanding a word she was saying, then – conscious of Peachey's impatient thrumming on the table – fobbed her off with a business card, wondering as he did so whether Nick Fitzgerald had also made her sign the necessary non-disclosure agreement. This inviting of random outsiders was not at all how they'd done things in the past. Plus, the truth was, he had taken a strong dislike to the spad and his lumpy hair, and found this antipathy extending to his invitee.

Fortunately the woman was heading to another meeting at the Department, and so did not leave with them, which meant, since the other externals had already escaped, that Peachey and Jon found themselves in the lift back down to the ground floor with no one but the same junior civil servant who'd shown them up. His presence was enough, however, to prevent any proper conversation, so it wasn't until they'd got past reception and back out into the open that Peachey let rip: 'What the fuck was that?'

It was most unlike Peachey to swear. He seemed shaken, and his face had grown paler than Jon had ever seen it before.

'I don't think I really understood what was going on,' ventured Jon.

'A battle of big dicks,' grumbled Peachey. 'Who has the biggest. That's what that was all about.'

'I thought you did very well.'

'Did you?' said Peachey – intoning it not as a question but as an expression of scepticism.

'You know, considering…'

'Considering the pile of shit we'd submitted.'

Jon hesitated. He was finding Peachey unusually hard to read – almost as hard as he'd found the meeting itself. 'I'm sorry about that.'

'I didn't mean it like that,' said Peachey. 'I'm not angry with *you*.' He let out a heavy sigh. 'Come on, let's go and get a cup of coffee. To make up for our breakfast.'

They walked in silence across Westminster Bridge to the café where they'd been due to meet that morning. The exercise seemed to do Peachey good, because he was back to his usual self, red of face and gruff of voice, by the time they sat down. Inevitably, their conversation focused on a post-mortem of the meeting just ended, and an effort to piece together some sense of where they now stood.

'Did Sir Andrew have a view?' asked Jon.

Peachey snorted. 'The Knight Commander scarpered before I could so much as say goodbye to him. I've no idea what he was playing at. Speaking colourfully? I'll give him speaking colourfully.'

'And that stuff about ministers meeting. What was that about?'

'God knows. I'll try asking him, but I don't expect he'll tell me.'

By the time they'd finished their coffee they'd agreed on a few key points of analysis. The first was that they'd gained a decisive advantage in their long-running struggle with the MTLA – though Peachey was keen to point out that this was by no means a complete victory. The second was that, while the Cobbett and Stone plan had been comprehensively dismissed, very much in line with their own reservations about it, there were positive signs that the Minister had understood Peachey's insinuation of Jon's idea and was at least open to considering it – though this had come at the cost of considerable personal discomfort for Peachey, along with all sorts of potential ructions with the civil servants at the Department which they'd now have to smooth over. The third point was that Nick Fitzgerald was, in Peachey's words: 'a snotty-nosed little twerp with a slide rule for a brain, but clearly his word counts with the Minister, so you'll have to butter him up a bit.'

'So what next?' asked Jon as they were leaving to walk to the station.

'I'll call Helen and try to smooth things over with her after all those "preposterous" things I said. And I'll call the Knight Commander to see if I can find out what the hell he's playing at. And you… why don't you see if you can set something up with Nick Fitzgerald. Become his best friend.'

'Thank you, I'm sure.'

'Apart from that…' He shrugged, spreading out his huge bear-paw hands as he did so. 'At this level, it's all about the next crisis or whim. So we'll see what happens next.'

'So it wasn't really a make-or-break meeting,' said Jon, unable to resist the temptation.

Peachey gave him an askance look. 'We could have been broken,' he growled. 'And we weren't.'

The next day at work was uneventful. Jon saw Peachey for five minutes after lunch, long enough to hear that Helen Gerrard was still furious, and that Sir Andrew had not yet returned his calls. After the long crescendo of preparation, and the absurdist drama of the meeting itself, its aftermath was – inevitably perhaps – an anti-climax.

But the calm did not last for long. The following day, after lunch, reception called through to Jon's office to tell him they had Jenny Macready, science editor at *The Guardian*, on the line.

'Who?'

'Jenny Macready?' repeated the receptionist.

'What does she want?'

'She didn't say.'

'OK.' He was about to suggest the call was put through, then hesitated. It wasn't normal for journalists to be calling Arexis, and certainly not equipped with Jon's name. 'Hold on a second, did she specifically ask for me?'

'Yes.'

'Tell her you can't get hold of me at the moment and take her details.'

Having fobbed off the call he dropped an e-mail to Peachey requesting guidance on what he should do. Twenty minutes later, Peachey himself was in his office, scowling and rubbing his chin.

'We need to act fast on this one. Have you reached out to Nick Fitzgerald yet?'

'No, I… Should I?'

'Call him.'

'Do you think…? I mean, we don't know it's actually a problem yet.'

'Call him anyway. I'm going to try the Knight Commander as well. If he answers the bloody phone. And well done for not taking the call. As you say, it may be nothing. But it looks pretty fishy to me.'

Jon didn't actually have a number for Nick Fitzgerald, only an e-mail address. But as Peachey was emphatic that he should try to call, he phoned the main Department of Health number and found himself put through to someone in the Minister's office.

'I can pass on a message,' drawled whoever it was that had picked up the phone, with the weary contempt of one who spends their days taking urgent and important messages that will end up unread or unresponded to.

'Just say: the press may be onto us. And give him my numbers.'

Brevity proved effective: Nick Fitzgerald returned Jon's call within the hour, firing off a series of questions to establish exactly what had happened – many of them suggesting a presumption that Jon might well turn out to be a complete idiot – and failing to acknowledge in any way that Jon might have done or be doing the right thing.

'How soon can you be in the Department?' demanded Fitzgerald.

Since it was already 4 p.m., Jon opened his diary for the next day. 'I can clear tomorrow morning pretty easily so... I could be with you first thing.'

'Today,' barked Fitzgerald. The arrogance of the man was breathtaking.

'I'm in Woking.'

'So how long does it take to get here?'

'I... guess I could be there by about five.'

'Five then. Clear your evening. And tell your people that if she calls again, they're to schedule a call with you for tomorrow.'

'You'd better get going then,' was Peachey's only comment when Jon relayed the conversation to him.

'And if I had plans for this evening?' queried Jon.

'Do you?'

'No, but...'

'Academic question then.'

So Jon, still bridling at the spad's high-handedness, set off, and an hour or so later was ushered into a meeting room at the Department of Health where Nick Fitzgerald and two other, older men were already locked in intense conversation.

'Ah, good,' said Fitzgerald as Jon entered. 'Jon Caldicot from Arexis,' he explained to the others, then, just as perfunctorily, introduced them to Jon: Mark Angel from the Department's own comms team, and Greg Lightfoot from Lightfoot Partners, another PR agency. 'So,' he continued, 'first things first. Did *you* leak it?'

Jon, who had only just sat down after shaking hands with the two new people, pulled back from the table, widening his eyes. A quick glance at the others, however, provided no evidence that this was a joke. 'Erm... no. I didn't.'

'Peachey?'

'You'd have to ask him. I wouldn't have thought so.'

'No. Well, you'll have to answer more questions when the enquiry proper takes place, of course, but let's move on.'

'Wait a minute. Do we know there's been a leak then?' While the possibility that Jenny Macready might have found something out had occurred to Jon almost as soon as he took the call from reception, he had not until now given even a moment's thought to the mechanism by which she might have done so.

Mark Angel, the comms guy, stepped in, striking a more conciliatory tone than Fitzgerald – though, in truth, it would have been hard to be less so. 'We're working on that basis. I'm afraid everyone who knew will be under suspicion.'

'Including him?' said Jon, pointing at Fitzgerald.

'Of course,' said Fitzgerald dismissively. 'Including the Minister. That's what "everyone" means.'

'We'll get to all that in due course,' continued Angel, as if neither Jon nor Fitzgerald had just spoken. 'If it were you then, obviously, it would be easier for everyone concerned, yourself in particular, if you told us now. Or if you had any other information you wanted to share at this point.'

'What kind of information.'

'Well, you know, any suspicions. Or anyone outside the... approved circles you might have said something to.'

'I hadn't realised I was coming here to be interrogated.'

Fitzgerald snorted contemptuously and started checking his phone.

'You're not,' said Mark Angel. 'As Nick said, the enquiry will come later. We just wanted to make sure you had an opportunity.'

'Right,' said Jon, still fuming. 'Well, there was some woman yesterday from the... Policy Unit? Policy Innovation Unit? I've no idea if she's signed anything.'

'She'll be investigated,' interrupted Fitzgerald impatiently. 'If we can move on... The purpose of this meeting is to plan a response and prepare you to put it into action. We're going to need you to behave like a grown-up on this one. Obviously, given your complete lack of experience in dealing with the media, that's quite a big risk we're taking. On the other hand, it's only a science editor, and the fact she's asked for you by name means parachuting someone else in too early would create its own risks. So we've provisionally come to the view that you should handle the first contact. Greg here can prepare you this evening, but if you think you're not up to it, or if you think you might have any trouble abiding by an agreed approach, then please say so and we'll consider the alternatives.'

'I'm up to it,' said Jon through gritted teeth. He had not realised it was possible to loathe another human being so completely.

'Good,' said Fitzgerald, picking up his smartphone and opening something on it. 'Greg, would you walk Dr Caldicot through the decision tree?'

The PR man, who had until now sat quietly with his eyes fixed on the table in front of him, now leaped to his feet and crossed to a flipchart on which had been scribbled a cascade of boxes full of indecipherable text linked by arrows. He got off to a bad start, from Jon's point of view, by asking if Jon knew what a decision tree was, then, when Jon confirmed that he did, set about over-explaining an entirely common-sense set of scenarios and responses, starting with the question 'Does JM ask about or allude to AN?' and explaining that, if she didn't, it was up to Jon how he responded. The interesting answers, however, all pointed to the bottom of the flipchart page, and when Lightfoot at last joined them there, he flipped the page to reveal another sheet of illegible scrawl, puffing slightly as he did so with the self-satisfaction of a sleuth revealing the murderer. Whereupon Jon found himself in the strange situation of having his own idea from earlier that week explained back to him, having passed through the filter of

Peachey's coded presentation, Fitzgerald's deciphering and, last but not least, Lightfoot's theft.

'I realise that right now this probably feels like a crisis to you,' explained the PR man, 'but, based on what's been explained to me about your current situation at Arexis, I think we can turn this into an opportunity. We just have to get on the front foot and make sure the story Jenny Macready gets is the one we want her to get.'

And that story? The story of how previous governments had prevented brilliant scientists from going public with discoveries that held out hope for thousands of people, hundreds of thousands, and would put Britain at the forefront of a medical revolution. Of how the current government had discovered this appalling situation and was now accelerating approvals for human trials through the system. Of how Gilbert Sword had taken a personal interest in the whole matter, listened to the scientists at last, and given them his unconditional support. In short, how a ministerial knight in shining armour had rescued a gaggle of scientific damsels from the dragon of the former administration.

Perhaps, thought Jon, he should have felt pleased that his approach had been embraced so wholeheartedly. It was just that, when he'd hit upon it, he'd envisaged it only as a way around the problem he and Peachey faced – and not as a tool of self-advancement for the likes of Fitzgerald.

'And if she asks me why the previous government prevented us from going public?' he asked, less impressed by his own idea than Lightfoot had clearly hoped.

'You have no idea,' said Fitzgerald, briefly looking up from his phone. 'You are completely apolitical in all this. That's critical. All you care about is the science. We'll deal with that side of things in due course.'

'We'll work through your key messages and responses this evening,' said Lightfoot. 'Don't worry, it's my job to make sure you're prepped for anything.'

It soon became apparent that prepping would involve a series of role-played scenarios, in which Lightfoot first took on the role of the journalist, then took to pieces and suggested improvements to Jon's untutored reactions to his questions. After about five minutes of this, Fitzgerald suggested he was no longer needed and left – at which point Mark Angel also made his excuses. Jon, it seemed, was expected to stay there for as long as it took – into the small hours if need be. Though with Fitzgerald gone, he at least felt his stress levels declining and was better able to listen to what turned out to be rather sensible suggestions from Lightfoot.

In fact, after about half an hour, he found himself starting to warm to the man. In part, perhaps, it was the contrast with the awful spad. But there was something about him as well: a charm, an eagerness, that made Jon want to be persuaded by him. It wasn't Lightfoot's fault he was there, he mused, and that decision tree… in his anger he'd perhaps been too quick to tar the man with a brush he'd brought for Fitzgerald. It wasn't all common sense, and even if it was, it was more convincing in Lightfoot's mouth.

'We can take a break when you get tired,' said Lightfoot after a particularly tricky set of test questions. 'It can be pretty exhausting this.'

'I'm fine,' said Jon. 'It's… good. Do you think it'll actually be this tough?'

'Not really. We're talking about a science editor here. But you know, there's a lot at stake so… it's worth prepping just in case.'

'Is this… normal?'

'How do you mean?'

'What we're doing. Is this… I mean, would you normally do all this?'

'Pretty normal, yes.' He narrowed his eyes slightly, as if trying to make out some detail in Jon's face. 'You'll be fine. Really you will.'

'You think?'

'Definitely. And don't let Nick Fitzgerald get to you either.'

'What do you mean?' said Jon, bridling slightly.

The corners of Lightfoot's mouth twitched upwards – not so much a smile as a gesture towards one. Actually, it now struck Jon, he had rather a kind face. 'Shall we get going again?'

'Sure.'

Lightfoot leaned over to study the scribbled notes in front of him, repositioning the top pages with his fingertips as he did so.

But just as he seemed about to start again with the questioning, he stopped, momentarily frozen, then sat back again and rested his hands palm down on the notes. 'Can I ask you something?'

'As you or in role?'

'As me. This fungus... I'd never heard of any of this until earlier today and, well, it's pretty incredible. In the original sense of the word, I mean. Hard to believe. Fantastic. And... Can it really do all this stuff? I mean, it replaces people's brains?'

'It replaces rats' central nervous systems,' Jon replied. 'So yes, their brains as well. We don't know about humans yet, but the assumption is that we'll see the same effects. But the point of stopping Annie at the synapse is precisely to ensure it's *not* the whole brain being replaced.'

'Annie?'

'That's what we call it. Saves time, I guess. You've not heard that before?'

'No. Everyone here seems to say *A.n.*'

'You can say that too. I suppose when you're working with her day-to-day the name makes a bit more sense.'

'Her?'

'Well, Annie, her. You know. Look, I do understand what you're saying about it all being... incredible. It's a long time ago, but I struggled in the same way when I was first told. And then, you know, you get used to it.'

'Sure,' said Lightfoot, dropping his eyes and knitting his brows as he did so. 'We just have to get seventy million people used to it, all at the same time.' He looked up again. 'And just explain to me... You see, I deal a lot with clients who have to get difficult news out, and often the real problem is something they should have done before and didn't, and while you can't go back and change that, it does sometimes help to know how they got into the situation they're in. So help me understand why this was kept secret in the first place.'

Jon hesitated, thrown by another recollection: years before, standing in that book-lined room in Hampstead before the withered figure of Anthony Cogan, wrestling with the same question and carefully avoiding the obvious answer.

He shook himself: he was, of course, still sitting in the windowless office in the Department of Health, with Greg Lightfoot waiting for him to say something.

'It's a good question. For someone like me it's… like a habit, I suppose. It's just how we do things. It's always been like that since I first started working on Annie. You know, I had to go through vetting and everything before they even told me about her. But… I think it was something to do with a… a kind of side effect. Well, no, that's not quite the right way to put it, but… Years ago, when the very first people were working on rats infected with Annie, there were cases of what's called violent sporogenesis. When Annie produced her spores, the rats basically tried to get their blood into any other living thing nearby, so they bit themselves till they bled, and then bit other rats – or even tried to bite researchers. I say there were cases: I mean, my understanding is that this was the norm at the beginning. Then it stopped. This is back in the seventies, so I really can't tell you exactly what happened. There's never been another case since – and the advances we've made since then mean that therapeutic uses would never lead to sporing anyway. But I think… I don't know. We'd have to ask someone who was there at the time.'

'Violent sporo…?' repeated Lightfoot, grabbing a pen as he did so.

'Violent sporogenesis.' Jon spelt the word out.

'Right,' said Lightfoot, finishing the word and dropping his pen. 'Brilliant. So basically you're telling me this fungus could turn people into flesh-eating zombies.'

'I'm not sure I'd put it quite like that.'

'Why the hell has no one mentioned this to me?'

'I think you're overreacting a bit. It's a theoretical issue and—'
He broke off, once again distracted by the shadow of that conversation with Cogan. 'Look, the therapies we're talking about here involve selective targeting of small areas of the brain. The engineered version of Annie we're using is incapable of sporing, just as it's incapable of spreading beyond the neurones initially infected. In fact the two are causally linked.'

'And I'm sure that's a perfectly good *theoretical* answer,' retorted Lightfoot, a tad sarcastically. 'But if I'm an editor looking to make something of this, then I might find flesh-eating zombies a lot more appealing.' He was clearly very put out by this new piece of information. 'I can't believe no one told me about this.'

'I'm sorry. It didn't cross my mind until now.'

'Not you. It's not your job to brief me. I'm sorry, I didn't mean to have a go at you. It's just… Look, we need to steer well clear of this for now, OK? Stick to the script.'

'And if she asks me about violent sporogenesis?'

'I don't know. I'll have to get back to you on that one. But the thing is, even if she doesn't, we're going to have to deal with this at some point. Once stuff starts coming out we won't be able to pick and choose. Is there anyone…? You said we'd have to ask someone who was there at the time. So who would that be?'

'There's… well…' There was really no avoiding where this was taking him. 'Here in the UK, Imogen Lazenby. My old boss up in Cambridge. Retired but… you know, still very… active.'

'Can we go and see her?'

Jon sighed. 'I'll drop her a line.'

10

The second call from Jenny Macready, the science editor at *The Guardian*, came as expected on the Friday morning. Jon, armed with Lightfoot's decision tree, got through it unscathed: not least because, as it turned out, Macready did not actually know very much – although, of course, she was unwilling to divulge who she'd learned even that little from. All she had was that Arexis was working on something interesting, potentially big, involving the engineering of a fungus – and that the outcome could affect what happened to the government's stake in the business.

'We could probably have hushed the whole thing up,' noted Lightfoot afterwards. 'If we'd not just happened to be looking for a way to go public, that is.' As it was, sticking to Lightfoot's script, Jon had done his bit to whet Macready's appetite. He would love to tell her more; they'd been wanting to go public for years, in fact; he personally thought it was long overdue and, with the new administration, the signs were looking positive at last – a breath of fresh air; a new spirit of openness – but he'd have to check with people at DH first all the same. He hoped she'd understand. He wasn't used to talking to journalists, and he wanted to do things right. If he could just make a few calls and get back to her.

A couple of hours later, he rang her back to ask if she'd be willing to meet him at the Department of Health the following week. 'They're happy to go ahead, but… well, like I said, I'm not really used to the whole press thing, so I'd be happier too if we could do it with someone else there.'

Macready, who had no idea how big a story was heading her way, agreed and a meeting was arranged for the following Wednesday.

In between Macready's call and his callback, Jon sent an e-mail to Professor Lazenby. It wasn't as if there had been no contact between them since he'd left the lab. A few times a year – though less often now she'd retired – there'd be some reason why they'd have to see each other: the Congress, a key meeting, even a social occasion like Maria's wedding. There was always an awkwardness about their encounters, but nothing to match the awfulness of his final days in the lab. Back then, like an animal caught in a flood clinging to anything that holds fast, Jon had clung to the belief that Lazenby had done him wrong, and Lazenby's clumsy attempts to persuade him to stay had parted around his high dudgeon like a river around a rock. Over time, though, even rocks are worn to silt. Jon had started a new life in a new world, where new things mattered – pipelines, portfolios, PowerPoint – and where Peachey wisely assigned him roles that kept his direct interaction with the Cambridge lab to a minimum. It was hard to keep reminding himself of the magnitude of Lazenby's transgressions – hard, indeed, to hold on to their reality – until at last he found himself wondering if she had in fact ever been so very unjust, and recalling his brief time in her lab not with anger but with the faintest pang of nostalgia for things he'd actually cared about. By now, all that remained of his rage, like the ash-tissue remnant of a flaming paper, was disinclination. He'd rather not engage with her at all, but he got through it when he had to, and the awkwardness of interacting with her decayed by half-lives.

He'd rather not have gone up to Cambridge this time either – especially not now, in the wake of Scott's funeral and the plumes of fertile thought it had stirred up. He even suggested as much to Peachey: mightn't Lightfoot manage better on his own? But Peachey was having none of it. 'Essential we're there.' Why it was essential was not clear to Jon, but there was no point arguing, and of course he'd get through it, like every other time.

And so, for the second week running, Jon started his Monday on the M11, driving up to Cambridge – this time in the passenger seat of Greg Lightfoot's car. It was a drab day: the sky dead-pigeon hued, the tarmac tones of the surroundings broken only by the blue blocks of motorway signs. Lightfoot spent the first part of the journey going back over ground they'd covered before: the questions about violent sporogenesis; the objectives for the meeting with Lazenby; confirmation of some key facts about her career and character. Sitting in the passenger seat, Jon ummed his assent as required, even as he flinched slightly as his attempt to describe his erstwhile boss was played back to him as adjectival bullets: dedicated, inflexible, hard to read. He'd not want to hear his own reduction at the hands of Lazenby: too quick to give up, perhaps; not a real scientist.

'I was wondering,' said Lightfoot as they passed the junction with the M25, 'the research into Annie – it started in the MoD, yes?'

'Yes. I think so. Porton Down.'

'And the MoD still fund you?'

'Partly.'

'What's that all about then?'

'I don't know really.' Another of those little cascades of memory washed through him, its spray throwing a momentary rainbow of sensations over the greyness: Jack Kapinsky's face as he talked to Jon about the past; the knot of dread in his stomach as he realised his error in infecting Cogan; the sudden but fleeting allure of revelation; the Plaza del Triunfo and the sharp shadows on the honey walls. 'I've been told that... well, to begin with, at Porton Down, what they were interested in was turning Annie into a weapon.'

'A weapon?'

'Yeah.'

'You mean... how? Based on the violent sporogenesis you mean?'

'I don't know, to be honest. I just know that to begin with... it was... Lazenby was the one who saw the therapeutic potential in Annie.'

'Hmm.'

'I mean, the Laws... You know about the Laws?'

'I know about the Laws.'

'Hayton's Laws. Except I was told that it wasn't really Sir Arthur Hayton who came up with them at all. It was Lazenby.'

'Right.' Lightfoot digested this for a second. 'So we're not just going to see someone who's old enough to remember violent sporogenesis? We're going to see the person who came up with the idea of mycotherapy?'

'Yes,' said Jon, wondering why he'd shared this. 'At least, that's what I was told. Years ago. It's not common knowledge. In fact... I think I wasn't supposed to repeat the story.'

'Who told you?'

'Jack Kapinsky. My old supervisor in the States. The guy who stopped Annie at the synapse. Same generation as Lazenby.' He paused. 'He died last year.'

'Right,' said Lightfoot again, glancing at Jon as he did so. 'I'm sorry to hear that.'

'He would have been good to talk to now.' How much better it would have been to talk to Jack. 'Great loss.'

'Hmm.' They drove a little further in silence. Lightfoot had perhaps picked up on the sadness in Jon's voice. Genuine, yet the flashes of memory did not come when bidden.

'I don't suppose you know...' began Lightfoot after a while, then broke off.

'What?'

'No, just... When Imogen Lazenby came up with the idea of using Annie therapeutically, I don't suppose you know how they reacted. The MoD, I mean.'

Jon hesitated. He'd told half the story now, and Jack was not around to tell him off for it. Besides which, it was Lightfoot asking, and hard not to give him what he wanted. 'I don't know about the MoD. But Sir Arthur Hayton... I was told he was very anti to begin with. Then he basically plagiarised her ideas and passed them off as his own.'

'Hmm.' Another pause as Lightfoot processed. 'It doesn't sound like Lazenby was the inflexible one, I have to say.'

'No.' He had a point. 'I guess she changed. Or...' He tailed off, unable to come up with another explanation.

If Lightfoot was again thinking through what he'd learned then it led to no further questions, and as the dull landscape slipped past them, Jon was left to his own erratic and fragmentary thoughts, following a trail of tangents from justificatory examples of Lazenby's rigidity to Jack again, in Seville; Jack's funeral; Scott's funeral; the meeting with Sword; the long e-mail from the woman at the Policy Innovation Unit he'd received on Friday and needed to respond to; three other e-mails that needed responses; not getting e-mails from Ryan Griffiths; Ryan, sitting in the pub with his pint, declaring they'd met for a reason; Kevin the lab assistant, also with a pint – he'd not thought about Kevin for years, not since he'd left Cambridge and, with it, the awkward aftermath of two stilted dates and a disastrous attempt at sex. Why had he done that? He'd not even fancied Kevin. And why – with everything that was going on – why was he thinking about Kevin now?

It was only as they were approaching the Cambridge exit that Lightfoot spoke again, interrupting Jon's unproductive reflections with the outcome of his own, more purposeful line of thought.

'Do you think we could persuade your professor to talk to Macready?'

'I don't know.' To Jon, things seemed complicated enough as they were, without getting Lazenby involved. 'Why?'

'Her story... I think it could help us.'

Jon frowned. 'You mean: would she let Macready write *about* her? I don't know about that. She's always struck me as, you know, quite a private person. The stuff I've told you today... so far as I know she's never told that to people herself. Jack knew because he was there. I'm not sure how well she'd react to us even knowing about it.'

'Hmm,' said Lightfoot. 'I guess we'll find out.'

Lazenby lived in a modest terraced house near the station: the kind of house that had been affordable to academics in the years before the city's boom. Despite their long association, Jon had never been there before, yet a shiver of familiarity passed through him as she let him and Lightfoot in, as if there were something of Lazenby in the air, prodding at his snoozing reptilian brain. It didn't help that the next thing she did was offer them a cup of tea; that she directed them to a low sofa while perching herself on a dining chair; that she brought her own tea in an oversized mug that was surely the same one she had carried round the lab.

'So,' she said, setting the mug down on the table. 'What's all this about?'

Age had made marked progress in her body in the last few years. The grey streaks in her hair – still pulled back tightly across her head – had fanned and merged; the fine skin of her cheeks had grown dusty with tiny wrinkles; and there was something about her movements that was no longer quite so fluid, as if somewhere in that intricate physical mechanism a tiny cog had lost a tooth. And as he sat there listening to Lightfoot's questions and Lazenby's answers, Jon found himself – incongruously – remembering the hollowed-out body of Anthony Cogan, strapped into his chair, that first day they'd met.

'I do remember the idea of some kind of military use being around in the early days,' Lazenby was saying, frowning slightly as she did so. She had picked up a pencil from somewhere but was not spinning it, just pressing it between fingertips and thumb. 'It was never really developed, I think. It was more that *A. n.* seemed like a potentially dangerous micro-organism, and in those days all potentially dangerous micro-organisms were seen as candidates for biological weapons. It wasn't until we noticed the copper aversion that any serious discussion of practical application began. Until then, from my perspective, *A. n.* was a curiosity. We weren't studying it with uses in mind.'

'And the secrecy,' said Lightfoot, 'how was that?'

Lazenby narrowed her eyes slightly. 'It was fine.'

'When you started working on the therapeutic uses, I mean...'

'Yes. It was fine.' She put the pencil down on a small table just to her right. 'Look, Mr Lightfoot, forgive me but... could you possibly explain what this is all about? Jon' – she nodded slightly towards him, without quite making eye contact – 'said in his e-mail that I could be of assistance, and I'm delighted to help in any way I can. But perhaps you could explain what it is you need from me?'

'Of course. Basically we're ready to go public with... *A. n.* do you say? Or Annie?'

'Either,' said Lazenby. She'd always preferred the abbreviation to the nickname.

'Right,' said Lightfoot. 'I've kind of got used to saying Annie now, so... We're ready to go public and I'm just trying to get all the facts straight.'

'I see. That's very... reassuring. I'm not sure there's anything I can tell you that Jon won't know.' Again the tilt of the head.

'Well, yes and no. Some of the history... I mean the things that happened back at the beginning.'

'Does any of that matter now?' asked Lazenby sceptically.

'It could do. It could matter a lot. It depends.'

'Depends on what?'

'On what happened. The story.'

Lazenby let out a little sigh. 'Well, you're the expert. It seems to me that good science should stand on its own merits, not on a story...'

'It should,' interrupted Lightfoot. 'But it won't.'

'Hmm,' said Lazenby, studying Lightfoot for a moment. Then she sat back in her chair, breathing out heavily as she did so. 'What do you need to know then?'

'Well, one thing I'm trying to understand is why Annie was kept secret.'

Lazenby had little to add to Jon's conjectures on this point. She'd been very young, she reminded Lightfoot, very junior, and not party to that kind of discussion. Very probably it was something to do with violent sporogenesis and the military interest. She was a scientist: he'd need to ask a general or a politician. 'Or Andrew Harper, maybe.'

'Yes,' said Lightfoot. 'We'll be speaking to him.' The Knight Commander had been proving very tricky to track down since the meeting with the Minister and had failed to respond to e-mails and calls from Lightfoot and Peachey alike. 'Tell me about violent sporogenesis.'

'What do you want to know?' said Lazenby, sitting forwards again.

'Anything really. We need to handle that part of the story carefully.'

'Yes,' said Lazenby. 'It was pretty disturbing to witness...'

'But it stopped.'

'Yes.'

'Just like that.'

'Yes.'

'Why?'

Lazenby let out a half-chuckle, picking up her pencil as she did so. 'If we knew that, it might have saved us decades of research.

But we don't. And I don't think we ever will. The key thing is not that it stopped, but that *we've* now stopped it. That's what the Laws were for: to get us to the point where we could say with certainty there was no risk.'

'Yes,' said Lightfoot, 'the Laws...'

'Which is where we are now. The Laws were the only way we were ever going to—' She broke off suddenly, frowning as she did so and staring at her knees. 'Well,' she continued – and for the first time in the whole interview looked directly at Jon – 'maybe not the only way.'

Before he could stop it, the puff of incredulity had escaped from Jon's nose and slightly open mouth. After all these years, was she really saying this? Hard on its heels, though, came a second emotion, something closer to embarrassment, and it was Jon's eyes that fell away first from their brief contact.

Lightfoot, who had noticed nothing, was already talking: 'That's another thing I wanted to ask about. The Laws. Hayton's Laws, yes? Except I understand that it was actually you who came up with them.'

Jon looked up to find Lazenby's eyes now firmly fixed on Lightfoot again. Her face, her whole frame indeed, had stiffened. She did not reply though.

'Is that right?' prompted Lightfoot.

'Who told you that?'

Lightfoot's eyes shot sideways towards Jon, and Lazenby's gaze followed them. He'd been well and truly dropped in it now.

'Jack told me,' he said, deciding in a flash that the only course of action open to him was candour. 'Years ago, at my first Congress. He told me that you were the one who came up with the idea, that Hayton rubbished it at first then presented it as his own.' Just as Lazenby had done to him. 'We call them Hayton's Laws, but really they were Lazenby's Laws all along.'

There had been no softening in Lazenby's features. 'Jack had no business telling you that,' she said quietly, calmly, but with an edge of something akin to menace.

'It's true then?' said Lightfoot.

'I don't see what it's got to do with anything.'

'Well,' replied Lightfoot, 'it seems to me that you've been treated pretty unfairly really.'

'Right,' said Lazenby, nodding slowly.

'And now we have an opportunity to set the record straight.'

'I see,' said Lazenby, and as she did so the slow nod switched to a slow shake. 'You don't get it, do you?'

'I'm sorry?'

'Science. How it works. How it should work. Maybe I have been treated unfairly. But it's not about me. It's not about you. It's not about Jon here.' She shot him a glance. 'There's enough big egos throwing their weight around already without my joining in, thank you. Self-aggrandisers. I care about science.'

There it was, thought Jon: what she'd always thought about him. Did she think he was incapable of caring about science too? Because he did care. Surely he cared. What he'd done – Scott, Cogan – surely it had not been just vanity that moved him.

'Of course,' Lightfoot was saying, his confident tone succumbing to the slightest perturbation, 'and that's exactly what we're trying to do as well. Support the science by making sure people really understand it.'

But he had miscalculated, offered a hook on which Lazenby refused to bite. He struggled gamely on but, as Jon could have told him, he'd already lost. Lazenby had him in her slippery grip now, reaching down from her moral high ground like a trout-tickler reaching from a riverbank. It was a good twenty minutes before they left again, but nothing further of consequence was achieved in that time. Lazenby would not be talking to any journalists about her creation of mycotherapy.

'We tried our best,' said Lightfoot as they walked back to the car. 'Shame.'

'Do you really think it would make a difference? If she were willing to talk to the papers, that is.'

'I think it could make all the difference. You can never tell with these things but... We need a good story, and the best stories always have heroes. If it's not your ex-boss then, in all honesty, I'm not sure who. Arexis? Too abstract. No one relates to an organisation. That Peachey guy? Forget it. Gilbert Sword? Knight in shining armour at a pinch. Our dramatis personae is pretty thin really. As things stand, we're kind of left with you.'

'Me?'

'Who else is there?'

'Hold on, no one has said anything about... I'll do the interview, as part of my job, but... It's not about me, OK?'

At some point he had stopped walking, and Lightfoot had swung round to face him.

'It has to be about someone.'

'It's about Annie.'

'Annie isn't a person. Not yet, at any rate.'

This was bullshit. For sure, Lightfoot was the expert: he probably knew what he was talking about. But this was bullshit. There was no way he was going to let himself be made the centre of this story. And have people digging into his past?

'There's no way I'm doing it. What's the story anyway?'

'Dogged young scientist fights the bureaucracy and sacrifices his own career in science to get a brilliant idea to market?'

Jon let out a scoffing half-laugh. This really beggared belief.

'What about if I persuade her to change her mind?'

'The professor?' said Lightfoot, raising his eyebrows. 'You think you could?'

'I—' began Jon but broke off. The suggestion had been a desperate one and, on reflection, ridiculous too. How exactly did he think he would do this?

'You didn't seem to make any effort just now.'

'You were doing all the talking.'

'I noticed.'

'I mean, I didn't think you wanted me to...'

Lightfoot let out a little sigh. 'What I *want* is to make my client happy. That means getting a story out that will help my client do what they want to do – which, as it happens, is what you want as well. Human trials. It's my view that your professor has the best story going for those purposes. So what I want is to persuade her to let us use it. I really don't care who does the talking.'

'Right,' said Jon. Maybe Lazenby's *was* the best story going. If the only other option was making it about himself, then certainly it was. 'Right,' he repeated. Lightfoot had had a point too, albeit one that had not chimed with Lazenby. It was an opportunity to set the record straight. 'So…' But he'd nothing to say, nothing to add. He'd kept silent because speaking would have been pointless.

'I can wait for you in the car,' said Lightfoot.

It seemed he really had no choice.

'Speak to her as a scientist,' added the PR man as he turned to go. 'She was right. I don't get it.'

Jon's return, mere minutes after his departure, took Lazenby by surprise.

'Ah. It's you again.'

'Yes. Could I come in for a minute?'

Lazenby had taken off the scrunchie that held her grey hair back, and in the living room a small pile of journals had made its way to the sofa, the top one open and face down on the page where her reading had been interrupted. 'Have a seat,' she said, gathering them up and placing them on the floor.

'Thank you.'

'No Mr Lightfoot this time,' said Lazenby, sitting herself in the chair she'd sat in before.

'No.' He had no idea what he was going to say.

'Has he sent you back to have another go at persuading me?'

'Yes.' There was no way he'd be able to keep up any kind of act, so no point even starting. 'I think that's exactly what's happened.'

Lazenby nodded. 'I've met the type before. Very persuasive.'

'It didn't seem to work on you.'

'No. I'm sure he's very good at his job, but—' She broke off, shaking her head at an invisible interlocutor. 'I've met the type before,' she repeated. 'Go on then. Tell me why I should say "yes" and talk to this journalist.'

'I'm not sure I know why you should. I can tell you what it would mean for… well, everything. I mean, everything we… you… well, the whole thing. Mycotherapy.'

'What it would mean for mycotherapy,' repeated Lazenby sceptically.

Despite his intentions, despite the prolonged talking-to he'd given himself as he walked back to her house, Jon bridled slightly. Boy, did she know how to press his buttons. 'Yes,' he said firmly. 'We're at an impasse. You know that. Unless we can unblock the human trials... I know it's not how you think things should be, but it's how they are all the same. We need to go public. And Lightfoot's view – and maybe I'm wrong, but I do think he knows what he's talking about – Lightfoot's view is that this is the way to do it. Your story. You could... you could save the whole project.'

Lazenby frowned and nodded. 'You're right,' she said, after a moment's thought.

Something told Jon she was not giving her consent.

'I don't think this is how things should be,' she continued. 'This is not some... celebrity talent show.' She spoke the words with contempt. 'It's not about people. It's about...' She caught herself and studied Jon's face – perhaps detecting in it his low-level irritation. 'I don't need to tell you this though, do I?'

'Not really,' said Jon, a little wearily. It was pointless: he already knew there was nothing he could do to get round her. Whatever he said, she'd make of it something that suited her own ends.

'So you understand,' Lazenby was saying. 'It may be how the world you inhabit is, but I'm not prepared to follow you into that world.'

Jon shook his head. Pointless.

Except, even as that judgement fell, a memory popped into his head, as if shaken loose by the slow sideways movements, and in such a way that the words were already forming on his lips by the time they were gathering shape in his mind: 'Call it a scientific pact with the devil, if you like. It's what we need to do to go any further.'

Lazenby reached for her pencil. 'From the way you say it, I get the feeling that is meant to mean something to me.'

'It's what you said to me. Years ago. When I first talked to you about engineering toxic spores. You said it wasn't in your hands, that we had to talk to Arexis, because that was our pact with the devil.'

'Right,' said Lazenby, tapping the pencil against her knee. 'I don't quite see the connection.'

'That it's never been just about the science. You've always had to compromise with the politics, the funding, the real world. Maybe it suited you then and doesn't suit you now. But it's the same compromise.'

Lazenby paused before responding, again studying Jon's face. When she did speak, it was not to reply to what he had just said. 'You're still angry with me.'

Jon's head sheared backwards, and his nose wrinkled upwards in disbelief. 'What? What's that got to do with anything?'

'You are though, aren't you?' insisted Lazenby. 'You're still angry. And I still don't really understand why.'

'No,' interrupted Jon, 'I'm not. I never—' But that would have been a lie. 'I can't see why it matters either way.'

'I totally agree,' said Lazenby. 'It shouldn't matter. Because – I'll say it again – it's not about me. And it's not about you either. We're not important.'

Jon snorted and rolled his eyes. It seemed to him that it had *always* been about Lazenby, however much she protested otherwise. But he had no inclination to argue. 'I'll tell you what, it *will* be about me if you don't agree to do this.'

'What do you mean?'

'Lightfoot reckons he needs a "hero"' – he added scare quotes around the word with his fingers – 'for his story. It's... I don't know. Human interest. He wanted it to be you. But he's told me that, if you won't do it, it has to be about me instead.'

'You?' said Lazenby. She carefully placed her pencil back on the table. 'You mean this journalist will write about you?'

'That's what he says. The best stories need heroes.'

'And you're the hero of this one?'

'If you say "no" then, yes, I'll be the hero.'

'In what way could this possibly be about *you*?'

Jon let out a half-laugh – not an especially amused one.

'I don't mean it like that,' continued Lazenby, growing a little flustered. 'It's just...' She broke off, turning her head slightly sideways and lifting both hands to smooth her hair across her scalp towards the nape of her neck, as if she were suddenly missing her scrunchie.

'I have no idea how it can be about me,' said Jon. 'For what it's worth.'

'And...' began Lazenby, dropping her hands again and looking back at him. She broke off, narrowing her eyes slightly as she peered at him. 'You don't want it to be?'

He didn't reply immediately but returned her scrutiny in equal measure. Of course that was what she'd have thought. 'That's how you've always seen me,' he said, unable to keep the bitter edge from his voice.

Lazenby frowned incomprehension.

'That I'm just trying to... That I'm just on some kind of ego trip.'

'What?' Lazenby seemed genuinely surprised by this comment. But he wasn't buying it.

'That's what you've always thought about me. Ever since I first came to see you about my... about the toxic spores idea.'

'I don't remember ever thinking that,' said Lazenby, firmly but without feeling. 'I remember being concerned about... well, your mental well-being.'

'Really?' said Jon, struggling to maintain a level, almost clinical tone. 'I don't believe you.'

'You don't believe I was concerned?'

'I don't believe you don't remember. I don't believe you've forgotten how you saw me. I don't believe you've stopped seeing me that way.'

'I'm sorry, but I don't really "see you"' – it was Lazenby's turn to scare quote words – 'in any way. I don't really know you that well. You were in the lab for less than a year, and... Six? Seven? What is it?'

'Six.'

'Six years ago. Exactly. So no, I don't think that about you. I don't really think about you at... I mean, I know it was a difficult time for you and that... well, I failed in my... pastoral... Well it's never been a strong suit for me. And I know you're still angry with me. But beyond that...'

As she spoke, Jon's head had resumed its slow sideways shake; his face flattened into a sneer of incredulity; his lips parted in anticipation of whatever futile retort would soon be bidden by his brain. He was all set to take another turn around the same vain loop – when, like the jolting wheel of a train that shakes its passengers awake, something slipped.

What if she were being sincere?

What is she had always been sincere, in her own inelegant way?

It was too much to process in one go, with Lazenby sitting there opposite him, waiting for his next move in their cross-purpose conversation. Even as the questions propagated through his thoughts, like fractures, so too echoed the creaking responses of a world view seeking to accommodate and persist: so many instances, so many examples, could he really imagine she had been sincere and open every single time?

It was too much to process but, all the same, he was awake now. Still sifting dream from fact; still wondering where he found himself, and why, but awake. Because it really had been one huge ego trip, hadn't it? The whole sorry episode with Scott, with Cogan. With Ryan. And it had *never* been Lazenby who had seen that truth. He had seen it himself, all along.

'Are you alright?' came Lazenby's voice.

He had, he now realised, lifted both hands to cover his face and was sitting like that with his head cradled. 'Sorry,' he said, dropping his hands again and pulling himself upright. He needed to say something...

Surely, though, there had been some kind of worthwhile motivation at the beginning. Perhaps by the time he sat by Scott in the bedroom, looking for a solution, it had already spontaneously brought forth the agents of its own corruption. Perhaps it had since been hollowed out by maggoty preoccupations. But if there had only been another him, covered over with muslin, was there not a chance he'd have done something good?

'I'm really sorry,' he repeated.

Lazenby indicated he should not worry with a small noise at the back of her nose and a slight raising of her fingertips, but she looked uncomfortable and did not speak.

'Can I ask you a question?'

'Of course,' said Lazenby, though with little enthusiasm.

'Why did you try to persuade me to stay?'

'In the lab, you mean?'

'Yes. In science.'

'Because you're good at it.'

'Good at what?'

Lazenby paused, her eyes turned down to her knees – perhaps considering what to say, perhaps weighing whether to continue with this conversation at all. Whichever it was, she eventually arrived at a conclusion and looked up.

'There's a great deal of art to experimental science,' she said. 'Getting an experiment to work is... well, there's a knack to it. You can't just set things up and read off the results. You have to... almost trick the world into behaving how you want it to. You have that knack.'

'Right.'

'I don't mean rigging the results, of course,' she added hastily. 'I mean all the things you have to do to get any results at all. Getting the experiment to work. Solving all the problems.'

'Yes, I... don't worry, I understand.'

'Not everyone has it. I've seen lots of people with brilliant minds, excellent grasp of the theory, fantastic hypotheses – but they just can't make the experiments work. That's what you're good at. And that's why I thought you should stay.'

Jon nodded. Whatever had passed between them in the past, he believed she was telling him the truth now.

'It's not enough though, is it?' he said, as much to himself as to her.

Lazenby shifted awkwardly in her chair but did not actually ask him to explain himself.

'If you're going to trick the world into behaving how you want it to,' he continued, 'then it matters what you want.'

'It always matters what you want,' said Lazenby, with the air of one who feels obliged to say *something*.

'I made a huge mistake leaving,' said Jon – and it felt so good to admit it at last, openly, to himself. 'I could have... I could have admitted I was wrong and... started again, from the beginning. You tried to warn me, and you were right. And Jack... I know Jack shouldn't have told me about Hayton and everything, but I think he was just trying to get me to see that... You know, he really admired you. That's why he told me the story. To get me to see that... well, to see that... The thing is, you believe in something, you always have, and you've worked for that, you've made things happen. And I... I admire that too.'

'Thank you,' said Lazenby. She was looking more uncomfortable than he had ever seen her, her fingers locked together in a wholly uncharacteristic position, her eyes fixed on the carpet in front of her. 'Look,' she said, glancing up for a second but unable to sustain eye contact, 'I don't feel like I'm equipped to deal with all of the... issues you're raising. In terms of starting again... I mean, with a view to your specific suggestion about engineering toxicity in spores, it seems to me you have the perfect opportunity to pick that up again – if you can get the human trials off the ground and gather some data on—'

She broke off – and suddenly, for no obvious reason, it was there again: the dark, curling smoke of suspicion, blackening his view of her even as it dulled his new-found clarity of perception. And as she belatedly wrapped up her sentence with the words 'the phenomenology of infection', he felt the drowsy lethargy in which he'd lived for so long overcoming him once more.

'Yes,' he said. The gestalt shift was complete: it was *now* that he was awake again, having slipped for a few minutes into some strange waking reverie. This was reality after all. 'You're right,' he continued, for the sake of saying something, remembering as he did so that he'd been sent here by Lightfoot with a clear purpose. 'Though, to be honest, I don't think the trials will be going ahead. Not if I'm the hero of Lightfoot's story.'

It was all bullshit: everything she said. All this pontificating about it not being about her, when her refusals kept her squarely at the centre of the picture. She'd never been sincere.

'You see,' he said, struggling to contain the edge that he knew was returning to his voice, 'that's the thing I suppose. All these years you've done everything you could to push things forwards, and now the thing you can do is this: share your story. I know it's profoundly unpleasant to you, and I know I'm arguing for self-serving reasons. But that's how things stand. And I just don't see why, after you've given your whole life to mycotherapy, why you'd stop now.'

'I'm retired,' said Lazenby weakly.

Jon gestured to the pile of journals on the floor next to him. 'You'll never retire.'

She sighed. 'You trust Lightfoot.'

'Not really. But I think he knows what he's talking about. So on this, yes, I trust him.'

When Lightfoot asked him, back at the car, how he'd managed to change her mind, he found himself unable to answer and really not caring about it. He'd officially had enough.

11

Annie was front-page news in that Saturday's *Guardian*, the prospect of a move to human trials not just a world-beating breakthrough for British science but also a personal triumph for pioneering scientist Imogen Lazenby. It was she who took centre stage in a two-page spread inside the paper, a photo of her looking unusually relaxed beside the headline: *The woman they tried to silence*. 'I don't do heroes,' began Macready's account of their interview, 'but if I did, I think my hero would be someone like Imogen Lazenby...'

Not Jon's though. Sincere or false, he was through with thinking about her. Through with her and the lot of them, gate-crashing his invitation-only life: Scott, Cogan, Ryan. Except the mere fact he told himself so was proof that, six years on, he was not. Six years on he was all stirred up again, the memories swirling like flakes in a snow globe.

And what was he to think about if not the past? The future? What promise did his future hold? Once, yes, he'd believed in his vocation; just as once he'd believed in love. But that was the past again: always the past.

Turning from past and future alike, he tried to bury himself in the present. He was kept busy enough by the unfolding drama around him. Lightfoot kept up a constant stream of queries as the story spread from *The Guardian* to other papers, other media, other countries. The MTLA, who had maintained a stony silence straight after the meeting with the Minister, reacted to the *Guardian* story with a welter of new concerns and issues, all of which landed on Jon's desk. And then there was the woman from the Policy Innovation Unit, who'd redoubled her badgering since the news story broke, until at last it became clear the easiest way of shutting her up would be to agree to a meeting.

'They're very close to the PM, you know,' said Peachey when he heard about it. 'Worth going to see her. Stay close.'

'Sure,' said Jon. Whatever, he thought.

'And what about these news stories? You need to be more active in all this. There's hardly anything being said about Arexis as things stand. It's Lazenby, Lazenby, Lazenby. Anyone would think she'd done it all single-handed.'

Jon said nothing. He was quite happy with his role in the shadows, leaving Lazenby to do the interviews, the shows, the shoots – with Gilbert Sword lapping up any spare credit as a cat laps up spilled milk. He couldn't see why it mattered to Arexis either: if they got their human trials at the end of it, and kept the funding flowing, then they had what they wanted, didn't they?

'Besides,' grumbled Peachey, 'I'd have thought you'd have wanted to be a bit more out there too. This whole approach was your idea, after all.'

Was that what Peachey too thought would motivate him? Was that what they all thought? He didn't remind Peachey of his previous big idea, long since patented, spiked and – in the shape of Cogan – committed to the flames. What Lazenby had said was true: with human trials finally on the brink of starting, now would have been the perfect moment for Jon to push for the idea to be resurrected. But that was the past. Always the past.

Fortunately Peachey too was preoccupied and switched without prompting to another topic. 'Sir Andrew is still on the war path.' The *Guardian* article had brought about a sea change in Peachey's political world. On the one hand, the civil servants at the Department of Health, who had left the meeting with Sword fearing that they were about to be made the fall guys, were delighted to find that Lightfoot – also in their Department's pay – had deftly shifted the focus onto the machinations of the Ministry of Defence. On the other hand, and by the same token, Sir Andrew was furious. Peachey, in response, had switched overnight from trying to get a hold of the Knight Commander to doing his best to avoid him.

'Does it matter if he's upset?' asked Jon.

'It could do.'

Jon nodded. He left worrying about that to Peachey, the master manoeuvrer, just as he left the communications to Greg Lightfoot. And the science to Lazenby. And his thing? Solving problems. Making the experiments work. If only there were a problem left that he cared about.

But there wasn't. He'd officially had enough.

It was in this frame of mind that he arrived for his meeting with the woman at the Policy Innovation Unit. She had a name of course: either Rebecca or Rachel. For some reason though, however many times he checked her business card (and found out that it was Rachel), the moment he put the card down again he found himself uncertain which it had been – and whether he'd perhaps got the name wrong on the e-mail he'd finally sent to her suggesting he pop round to her offices in Westminster first thing one morning. Rachel or Rebecca: which was it and which had he written?

He was still wondering when he finally met her, though he'd spent the walk across from his flat repeating the word 'Rachel' under his breath.

'Thank you for coming in,' she enthused. 'Did they offer you coffee?'

They had, and Jon had declined but now had second thoughts. 'Yes, but…' He'd spotted a fancy machine in the plush reception area. 'Could I have a double espresso, please?'

R ushered him to a smoked glass box labelled Meeting Room C and headed off in search of his coffee, leaving him to stare at the blank, semi-translucent walls and round wooden table with, at its centre, the obligatory medusa's head of cables and spider phone.

He had no idea why he was here. But then, he had little sense of why he was in any part of his life right now. The wheels kept turning, carrying him nowhere, and he just had to find a way to get off.

'Here you go,' said R, returning with an over-engineered thimble full of black liquid. 'Thank you for making the time to come in,' she repeated, handing him the coffee.

'Not at all,' said Jon insincerely, lifting the cup and inhaling. It was very good coffee.

'So how much do you know about what we do here at the Unit?'

'Not much,' said Jon as, in his pocket, his phone started ringing. 'Sorry.' He pulled it out: a number he did not recognise. He switched the phone to silent and put it back in his pocket. 'Sorry. Not much at all I'm afraid.'

She launched into what was surely a standard spiel about the Policy Innovation Unit's role in driving the cross-departmental strategic deployment of new policy levers, along with a brief potted history of its origins within the Cabinet Office before being spun off as a private company. She was, Jon guessed, a little younger than him, perhaps still in her late twenties: a smart, personable woman, although there was also something about her that reminded him, incongruously, of Nick Fitzgerald, the spad. It was as if she had been coloured in by a child, and the waxy sheen of self-assurance strayed across the lines here and there into places it should not have been.

'My focus, as you know, is behaviour change,' she was explaining.

He did know that, it was true: it said *Director of Behaviour Change* on her business card. He didn't know what that meant though. 'Yes,' he said.

'Which is why Nick alerted me to the work you're doing.'

'Yes,' he repeated. 'Well, actually... sorry, it's not my field so... could you just talk me through that?'

'Talk you through what?' said R, narrowing her eyes a little as she did so.

'Why he alerted you.' A question shot across his mind as he spoke: had they interrogated her about the leak yet? He still didn't believe the spad would be investigated. 'We're not really used to having our work talked about like this.'

R nodded. 'Although I see that's now changing.'

'True,' said Jon. Maybe it *had* been her who'd leaked it.

'Fascinating story,' she continued. 'This Professor Lazenby must be an incredible woman. Really inspiring. Do you know her?'

'Yes, I know her.'

'Amazing. To stick to her guns against such... well, "stick to her guns", maybe that's not quite the right phrase in the context.'

Jon forced a smile. 'She's certainly… not one to give in easily. Coming back to your involvement though…'

'Yes,' said R. 'Well it's obvious, isn't it? I mean, what you're doing is behaviour change.'

'Is it? I think of it as a form of therapy.'

'Well, yes, therapy – I mean, the two overlap, don't they?' She paused, and though her face registered no change of expression, Jon could not help but feel that, in that brief moment, she was rapidly calculating whether he was actually worth talking to. 'Your Professor Lazenby, for example. Why did she start this whole thing in the first place?'

'I'm not sure I know her that well.'

'But her mother. I mean, it's in the papers. That's true, I assume? The alcoholism.'

'Yes, I… She had a personal… connection.'

'She wanted to change her mother's behaviour. That's what this is about. Behaviour change.'

'Well,' said Jon, 'when you put it that way…' His idea though, the toxic spores, that hadn't been about changing behaviour. That had been about saving lives. And that was what they were all doing, wasn't it?

'The thing is, Lazenby's mother died. I think that's what she wanted to prevent. Not her own mother, of course. Too late for that. But other people.'

'And the way to do that is by changing their behaviour,' said R, just a little impatiently. 'I don't think there's really a question about whether the current intervention qualifies as behaviour change. The thing I'm interested in is its broader application.'

'Right. To other addictive behaviours, you mean?'

'Ye-es,' said R, drawing the word out until it meant 'no'. 'Those and… Well, what *is* addiction, when you come down to it?'

'Wow,' said Jon. This was definitely not his field. 'That's a big question. I mean, you'd need to talk to the experts on this, but my understanding is that there's not a universally agreed definition. It's actually very hard to pin down.'

'Yes, yes,' said R, waving these technicalities aside with a slightly raised hand. 'But what *is* it, in its essence?'

Jon hesitated. Wasn't that the question he had just been responding to? 'That's what I'm saying,' he tried again. 'It's complicated.'

'I'm sure you can *make* it complicated,' said R. 'But in its essence it's... what? A disease of the will. A chronic inability to be who you want to be, to do what you want to do, to live how you want to live.'

Jon said nothing.

'And when you think about it like that,' she continued, 'well, who among us isn't a little bit addicted? We all have such good intentions but... we're lazy, irrational, stupid. I'm not being cynical here. I'm just stating the scientific facts.'

It struck him that this woman wouldn't recognise a 'scientific fact' if it walked up to her and slapped her in the face. But he just smiled and nodded.

'The thing is,' she was saying – she was on a roll now, into her script – 'all the really big policy problems facing modern Western governments – climate change, economic instability, obesity, physical inactivity, medicines overuse – what's the basic problem in every case? Human behaviour. Irrational, lazy human behaviour. If people just behaved differently, en masse, then most of the issues we face would disappear overnight, just like that. Human behaviour is the basic problem that government has to solve. But now look at the policy levers we have at our disposal. Back in the nineties, we still thought we could do it by changing people's minds: campaigns, information, incentives. And we did a lot of that – until eventually we realised just how lazy and irrational people really are. So then we tried nudging people, changing the context instead of changing minds. We rewrote the letters so they turned up to their appointments, redesigned the forms so they saved for a pension. And we did a lot of that too – until eventually we realised just how many contexts lay outside our control. So we started talking about networks and systems, and how everything affects everything else. And we talked about that a great deal, until eventually we came to the conclusion that it was all just too complicated. My colleagues won't thank me for saying any of this: they're all still passionate about this approach or that. But it seems to me we keep coming back to the same basic problem: lazy, irrational, stupid people. Human beings are weak-willed. They want to be better than they are, but they fail. Again and again and again. Weak-willed. And your fungus… Your fungus is willpower.'

As she spoke, another of those unbidden memories had swirled into view in Jon's head. This time it was Kapinsky, reminiscing about his visit to Sir Arthur Hayton's club, a world run from armchairs. Except it was as if he were himself remembering as Kapinsky: the smoked glass of their cubicle clearing to reveal dark wood and gloomy paintings; the spider phone morphing into a tray of small cakes; their chairs growing wings and high backs; and R herself sinking back into the worn upholstery with unrufflable self-satisfaction.

He couldn't fault her logic. Well, he didn't actually know enough about the topic to be able to tell whether she was talking bullshit. But it all *seemed* logical enough. And she'd set about the problem just as he would have done. She'd found her hidden constant: people. It wasn't the logic that was at fault.

But this world, this world of dark wood through smoked glass, this world in which he too had grown so at ease – at least, his hollow, soulless body had – this world, it was not right.

And what she was saying was absurd.

'Let me check I'm following you here,' he said, becoming aware as he started to speak that his breath had quickened and threatened to crack his voice at any moment. 'You're suggesting that – let's say I want to lose weight – I might use Annie to give myself an aversion to, say, complex carbs?'

'Why not?'

'Because… This is a major intervention. We're planning to use it for people who have a serious, life-threatening condition. People for whom every other therapy has failed. Even if they do live, their lives are destroyed.'

'Being overweight can kill you.'

'Yes, but… you don't rewire your brain just because you keep eating cakes.'

'Why not?'

'Because… because it's ridiculous.'

'Why? People take drugs to keep themselves healthy: they re-architect their own physiology. Doctors tell them to do it. And they re-architect their psychology all the time: self-help, coaching, CBT. What's the difference?'

Jon opened his mouth, but the words did not come. The logic again: he could not escape the logic while he was still in this world.

'OK,' he said weakly, 'so maybe in that case... But the other big issues you talked about? I mean, what are you proposing here? That we somehow engineer an aversion to using too many fossil fuels? Or to putting things in the wrong recycling bin? We're using a primitive aversion mechanism here. You do understand how that actually works?'

R, whatever her name was, nodded slowly, looking at him as a hotel guest might look at a concierge who is clearly just not going to understand. 'I've no wish to make light of the *technical* challenges,' she said, imbuing the word 'technical' with as much distaste as she could muster. 'I'm offering a *strategic* perspective on what is, undeniably, an entirely new policy tool.'

There was an awkward pause. It was obvious that the meeting had been a complete waste of time for both of them; moreover, that each knew as much about the other. But, like a blind date that is clearly going nowhere before the first round of drinks has been drunk, each felt the need to drag things out a little longer until an appropriate moment presented itself, and somehow they occupied a further ten minutes with discussion of the progress towards human trials and brief profiles of R's other projects.

'A disease of the will,' he muttered to himself contemptuously as he passed back out through the lobby. But the contempt bounced straight back on him: a chronic inability to be who you want to be, to do what you want to do, to live how you want to live. That just about summed him up, didn't it? Someone who managed to live by not living.

Life, wrote Edith Markham, is a far better teacher of philosophy than ever Socrates was. Like him, it brings us through absurdities and contradictions to a state of aporia, in which we admit not only that we do not know anything, but also that we do not really care any more. Yet that very stasis, paradoxically, is the pre-condition of movement. The future, paradoxically, is unlocked only by memory. To change, paradoxically, is to stay the same. And the paradox is life itself: because life always finds a way. It clings to the rock face. It stains the ice. It stirs in the ash, explodes from the desert and teems in the dark oceanic vents. It endures even in the vacuum of a human being who has given up.

Life finds a way, but it does not generate spontaneously. Francesco Redi despatched that idea with his jars of meat and pieces of muslin: *the earth, after having brought forth the first plants and animals at the beginning by order of the Supreme and Omnipotent Creator, has never produced any kinds of plants or animals, either perfect or imperfect; and everything which we know in past or present times that she has produced, came solely from the true seeds of the plants and animals themselves, which thus, through means of their own, preserve their species.* Seeds of the past. Always the past.

Out in the street Jon pulled out his phone to check the time. There was a voicemail from the call he had not taken, so he listened to it as he started walking.

'Hi. Jon. I'm not sure whether you'll remember me but this is Ryan Griffiths. I'm... I used to work for Tony Cogan. Look, I'm sorry to call you out of the blue like this, but I was hoping I could talk to you. I'll try you again. Or if you prefer you could call me back on this number. Either way. So... Hope to speak soon.'

12

Ryan's voicemail prompted two contradictory impulses in Jon: on the one hand, a visceral urge to phone back immediately; on the other, a more cerebral imperative to resist that first desire, to prove himself. Though that was absurd: prove himself to whom? Besides which, Ryan would have no way of detecting the desperate lack of interval between hearing and reply.

Yet resist he did, for long enough at least to fill his imagination with dough scraps of motive and knead them into every crevice of possibility. He held off during the walk to Waterloo and the train ride to Woking, working back and forth across the same unanswerable question: why had he called? He held off through a dragging day, though he did no real work to speak of: when he had to speak to colleagues it was with the minimum attention required to make their exchanges viable, and when they'd gone, and he sat again staring at his computer, it was with an eye before which the to-do lists and inboxes fell out of focus, to reveal like a magic eye puzzle his memories of Ryan Griffiths, fragmentary perhaps but still more three-dimensional than this flat life he had constructed for himself. He held off for the whole day and somehow made it home again: it was not the kind of call one would make on a platform, or on a train, or in the milling crowds outside Waterloo. But the moment he was through the door of his diving-bell apartment, he knew the game was up.

'Jon,' came Ryan's voice at the other end of the line. So he'd put Jon's number into his mobile. Maybe had it there all along. One of the two asymptotes towards which Jon's lines of thought had been tending, impossibly, was the crazy notion that Ryan was in love with him, had always been in love with him, had himself been resisting all these years, but – with the papers full of reminders – could resist no longer: they'd met for a reason, and Ryan had at last made sense of it. The other was that Ryan might be going to blackmail him.

'Ryan,' said Jon, wondering if his voice would hold. He needed to breathe. 'I got your message.'

'So you do remember me.'

'Of course I... How are you?'

'Very well. Listen, I can't really talk right now. I didn't want to miss your call but... can we arrange a time to meet up?'

'Sure.'

'Where are you these days?'

'London. Elephant and Castle.'

'Right, great. I can come to you then. When would suit you?'

Any time suited him. Right then suited him. 'Tomorrow evening?'

'Tomorrow evening is fantastic.'

'Do you want to grab a bite to eat?'

There was a fractional hesitation at the other end, and mentally Jon kicked himself. It was years since they'd met, and they'd met just a few times, albeit in circumstances that hot-housed intimacy and left Jon pinning dreams to the memory like posters of Old Masters to the walls of a student bedsit. Dinner was disproportionate to what had actually passed.

'Sure,' said Ryan. 'Why not?'

'Like a pizza or something. I'll be hungry after work. I get back late and—'

'Sure. Listen, I've really got to go now. Text me a place and I'll meet you there.'

'OK.'

'And thanks for calling back.'

'No problem. See you tomorrow.'

And that was that. Apart from the agonies of deciding where to suggest – somewhere sufficiently everyday and ordinary, as if he'd given it no thought, but which could at the same time afford them privacy, perhaps even an air of romance – apart from that, there was nothing for him to do but run over his speculations until they were worn into deep grooves, along which his fitful, half-sleeping thoughts continued to run long into the night.

Yet strangely, when he did sleep, it was not Ryan he dreamed of but Scott. They were back in his flat in Cambridge, eating dinner, except the food was burned to a blackened, inedible mess. 'I'm so sorry,' Scott kept saying. 'I don't know what happened. I'm so very sorry.'

'It's not a problem,' Jon tried to reassure him. He couldn't see why Scott was so upset. It bothered him. And when he woke, with a start, the agitation remained, knotted in his stomach.

By the time he sat waiting the next evening in the Lebanese restaurant he'd finally plumped for – an inspired choice, its melamine tables offset by the sensuality of the food – he'd at least begun to reconcile himself to the likely realities of the meeting. Ryan wasn't in love with him, and he didn't seem the type to blackmail either. He'd have his reasons for calling, but they'd be unexceptional, boring. Most likely, once they'd finished their baklava, they'd continue on their own glancing trajectories, unconnected.

And yet he could not shake the thought: we meet people for a reason. And if he could just work out that reason, perhaps there was still hope for him.

Ryan himself had not changed much. The shine of youth had passed from his cheeks, the angles of his jaw grown a little more pronounced, his figure swelled from slender to athletic, but his smile as he spotted Jon through the window from the street was as unaffected and disarming as ever, and his green eyes, shining beneath dark brows, still quickened Jon's pulse in a way no dose of reality could dampen.

They greeted each other warmly, as if they were old school friends who'd fallen out of touch – as if their last contact had not consisted of Jon writing ever more desperate e-mails and Ryan resolutely ignoring them.

'Great choice,' said Ryan, looking round the room as he took his seat. 'I love Lebanese.'

This was a relief.

'It's been ages,' he continued warmly. 'So much to catch up on. Let's order first or we'll never get to it.'

Jon suggested that they each select a few dishes, but Ryan insisted that everything looked good and that, given Jon knew the place, it would be better if he ordered what he knew was best. So Jon put in a meze order, finding now it actually came to it that he was in no particular hurry to ask why Ryan had got in touch with him.

'I hope that's enough,' he said, when the order had been made.

'I'm sure it will be,' said Ryan. 'So how are you?'

'I'm good, thanks, yes. You?'

Ryan nodded. 'I see things are moving forwards with… you know, all the stories in the press.'

'Yes.'

'Are you still involved in it?'

'I am, yes. I'm not in the lab any more. I work for the company behind it. Arexis. You may have seen the name if you've been reading the articles.'

'Yes,' said Ryan. 'I think so.'

'I'm guessing that's why you got in touch.'

'Hmm?'

'The articles in the paper.'

'Yes,' said Ryan, a little vaguely. 'So you're down in London now, then?'

'I live in London. The office is out in Woking. I reverse commute.'

'And… are you with anyone?'

Jon shook his head. Though part of him yearned to believe that this was the question Ryan most wanted to ask, it was clear that, with these trite enquiries, Ryan was merely circling around whatever he wanted to talk about.

'Too busy, I suppose?'

'Something like that.' The meze plates arrived, and it seemed a good opportunity to change the conversation. 'What about you? What have you been up to?'

'Oh, you know. This and that. I travelled for a bit and then… back here in the UK. I work in a care home now. Nothing much to report really.'

'And… are *you* with anyone?'

A slight, shy smile played across Ryan's lips. 'Yeah. I'm with someone.'

'That's great. More than I've achieved.'

'Well, you know.' He reached across to take a plate of hummus kawarma which had been placed next to Jon. 'It's luck really, isn't it? I love this stuff.' He scooped half of the smooth, fawn paste, studded with lamb and oozing oil, onto his plate. 'I'm sorry to contact you like this out of the blue. And I'm sorry I... you know, didn't respond. To your e-mails I mean.'

'It's all a long time ago,' said Jon factually, wondering as he said it how much difference that made. 'I mean, I should have respected your not wanting me to contact you as well.'

'Yeah but... the risks you'd taken – it wasn't very fair to you. I can see that now.'

Jon smiled wryly. If concern about risks had been his primary motivation in writing all those e-mails then maybe Ryan would have had a point. 'Well, let's not talk about it any more. You've responded now.'

'Yeah.'

'A bit late, but... you know...'

Ryan laughed.

'What did happen?' continued Jon. Since they were here at last, talking, he might as well find out how his one-time great project had perished.

'Oh,' said Ryan, reaching for the dolmas. 'Yeah, like I said really.' With a stuffed vine leaf transferred to his plate he scanned the rest of the table before taking up another plate. 'Heart failure.'

'But just like that? No connection to... you know, the infection.'

'No,' said Ryan, busying himself with more plates.

'And he was cremated. Without embalming. Like we agreed.'

'It was all... Everything was sorted.' There was now no space left for more food on Ryan's plate, and setting down the dish from which he'd just helped himself, he again made eye contact with Jon. 'I do want to ask you about something though. Not about... what happened at the end, but about the fungus.'

'Uh-huh.'

'You're sure it had never been in humans before?'

It was Jon's turn to reach for a plate and serve himself. This struck him as a very strange question. 'Yes. Absolutely. Why?'

'I just wondered, that's all.'

'Six years later you suddenly just wondered?'

Ryan frowned. 'No, OK, that was a stupid thing to say. The stuff in the papers and… I've been doing some reading.'

'Reading.'

'Yeah. I think I mentioned to you once before someone called Edith Markham? An anthropologist?'

'She spent time on Teobeka, yes? You told me one of the stories of the tribe that lived there.'

'That's right. So with all the news and… I don't know why really – anyway, I started rereading her book. She describes this ritual they had in the tribe when somebody died. The blood of the dead person was smeared on the faces of other people in the tribe. And it struck me, that could be a way for the spores to spread, yes?'

'I suppose so,' said Jon. 'In theory, at any rate.' Was this really why Ryan had got in touch? To share some far-fetched idea about the Teobe? 'I mean, the blood would have to get into another person through a cut or something.'

'Or through the eyes?'

'Well… OK, there are a lot of nerves in the cornea, and I suppose…'

'Because the blood goes in the eyes,' interrupted Ryan. 'That's a key part of the ritual.'

'Right. OK. Well then, technically yes, you may be right. The spores conceivably could spread that way. If the dead person were infected to begin with. But that doesn't mean they *were* infected. I mean, the spores could spread through blood transfusions too, but that doesn't mean blood donors are infected.'

'No, I know,' said Ryan a little impatiently. He seemed peculiarly animated about the whole topic. 'But if they were—'

'If they were then, yes, the spores could spread that way,' interrupted Jon. He was starting to feel a little irritated by the conversation – not one of the many emotions he'd anticipated feeling in this conversation. 'But they weren't. I mean, we'd know if this had been in humans before. How would you hide something like that?'

'You've kept the fungus a secret for years.'

'Yes but… OK, so it might not be common knowledge. But people who work in the field would know. I'd know. How could I not know?'

'I don't know. The same way the rest of us didn't know about the fungus, I guess.'

'Look, I'm sorry,' said Jon, putting down his fork and leaning back in his chair, 'but this is… ridiculous. It hasn't been in humans before, OK? Anyway, what difference does it make if it has?'

'Well that would be quite a big deal, wouldn't it?'

'Yes, it would, but… Sorry, this may come out wrong but what difference would it make to you?'

'What do you mean?' retorted Ryan, a little defensively.

The feeling of irritation was not passing. He'd prepared himself for Ryan failing to declare undying love, but he'd still expected something a bit more substantial than this. 'I'm trying to work out why you've got back in touch after all these years to describe some ritual you've read about in a book. I mean, I really don't mean to be rude but… why are we here?'

'Hmm,' said Ryan, folding his hands together and pressing the knuckles of his thumbs against pouting lips. 'Hmm,' he repeated. 'Well,' he said, lowering his hands to the table again, 'to be honest I haven't told you everything yet.'

'OK.' So there was more: he'd known there had to be.

'Markham took part in the ritual herself. And she describes what happened to her after it. Hallucinations, voices in her head, periods of paralysis. Weird stuff, lasting for a couple of weeks. That's the infection taking hold, yes?'

'It might be, I suppose. Or it might not—'

'There's something else,' continued Ryan, not letting him finish. 'I know years ago you said there were no side effects or anything, but… in the newspapers, this professor, she talked about, at the beginning, some kind of… behaviour issues in the rats?'

'Right,' said Jon. It was true: under Lightfoot's instruction, Lazenby had skirted around the details of violent sporogenesis, referring only in the vaguest terms to erratic behaviour in early test subjects. 'Yes, at the beginning there were some… issues.'

'What kind of issues?'

'Why are you asking?'

'Were they violent? Did they cut themselves up and then attack others?'

Jon froze. Nothing in Ryan's demeanour or tone suggested he knew the nerve he was hitting with this question. He could not know. How would he know? There had been no details in the papers. 'Why do you ask?'

Their eyes locked across the table. In Ryan's, he detected that same, contained passion that many years ago he had found so attractive. Only now he found it scared him too.

'Is that what happened?' persisted Ryan.

'No,' said Jon – then, unable to maintain the lie any longer, added: 'I mean, it hasn't happened for many years.'

Ryan stiffened. 'But it happened at the beginning.'

'Right at the beginning – in the seventies – there were some instances of... violent sporogenesis.'

'Violent what?'

'When Annie spored, the hosts engaged in violent behaviour. Well, self-harm first, as you say. And then harm to any other living creature nearby.'

Ryan closed his eyes and took a long deep breath.

'But it was years ago,' insisted Jon. 'Decades.'

Ryan opened his eyes again, but they were fixed on some far-off projection of his own thoughts. 'What have you done?' he whispered, possibly to Jon, though it wasn't clear.

'Did something happen? Before he died, I mean. Was... Did Mr Cogan become violent?'

Ryan's eyes snapped into focus, fixing Jon in an uncompromising stare. 'Why the fuck did you not tell us?'

'I...'

'We asked about side effects. I asked you directly. This is why the people you worked with resisted your idea, isn't it?'

'Partly...'

'What gave you the right?'

'I didn't think it was relevant. It was all so long ago and... just those first cases. An anomaly. Look, I know you're angry and you've every right but... what happened?'

'What do you mean?'

'Cogan. Something happened before he died, yes?'

For a moment, Ryan stared at Jon as if he did not understand what was being said. 'No,' he said at last. 'Nothing happened to Tony.'

'Then why did you ask about violent behaviour?'

Again, the long look of incomprehension. Only this time, when it ended, it seemed to take with it all the righteous anger. Suddenly, Ryan seemed almost business-like in his manner – even reaching for some flatbread and pressing it into his hummus. 'Because of what I've been reading,' he said. He took a bite of the flatbread.

It was Jon's turn not to understand. 'You mean… you read about the violent sporogenesis? Where?'

Ryan's appetite seemed to have returned as, although he still had food on his plate, he now reached for the kibbeh. Jon, for his part, had given up on eating.

'I read what happened to Edith Markham,' said Ryan, matter-of-factly. 'I'm guessing you didn't know about that either.'

'No. What happened to her?'

'She went mad. Got a kitchen knife, cut herself all over, then ran down the street stabbing other people and rubbing herself against them. And then there's the Teobe. The entire tribe was shipped to another island and, a couple of years later… well, we don't know exactly because the authorities kept it quiet, but it seems like the whole tribe went mad and… you know, violent whatever you called it.'

Jon said nothing. He had nothing to say. He was paralysed. If what Ryan was saying was true then… The pieces all fitted together, yes, but how could he not have known? How could something like that have been kept secret? It wasn't possible. And who *did* know?

Except he already knew one person who did. Professor Imogen Lazenby. Demanding evidence of the phenomenology of infection when she knew that evidence already existed. At the heart of all the layers of uncertainty, she was a liar: a liar and a cheat.

'Why did it stop?' asked Ryan suddenly, bringing Jon back to the room.

'Why did what stop?'

'The violent… You said that it happened ages ago and hasn't happened since. So why did it stop?'

'Nobody knows. At least…' Could he be confident of statements like that? 'I mean, if anybody does know, they've not told me. Most people now think it was some other factor – a secondary infection, or something in the environment. No one's been able to replicate the behaviour so… We don't know what caused it, and we don't know why it stopped. That's why so much effort has been invested in creating a version of Annie that doesn't spore at all, so there's no risk.'

'But the version you injected into Tony does spore.'

'Yes. But you said nothing happened, right?'

'Nothing's happened,' repeated Ryan.

'I feel like… I feel like there's something you're not telling me. I mean, I accept what I did was wrong, and if I'd known… I mean, if what you've told me tonight is true then that changes everything. I'd never have dismissed the risk if I'd known that… I'm not trying to make excuses. It was wrong of me anyway. And I understand why you're angry with me. And I'm sure… I'm sure you won't want to see me again after tonight. But if nothing happened—'

He broke off. He was starting to repeat himself. And he could not bear Ryan, whose smile and sparkling eyes could be so enchanting, regarding him with such coldness.

'I do want to see you again,' said Ryan suddenly – flatly, and without any warmth. 'But first I want you to do something for me. It's the least… I think you owe it to us.' He paused. 'Will you do that?'

'What do you want me to do?'

'I want you to find out why it stopped.'

Jon faltered. 'I don't know if I can.'

Ryan leaned forwards and, reaching out his right arm, grabbed Jon's wrist. 'You're a scientist,' he said, pushing his face forwards, as he might have done had he been about to kiss Jon. 'You find things out. I'm not. I can't. You have to do it.'

'Why?' said Jon, almost whispering. 'Why does it matter?'

They sat like that for a long moment, then Ryan released his grip and, in the same movement, stood up, his chair sliding back across the floor with an ugly, grating noise. 'I'm going now,' he said. 'I'll see you when you've found out.'

Then, without so much as a look back, he went, leaving Jon with a table of half-eaten meze plates.

Jon didn't sleep much that night. He spent the first few hours at his computer, trawling the internet for anything that might either – as he hoped – disprove or – as it turned out – lend credence to what Ryan had told him. When at last, well after 3 a.m., his eyelids drooped so low he could no longer focus on the screen, still his mind turned over, like an idling engine keeping weary residents awake and clouding their air. He must have drifted off at some point, because when his alarm went off it woke him, but he awoke from dreams that were hard to distinguish from twisted trains of thought, and lay for a good ten minutes unpicking the real from the fabricated.

Such was the pattern of the coming days. He did sleep each night, of course – but badly, and only after more hours of turning over facts and possibilities in an increasingly agitated search for connections, as if he were playing a convoluted game of Memory where none of the cards seemed to match. In the day, he hauled himself to work and did the least he could get away with to keep the plates spinning, devoting the rest of his time to his researches. In the evenings, he'd grab food on the way home and sit down again with his laptop, searching. Though there wasn't very much to be found: confirmation that Markham had committed suicide after going mad, but not enough detail to substantiate or disprove Ryan's account; confirmation that some kind of Teobe uprising had taken place on Madenu – that name rang a bell, though he could not remember why – but again, a lack of clarity about what had really happened. In the latter case, there had definitely been some kind of cover-up, though nuclear tests and colonial high-handedness provided more than enough of an explanation for that. In the former case, it was more that the events in question had happened long before the internet existed, and whatever records there were had never made it into the digital realm. The

240

brief Wikipedia entry on Markham, for example, cited an article in a contemporaneous *Cambridge Evening News* as a source for the claim that she had killed herself after she 'became violent and delusional', but the article itself was nowhere to be found.

He *was* able to order a second-hand copy of Markham's book, which he had delivered express to the office so he could be sure there was someone to sign for it. He jumped straight to a chapter on blood-sharing – to find that Ryan had already told him the most important things: the ritual smearing of blood, the importance of the eyes, the hallucinations and voices. Markham had embroidered her account with a mix of Teobe mythology and philosophical speculation, but picking through these to the basic facts it was clear enough that, yes, Annie could in theory have spread through this ritual and, yes, it was not impossible that Markham was giving an account of the phenomenology of infection. But there was no proof. And when he tried to read the rest of the book, he soon found himself mired in speculations on the nature of human existence.

It was ironic that Jon's new-found anxiety about Annie's past coincided with a near total lack of public concern at the revelation of her existence. It was early days of course, but the consensus was that, so far at least, Lightfoot's management of the news had been a resounding success. Focus groups showed that people were intrigued rather than panicked. There were noises in the press about Lazenby featuring on the next Honours List. The existence of 'behaviour issues' in the past had registered without causing alarm – though only because the details of violent sporogenesis had not been made public, and journalists, distracted by the story of Lazenby's fight against intransigent authorities, had so far failed to ask good questions about them.

And when they did? Lightfoot – whose queries to Jon continued, though less frequently – was sanguine. 'The story shapes the information, not the other way round,' he opined, and Jon had neither the knowledge nor inclination to argue otherwise. Though he couldn't help wondering: what if the mole who'd first broken the story chose to go to the press again? What if they decided to stir things up?

Because – among the many other conjectures now swirling about his head – Jon found himself returning again and again to the thought that it might have been Ryan who'd tipped off the journalist at *The Guardian*. It made no sense, of course. Why would he have done so? Why now? And why then follow up by getting in touch directly? But it might explain why Jenny Macready had asked for Jon by name when she first phoned, and with so many facts up for grabs, that slender thread of explanation kept the possibility alive in Jon's head.

Throughout, he wrestled with the constant desire to call Ryan again. Which he knew was ridiculous. Even before they'd met over meze, he'd worked hard to set aside the fantasy that Ryan might be about to reveal long-hidden love, and to the extent that he'd failed, Ryan's behaviour had amply disproved the hypothesis. And yet, despite all that, some childish part of him that insisted the world conform to its grasping little hands still declared with petulant self-confidence that this was what was really at stake. Ryan had said he wanted to see Jon again: he'd set a task, and tasks have rewards, and quests end with everyone happy ever after. Every rational fibre in Jon's body protested, yet still the infantile voice prattled on in its playpen.

The weekend passed, simultaneously indolent and exhausting, as Jon barely made it out of his flat but instead lounged around on his sofa, poorly slept, re-pursuing links he'd already read, hauling his eyes across the pages of Markham's book, and – when he could bear no more – watching hours of shit television.

On the Monday morning, back at Arexis, Peachey dropped into his office.

'Do you have a moment?'

'Sure,' he said, closing the browser window he had open on his computer, every tab of which related to Markham or Madenu.

It wasn't a large office, and Peachey, whose frame would have seemed lumbering in any context, lowered himself awkwardly into the other chair like a grown-up joining their child's toys at a tea party.

'How did it go with the Policy Innovation Unit?' They had not had a chance to catch up since Jon's meeting with the R-woman the previous week.

'OK. Well, a waste of time really. She had some... pretty mad ideas.'

'Hmm. Any idea why Rachel Bailey has written to me asking for a meeting?'

'Rachel Bailey? That's who I met.'

'That's what I thought.'

'So why is she writing to you now?'

Peachey shrugged, his elbows brushing the bookcase on one side of him and the wall on the other. 'That's what I was hoping you could tell me.'

'Incredible,' said Jon, more to himself than to Peachey. 'She had these crazy ideas about using Annie to tackle... I don't know. Pretty much anything. Like... obesity and things. I told her... well, I didn't actually say she was crazy, but she clearly was.'

'Hmm.' Peachey rubbed his fleshy palm across his fleshy chin. 'Could be useful though. I might meet with her.'

'As you wish,' said Jon. Peachey the politician, he thought, with more than a little contempt. What had *he* known all along and, politically, decided to keep to himself?

'Is everything alright with you?'

'It's fine,' said Jon. He'd been expecting this conversation – not quite so soon, perhaps, but his bare minimum performance had been bound to attract attention eventually.

'I feel like you've... not been entirely present of late.'

'I'm pretty tired. The last few weeks have been a bit full on.'

'If you need a few days off...'

There was no particular reason to doubt the sincerity of Peachey's concern. But Jon didn't trust the man any more; he didn't trust any of them.

'I'm fine,' he said. What *did* Peachey know? 'Actually, I have a question.'

A grunt sounded in Peachey's throat.

'Why did violent sporogenesis stop?'

Peachey took a moment before responding, studying Jon's face. 'You ask as if you thought I knew the answer.'

'Do you?'

'No.'

'Really?'

'Really,' said Peachey, his voice all rumbling undertones. 'You know I don't. None of us do. Why are you asking?'

'We're thinking about putting Annie inside people. It seems like a pretty important question to me.'

'We've been thinking about putting Annie inside people for years. As I recall, you once thought we should be putting a strain of Annie that wasn't even stopped at the synapse inside people. My question is why you are asking *now?*'

It wasn't so long ago that the animal quality of Peachey's voice, emanating from that hulking body, would have intimidated Jon. He'd have backed off, not wanting to cause trouble. Now it felt like a challenge.

'I've been doing some reading. Edith Markham.'

'Who put you onto Edith Markham?'

'No one. Personal interest. I was reading about Teobeka.'

'Personal interest,' repeated Peachey, before letting out a sigh. 'I somehow don't think I'm going to have the answers to any of your questions. Violent sporogenesis, Edith Markham, Teobeka – these were all before my time.'

'And no one ever told you? You never asked?'

'Told me what?' said Peachey, eyeing Jon with a wide frown, as a frog might eye a fly. 'Asked what?'

Jon let out an airy snort of contempt, shaking his head. Peachey the politician. 'You really don't know anything, do you?'

Peachey leaned forwards slightly, his shirt front crumpling along its many creases, his flesh pressing up against the folds. 'You've been in my office. You've seen the photo on my desk.'

Jon had. It was a photo of Peachey's three smiling daughters, none of whom remotely resembled him. Quite an old photo, taken when the eldest, who had started at university earlier that year, had still been on the brink of teenage, before mobile phones and make-up kicked in.

'It's there to remind me what matters in life,' continued Peachey. 'Why I do any of this. There are lots of interesting questions one could ask but, if they don't get you where you want to go, why ask them? They're not going to pay Alice's tuition fees. They're not going to buy Millie those shoes she's been pestering me about for weeks. They're not going to put a smile on anyone's face.'

'So you're telling me I should just... stop asking.'

'It's up to you, lad. But when I come in here, I don't see any photos anywhere. So when you start with all these questions about things that happened fifty years ago, I can't help wondering: why's he asking? Why now?'

'I told you,' said Jon, astonishing himself with his own calm – even though he knew Peachey didn't believe a word he was saying. 'I've been reading Markham. And... about what she did, at the end.'

'Hmm,' said Peachey, leaning back in his tiny chair. 'I think you *should* take a few days off, like I said. We've been running you ragged with all this press work.'

'I'll think about it...' began Jon, but Peachey interrupted: 'It's not a suggestion.'

There was a momentary pause, as Jon failed to form any further words or, indeed, facial expressions. Had Peachey really just said what he thought he'd said?

'Take some time off. Starting now. The rest will do you good.'

'Are you serious?'

Peachey was, and sat there watching as Jon angrily got his things together, intervening only to suggest – though doubtless this too was no suggestion – that he leave his laptop: 'Don't want you being pestered with e-mails and things. If you're going to take a break, take a break.'

'How long a break do you think I should take?' snapped back Jon, swinging his bag up onto his shoulder as a warrior might swing a mace.

'I'll call you next week and see how you're feeling.'

He left the building in a trance-like, cinematic state of disassociation: as if he were watching his own progress downstairs, past reception and out into the car park from a series of camera angles; as if he could hear the made-for-movie music that would accompany these shots; as if the best he might hope for was to identify with himself. What had just happened could not be believed. And what *had* just happened?

He was already on the platform and waiting for a train back to Waterloo by the time his consciousness, cut loose by its own incredulity, came slamming back into his body and reconnected with the undifferentiated mass of emotion therein with a jolt that left him nauseous. He was nearly sick, right there on the platform: and when the train came, he sat on it red-faced and sweating, feeling his stomach might revolt at any moment.

What had just happened?

He reached Waterloo a bit before 3 p.m. The weaving throng was thinner, less frantic than at rush hour, but its agitated dance did nothing to alleviate the inchoate, emetic sensations coursing through his body. It wasn't until he was in the dark hallway of his building that he felt able even to take a full breath, and reaching his flat, he flung himself on his bed without so much as taking off his shoes.

Had he just been fired? Suspended? For asking a question?

There could be no doubt now. What Ryan had told him was true – or if not true, then no worse than the truth. Perhaps Peachey really didn't know anything, but he *knew* there was something he didn't know, and to that extent was as complicit as anyone else in the... what? Conspiracy? He shook his head, feeling the soft resistance of the pillow beneath him. Was he really about to sign up to some lunatic conspiracy theory?

How else, though, could he explain what had happened. Even if Peachey had chosen not to ask questions, there would be others who knew the answers, and first among them Professor Imogen Lazenby, more manipulative and deceitful than he'd ever imagined. He'd only doubted it because Jack Kapinsky had so admired her, Jack whom he'd trusted – but Jack too must have known. How could he not have? He too had been there at the beginning, in Sir Arthur Hayton's lab. Hayton and – how had Jack described them? – the old guard, the people who knew people who could pull strings, running the world from their armchairs. Just the kind to hatch a plot. Although that account would have suited Jack too, got him off the hook. He couldn't trust what Jack had told him any more. He couldn't trust any of them.

So how the hell was he going to get an answer to Ryan's question?

And as that thought cut into his head, so his body involuntarily jerked in on itself and sent an empty, retching spasm up from his gut. 'Oh God,' he let out, as it passed. Then again, the heaving contraction this time propelling him from the bed and towards the bathroom, though nothing came up. He stood for a minute, bent over the sink, just in case. Then, with no further sign of revolt, he turned on the tap and splashed his face with cold water.

And as the coolness struck his hot face, so too one clear thought shone through the miasma. He was not being honest with himself. He never had been. It was his own lie, his own conspiracy of one, that had fretsawn his sleep to pieces those last few days. Yes, the possibility that Annie had once infected an entire tribe plus visiting anthropologist, that violent sporogenesis had occurred in all of them, that this had then been kept secret – all this was startling, disturbing. But it was not these possibilities that now commanded his enteric nervous system.

Why was Ryan so keen to have an answer? Something must have happened to Cogan. Not so, Ryan had insisted: Cogan had died with no symptoms, he said. But why, then, was he so exercised by Jon's admission? Why did he need to know how violent sporogenesis had been stopped? It simply did not add up. Something had happened to Cogan. Or… to Ryan. Something had happened to Ryan.

Swiftly wiping his face with a towel he returned to the main room of his flat and found his phone. Sitting on the end of the bed, he composed a text to Ryan: *It looks like you're right about everything. I need to know why this matters so much.*

He'd no real reason to expect an immediate response but waited nonetheless, turning the phone over in his hands and staring at the skirting board. And as he waited, he thought of Scott, and Scott's diagnosis, and his idea for how to fix things, and everything that had followed; and from that narrow walkway of choices, the manifold branching realities that might have been, and where they might have taken him, if only he had not done as he had.

Then the phone buzzed. Ryan.

Have you found out why it stopped?

He typed his answer: *No.*

A few seconds later, another response. *Call me when you have.*

He fell back onto the bed, letting the phone slip from his hand as he did so.

There was nothing else he could do then: he would have to ask Lazenby. For sure, she would not answer his questions, and even if she did, he would not trust her answers. But there was no other way. Jack was dead. Peachey knew nothing. Lazenby was the last link with the past.

Then suddenly he remembered where he had heard that name before – Madenu. Not Lazenby talking, but talking *to* Lazenby: 'Have you gone mad? Have you forgotten Madenu?'

'Georges Durand,' he whispered to himself. The man who had never signed up to Lazenby's mycotherapeutic dream. The man who had never been at Hayton's lab, but whose history stretched back – how far? To the beginning?

He sat up like a bolt.

It was time to move again. Better to try anything than carry on like this.

'Georges Durand,' he repeated, nodding to himself.

13

The next morning Jon was woken by his doorbell after the closest he'd had to a good night's sleep in over a week.

Galvanised by the idea of making contact with Georges Durand, he'd spent the rest of the evening working out how to make that happen. He knew the man slightly, having met him on a number of occasions since his first Congress in Seville, and was fairly sure he had contact details somewhere on his work laptop, but since he'd had to leave that in the office, this was of little help to him. He knew Durand had been a professor at UPMC in Paris, but since, like Lazenby, he was now retired, that didn't help him much either. After wasting a good hour looking for contact details online, he cut his losses and called Maria on her mobile.

'Listen,' he explained after the usual opening pleasantries, 'I'll get straight to the point.' He could hear the noises of Maria's family in the background. 'I need to get in touch with Georges Durand, and I wondered if you had up-to-date contact details anywhere in the lab.'

'Possibly,' said Maria, then added in a puzzled tone: 'Don't you have them?'

'Not personally.'

'But at Arexis. Surely you have them.'

'Yeah. I wanted to get them a bit sooner.'

'I won't be able to look until tomorrow.'

'I know. It's a bit... Look, could you just check for me? A phone number ideally. Or an e-mail.'

'Sure. I'll check. But... Is everything OK?'

'It's fine.' If only people would stop asking him that question. 'It's just...' Not for the first time in his life, he found himself wishing he could tell Maria more. 'Look, I can't really talk at the moment, I'm afraid.'

'OK.'

'If you could just check the details for Durand…'

'Don't worry, I'll do it. First thing tomorrow. I'm just worried about you, that's all.'

He hesitated: she had good reason. 'Well, don't be,' he said. 'I really appreciate it. This and everything you've done for me.' God alone knew what he'd done to deserve Maria. 'In fact… I'm not sure I ever said a proper thank you for all the support you gave me. You know, back when I was at the lab.'

'OK,' she said, 'now you're really freaking me out. You sound like you're saying goodbye or something.'

Jon laughed. 'Not at all.' Unless, in a way, he was. 'Just reminiscing. Sorry. Talk in the morning, yes?'

There had not been much more he could do that evening except check out the price of Eurostar tickets: no point booking one until he could be sure Georges Durand would be at the other end. But it felt like he at last had some kind of way forwards, and though when he went to bed he again lay awake for an hour or two before falling asleep, his thoughts were at least focused on a plan and the best ways of putting it into practice.

When the doorbell sounded, it roused him not from fretful dreams but from blissful unconsciousness. It was 9.30 a.m. He'd not bothered to set his alarm, having nothing particular to get up for and, in light of recent experience, no expectation of sleeping so late. For a moment he was not quite sure what had happened – just that he had been asleep and was now awake. Then the bell rang again, this time startling him from his bed and, in a single rapid movement, towards the entryphone.

'Hello?' he said, doing his best not to sound like someone who had just woken up.

'Jon Caldicot?' came a voice. It would be a delivery driver. He pressed the button to buzz the person in, then quickly threw on a dressing gown before heading out into the corridor to meet him.

It was not a delivery driver. It was Sir Andrew Harper.

'Ah,' he said, smiling slightly. 'I see I woke you up. So sorry.'

'No…' said Jon, too taken aback even to wonder what the Knight Commander was doing there. 'I was just…' he tailed off. 'I'm not at work today.'

'No,' said Sir Andrew. The peeling, poorly kept common parts of Jon's building looked shabbier than ever in his immaculate presence. 'Matthew Peachey told me. I was passing by on my way to the Ministry so thought I'd drop in. Seeing as, you know… I know where you live and all that.'

He smiled. It took Jon, still not entirely awake, a few moments to register what Sir Andrew had said. A joke? A threat? An infelicitous turn of phrase? This being Sir Andrew, only the last seemed unlikely.

'Right. Would you like a cup of coffee?'

Sir Andrew narrowed his eyes slightly, as if to underscore the absurdity of his passing any further into such accommodation. 'I noticed a nice little café sort of thing just across the street. How about you join me there as soon as you're dressed?'

Returning to his flat, Jon hastily threw on some clothes. So it was worse even than he'd thought. Asking questions about Annie's past hadn't just seen him suspended from his job: now Sir Andrew was paying him a visit in his flat. Talk about an overreaction. What next? Would they be bugging his phone? Sending someone in to search the flat? He was already in the hallway and locking the door behind him when the possible consequences of these crazy thoughts being true struck him. What if they really did search his flat? Now, while he was in the café?

He unlocked the door again and swiftly crossed to the chest of drawers on the far side of the room, opening the drawer in which he kept his underwear and rummaging at the back for the sealed jiffy bag that had lain there undisturbed ever since he'd moved in, and the contents of which had previously spent some months in his sock drawer back in Cambridge: nine unused vials of spores, still in their misnumbered plastic case. Glancing over his shoulder as he did so to check no goons had slipped into the flat behind him, he shoved the padded envelope to the bottom of his ruck-sack, swung the bag over his shoulder and left again.

He found Sir Andrew waiting, as promised, in the café oppo-site, a one-time greasy spoon that had been bought by a young man with an elaborate beard and refurbished with equal parts reverence and irony. Sir Andrew had taken a table in the corner and sat there groomed and tailored, sipping on a mug of tea beneath framed prints of antique horse-full streets, as if he were part of the décor.

'Awake?' he said, smiling, as Jon approached.

Jon took a seat without responding. As he did so, a waitress arrived with a take on a bacon sandwich, made with two slices of char-hatched toast and accompanied by a ramekin of brown sauce.

'Have something to eat,' suggested Sir Andrew.

'It's OK,' said Jon. 'Just a coffee please,' he said to the waitress. 'Double espresso.'

'You should eat breakfast,' said Sir Andrew, looking intently at his own as if checking it for imperfections. 'The most important meal of the day.' He took a knife, fork and paper napkin from the glass of cutlery that stood in the middle of the table, next to the cruets. 'It seems your idea has worked rather well. The press seem to be lapping it up. Perhaps not quite in the way we envisaged, but... Was it your idea to make the MoD the villain?'

'No,' said Jon. 'That was Greg Lightfoot.'

'Hmm,' said Sir Andrew, dipping the small square of sandwich he'd cut off in the brown sauce and popping it in his mouth. He chewed swiftly and swallowed, dabbing his lips with the paper napkin before continuing: 'Yes, I suspected as much. Very much a creature of DH. Can't blame him: that is his job.' He gave Jon a slightly severe look. 'You need to learn how to manage people like that.'

'I do?'

'You do. Although with hindsight I can see that I was expecting a little too much of you.'

Jon's coffee arrived – opportunely, as he was not quite sure what was going on. What did Sir Andrew mean, he had been expecting too much? Then, as he lifted his coffee to his mouth and its bitter aroma reached his nose, it suddenly hit him: 'You were the leak.'

Sir Andrew, who was busily chewing another neatly cut cube of toast and bacon, said nothing.

'I don't get it,' continued Jon, putting the cup back down, untouched. 'Why?'

Sir Andrew swallowed and dabbed his lips again, before taking another sip of tea. 'How long do you think it would have taken Gilbert Sword and that ridiculous pet monkey of his to do something? Sometimes we have to take firm action in the public interest, even if – as in this case – the consequences are not personally beneficial.'

Jon said nothing, instead taking his delayed drink of coffee. The tone of Sir Andrew's voice was that of a tutor, as if Jon had come down to the café to learn from him about the ways of the world.

'Anyway,' said the Knight Commander, 'I didn't come here to talk about all that.'

'No. I assumed you didn't.'

'I'm sorry Matthew rather... exceeded himself. He can be a little overzealous at times, as I'm sure you know.' The didactic tone was gone now, replaced by an intimacy of equals which Jon found no less disorientating. 'You have to remember that this is a very challenging time for him. He enjoys his little empire. Likes running things. And the lack of public attention was what made that possible for him. It insulated him from reality, carved out this little space for him to rule. And now that space has been blown wide open, thanks to your clever idea.'

'Are you saying he didn't want to go public?'

'No. Good Lord. He's a good fellow. He knew what his job was. But... The war of attrition quite suited him really. Of course, it was all an illusion. He never really had control of anything, and I imagine he knew as much. But so long as he was willing not to ask the kind of question you have started asking, he could carry on pretending to himself.'

'Right,' said Jon. His coffee, double as it was, was almost gone. 'I think I might order something to eat after all.'

'Be my guest,' said Sir Andrew, passing him the menu and waving the waitress over.

Jon ordered poached eggs and smashed avocado on artisan toast, along with another coffee. Now that Sir Andrew had at last mentioned the questions he'd been asking, he was expecting further discussion of this point, but the Knight Commander was busy with another morsel of bacon sandwich and did not appear in a hurry to take things further.

'So who *is* in control?' asked Jon at last.

Sir Andrew shook his head and swallowed. 'I suppose you think I am.'

'I really don't know.'

'When I was a young man – younger than you are now – I was fortunate enough to be taken under the wing of a very senior member of the service. A mentor, he would be called now: though now of course we'd be matched objectively by Human Resources and tracked with forms and indicators. Back then it was a friendly word, an invitation to dine at the club. And when I was singled out for attention, and by someone so… powerful, I thought: well, the sky is the limit. I could run a department, run the whole civil service.' He chuckled in a hollow, performative way.

'Yes,' he drawled. 'So, one evening, over dinner, my mentor, let's call him, asks me about my ambitions. So I told him: "I'd like to run something really big. Something that makes a real difference in the world." I'll never forget what he said to me. He began by applauding my desire to make a difference: that, he assured me, was the very essence of public service. Without that core conviction, I might as well go off and work in the City. But running things? "The world is getting too large for that. One doesn't run things any more: things run away with themselves." I've thought about that a great deal since. The world is getting too large. Of course, his wisdom is entirely lost on the modern civil service: these days it's *all* about running things, preferably without knowing the first thing about them. Maybe I'd have risen through the ranks if I'd stuck to my ambition. But I think I was right. And I think I've been happier. Things run away with themselves, and my role is… a shepherd. Or a sheepdog perhaps.' He laughed, as if he had made a tremendous joke. 'Of course,' he added, 'even a sheepdog needs to be a wolf sometimes. But what can we do?'

Jon did not reply. He had no idea what Sir Andrew was up to: was he being threatened now? Or mentored? Or something else?

He was starting to feel rather irritated by the whole conversation: after all, he was under no obligation to sit here and listen to Sir Andrew's reminiscences.

'You do know why Matt Peachey exceeded himself, as you put it?' he said, willing the man to show his hand and get on with it. 'What questions I was asking?'

'Of course,' said Sir Andrew – then stopped, as Jon's eggs had arrived. The artisan toast bore no obvious signs of exceptional craftsmanship, but they assured the waitress they were happy with their food and needed nothing else. Then, as soon as she was gone, Sir Andrew continued: 'You wanted to know about Edith Markham. He phoned me and told me the moment you'd left. He knew it was above his pay grade.'

'And you're… angry with me?' asked Jon, grinding pepper onto his eggs.

'Angry? Because you asked a question? We do live in a liberal democracy, you know.'

'Not angry then. But bothered.'

'Bothered?'

'That I found out. That I want to know. I don't know.'

'Hmm,' said Sir Andrew, setting down his cutlery neatly on either side of his plate. 'I see what you mean. I suppose I might be bothered. It partly depends on *why* you want to know. But I'm assuming that has something to do with an idea you had about six years ago. Rather a good idea.'

Jon, who was cutting into his eggs and toast, had to make a conscious effort not to slow or stop the movement. Where was this going? How much did the Knight Commander know? As he popped in a mouthful of egg, he dropped a hand and pulled his bag, which lay on the floor by the side of his chair, between his feet. In it, and in the corner of his own consciousness, the nine vials.

'You wanted to make a difference,' continued Sir Andrew, 'but you were told you had to wait. How could one possibly replace a person's entire brain with Annie without knowing what that would be like for them? Whether it would even *be* them, in fact? So you waited, and you worked, and you did your bit to fill in the gaps – even though your idea was no longer officially yours but now belonged to Arexis. You did what was in the public interest. And when it came to the final hurdle, actually telling the public, you came up with the idea that saved the day – and then let others take the credit for it. And then, when you were researching some question or other about Annie's history for Greg Lightfoot, you stumble on a book and, in that book, a detailed, first-hand account of what it is like to have your brain replaced by Annie. And you feel… well, what would I feel? Furious, I think. So furious I might not stop to think before asking my boss lots of questions I really should have been much more careful about. They lied to you, after all. The evidence of what it was like was already there, and they didn't tell you.' He picked up his cutlery again and started sawing another chunk off his slowly shrinking sandwich. 'Do I have it about right?'

Jon hesitated before answering. Sir Andrew had got one thing right: that he should have been much more careful about asking Peachey all those questions. And he needed to be careful now as well, because Sir Andrew had got it completely wrong, but he'd also been terribly clever about it. Too clever for his own good, in fact. He had handed Jon the perfect cover story.

'Yes,' he said slowly, frantically checking for any inconsistency that might later catch him out. 'You've got it about right.'

Sir Andrew nodded, the slightest flicker of a self-satisfied smile on his lips. 'To be honest with you, I'm astonished no one's asked questions about Markham before. She's been hiding in plain sight all these years. If you scientist types were just a little more curious about the world you live in…'

'I'm not sure I'm a scientist type.'

'No? Well, I suppose that leads me to the other thing that might possibly bother me a little. Which is what you intend to do next.'

For some reason, though he heard the words, Jon entirely failed to engage with what this last question actually meant and looked blankly at Sir Andrew.

'Now you know about Edith Markham. What do you intend to do?'

'Ah,' said Jon. The truth, of course, was that he wanted to see Ryan again. But that was not part of the cover story. Nor did he yet have an answer to the question Ryan had set him. And Sir Andrew was one of the few people around who might just have that answer... But he had to be cannier this time, make it seem like his focus was on the phenomenology of infection.

'Well, I'm not sure I do know about Edith Markham really,' he said, feeling his way. 'I mean, I'd like to know more.'

'And then?'

'And then...' Then Ryan. But canny, careful: 'It depends what happened. But I think we should be looking again at the idea.' He hesitated. 'My idea.' The pronoun felt strange in his mouth, insincere even, but he pressed on. 'I went to a funeral a couple of weeks ago. An ex of mine. He died of Scander's disease, a neuro-degenerative condition. And he shouldn't have died at all. None of this needed to happen.' As he spoke the last words, a ripple of the same nausea he had felt the day before washed through him, but he gritted his teeth and it passed. This was what he had to do now: lie. Lie to them. Lie about everything.

Sir Andrew was nodding, apparently satisfied. 'So what do you want to know?'

'What happened?'

'I'll tell you what I know. You have to remember that I didn't myself become involved until a year or so after Markham's death. What I understand, however, is that Markham had come back to Cambridge from Teobeka and there resumed the life of an academic. She acquired, I believe, a reputation as something of an eccentric, but nothing especially unusual in a don, especially not one who's spent the last decade on a remote Pacific atoll. She was also very active in the campaign to stop the planned nuclear test on Teobeka, and when the test went ahead, it seems to have tipped her over the edge. At least, that's how it was explained at the time. She took a carving knife, cut her own body horribly, then ran through Newnham village attacking passers-by at random until she was finally overpowered and restrained. A few days later she died in hospital and, partly because of the risk that she might be carrying some kind of tropical disease, an autopsy was ordered. It was during this that the pathologist noticed her brain was of a very peculiar texture, and that, under the microscope, it looked even stranger. By coincidence, this pathologist was a fellow of Gonville and Caius, the same college as Sir Arthur Hayton, and he'd recently attended a lecture by Sir Arthur at which slides of fungal hyphae had been shown. Noticing a resemblance, the pathologist asked Sir Arthur to take a look, and so Annie was discovered. Of course, it took a lot more work before anyone even began to realise what they were really looking at. The initial assumption was that the fungal infection was recent and had caused Markham's violent behaviour, not that it might have been there all along – and certainly not that it might in fact have taken over the normal functions of Markham's central nervous system. But from here on, I think you pretty much know the story. Just replace the shrew with Markham, really, and you have it.'

Jon had been thinking carefully as Sir Andrew spoke. If his motivations had indeed been as Sir Andrew hypothesised, what part of this story would most grab his attention? 'So, prior to the violent sporogenesis, Markham lived for some time with full substitution of her CNS with no noticeable symptoms, apart from being a bit eccentric.'

'It would seem so. It depends when she was infected really.'

'Well she got it from the Teobe presumably. Through blood-sharing.'

'One supposes so. Markham's book came out a year later, edited and published by a colleague. It took us by surprise: we'd no idea it even existed, otherwise we'd have stopped it. Although, as we've seen, no one read it anyway. However, yes, by the time it came out there was clear evidence of rats with one hundred per cent substitution and full functioning, so when we read the account of blood-sharing, we came to the same conclusions you have.'

'You were involved by this stage.'

'Yes. My mentor had suggested I take on what he described as a "small but unusual project" in Cambridge. My original job was to handle the quarantine cases.'

'Quarantine?'

'The people who Markheim had attacked. We managed to keep everything under wraps, but there was plenty of concern at the time. Remember, to begin with we'd no idea what this infection was, how it had started or how it had spread. It took Sir Arthur a good year to come up with the first version of a test for infection. During that period, we had to keep all those victims under a very close watch without raising too much alarm.'

'And none of them were infected.'

'None of them were infected. We were lucky.'

'But the Teobe. They were.'

'Yes. Though of course, not long after that things all went horribly wrong on Madenu. We shared the test with them, and they confirmed that infection was widespread among the Teobe. But I'm afraid I don't know much more than that. Our French colleagues chose not to divulge any details of what happened on the island. The little I know mostly comes from Georges Durand shouting at me at Congresses.'

'Georges Durand?'

'Yes. Well, you know what he's like. The grit in everyone's oyster.'

'But what does he know about it?'

'He was on Madenu. He conducted the tests. Seems to have been a rather traumatic experience for him, poor chap. Left him vehemently opposed to mycotherapy. It's another of those things that astonish me really: that he's never gone public and blown the whole thing. I suspect someone somewhere has been leaning on him all these years. It can be arranged, you know.'

Another threat? There was, it occurred to Jon, something rather impressive about Sir Andrew's ability to be both avuncular and menacing at the same time. Impressive but disorientating, and right now he had to keep on track, hold true to the lie he'd been handed. That also meant holding at bay the excited thoughts triggered by this new information about Georges Durand: if he'd been there on Madenu... But no, he could think about that later. His focus now had to be on whether his old, abandoned idea could be resurrected. That was the motive he had to project. Besides, it struck him that there might be a way through that to the question he really wanted to ask Sir Andrew.

'So the Teobe were infected,' he said firmly, going back to what should have been the thing that interested him. 'More evidence that human beings can thrive with one hundred per cent substitution. We have the phenomenology, we have the function, and with my idea we have the check on violent sporogenesis. All the pieces are there.'

'So it would seem.'

'Incredible,' said Jon, shaking his head as if angrily reflecting on the way these details had been hidden from him six years previously. Then, as if the thought had just occurred to him, he added: 'The thing I don't understand is... The Teobe lived peacefully for many years, yes? They caused no trouble when they first went to Madenu. Then suddenly all these outbursts of violent sporogenesis: Markham, the Teobe, the first rats. And then it all stopped again.'

'A mystery,' said Sir Andrew, widening his eyes slightly as he did so.

Jon hesitated: Sir Andrew had handed him his cover story, but did he actually believe it himself? Jon couldn't quite remember now, but he was fairly sure the first question he'd asked Peachey the day before was not about Markham at all: it was why violent sporogenesis had stopped. If Peachey had passed on that detail, Sir Andrew was far too clever not to have picked up on it. If Peachey had even *noticed* that detail, of course, which it was quite possible he hadn't. This game was proving very hard to play: too many possibilities, too many variables. And he was playing it against a grand master.

'One I suppose we'll never resolve,' he said, retreating. Better to change the subject quickly. 'Why did you keep it secret?'

'The human infections? I'd have thought that was pretty obvious. At first it was a military secret, but even when Sir Arthur had come up with the idea of mycotherapy, can you imagine the public reaction if they'd known?'

Lazenby, thought Jon, unaccountably rankled by this inaccuracy. It was Lazenby who had come up with mycotherapy. But he let the point pass. 'Yes, of course, but I don't mean the public. Why did you keep it secret from us? All the people working in the field.'

'Ah,' said Sir Andrew. He speared the last oblong of his bacon sandwich, dipped it in what was left of the sauce, and popped it in his mouth.

'We all knew about Annie,' continued Jon, since Sir Andrew was not now going to say anything until he had swallowed. 'We were all signed up to non-disclosure. So why not give us all the facts?'

Sir Andrew repeated the ritual dabbing of his lips with his paper napkin, then folded it neatly and placed it on his empty plate next to the carefully aligned knife and fork. 'I'm afraid that was my idea.'

'Right. And... why?'

Sir Andrew drained his mug of tea. 'We were at a point where it was clear we would need to establish a long-term research programme for Annie. That would mean bringing new people in. People like yourself. Or Matthew Peachey. And when you do that, you always increase the risks that someone will take it on themselves to go public. You know how it goes: it's in the public interest to know, even when it's manifestly in the public interest to be spared knowing for a little longer. My judgement was that stories about rampaging tribesmen or murderous dons with kitchen knives would greatly increase the risks of that happening. Moreover, it was my view – and Sir Arthur eventually agreed – that the knowledge of prior human infection had no bearing whatsoever on the research to be undertaken. I believe that remained true until you had your idea, some decades later. There were only a few people in the know at the time, here and in France, and the French authorities already had a strong incentive to keep the events on Madenu quiet. So... we came up with the shrew. And I never thought the shrew would live this long, but it has. Rest in peace, noble shrew.'

'Hmm,' said Jon. It was all plausible enough, though he doubted he'd ever be able entirely to trust anything Sir Andrew told him. 'It was Lazenby, by the way,' he added, finding himself unable to leave the record uncorrected. 'Not Hayton.'

'It was Lazenby what?'

'Who came up with the idea of mycotherapy.'

'Well,' said Sir Andrew dismissively, 'if you believe what you read in the papers.'

'You don't?'

'Sir Arthur Hayton was a great man, and also, I believe, a great teacher.'

'Jack Kapinsky told me that Hayton had basically plagiarised Lazenby's ideas.'

'Did he really?'

'He told me quite a lot actually,' said Jon, growing even more irritated.

'I'm sure he did. Always the talker, our Jack.' Sir Andrew lifted his hands and with elegant fingertips – the man surely had manicures – pushed his empty plate a few millimetres further away from him. 'May I give you a word of advice?'

Jon nodded, checking himself: careful, canny.

'Your anger is understandable, but… don't feed it. It will hurt no one but yourself. Professor Lazenby wronged you by keeping these things secret from you, but if things were as you believe, then she is also a model of how you might now behave. That woman has starved her anger for decades, and all for the greater good. Angry people do regrettable things. Shall we ask for the bill?'

Ending the conversation suited Jon, though he'd been so intent on it that he'd eaten only half his eggs on toast. 'I'll pay,' he said, waving a hand.

'I'll leave some money with you,' insisted Sir Andrew, taking a portfolio wallet from his coat pocket. 'We wouldn't want anyone accusing you of bribing me.'

'With a bacon sandwich?'

Sir Andrew smiled, placing a ten-pound note on the table and getting to his feet. 'I'm pleased we had the chance to talk. Let's find another opportunity soon.' He turned to leave – then, perhaps only just remembering or perhaps as a last little piece of theatre, stopped and turned back: 'Ah yes, and Matthew Peachey. You can assume he'll be expecting you back at work tomorrow.'

'OK,' said Jon, maintaining his own little act to the end. Because he wasn't going back to Arexis. He was going to Paris.

As concrete walls rose up either side of him and the train lowered itself into the tunnel, Jon felt a tingling sensation run through his body, spreading from his back around his sides and out into his limbs, not quite unfamiliar but so long unfelt that for a moment he did not recognise it.

The practicalities of the trip had been easy enough to arrange. Maria had a telephone number for him; Georges Durand picked up the phone and agreed to a meeting with barely any questions; there were plenty of seats on the Eurostar; and Peachey did not argue, though he sounded as if he might want to, when Jon phoned to say he needed a few more days to recover his composure. He'd even bought himself a new, pay-as-you-go mobile, just in case someone was tracking the numbers he dialled – though he realised that, if they'd gone further and bugged him, they'd already know pretty much what he was up to. Before setting out, he'd texted Ryan from the new phone: *Use this number from now on. Safer.*

Ryan had responded with a thumbs-up emoticon, but the brevity of the response had not troubled him. Because his mind was steadily clearing too. For all that those around him might be lying to him, they'd all had their own chip of truth to offer: he really did hurt no one but himself if he fed his anger; there were no pictures hanging in his office; and, in the final analysis, none of what was happening was about him anyway. He'd blundered into someone else's life story: Lazenby's, or Ryan's, or Annie's – it barely mattered. Free from the weighty duties of a protagonist, he could feel his body loosening its tight grip on his bones and opening itself once again to that long suppressed thrill.

Nothing had changed as such. He was still at a professional dead end and, once this trip was discovered, quite likely to be kicked out of the job he had. He still lived in an oppressive flat he should never have bought, frayed by the noise and light and toxic air. He was still alone. But hey: he was young, and healthy, and – compared to most humans who had ever existed – wealthy beyond measure. He was speeding through a tunnel to the City of Light. He'd have food on his table that night and a roof over his head. And he had a mission: to answer Ryan's question. He didn't know why, and he didn't know where it would take him. It would take him somewhere though. Nothing had changed, and yet, in a way, everything had.

And now, as they hurtled into the darkness, he felt it: the simple joy of being alive. For a moment, even the plastic curves of the seats seemed comely, the branded colours of the upholstery bright and jolly, and the passengers – talking and eating and sleeping and watching videos and working at laptops – even the passengers were, in that instant, brothers and sisters in creation.

It couldn't last, of course. They had not been long above ground again, in France, before he started to remember some of the things he still had to worry about: chief among them, the unresolved puzzle of why Ryan cared so much about his question in the first place. Plus he still had to give a bit more thought to how he was going to approach his meeting with Durand. And soon they would be in Paris too, and those concerns would in turn be overtaken by practical matters, like getting something to eat or finding the right Metro line. There was no firm foothold at the summit of his hierarchy of needs, but merely to have perched there for a little while, to have seen the high views, was enough to make life in the lowlands more liveable.

So his ecstasy in the tunnel could not last, but still he emerged later from the Metro with a spring in his step that the wind and rain waiting for him could not check. The cafés had rolled down their thick plastic tents, and here and there the heat lamps shone red through the blear of condensation and raindrops, but though he'd rather have been inside, his spirits held. Twice on his way to Durand's his umbrella blew inside out, and when he tried to check the map he'd scribbled on a piece of paper it flapped about unhelpfully and blotched with the wet. The gods had not chosen to match the weather to his new mood of hope, but it wasn't so far he had to walk, just a few minutes from the station exit. And he had a destination: that was what mattered.

He'd arrived pretty much on time, and Durand buzzed him through the main door of the building without even confirming it was him. Out of the rain he stood for a moment in the darkened hallway, his trousers wet from the knees down, wondering what he was meant to do now. Then a door creaked and a light went on somewhere above him, and Durand's voice shouted down to him: 'Up. Come up.'

There was an old-fashioned grille-gate lift at the end of the corridor, but, not knowing which floor he was aiming at anyway, Jon instead took the stairs, climbing three flights before he at last drew level with the light from Durand's apartment.

'Young legs,' said Durand, who was waiting for him in the open doorway. 'Something to drink? Tea?'

'Thank you.'

'Milk? Sugar?'

'Just milk please.'

He followed Durand into the cosy apartment and, as directed by his host, went on through to the living room at the end of the little hallway. It was a small room, painted white and dimly lit, with high ceilings and a tall narrow window at the far end. Carved wood featured prominently in the elegant furniture: a sideboard, a bookcase, and a tight circle of chairs and coffee tables arranged on a threadbare Persian rug which covered most of the woodblock floor. There was no television. Unsure where he should sit, he hovered instead by a table of framed photographs of what he assumed were Durand's family: wife, children, grandchildren.

'Sit down, sit down,' said Durand in his accented but excellent English, entering with a cup of tea for Jon and, for himself, Jon noticed, a cup of black coffee – which Jon too would have preferred, had it been offered.

'Quite a collection,' said Jon, gesturing to the photos as he sat at one end of the sofa. 'Thank you,' he added, taking the cup of insipid-looking tea that Durand was holding out to him.

'My clan,' said Durand, lowering himself a little stiffly into an armchair facing Jon. A wiry, fidgety man with an unkempt beard, he had – like Lazenby – aged since Jon first met him at the Congress in Seville, though his eyes remained as bright and his face as animated as ever. '*Bien, alors.*' The words had an interrogatory tone: Jon had asked for this interview, so it was up to Jon to make the running.

Jon, however, was in no great hurry: he suspected that rushing things might be a bad idea, as it had been with Peachey, and had already decided on his way there to circle around his topic before attacking it directly. 'You've seen that we've gone public, I suppose.'

'I have. It's in the French papers too. I have been contacted by a few journalists already.'

'Have you spoken to any?'

Durand lowered his face, giving Jon a stern look from under his bushy eyebrows. 'Did they send you here to check up on me? That I'm staying "on message", as you say.'

'No,' said Jon. 'Not at all.'

'I am glad to hear it,' said Durand, taking a sip of his coffee. 'Why *did* they send you?'

Jon hesitated: his circling plan seemed to be backfiring. 'No one sent me. I came here of my own accord.'

Durand raised his eyebrows and frowned, his mobile features unable to hide his scepticism on this point. 'With some purpose, I suppose.'

'Yes, I have a… purpose.' One could argue, of course, that he had been sent: by Ryan. Not directly, but Ryan had given him the mission which had brought him here.

'Go on.'

The other question which Jon had considered as he'd prepared for this meeting was one that had stalked him, with changing indirect objects, since his first fatal resolution to save Scott: how much should he reveal? Posed in the abstract, the answer had seemed obvious enough: as little as necessary. But now he sat here, a feeling – a memory of a feeling – stirred within him. He could tell Durand, a virtual stranger, *everything*, as he had not told Jack, whom he'd trusted; or Maria, who'd cared; or Peachey, to whom it was now hard to imagine he'd ever considered opening up; or Lazenby, whom he never had considered. He could tell him everything, and end once and for all this dark secret that, so long out of mind, had returned to trouble him – like the nine vials, long forgotten in his underwear drawer, that he now had to carry around in his bag just in case they really did search his flat. He could lay it to rest and, free at last from its subtle checks, move forwards, as he had not for so long, to embrace the possibilities he had glimpsed in the tunnel.

But it was so hard. So hard to tell the truth.

'Where to begin?' he said, meaning to think it but finding the words had slipped from his mouth.

'I am retired,' said Durand, his shoulders and elbows inclining towards a shrug. 'I do not work. My wife is out with her friends and will not be back for at least three hours. I have no other calls on my time. Begin as far back as you feel you need to.'

The problem was, though, if he once began stepping back, there would be no end to the regress. 'Actually, I think… The easiest place to start is yesterday. I had a long conversation with Sir Andrew Harper.'

At the mention of this name, Durand's face seemed to retract inwards, his lips puckering at its centre as if he had just bitten into an unripe lemon.

'Well,' continued Jon swiftly, keen to avoid any impression that he was in any way aligned with Sir Andrew, 'a long lecture from him really. I had been asking the wrong questions. About Edith Markham and the Teobe.'

Further creases layered themselves into Durand's forehead. It was hard to track the significance of the fluid contortions of his features.

'He was—' said Jon – then broke off. Describing it as a lecture wasn't entirely accurate either: Sir Andrew had at least *seemed* very open in answering his questions. 'I was actually expecting him to be angry with me, but in fact he didn't seem to be.'

'Sir Andrew is above anger,' observed Durand drily. 'It is not in the repertoire off his class. Or rather, if one day he does become angry with you, you will not find out about it because he comes to lecture you.'

There was something about Durand as he spoke – the knowing tilt of the head, the hardened set of the muscles either side of his mouth, the distant focus of those gleaming eyes – that suggested a long tail of history behind this remark. And it suddenly struck Jon that there were whole worlds, whole lives, behind and beneath this all-consuming moment, like the deep rolling waves beneath the cresting foam. These people had lived so much longer then him, pursuing their own trajectories, crossing with others who had lived still longer and had now departed, weaving the meshwork upon which he laid his own slender fibre of action.

At some point, he would have to decide which one of them to trust.

'He told me… I've no way of knowing whether he was telling me the truth, but he told me what happened to Markham at the end. And as much as he knew about the Teobe. On Madenu.'

At the name of the island, Durand closed his eyes, then opened them again, fixing Jon with a searching gaze: 'What are these things to you?'

'Well, it's… quite a big deal really, isn't it? I mean, I've always been told that Annie had never been in humans before. That's what we're telling the public now too.' He broke off. It was true enough, what he was saying, yet still a kind of lie. 'And the thing is… I had this idea, years ago. Taking it forwards depended on knowing more about the phenomenology – how it would feel to be infected. I was told we had no data, whereas in fact… Do you remember, the Congress in Seville, Lazenby's presentation, and you challenged her about Madenu?' Again he broke off. These were all facts, but he was still lying. 'And also…' He hesitated: after everything, was he really going to trust someone he barely knew? 'The thing is,' he said, dragging the words from his mouth as his breath seemed suddenly to desert him, 'I… Well, I made… a mistake.'

'A mistake?' repeated Durand, his eyebrows sliding upwards.

'I don't know… I don't think I can… talk about it.'

There was a long pause, as Durand examined his face – a plethora of twitches and contractions pulling his own features this way and that as he did so. Then, from the muscular dance, a kind of calm emerged, starting from Durand's eyes and rolling outwards: a look that Jon was surely not wrong to identify as sympathy.

'So we are, as you say, in the same boat,' said Durand quietly. 'Mistakes we do not wish to talk about.'

'Maybe so,' said Jon, grateful to Durand for not pushing him: for he could not go further. 'I do appreciate it's unreasonable to ask you to talk about the past when I'm not prepared to talk about things myself.'

'Because that is what you want to know about.'

'I think so.'

Durand let out a long sigh, lifting his hands to his head as he did so, as if to run his fingers through his hair – though he stopped short, instead letting his arms swing back down again. 'It is unreasonable. But if reason were the measure of what we do and don't do we would live in a very different world. Ask what you want to ask. I may not answer, but ask anyway.'

'I suppose... anything you can tell me really. I want to... Well, the question I really want to get an answer to is why violent sporogenesis stopped.'

Durand let out three rapid tuts, waving a finger at Jon as he did so. 'That is the wrong question.'

'It is?'

'*Oui.*'

'Why is it the wrong question?'

'Because we do not have an answer to it.'

'Right,' said Jon. 'So what is the right question.'

'Why did it start?'

'In the Teobe, you mean? Yes, I'd wondered about that as well. When you say that's the right question... does that mean we do have an answer to it?'

Durand nodded slowly, sucking air through his teeth as he did so.

'And what is it?' said Jon. 'The answer.'

For a moment longer, Durand's nodding continued. Then he stopped and drew himself forwards in his chair. 'I will tell you what I know.' He picked up the cup of coffee from the table at his side and took a sip. 'The first I knew of Annie, as you call her, was when I was despatched to the island of Madenu to test for a fungal infection in the Teobe people. This infection, I was informed, had been found in a British academic, Edith Markham, and had affected the brain – I did not know then just how completely. In Markham, they told me, it had been associated with violent behaviour – again, I was not told all the details. It was now necessary to test the people with whom Markham had been residing for many years, and from whom it was believed she might have caught the infection: the Teobe, now living on Madenu in, as I discovered on arrival, a kind of refugee camp. I was puzzled: everything I had read about this tribe suggested that they were unusually lacking in violent behaviour. Indeed, they were renowned for their... peaceability? Is that a word?'

'I think so.'

'You understand me though. The opposite of violence. Why, I wondered, was I being asked to test these people? But I did my job: I took the samples of blood, I analysed, and again and again the results were positive. More than half, maybe sixty per cent of the Teobe appeared to be infected; even more of the older generations. I wondered if perhaps I had made a mistake, and communicated the findings to my superiors here in France with a caution to that effect. An autopsy is necessary, came the reply, to confirm these results. This was not as easy as it sounds: the Teobe were most particular about their funeral rites – I assume that if you have read Markham you know about the *koaniki*.'

'The blood-sharing.'

'*Exactement*. Acquiring a body for autopsy was no easy matter. However, after some weeks of careful negotiation, we were given permission to carry out an autopsy on an elderly woman after her *koaniki*, provided her body was returned within two days. I had been instructed to look specifically at the brain, so examined that immediately. You already know, of course, what I found. But remember, nothing had prepared me for it. A fungal infection I had anticipated. But the complete replacement of all neuronal tissue by the fungus? I was astonished.

'I noticed one other thing under the microscope: clear evidence that some of the fungal cells had ruptured. I checked a sample of blood and discovered plentiful spores. I wrote all of this in my report to my superiors, along with the obvious hypothesis that the fungus was spreading from one member of the tribe to another via the *koaniki* ritual.

'A few days later, a response came: not to me, but to the soldiers who had been stationed on the island ever since the Teobe evacuation, to ensure there were no problems between the new arrivals and the indigenous population. Their orders were simple: the *koaniki* was to be banned with immediate effect. I was horrified by this outcome, and at once contacted my immediate superior: such a heavy-handed measure was not proportionate to what remained at this stage only a hypothesis. We cannot take the risk, he replied. What risk? The Teobe were peaceful and sociable.

There was none of the violence seen in the English academic. Indeed, there was no evidence the infection had any deleterious effects. This, he told me, was immaterial. The infection had to be contained, as a matter of priority. And so it began.'

He broke off, his eyes turning to one side and again losing focus. Jon waited for a few seconds before prompting him: 'Violent sporogenesis, you mean?'

'Eh?' said Durand, rousing himself.

'It was then that the violent sporogenesis began. After the *koaniki* was banned.'

'*Oui.* Yes.'

'But I don't understand. Why?'

'I don't know,' said Durand. 'I have told you the facts. Why they are the facts...?' He shrugged.

Jon shook his head. There was one rather obvious possible explanation, but surely it could not be true. 'Are you suggesting that Annie somehow reacted to being deprived of her usual transmission route?'

'I am suggesting nothing. But that hypothesis suggests itself, no?'

'And then in the lab, it stopped again because...' He did not complete the thought out loud: because Annie realised the scientists with their needles had supplied a new transmission mechanism? 'No, though,' he continued, as much to himself as to Durand. 'That's ridiculous, surely?'

'And yet we are drawn to that explanation.'

'But how?'

Again Durand shrugged. 'I have said for many years now that this organism is too complicated to be controlled by Sir Arthur Hayton's Laws. I have argued against the arrogance of this so-called mycotherapy. We have not yet understood, and what we have not understood we must respect. But they respect nothing. For them, the fungus was from the beginning a weapon, and so it remains. That is all they see. Perhaps the enemy is no longer a foreign power; perhaps it is the foreigner within us. A weapon, though, is a weapon. I have told them. But they would not listen.'

Jon too was only half-listening by now, struggling as he was to process what Durand was saying amidst the torrent of his own thoughts and speculations. There was a critical new fact here: that violent sporogenesis had started straight after the banning of the *koaniki* ritual. But what did that new fact signify? On every rung of interpretation – from correlation to causation; from causation to generalisation; from generalisation to explanation; from explanation to implication – the questions multiplied and ramified. And as those questions neared the present day, and the consequences of his own injection of spores into Anthony Cogan and whatever had happened thereafter – for why was Ryan demanding answers if nothing had happened? – so too the variables proliferated, the error bars widened, the bounds of statistical significance spread until they encompassed pretty much whatever meaning might occur to him. There was a critical new fact here, but it left him in state of perfect uncertainty.

'Would you like some more tea?' said Durand, who he now realised had been watching him for… how long had he been sitting there silently?

'Thank you.' He picked up his empty cup and held it out. 'Actually, if you don't mind, what I'd really like is a cup of black coffee.'

'Ha!' said Durand, throwing up his hands. 'You see, I have made assumptions again about the English. I try so hard to understand you, but you are always defeating me. A coffee it is.'

Left alone, Jon pulled out his new phone and began composing a text to Ryan: *I have info. Violent sporogen started in the Teobe straight after blood-sharing banned by authorities. Almost as if Annie found new transmission route when old one closed off. If so, could end of v sporogen in rats be because new route supplied by researchers transferring spores? Hard to believe – how would Annie *know*?*

Noises from the kitchen alerted him to Durand's imminent return, so he hastily concluded the message: *Is this helpful? Why do you need to know? I'm worried something has happened to you. Please can we talk again?*

'Black coffee,' said Durand, returning with not only the coffee but also a small plate on which he had placed four macarons, two a dark chocolate colour, the other two pale yellow.

'Oh, wow,' said Jon, pressing send and putting his phone away again. 'Those look delicious.'

'My assumption is correct this time?'

'Your assumption is spot on.'

'Spot on,' repeated Durand with satisfaction. 'I had forgotten this phrase.' He placed the macarons on a small table by Jon, transferred one of the pale ones to the saucer of his own cup and returned to his seat. 'I hope what I have told you is of some interest to you.'

'Yes. I'm very grateful.' He took a bite from one of the chocolate macarons, its sweet structure yielding easily between his teeth, the rich flavour spreading across his tongue. 'Delicious.'

'Try the lemon one as well.'

'I will,' said Jon, taking a sip of coffee. It was a little overbrewed for his liking, thick and bitter, but still welcome. 'It is very interesting, yes. And I understand now why you have been... well, opposed to mycotherapy.'

Durand inclined his head slightly but said nothing.

'When I spoke to Sir Andrew yesterday he mentioned that he was surprised you'd never gone public with what you know. He implied... well, I wondered if you'd been... you know, threatened.'

'Threatened?' said Durand, stretching his face as if he were surprised to hear the word spoken. 'I don't think that's quite how it works. If there are threats, they are like the sound of a... what do you call it in English? *Une chauve-souris?*'

'I don't know, I'm afraid.'

'The little animal that flies at night. Vampires.'

'A bat?'

'Yes, a bat. It is like the sound of a bat. You cannot actually hear it but somehow you have the sensation it is there.'

Jon nodded: this was a pretty accurate description of his own conversation with Sir Andrew the day before.

'Perhaps I was threatened,' continued Durand thoughtfully. 'But I always had the choice, you understand? I could have put a stop to this at any moment. It is not enough to say I was threatened, I think. That is not an excuse.'

'So why didn't you? Put a stop to it, I mean.'

'It's a good question,' said Durand. 'It is one I have often asked myself. And I think the answer is...' He paused, frowning at the floor – then, looking up again, said: 'Indecision?'

This did not seem to Jon like much of an explanation either, but he did not challenge it. 'You could do so now,' he said instead.

'Are you inciting me?'

'No,' said Jon quickly. He wasn't actually sure why he'd said that. 'I just meant...' He tailed off, unable to say what he had meant. 'You know, you could, if you wanted to.'

'And with all the stories in the paper, with everything going so well for your company, do you think I should? Should I set off this bomb? Boom!' He mimed the explosion as well, with wide-spread hands on either side of his face.

'I don't know.'

'But you too have begun to doubt the wisdom of mycotherapy, no?'

Had he? He'd come here because Ryan was asking him questions, because he was worried about what had happened after he'd infected Cogan. But Durand was right as well.

'If what you say is true... I mean, I believe what you say, that the violence began after the blood-sharing was banned, but if that really does mean... If Annie somehow has an awareness, a point of view... I don't know. I don't know what to make of any of it. We've always treated Annie as a mechanism, something we could engineer. But if she makes her own choices...'

Durand nodded. 'I think the problem goes deeper. You have always treated *human beings* as mechanisms.'

Jon let out a sharp sniff of air, frowning. 'Just the other day I was told that the basic problem governments have to deal with is human behaviour.'

'They respect nothing,' said Durand bitterly. 'This should be the starting point of our science: respect for what we do not understand; respect for what we will never understand. But my views are not in fashion, so, who am I to say? Maybe I am wrong after all.'

'I don't know,' said Jon, suddenly remembering the other half of his macaron. He popped it in his mouth: slight and sugary as it was, its warm flavour enveloped his tongue and, in a way he could not explain, recalled the sensations he had felt earlier in the tunnel. 'It's always been my mantra that the way to solve problems was to find the hidden constant and turn it into a variable. I'm very good at it, you know. Solving problems. But maybe it's that way of thinking that's been the hidden constant all along.'

'You are young,' said Durand. 'You are still working things out.'

'I'm thirty-four.'

'That is young. You have choices still. For what it is worth, I have come to the conclusion that there is only one problem we must solve in this life, and that is the problem of how to live well. *Il faut cultiver notre jardin.*'

Even had he not been in this strange, reflective state, Jon's French would not have been good enough to catch immediately the meaning of what Durand had just said. By the time he had worked it out and was wondering why he'd said it, Durand was speaking again.

'I would like to ask: what was the mistake you made?'

'I infected someone with native spores,' said Jon, before he even knew what he was doing. A long moment passed: the words had been spoken and the world had not caved in. No panic had come upon him: only a fractional sense of release somewhere deep in his chest. 'It was someone with a neurodegenerative disease. My boyfriend of the time had the same condition. I thought I had found a way to save him – it was a brilliant idea, though I say so myself; it still is in fact – but they told me that without evidence of the phenomenology of infection, nothing could be done. So I took things into my own hands. I found this man, stole the spores and infected him.'

'And this was your mistake?' said Durand. He seemed surprisingly calm for someone who had witnessed first-hand the horrors Annie had once been guilty of.

'No,' said Jon, realising as he spoke. 'That wasn't it. My mistake was... This man was on the brink of death. He was so full of hope. And... I lied to them.'

'To them?'

'To him and his carer. I didn't tell them about violent sporogenesis. I didn't think it was relevant. No, I *decided* it wasn't relevant, because it would have got in the way of what I wanted. And that was wrong.'

Durand nodded but said nothing.

Then the panic hit him. 'I've never told anyone this before,' he said, just holding his voice together. 'Are you going to tell them?'

'Tell whom?'

'I don't know. Them. Anyone.'

Durand shook his head. 'I have been silent so long it has become a habit. You must live with your mistake, and I must live with mine.'

'Even after… I mean, you've seen what Annie can do in the wild.'

Durand pulled a face. 'I'm not sure it's Annie I'm frightened of. The monster is already in the wild, don't you think?'

'Huh,' said Jon. So that was to be it? And suddenly he realised that the panic had, with the slightest muscular adjustments, become something else entirely: indignation. He'd confessed his crime, so where was his punishment? But he was watching it, this indignation. It was only a part of him. He could recognise it yet choose not to be it. 'Thank you,' he said, not quite excluding the emotion from his voice but not succumbing to it either.

'Don't thank me,' said Durand, lifting his hands to dismiss the idea. 'It is not a favour I am doing you.' He let his hands fall again, letting out a little sigh as he did so. 'You must try the lemon one.'

'Oh. Yes.' As there was also another chocolate one, Jon picked up the plate and, half-rising from his chair, held it out to Durand, and as he levered himself up, he could feel the emotional tension in his body dissipating through the movement.

'*Merci*,' said Durand, taking his cake.

'What was your mistake?' said Jon, sitting back down and taking his own. 'If you don't mind me asking.'

Durand frowned, chewing and swallowing before he spoke. 'I did not see the whole.'

Jon nodded, though he did not understand. He was not going to get anything less cryptic out of Durand. So instead he popped the macaron into his mouth, and it really was even better than the chocolate one.

Jon's journey back to London was marked, not by spikes of euphoria as the outward journey had been, but by a calm and consistent conviction that he was returning a better person than he'd left.

A reply from Ryan had arrived on his phone while he was still at the Gare du Nord, awaiting his train: *Yes, it's time to meet again.*

Could you come to me this time? It's a train journey, I'm afraid. Two seconds later, an addendum: *And yes, it is helpful.*

It was a sign of the change in him that Jon did not react with the anxious analysis of motive and consequence that had hobbled his decision-making ever since he'd first weighed himself down with secrets – and that he had for years now avoided only by living a life from which meaningful decisions were largely absent. In fact, he now found, he did not need to decide at all. He merely needed to consult himself, and discover in himself what he was going to do anyway, and then to share these observations with Ryan.

OK. Where am I coming to?

And then? He did not know, but it did not matter. He was all readiness, unfettered by intent, and the facile desire to know what to do no longer constrained his ability to do it. A third of a century into his life he had, at last, coincided with his own body, and could advance in lockstep with the world.

He did not return to his flat that night. It was not so much that, following his no-show at Arexis, they might have sent goons to watch his flat and follow him when at last he returned. That remained a real possibility of course, but it no longer seemed very likely to him. What was it Durand had said about bats? Yes, he could imagine darkly clad agents ranged along the railway arches opposite his building, but only because he'd watched too many movies. It was not fear of the world of high politics into which he had stumbled that stopped him going home. It was the simple fact that the flat was small, gloomy, depressing; that it had been the site of his years of stasis; that returning might knock him off this new point of equilibrium; that, knocked off so soon, he might not find it again.

So instead he went to a chain hotel round the back of Euston, from where he would need to take a train the next morning to get to Shrewsbury, the destination Ryan had given him. Much further away than he'd expected when he'd agreed to go, as he found when he checked first train times and then a map. Then again, it struck him, he'd have gone if it had been twice the distance. More.

It was late when he checked in, and he'd eaten on the way, so he went straight to bed – though he again lay for a long time awake, not thinking so much as replaying on the dark screen of the night episodes from that day, from the last few weeks, from his time back in Cambridge. We meet people for a reason, he told himself. That reason was sunk so deep beneath the froth and circumstance that he could not trace it, but it was of no consequence. All that mattered was to know that it was there.

He woke around 6.30 a.m., well before the winter sun took over its brief shift from the street lamps. For a few minutes he lay there in the dark of the small, impersonal room, fancying that he could project into the emptiness whatever he chose. It was not true, of course, but there was no harm in imagining just for a moment that he was no longer who he was. Then he switched on the light and showered before putting on the same clothes he'd arrived in, thankful he had at least thought to pack a change of underwear, just in case.

His morning passed in a blur of mundanity: the warmed trays of hash browns and scrambled eggs at the breakfast buffet; the polite enquiry if everything had been to his satisfaction as he checked out; a proper coffee on the station concourse, as he worked through the touch-screen ticket-machine menus; the long trek through the train, checking the screens on either side for an unreserved seat; the failure of the indifferent grey countryside they sped by to hold his attention, leaving him free to muse, and wonder, until a change at New Street interrupted.

He'd paid for the hotel with his credit card, and even as he did so found himself wondering how he'd pay it off now he had no job. Then he caught himself: he did still have a job, just about. The question was whether he would go back – and that, he discovered when he looked into himself, was not yet decided. It would have to be soon, of course; there were only so many days he could take off before they'd start asking questions. But all in good time.

There were other decisions that would have to happen first. The visit to Durand had left him with a clear picture of a possible future in which he'd pick up the phone to Jenny Macready at *The Guardian*: 'You don't know the whole story yet: it begins before we thought it began.' Was that what he was going to do then? Perhaps. The decision would come. All in good time.

Ryan, whom he'd warned of his arrival time by text, was waiting for him in the station car park.

'Thank you for coming,' he said as Jon approached him.

'That's OK. But I want to know what's going on.'

Ryan nodded. 'Yes.' He gestured towards the car he was standing by. 'Do you need to put your bag in the boot?'

'That's OK.'

'It's a bit of a drive. Thirty minutes or so.'

They drove through the town and out into the countryside, soon turning off the main road onto smaller ones, then onto a lane, then onto a rough track that led between two hedges to a farmhouse that stood by itself in the middle of fields. The journey, as Ryan had warned, took half an hour, and in all that time, they barely exchanged a word. For Jon's part, although there were so many things he could have said, he found himself disinclined to make the running. He'd put his job at risk for Ryan, gone to Paris in search of answers with his own questions unattended to, and now it was Ryan's turn to put something on the table. Beautiful Ryan. Slyly he watched his driver's profile from the corner of his eye and wondered: what was Ryan waiting for? For Ryan, who had bid him travel all this way, showed no signs of initiating conversation either, instead keeping his eyes fixed firmly on the road – as if there were no passenger searching his face for clues.

'Here we are,' said Ryan as they pulled up in front of the house.

'And where is here?'

'Home,' said Ryan, releasing his seat belt and opening his door. 'This is where we live.'

'I thought…' began Jon, following his example. 'I assumed you still lived in London. I don't know why.'

'No.'

'So when I saw you the other week…?'

Ryan gave him a slightly confused look. 'I got the train. Like you just have.'

He turned to enter the house. Behind him, Jon hesitated: so Ryan had made a six-hour round trip just to ask him about violent sporogenesis? 'Did you get infected?' he blurted out.

Ryan stopped and turned. 'What?'

'I need to know what this is all about and' – even now he baulked at the words – 'what I've done. I need to know what I've done. Why do you care so much about Annie?'

For a moment his eyes met Ryan's, but he could not hold the contact and quickly looked down at the gravel. It was going to be so hard: life, really living, it was going to hurt.

'Love,' said Ryan. 'I care because of love.'

Jon did not look up. He knew that love was not for him but did not need his face rubbed in the confirmation.

'I'm sorry I lost my temper when we met,' continued Ryan. 'What you've done is… given us a chance. It's not your fault that that chance will get taken away again sometime. That's just the deal, isn't it? Better to have loved and lost—'

'Stop,' interrupted Jon. 'Please, just stop. Let's… go in.'

He did not look up – he didn't want to see the expression on Ryan's face – but waited with eyes turned down until he saw the lower half of Ryan's body turn and leave, then followed him into the house.

They passed through a hallway lined with boots and coats and into a whitewashed living room with spare, rustic furnishing. At the far end, French doors opened into an old-fashioned dwarf wall conservatory that brimmed with tumescent palms and eager vines, their fronds and tendrils blocking all but a few glimpses of the garden beyond. And in their midst, sat in a small, upright armchair, a man in his late forties or early fifties.

He smiled as soon as he saw Jon, setting down the book he'd been reading and getting up to greet his visitor. 'Hello, Dr Caldicot.'

Jon had stopped at the other end of the living room. He'd not have recognised the man in the street – he looked so different, *so* different, from the last time they met – but here… he already knew who it was. He'd known before he even saw him.

'Mr Cogan? It's you, isn't it?'

14

Was it me? Is it me?

Perhaps I should say, as it was once put by or to me: yes, it's me, of course it is, but I'm not quite sure who that is.

There are days, good days, when I feel I am assuredly more than I was. More even than I am. Those are the days when it feels like anything is possible; when by the simplest acts – sowing seeds into the warm dark earth, watching a bee on its desultory way, kissing the eyes of the man I love – I am plumbed into the wellsprings of potentiality; when, as Schiller put it, 'the stimulus is the sheer plenitude of vitality, when superabundance of life is its own incentive to action'.

But there have always been days like that. And on the others, I know I am pretty much what I have always been, and that the only difference is that this is alright. And it's alright not because I am now some human-fungoid hybrid but because, against all the odds, someone loves me, and because I have learned to love life in return.

I'm totally changed, of course. The rewiring was the easy bit, after which came the months of recreating a body: building muscles where mere fibres remained, learning to talk and walk again, mastering tasks that most two-year-olds have off pat. Everything had to be replaced – like the planks of Plutarch's ship. Edith Markham's paradox was my day-to-day life.

So is it me? Such an odd question. Who among us can really answer it without a moment's hesitation?

And does it matter? This story isn't about me anyway. When I said it was my life story, I did not mean it was a story about my life. I meant it was a story about life, and mine.

Right then though, seeing Jon Caldicot for the first time in six years, it didn't seem the moment to confuse matters with philosophy. So I just said: 'Yes. It's me.'

It had been my idea to bring him in. Ryan would happily have cut him loose again. 'All I have to do is throw that away,' he'd said, pointing to the pay-as-you-go mobile he'd bought to make contact. But, lied though he had to us, I thought we owed Jon better than that. He'd saved my life, after all, and now he'd found the information we needed to stop that life ending very badly. Besides, I still needed him. Ryan would have done anything he could for me, but it was Jon's skills that were called for now.

Of course, I could not then predict just how important his last act in this story was to be. But something told me... Was it Annie? I don't think so. Annie is me. It was, I think, my gut. Though my gut too is me. It's all me. Or not me. Draw the boundaries where you will.

Nor did I predict how Jon would react to finding me alive and well. For a few seconds after I answered he stood there, the look of astonishment fixed upon his face. Then, slowly, the tone drained from the muscles around his eyes and mouth, releasing his features into a blank, almost dumb expression. He just about managed to totter sideways before his legs folded beneath him and he slumped into a chair in the corner of the room. And there he sat, motionless, expressionless, his eyes fixed on space.

A few seconds passed. Both Ryan and I were waiting for him to say something, but nothing happened.

'Dr Caldicot?' I said.

Still nothing.

'Dr Caldicot?' I repeated, rising from my chair.

'Jon?' said Ryan at the same time, crossing to the collapsed figure. 'Jon?' he repeated, gently tapping his cheek with his fingers.

But Jon had checked out, headed off somewhere else, leaving his body behind to be cared for by his autonomic nervous system.

'His eyes are still open,' I observed, joining Ryan at Jon's body's side. 'Do you think we should splash water on his face or something.'

Ryan shook his head. 'I think... Just leave him for a bit?'

So we did, but to our growing alarm he had still not moved ten minutes later.

'Should we call a doctor?' I suggested. We'd returned to stand on either side of him.

Ryan shrugged. 'Jon?' he began again, shaking the body by the arm. 'Jon? Can you hear me?'

Then suddenly the eyes snapped into focus and, almost in the same moment, turned towards me.

'Jon,' I said, with some relief. 'Are you alright? You gave us a bit of a fright there.'

The eyes studied me, but the mouth said nothing.

'Get him a cup of tea,' I said to Ryan, sotto voce. I've no idea what I thought either the whisper or the tea would achieve: it was just what came to me in the moment.

'You seem to have passed out or something,' I continued, leaning down so my face was on a level with his. I was almost sure that he could hear and understand me, but he showed no sign of responding. 'It's Tony Cogan,' I tried, speaking in that loud, deliberate voice we usually reserve for the elderly. 'Do you remember?'

I'd made no further progress by the time Ryan returned with the cup of tea. He held it out as temptingly as he could, explaining as he did so: 'Cup of tea.' Jon's eyes shifted briefly, first to him, then to the cup, then flicked back to me, on whom they'd been fixed the whole time.

I gestured to Ryan to put the tea down on the small table beside Jon's chair and follow me into the hallway, shutting the door behind us.

'He seems to be...' I began but wasn't sure what the right word would be. 'I don't know. Catatonic.'

'Maybe if we leave him for a bit longer?' suggested Ryan. 'I suppose it's the shock. Is that what shock does?'

'I've no idea. I'm still wondering if we should call a doctor.'

'He doesn't actually seem to be ill or anything. I mean, he's breathing normally, looking around.'

'Looking at me mostly.'

'That's what I mean by the shock. Maybe I should have prepared him before I brought him in.'

'I don't think it's your fault,' I said. 'Let's leave him a bit longer, like you say. But I think... we should keep an eye on him, no? In case something happens.'

We agreed this would be the best course of action: so I fetched my book from the conservatory and sat down opposite Jon – the eyes followed me everywhere – where I could see him and read at the same time.

'I'm just going to sit here and read,' I explained superfluously. 'As soon as you're ready to talk again…' I began – but it didn't seem necessary to finish the sentence.

That was pretty much how we spent the next few hours. At first I'd look up after every few sentences, which made it hard to make real progress with the book. As the time passed, however, I quickly grew used to Jon Caldicot doing nothing but watch me. It was unnerving, when I did look up, to find those eyes still locked on me, but I'd do my best to smile back and, when I got no response, carry on with another chapter.

Ryan too had joined me at the beginning – then, after a while, left again, remarking that he might as well get a few things done before he went into work. At about 4 p.m. – he was on the late shift and would need to be heading off in the next quarter of an hour – he returned and beckoned me back out into the hall.

'So what are we going to do?' he asked when I joined him.

I shrugged.

'Are you OK with me leaving him here with you? I can call in sick.'

'I don't think that's necessary. I don't think he's going to turn violent or anything. In fact, if anyone is in danger…'

Ryan gave me a dark look. He did not find consolation in black humour.

'We'll be fine,' I said hastily.

'And later? I mean, I guess he'll have to stay here tonight.'

'It looks like it.'

'So what will you do?'

A good question. 'If he's still not moving, I guess I'll bring a duvet down and throw over him. Surely he'll have come to by then though.'

Eventually I persuaded Ryan that I'd be able to deal with whatever happened. Not for the first time, I gently reminded him I did not need caring for these days, and not for the first time he smiled at his own delightful faults.

I went back into the room to find the eyes waiting for me.

'Still not speaking?' I said, just a little impatiently now.

Nothing.

I resumed reading, hearing the front door a few minutes later as Ryan headed out. Then, less than a minute later, the front door again.

'His bag,' said Ryan, appearing in the doorway with said item. 'He left it in the car.'

I jumped to my feet and crossed to take it, taking the opportunity to give Ryan another quick kiss before he left. 'Have a good shift,' I said, waving him off again, then turned back to Jon Caldicot. The eyes, of course, still followed me, but in the face now... was there the hint of a shift in those features, a slight flattening and widening of the mouth?

'Your bag,' I said, holding it up. Then I crossed to his chair and bent down to place the bag by his side.

Which was when he moved: the arm nearest me suddenly lifting and the hand reaching out towards my face. Instinctively I pulled away sharply before he could touch me, startled by the unexpected motion. The arm fell again as I retreated out of reach, though the eyes remained as they had been all along.

'You made me jump there,' I said. And now I was sure: his mouth was edging towards a smile. 'Can you understand me?'

I was certain he could, and I was desperate to talk to him, so I pulled my chair over – and as I did, he suddenly folded his splayed legs at the knee to make more room for me.

'There you go,' I said, sitting down. 'Would you be more comfortable sitting up a bit?'

He stared at me for a few seconds, then levered himself upwards in the chair on his elbow, so he was sitting more upright.

'That's it,' I said. It crossed my mind that perhaps I should call or text Ryan who, after all, would not have got very far. But no: I really didn't need caring for, much as I might crave and encourage it.

'So,' I said. 'Here we are again. Only this time you're the one who can't speak or move.'

The slight smile had not shifted from Jon's face. It neither waxed nor waned at this observation. Still, I fancied he too was amused by this turn of events.

'I suppose I should start by apologising. We should have told you what we were doing. But we couldn't be sure we could trust you. And as things have turned out, perhaps we were right. You should have told us about violent sporogenesis.'

The faint, unwavering smile, which a moment earlier had seemed so apposite, now seemed out of place, almost offensive.

'However, we are where we are. We'd have been none the wiser if it hadn't been for that mention of behavioural issues in the newspaper. God alone knows why but, the moment I read that, an image of Edith Markham running through Newnham brandishing a kitchen knife popped into my head. Perhaps that was Annie. I never know these days. Either way, I reread Markham, and I have to say Anthony Cogan could not have read it properly, because the account of what it's like to be infected is unmistakeable. Though of course, he hadn't had that experience at the time, so I suppose he wouldn't have known. I have, and when I reread it everything fell into place: the Teobe, Madenu, Markham. The conclusion was unavoidable: this quiet, happy life of ours is heading inexorably towards…'

I stopped. The idea of death did not scare me: there had been plenty of time in my previous life to grow used to that. But the thought that I might one day become something worse, something feral, that I might hurt Ryan… it was still too ugly, too raw.

And still that idiot smile. It was starting to annoy me now.

'So we talked,' I continued briskly. 'Ryan and I. We discussed our options. I suppose there are many couples who have to work through the news that one of them will turn into something else, and I'm sure, like us, they clutch at straws. There must be some way of stopping it. And Ryan, bless him, Ryan took it upon himself to find out, whatever it took. The rest you know.'

I waited. There was still no change in his expression. Was I wasting my time here?

'Are you understanding all this?'

Still he did not speak, but his eyes closed then opened again. Not a rapid, reflex blink, but a slow, deliberate movement.

I nodded. 'That was one of my last movements, you know. Blinking. I'd try to invest it with such meaning.'

The smile: it had not changed but, it now struck me, perhaps I had read it wrongly. There was something sad about it too.

'The thing is,' I said, 'we need your help again. Ryan thinks we can manage without you but... I don't think so. To convince Annie... That is' – I find the grammar so hard these days – 'to convince myself, I suppose... I'm not sure. Either way, the thing I realised when I read your text is that Annie is not a parasite – or an *aeisite* – of human beings. Not of *individual* humans, I mean. She's a parasite of culture. At some point in the far distant past, she found a home in our most ancient act of meaning-making: mourning our dead. Now she lives in one of our most modern: medical science, the rats in your lab. She's carried not in a body but in a collective practice. And that's the problem I face: the collective. The same problem that felled Edith Markham. Because you created me all alone. You threw me into this world without... a home. Just me. And that's why... that's why it will happen. The violence. It *will* happen.'

I don't pretend for a moment that everything I said made absolute sense. The thing is, I have come to realise that making sense is overrated. I always made lots of sense in my last life, and what good did that do me?

Jon, of course, said nothing either way. He just kept looking at me with that slight, sad smile.

'Unless...' I continued. 'Unless I can find a place in this world. A place for me and for Annie. Of course, in an ideal world I'd fly off to Teobeka or Madenu and join my people under the palm trees, but the bombs and imperialists did for that option. I've no people left these days except your rats. That's my tribe now: rats in a lab. But... it's better than nothing. If it staves off the madness. Which is why I need you to make me a promise: when I die, harvest the spores as you would from a rat and smuggle them back into your lab. Convince me, convince Annie that you'll do it. We have to believe you.'

I searched in vain for some flicker of a response in his face. I was sure he had understood me, and if he had, then surely he must also realise how important this was.

'Ryan said he'd do it with a rat from a pet shop but... I don't think she'd fall for that.'

At last Jon spoke, a single word: 'No.' It slipped out quietly, a word escaping a larger thought that remained unspoken, and for the first time in hours, Jon's eyes fell away from the close watch on my face and rolled out to some far-off possibility.

It was so long since he'd spoken that the noise startled me.

'No what?' I said cautiously. 'You don't think she'll fall for it either.' At the same time, another hypothesis had gripped me, feeding the fear I'd been living with ever since I read that article in *The Guardian*: that he was saying no to my request.

Jon's eyes shot back to me, as if he were slightly surprised to find me there. For a moment he looked at me, his face now changing easily to an expression of puzzlement. Then suddenly he twitched upright, his gaze pulling inwards, as one suddenly becoming aware of himself.

'I need the toilet,' he said.

'Of course, it's... I'll show you.'

He struggled a little to get to his feet and walked as one whose balance is precarious. I led him to the downstairs loo and waited outside while he used it, just in case, conscious of the intrusion as I tried not to listen to the sound of the stream of urine swaying between bowl and water. A memory of being taken to the toilet by Ryan passed through my mind: that unwelcome, soiled intimacy transfigured by Ryan's care.

The toilet flushed, and Jon emerged. 'Could I have something to eat?' he asked.

'Of course,' I said. 'We'll have some dinner. I'll make us some pasta.'

'Could I have something *now?*'

'Erm... yes, of course. Toast?'

'Bread's fine. Anything. I just need to eat something.'

We went to the kitchen and I cut him a slice of bread, which he began tearing into even before I could pass him the butter and jam.

'Tea?' I said.

He nodded, his mouth full.

'I wonder if I should put sugar in it?'

He nodded again. I put on the kettle.

'Sit down,' I said, gesturing towards the table. 'I'll cut you more bread.'

It didn't seem like the right moment to pick up our conversation – well, my monologue, I suppose – so I limited myself to further practical questions and observations as I set about attending to Jon's basic needs, joining him at the table with a cup of tea for myself and watching as he filled his face with bread, butter and jam.

'Is this yours?' he said suddenly, pointing to the handwritten label on the jam jar.

'Yes. We have a plum tree.'

'It's very good.'

'Thank you.'

'Very good,' he repeated. 'I'd forgotten how good—' He broke off. It seemed to me that the inner corners of his eyes were shining, as they might have if tears had formed in them. 'Very good,' he repeated, taking another huge bite of the sandwich he'd made for himself.

We sat like that a little longer: Jon eating, me watching. He was not looking at me now but instead switching his eyes back and forth between his food and empty space. Then, suddenly, he turned towards me and spoke: 'I did care, you know.'

I wasn't sure what this meant, but since he seemed set to go on, I decided not to ask questions, merely to nod encouragingly.

'It wasn't only pride,' he continued. 'My ego, I know it's there, and yes, it was a big part of it. But I did care too. It's true that I never loved him. Not really. I'm not sure I've ever really loved anyone. But when he told me he was dying, I genuinely, genuinely wanted to save him. And that's… that's a good thing, isn't it?'

'It is,' I said.

'It is,' he repeated.

'Are you… talking about your boyfriend? The one who got Scander's? What was his name?'

'Scott.'

'What happened in the end?'

'He died. A few weeks ago.'

'I'm so sorry.'

Another silence, as Jon finished the sandwich. I desperately wanted to return to my question now: would he help me? Had he already said no? But I held off: still it did not seem the right moment.

'You were talking,' said Jon, pushing his plate away. He sipped at the tea, pulling a face as he did so. 'Hnnn. Sweet.'

'Too sweet?'

'No I... I think it's a good idea.' He put the cup down again. 'You said that Annie found a home in... how did you put it? The oldest act of meaning-making.'

'Ah. Yes. Mourning the... Yes.'

'Why did you say that?'

'Why? Because... well, I'm not sure if I've remembered this right, but I think that burial rites are as old as... well, as us. The species, I mean. They're a fundamental part of what we are.'

'But what did you mean about meaning-making?'

I hesitated. I had used the phrase without really thinking, and if Jon hadn't already grasped what it meant then I wasn't sure I'd be able to explain it. 'I mean that... it creates another world. A human world. Which is the world we actually live in, so really it's not another world at all...' I was making a bad job of this.

'Edith Markham has this phrase,' I tried again. '*Meaning*, she writes, *is rooted in the excess of life over subsistence.* We don't have to do it to survive. Burial, for example. I suppose you can make an argument that burying the dead helps to limit the spread of disease. But what about the grave goods? The tools, the trinkets? Burying precious, useful things is, if anything, bad for your own survival. At best it's a waste of time and resources. Yet, for as long as they have existed, humans have done this. And any human you ask can tell you why. Well, any human that's not been indoctrinated with modern scepticism. "We don't actually know what was going through the minds of those first humans," they say. "We only have the material remains." And it's true, we don't know. Except we do. It's obvious. They did it because they cared. They did it because it mattered. Their act suffused the world with meaning, and the meaning explains their act.'

I studied Jon's face. He was listening closely, intently, but it was hard to work out if he also comprehended. Now, sensing I'd no more to say, he nodded slightly.

'The way you see the world is... different.'

'How so?' I said.

'From how I see it.'

'Right.'

He nodded again. 'Interesting.'

'I haven't always seen things this way,' I added. 'It was only... I don't know. There was Annie. There was Ryan. Something shifted. It didn't happen all at once but... underneath, if you will... Yes. Something shifted. We went on this trip to the jungle, when I was better again, and this monkey... I don't know, it was like I was suddenly seeing nature when I'd never seen it before.'

'That must have been wonderful,' said Jon.

'It was. It was wonderful and... terrifying.'

'I see problems,' he said thoughtfully. 'Problems and solutions. I'm not sure I always see what matters.'

'That's true of most of us.'

'Is it?'

'Yes. Most of the time. We can't live life as a constant epiphany.'

'I do sometimes see though. I did want Scott not to have to—' He broke off, catching something in his throat. 'I did care.'

'Of course.'

Another silence. Again I could not see how to turn the conversation back to where I wanted it.

'I'm going to make myself some pasta anyway,' I said instead. 'I don't know if you're still hungry, but you're welcome to join me.'

'Thank you. Yes.'

He hesitated: clearly food was no longer top of his mind. 'How is it then?'

'How's what?'

'Being Annie. I mean, having Annie... Living with Annie. That was the point of the whole thing, after all, so now we're both here... I may as well ask you what it's like.'

'It's like... being me. But I would say that, wouldn't I?'

'I suppose you would,' said Jon. 'And Ryan? He once told me he'd look into your eyes and know. So what does he say?'

'He says it's me. He says I've changed. I say he's changed. You know. Pretty normal really. Right now the main difference is the anxiety. Worrying whether and when the violent sporogenesis will hit. So far as I can see it could be any day.'

'Yes,' said Jon. 'Unless we can stop it.'

'Will you help me?'

'Yes.'

'By harvesting the spores when I die. Taking them back in.'

'No.'

'No?'

'That's not the right way.'

'It isn't?'

Jon looked at me. The faint smile had returned to his face, and his features returned to something close to the expression they'd borne all that afternoon as he'd sat slumped in a chair, watching me reading. Only now, somehow, they seemed to me not blank and inexpressive but suffused with an almost paternal care. And when his arm again lifted and his hand reached until the fingertips lightly touched my check, I did not pull away.

'I'm sorry I threw you into this world on your own,' he said. Then dropping his hand again, he pushed his chair back and stood up, purposefully. 'I have a present for you. Where's my bag?'

I followed him back to the living room and stood behind him as he lifted the bag up onto the seat he'd been sitting in and started rooting through it. It was already dark outside, the winter drawing in with its annual hinted threat that, this year, it might decide not to leave again. But I'd left a light on in the conservatory, and the lush fronds cutting up from the deep shadows told their own tale of unending equatorial plenty.

'Here it is,' he said, turning to me and handing me something.

I took it. It was a blue plastic case containing nine small glass vials, with an empty slot for a tenth. I had seen such a vial once before, on the day that Jon infected me.

'You found the hidden constant,' he said.

I could not quite believe what I was holding. 'Is this what I think it is?'

He smiled and nodded. 'No one should be alone.'

*

Meaning is rooted in the excess of life over subsistence.
I often go back to that line of Markham's. And when I do, I remember my monkey.

My upbringing, Antony Cogan's upbringing, equipped neither him nor me to appreciate the strange truth that Markham was struggling to express. For Cogan grew up in a secular, rational household, where conversation was conducted by the late rays of the Enlightenment. He was taught that strangeness was nothing more than a species of ignorance. To think of it as something real and in the world would have been to admit an imperfect relationship with Science, that exalted beacon of Law from which shines forth the light of Explanation, driving the fell creatures of Mystery from their dark holdfasts in the mind of man. It would have been a form of heresy.

To assure the rectitude of this faith, his family would regularly assemble to watch the gospel according to David Attenborough. A host of living creatures, ranged across the TV screen like saints across a reredos, testified to the truth of their creed: the plants captured the sunlight; animals ate those plants; other animals, progressively redder in tooth and claw, ate the animals that had eaten the plants; and everything, from the Amazon to Hampstead Heath, the Serengeti to the Serpentine, was bound by the iron law of function. Everything had its use. Everything made a marginal contribution to genetic reproductivity in the unforgiving free market of nature. The weak perished and the fittest survived, and no benefits were dispensed. Activity without useful outcomes was a drain on scarce resources, a waste, an evolutionary death sentence. To observe such activity in nature would have been... well, strange.

All this he took for certain fact, and, in so doing, embarked upon adulthood in a state of exquisite cognitive dissonance. He clung to the music, the poetry, the philosophy, even as they shrank into the just-so stories of sociobiologists and evolutionary psychologists – or, if they could not be explained away, were dismissed as 'biologically frivolous and vain'. He stopped his ears to the snub-nosed economists knocking at the door, even as he met their requests to enumerate how many pins he'd manufactured and how many hours spent counting angels on their heads. He blithely, if largely unsuccessfully, pursued a penchant for necessarily fruitless sex. He carried on as if it all still meant something. Yet, at the same time, he knew in the back of his mind that he was just a dysfunctional vessel for doomed genes; that it was dog eat dog out there; that Science had proved as much; such was Life.

Then something shifted. Was it Annie? Was it Ryan? Was it the monkey? It's impossible to say. But somewhere along the way, Cogan turned into me. Of course, there were the physical changes as well: the physiotherapy sessions, the lessons in how to hold a fork or tie my shoelaces. I was changing my body, changing my skills, like an overgrown neonate, and on the inside, changing my mind too, wondering what it all meant and how I could make sense of it.

Somewhere amidst it all a resolution took shape. To get the measure of life, I would visit what I fancied were its two extremes: the desert and the jungle. There, I told myself, I would find the answers I had lived without, even if I didn't know what questions I was asking.

We went to the desert first. Sitting on a high dune as the sun set and an untainted, voluminous darkness brought forth planets, galaxies and supernovae, sitting there I knew for the first time what it was to feel awe. The universe, in its incomprehensible vastness, opened up around me, and my heart sang: 'Behold, thou hast made my days as an handbreadth; and mine age is as nothing before thee: verily every man at his best state is altogether vanity.'

The desert supplied the starry sky above, but it was in the jungle that I would encounter the moral law within. There I was not opened up but overwhelmed by the obscene proliferation of living creatures. In the desert there had been space, clarity, a single point of consciousness in a vast, lifeless clearing. In the jungle, I felt that the trailing vines would grow into my eye sockets if I looked at them too long, that insects would burrow under my skin and aerophytes sprout from my sweating armpits. If the desert was sacred, the jungle was profane – and life was its profanity.

To be honest, we did not even see the jungle proper. We stayed in a lodge, a few hours upriver from the nearest airport, with tidy wooden walkways running through the canopy and linking our air-conditioned tree house with a central complex where we could dine on fruit and freshly caught fish, write postcards home and check the internet. My original plan had been to go further, deeper into the heart of darkness, but that intention soon sublimed in the hot, humid air of the rainforest. Gone was the cool apprehension of my days as an handbreadth: I could feel the sweaty palm closing around me.

Above the central complex rose a tower, up which one could climb to watch the sun set over the bewildering, undulating canopy of trees. Every evening I'd leave Ryan chatting to a Polish couple we'd befriended and head up there in the hope of some moment of reflective clarity, such as I'd experienced in the desert. Every evening I'd find myself surrounded not only by a clutch of my own species, chattering and snapping, but also by a troupe of insolent monkeys who spent their time jumping on people's heads and snatching food from their hands. There was no peace in the jungle.

Then, one evening, I noticed one of the monkeys clinging to a post at the very far corner of the tower, some way off from her reprobate fellows and the tourists they were tormenting. If she'd climbed up there in pursuit of food then she'd lost interest, but I fancy that had never been her purpose to start with. Instead she was hanging with her eyes set on the red horizon, and when an especially loud shriek, simian or human, distracted her, she'd glance across with a weariness I recognised all too well before rolling her eyes back to the splendid, fading colours of the dusk. Like me, she lingered a little longer than the others. As the humid night pressed up against us, only we two remained. Then, without so much as a glance at me, she drew her gaze back from infinity and swung herself back down into a world of grooming and bananas.

In that moment, I understood. That monkey had done everything she had to do to survive that day. She had subsisted to the full, and it simply did not matter what she did with the last few minutes before she slept. The blind watchmaker, groping in the dark, would never lay his thieving fingers on these precious moments. They belonged not to her genes, her species, her lineage, but to her. The excess of life over subsistence, the fertile soil from which meaning grows.

I turned my own gaze away from my monkey double and out towards the darkening canopy. All my life I had been told what to see: the struggle for survival; marginal productivity; the law of the jungle. Yet here was the real jungle, and what I saw was lawless, ebullient, exuberant, obscene, organic, chaotic, unclean, uncontrollable excess.

They had hidden it from me: the high priests of Science. They had pruned the roses in my parents' garden, trimmed the lawn's edges with a half-moon spade and strafed the liverworts between the paving slabs; they had measured and weighed and oxidised and analysed, and thrown the residue in the bin; they had boiled up value in a retort and reduced it to a clear, odourless utility; they had knocked at my door with their checklists and proformas; they even patrolled the high walkways through the canopy each morning, before we tourists awoke, clearing away the serpents. They had hidden it from me, but now my eyes were opened, and I beheld 'wondrous things out of thy law'.

What they'd taught me had never been science. It was a meagre, bloodless ideology, and like all ideologies it grew not from truth but from blindness and fear. For tell me: what kind of sage looks at another person and finds it in himself to wonder if they might be nothing more than a machine?

It was not till some years later that I'd learn that Annie lives not in a body but in a practice; that she makes her home not in an individual but in a culture. In this, of course, she is not alone. Far from making zombies of us, Annie is just another way of being a person. Yes, I am Annie, but only because I always was. You are Annie. We are all Annie, and we thrive in the rich, decomposing excess.

This is the life I wanted you to know. The life of reefs and rain-forests, of rotting trees and deep-sea vents, of Gordian worms and zombie ants, of vesicles, reticula and spindles. The life of Annie. The life of us.

And this, I think, is why you came to me. Not because your body fails. Not because the darkness draws in on you – though it draws in on all of us. Because you thirst for living wisdom, vital science, a biology of truth.

And now you can decide.

The vials are ready. Annie is ready.

You are the only variable.

ACKNOWLEDGEMENTS

A novel too makes its home not in an individual but in a culture. In writing this novel, I have parasitised the genius and goodwill of so many, not least: Jonathan Siklos, Ingrid Wassenaar, Richard Stemp, Robert Douglas-Fairhurst, Robert West, Alison Bomber, Kate Weinberg, Maddie Holmes, Douglas Pretsell, Sue Weaver, Kit Roberts, Tara Montgomery, Ayesha Christmas, Gil Bomber and Laura Kincaid.

A novel makes its home in a cover too, for which thanks to Matthew West and Geoff Harrison. I'm humbled that an artist as talented as Geoff would give me a painting as brilliant and apt as *Control Group*.

ABOUT THE AUTHOR

Simon Christmas was born in Shrewsbury in 1969. He lives in Abergavenny and Bloomsbury.

Printed in Great Britain
by Amazon

83163433R00181